BEHOLD THE MAN

BOOKS BY N. RICHARD NASH

Novels

RADIANCE

APHRODITE'S CAVE

THE LAST MAGIC

EAST WIND, RAIN

CRY MACHO

Poetry

ABSALOM

Plays

MAGIC

THE TORCH

ECHOES

GIRLS OF SUMMER

THE RAINMAKER

SEE THE JAGUAR

THE YOUNG AND FAIR

SECOND BEST BED

Nonfiction

THE WOUNDS OF SPARTA

THE ATHENIAN SPIRIT

BEHOLD THE MAN

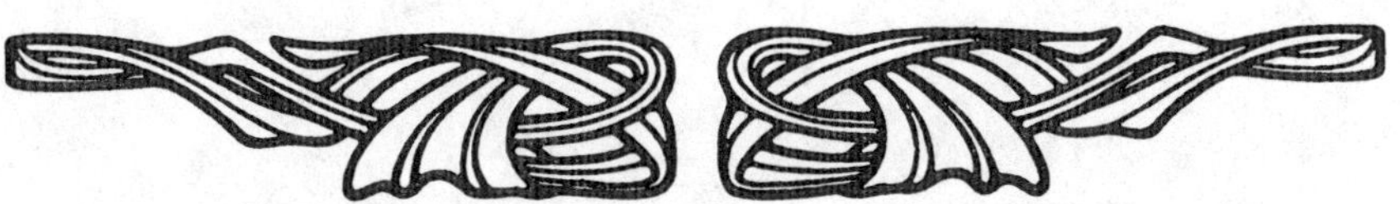

N. RICHARD NASH

DOUBLEDAY & COMPANY, INC.
GARDEN CITY, NEW YORK
1986

Designed by Wilma Robin

Library of Congress Cataloging-in-Publication Data

Nash, N. Richard.
Behold the Man.

1. Mary Magdalene, Saint—Fiction. 2. Judas Iscariot—Fiction. 3. Jesus Christ—Fiction. I. Title.
PS3527.A6365B4 1986 813′.54 85-30772
ISBN 0-385-14296-X

PRINTED IN THE UNITED STATES OF AMERICA
FIRST EDITION

The words *Ecce Homo,* said to have been spoken by Pontius Pilate when he witnessed the revilement of Jesus, have generally been translated "Behold the Man." In Latin, however, there is no definite or indefinite article, so *Ecce Homo* may be translated either "Behold the Man" or "Behold a Man" or "Behold, Man." Regrettably, this engaging ambiguity does not obtain in English.

Someone has remarked that it is difficult to write a life of Jesus without writing a gospel. This book, however, is not a life of Jesus, but a novel about two of his followers, Mary Magdalene and Judas Iscariot.

The Gospels, which are the initial and ultimate source, offer few facts about the harlot from Magdala and the betrayer from Kerioth. None of the biblical accounts devotes more than ten verses to Judas, less than a half page. As to Mary Magdalene—even if one adds references to Mary of Bethany and the unnamed fallen woman in Simon's house, both of whom are sometimes associated with Mary of Magdala—she is given scarcely more space than Judas.

Little space except the vast spaces that imagining may fill. A work of the imagination, then; a fiction.

1

Thorns and thistles! the boy cried, like a crazy thing, thorns and thistles! The soldiers pursued the felon, shouting, Zealot, filthy Jew, seize him!

She watched from the passageway that led to her father's counting chambers, saw the boy scurrying in one direction and then another as more soldiery, horsemen too, came charging down the high street from the mount and into the main thoroughfare from the alleyways. He will get caught, she thought, beaten to death. Serves him right.

She hated the Zealots, as her father did. They make trouble for all of us, he said. There was not a Jew of quality who did not suffer because of the barbarity of those Galilean cutthroats. Freedom was forever doomed if it had to depend on fanatics with poisons in their belt pouches and knives hidden in the folds of their mantles. Sooner or later the Romans would discard their indulgent distinctions among Sadducees, Pharisees, priests, Levites, scribes, rebels, rich, poor, and lump them all together: "Jews." Treacherous Jews. All of a single stripe, crafty and falsehearted, all Zealots, open or secret, men of mischief.

Thorns and thistles! the unruly clamor continued, with the soldiers cutting down their distance from the boy. But he was cunning—swift turns and twists, in and out of crowds and under porticoes where the horses could not follow, darting like a harried swallow.

She saw the young man clearly now, closer, no older than she was, eighteen perhaps. Get him! they yelled. And he was no longer a rebel emblem, but a country lad with a shock of coppery hair and a disarray of many panics, each limb with its own terrors, and his eyes most terrible. Good, she said; be frightened and get caught. Get him!

Thorns and thistles!

The young man twisted toward the steps that led upward to the Temple, changed his mind, cascaded downward, ran across the pathway of the horses, and suddenly was racing toward her, fifty ells away, thirty, twenty, so close that soon she caught a breath of sweat and fear.

She almost laughed. You *fool,* you've run into a blind alley on the Sabbath, everything locked tight. No egress, and they have got you now, stoppered in a bottle.

There was a yell and a trumpet, the crowd pressing into the main thoroughfare, the thud and clatter of hooves, shimmer of heat and summer dust.

The boy was knocking on locked doors. Let me in, I'm a Jew, let me in! One entrance and another, pounding, kicking at the doors, smashing at lock and iron, let me in, oh God.

He stopped. It was no good. The vigor of his madness withered. Sane, he knew that he was doomed; all that was left was stillness. His fright was a ghastly quiet. Yes, he is my age, she thought. She turned her eyes away, not wanting to pity him.

Suddenly her keys were in her hand, and she stood by her father's door. She unlocked it.

"Hurry!" she said.

She tried to stop herself: Oh, Lord, what am I about to do? "Hurry, you lunatic!"

He rushed into the darkness of the counting chamber. She slammed the door shut but did not enter; ran a few paces on the hot cobblestones. When she came to a halt, she trembled. What to do now, dear heaven, what?

She saw the dust at the head of the alleyway. The horseman came first, then the three men on foot.

"Where is he?" one yelled. "Where did he go?"

The horseman dismounted. She knew him. His name was Tullius, but he was called the Crippled Centurion. He limped toward her. He had a surly charm and busy lips with a mouthful of appetites. The lips were now dry and he licked at the Judean grit.

"Where did he go?" he asked.

"The trellis," she said.

He looked where she pointed. At her again. Back to the trellis.

"That lattice wouldn't hold a man."

"He was a boy."

No time to doubt her. He gestured to the smallest of the soldiers to climb the trellis and crawl across the grain merchant's roof, then directed the other two to go back the way they had come. He mounted again, looked down as if to fix her in his mind, and was the first out of the passageway.

More soldiers came and went. She was easier with them than she had been with Tullius. When they were all gone, her composure went with them. What stupidity have I done? What will come of it? There would be trouble; there was bound to be. She had an impulse to rush after the soldiery and shout, I have found him, come back, I have caught your troublemaker. But even if she hated the criminal and knew that sooner or later such Zealots meant catastrophe, he was a Jew and so was she, and the thought of betraying him to the Romans was like vermin on her skin.

At the rear entrance of her father's counting chambers, she stood a moment to overcome her anxiety. She opened the door. The boy stood at the far end of the lightless vestibule, dwindled in the shadows. She barely saw his eyes and the shine of his bright hair.

"Have they gone?" he whispered.

"Yes."

He started for the door. Her hand reached out and grabbed his arm. It was wet with perspiration. "You can't go that way. They may come back."

Without waiting, knowing he would follow, she walked past him and opened the door to the counting room. It was a long and narrow chamber, with lamps unlighted on the Sabbath, but shafts of sunlight angling down from the high, barred transoms, with golden motes dancing in them.

She heard him mutter in contempt. Turning, she saw what he was gazing at: the long tables with great leather accounting scrolls, all locked with gilded hasps; the shelves stacked with papyri, with parchment upon parchment, ribboned and labeled, telling tales of old ships and long-forgotten ladings, of cargoes bought and paid for, of merchants in foreign ports and tallymen long since dead.

"Whose place is this?"

"My father's."

"Who is he?"

"Joram of Magdala."

"A Sadducee." The boy spat.

She looked at his spittle on the white-tiled floor. She gestured to it and to his bare foot. "Wipe it," she said.

"Your father is worse than a Roman. He's a Jewish pander."

"Wipe it or I'll turn you over to the soldiers."

"To hell with you."

He pushed her out of his way and started for the front door, leading to the main thoroughfare. Halfway, the fugitive stopped as if stricken. He reached to grab for a support that was not there, lurched, laid both hands on a table. For the first time, she saw a crescent stain of scarlet spreading on the bottom of his tunic.

"My leg," he said.

In a spasm, he thrust his arms upward, as if to snatch at a bough that might keep him from sinking to his knees.

"Not fall," he said. She stepped forward.

With a moan, he reached for her and was in her arms.

She was afraid to hold him, and equally afraid to let him go. His body shuddered; she tightened her embrace to steady him and give him comfort. It was different then; he was close, his trouble was hers, and she was charged to keep him safe. He's dying, she thought, and she murmured nonsense words in healing tones, as if he were a sorrowing child or a wounded lamb—I won't let you fall, she said, I won't let you.

He began to cry.

"No," she said softly. "Please—don't cry—no."

She placed her hand on his cheek. What shall I do with him? He moaned a little more, a muffled sound. No, she kept saying, trying to console, but there was no help in it. Where was she to go?

As if she had stanched his wound, he steadied.

"Let me go."

"You'll need tending. I'll find someone to look to you. Wait here."

"No. I'll get caught."

"The wound . . ."

"What is your name?"

"Mary of Magdala. . . . Who are you?"

He shook his head to let her know: forbidden. He was not allowed to reveal his name.

Her question about his identity quickened his sense of danger; he moved clear of the girl and started toward the door.

"Wait—you're bleeding."

"I'm sorry that I spat."

"Wait—please wait."

She was unfastening her mantle, letting it fall to her waist. As she loosened the lace-and-linen underbodice, she saw him staring at her breasts, but there was no time for modesty. Bodice in hand, she hurried to him, knelt on the floor, raised his tunic and started to bind him. A knife wound, clearly; she could not tell how deep. She tightened the dressing and he groaned in pain; his hand gripped her bare shoulder. She thought he might not be able to endure any more, but there was more to do. So she reached for his other hand and placed it on her breast, as if he were a child who needed the comfort of a mother. But when she pulled the knot still tighter, his hand clenched and she, too, was in pain.

She had a lightheaded instant of pleasure and ache and anger, and a bright, clear notion: Pain shared is a kind of ecstasy.

She finished her work and he was gone.

If she did not get invited to Herod's party she would perish. No question, perish. The tremors were already telling her so: be one of the guests or one of the dying.

Before long, she would know; as soon as her father returned from the meeting. He had promised to be back by midafternoon, and the sun was already westering, the shadows lengthening in her bedchamber. She fretted over his lateness. Magdalas are never tardy, her father always said; his family pride was overweening in everything, even punctuality. But where was his time-punctilio now, when her nerves were quivering? Something might have gone wrong: Herod had not offered the invitation.

No, her father would wangle it out of him; he was a good bargainer. Put a little extra honey in the covenant, she had begged, make it worth his while to have me come.

"Bribe him, you mean?" Joram had asked.

"It's not bribery, Father, if you openly make it part of the transaction."

He had patted her lightly on the cheek; the touch was meant to tell her she was precious to him but not too weightily considered; she was not yet eighteen, and merely a woman. "Shall we offer an extra ship or two, in return for a party invitation?"

"Don't be a thorn, Father. Herod doesn't come that high. A crate of crockery—a packet of saffron—and he'd sell his cousin."

"Pontius Pilate is not his cousin."

"But he's not *selling* Pilate. He's merely inviting me to a party where Pilate is the guest of honor."

"No Jews allowed."

"But Herod himself is a Jew."

"Don't call him that—he has no right to the name. He's an Idumaean scum who wears a Jewish *tallith* as a thief wears a mask."

"But you deal with him."

"I have to deal with him, because it is said he will be our king. I'd rather deal with pigs . . . or Pilate."

"If I go to the party, I will *meet* Pilate—and make myself pleasing to him, and soon he'll be our friend—and you'll be able to deal directly with him."

"Don't be naïve."

She was not naïve. If her father needed to believe she was still an innocent, Mary indulged his credulity, but she had an artful mind and was sophisticated in the ways of men, and Jerusalem. Had she continued to live in the countryside near Magdala—in a house they still owned but rarely used—she might have remained guileless. But when her mother had died, her father had brought her and Caleb, her brother, to live in the capital, which was the center of his worldly business, so that he could look after his motherless children. But his trade was in Alexandria and Rome and as far as Cathay, and the orphans had to make do with the attention of strangers—slaves, for the most part, and tutors some of whom did not even speak Aramaic.

Even ten years ago Mary of Magdala was no longer a child. Her mother once said that when the little girl's questions turned from wondering to doubting, she had lost her childhood. But it wasn't then; she lost her childhood when her mother died. Mary knew it was gone because her joy was gone. She thought she had recovered it when she moved to Jerusalem. She was wrong, however; the city was exciting, but not joyous. And she sensed that adult joy was a kind of insanity.

Which she shared. The din and hubbub of the frenzied city was a delicious lunacy. On the day of her arrival, there was a spectacular parade of the Roman military, ten centuries of men with shields blinding-bright in the sun, and cavalry boasting in clouds of dusty magic—riders appearing and vanishing—silver soldiers on silver horses, prancing, whirling like silver centaurs. The martial profanity of trumpets and drums, the racket of rattleboxes, the shouts of the centurions louder than the brasses, and her own voice screaming to tell herself that she was *there.* In the evening she went to bed quivering as if in a seizure, and her father stood over the bed, feeling her brow for fever. The child is ill, he said over and over, but she prayed that night for many such illnesses.

Another day, she saw her first fair, a cargo from India, in the bazaar not far from the Temple, great hills of velvets and laces in colors to blind the eye, and mounds of saffron as shiny as egg yolks, and betel nuts and Damascan almonds and candle flowers, and an east wind of spices that inflamed the nostrils, cardamom and cumin, turmeric and white pepper and capsicum. And her father, in a light she had never seen him, talking to turbaned men in a language she had never heard him speak, threading his way among kiosks and pavilions, making bargains, writing numbers on his forearm, bowing as the Hindus bowed. And she wondered—envying—how many languages he could converse in, and how many embraces and salutations he had mastered.

When the afternoons were hot and the portals of the Temple were left open, she would often mount the steps and stand at the doorway, gazing in upon the tremulous lamp glow, eavesdropping on the men at their sacrifices. Often she had an urge to enter but was, of course, forbidden except on the highest of Holy Days, when females were allowed access to the prayers by a separate entrance. There was one portal of the Temple where spying was even more titillating, and hazardous: the entrance to the Chamber of Hewn Stone, the hall of the Sanhedrin, highest council of the Jews. It was an awesome place, like a hollowed-out mountain, austerely unreceptive to inquisitive young girls. Once, she got caught. Two elders, friends of the family, said they would tell her father she was behaving in an unbecoming way.

But they didn't. Her father was one of the Sanhedrin's unofficial advisers—on the Sadducee side of the chamber, where the rich men sat on chairs that looked like thrones. The Pharisees, many of whom were just as rich but claimed not to be, sat on the other side of the room. They forswore the ostentation of the great gilded chairs and sat upright on backless planks of wood, calling themselves "bench-proud." Her father said that Pharisees were proud only in their buttocks; in their souls they were hypocrites.

He did not make such statements behind his hand, but declared them brazenly, often on the open floor of the Sanhedrin. While we deal overtly with the Romans, he declaimed, the Pharisees deal with them shiftily in alcoves and alleys. The same with our dealings with the Deity: we forthrightly keep our covenants; the Pharisees extenuate. Claiming they have a more tolerant view of the Law, they are intolerant of life, except of their own false pieties.

Always, what her father said in the council chamber was provocative; sometimes, even true. Mary tingled whenever she heard him brazenly insult the Pharisees. She studied how her father drove an argument to its extremity—but artfully, without cutting off an avenue of retreat. He was a daring, yet a shrewd, negotiator. She admired this in him.

As she admired the traders at the crossroads of the well. It was the main watering place of the capital, where the caravans came to barter. Hardly a day passed that she did not sneak down from their fine house on the mount, down through the center of the city, to the disorderly *plateia,* where the crude wagoneers and the scratchy camel drivers brought their cargos from every corner of the world. There, more than at home with her tutors, she learned by stealth to speak a number of languages. Jargon, for the most part, the vulgarisms of peddlers and sailors and donkey dealers, racier and more vivid than the Pindaric Ode she could recite, verse for verse, or the Invocation to Ra, or the *katalogos* of Greek muses. And more useful, too, for it was not until recently that she realized that cultivated speech was a sharper-cutting instrument of negotiation than patois could ever be. And now, in her eighteenth year, she knew that negotiation was not only useful but the greatest art of all; negotiation was everything.

How sad, she thought, that criminals had not learned this to be the case. Not a woman got flogged in the prison courtyard who could not have negotiated her way out of it if she had had the skill to bargain.

Once, during Mary's first year in the city, she had seen a grave-looter being nailed to a cross. Her heart had stopped beating. She felt that she must vomit and scream and flee, everything at once, and all she could manage was a cry as quiet as the fall of an eyelash. She had vowed never to view another crucifixion, but had reconsidered: it was a fact of existence, and she had better get used to it. Nowadays, her pity for a crucified man had given over to resentment. There was hardly an occasion when a convicted prisoner could not have saved himself by recanting or disavowing or turning his coat a little or eating a morsel of dirt. By *negotiating.* Life was worth the haggle.

Life was worth anything. Even in these times, grown into young womanhood and filled with the nagging void of existing without an errand, she felt in some hopeful, inexpressible way that the hurt was the price she was paying in the present for an excitement in the future. An exciting life would be worth any pain she had to suffer for it. And if she was in some sort of trap she did not fully comprehend, she would ferret her way out. She would fight, she would bargain, she would trick her way into a world she could be free to explore. Escape.

And Herod's celebration was a good place to begin.

Celebrate or die. Not that she particularly enjoyed parties or feasts; even as a child she had noticed that, at holiday celebrations, she turned into someone she did not know or like. But there would be attractions at Herod's festival, fascinating foreigners, two men who had delivered orations to the Roman Senate, an astronomer from Alexandria, a Phoenician cartographer who had charted a freakish map of an odd-shaped world, Greek philosophers and poets, and a Corinthian scholar who had come upon a fragment of a buried drama of Aeschylus. She needed, she desperately needed to see them all and hear them speak, to catch a spark of their foreign fire, to smash her way out of imprisonment in Jewish Jerusalem.

She could feel her cell getting smaller. Sooner or later, to escape, she would have to marry—and barter one set of chains for another. But she could not imagine herself married to anyone. When her mother died and Mary had ceased being a child, she had almost ceased being a female. Her brain-proud father had raised her as he had raised Caleb, with tutors of the same cast, and a view of the world that tacitly promised Mary would live in it, travel in it and negotiate in it as her brother did. Which promise was not kept. All that was left to her of the unspoken pledge was a vista broader and freer than a woman's world could be.

She was different from all the girls she had grown up with, and estranged from them; her hungers made them nervous. Among women her age she was the last one unespoused, except for those who were already acknowledged as spinsters, the ugly or the sick or the malformed, objects of pity. Girls in their late teens, Sadducees and Pharisees alike, were mothers now. Her only friend, Sarah the Levite, had just had her third child. She had been the brightest person Mary had ever known, quivering with words and numbers, measuring the breadth of sound and the depth of light, a heaven-gazer, foretelling the traverse of every star as if she had personally dispatched it. I'm going to ride up there, Sarah had said, and hew a pathway to Hyperion. Then her parents had married her off, and she had become a housewoman—her journeys, poems, meteors forgotten. Not that Mary decried motherhood. She wanted to have children, many of them, wanted children with an anguish that sometimes awakened her at night. But she wanted Rome and Alexandria as well.

Her father said she was greedy. He was right.

She was greedy to *know.*

What she needed to know was a mystery to her, so she told herself she needed to know everything. How the world was made, and what was the first word ever spoken. Is there a language of men and a language of women and a language of the Lord? Since the gift of being God's chosen people had brought the Jews all the penalties of pride, could the gift be returned? Was their destiny, as the Jews claimed, preordained—and was *that* returnable? If I reject the life of Sarah the Levite, what am I to be? An idle woman of the rich Sadducees, dawdling in safe rooms, dozing in sheltered gardens, strolling in the shade of time, eyes averted from the embarrassment of being alive?

A hunger to know. Once, when she was just past fourteen, she had a tutor who seemed to know all that she wanted to find out. He was Abaris, a thirty-year-old Mesopotamian Jew who taught her geography. He devised intricate schemata of life on strips of papyrus that he tacked to the wall of her study chamber. There could not be so many worlds as he described to her, hidden continents and shoreless seas, and infinite realms of beasts and birds, and lands where only tempests dwelt.

She fell in love, not with him, for he had wens on his cheeks, but with the mystery of what he knew and was withholding from her. One day, sensing her hunger, he offered a bargain: he would tell her the greatest secret ever left untold if she would lie naked with him.

How incongruous it was to be a virgin undressing for the rapture not of her body but her mind.

In lovemaking, too, Abaris was a good geography teacher, revealing to his student the uncharted places of her person, the mounds and promontories of pleasure, the caverns of dark delight. She had not expected the pain that began it, or the pleasure in the strife that finished it. It was as if she had been set ashore in an ominous, unexplored country that was hot and loving and barbaric.

She discerned then that her need to be caressed was like a constant state of emergency; she had a physical necessity to be loved—her flesh, her bones, her organs—her skin had a famine for the touch of hands. She was grateful for every sensual gratification, knowing instinctively she was getting imitations of the real thing . . . whatever that might be. Meanwhile, the love in a man's fingers was magical with lotions and unguents that would make her smooth and glowing and beautiful. Even, perhaps, happy.

The tutor kept the bargain and told her his secret. First, however, he made her promise not to repeat a word of his revelation, for what he had to say was heterodoxy, and if the Sanhedrin were to hear of it he would come to unimaginable grief. The world, he confided, was not the Lord's sole creation, but one of a limitless number of creations, and not a vast star but only a tiny, forlorn midge, a lost speck of astral dust whirling in an endless universe. Insignificant enough to have been formed in the six days of the Scriptures, it had in fact taken many millennia to create, and had never been finished but was still being patched and tinkered with, remade and worsened by a Creator who had no pattern to follow and was either confused or unconcerned or feckless. We were, the teacher said, in unreliable hands.

It was a stunning contradiction of what he had taught her, and while it disturbed Mary, it thrilled her; it snapped some shackles in her mind, set her racing to a hundred wild and brain-bustling supposes.

The secret of Abaris was, she thought, fair value for her virginity, to say nothing of the pleasure she had derived. For the first time, she had a sense of the worth of her body, which could yield so precious a profit.

She struck other such bargains. With a Greek poet who showed her how to fling words like arrows. With a philosopher from Rhodes who described the difference between a Cynic and a Stoic. With a mathematician who taught her probabilities and the enigma of zero. Each time, she tried to convince herself she was in love with a man; but she had no gift for self-deception, or for deception of any kind, and knew it was not a man who was her passion, it was the touchings, the caressings. And most of all, the *knowing.*

Where knowing was concerned she was insatiable. It was like sexual starvation. Worse. And she had a sickly dread that she might never be gratified. This void had grown more frightening of late, and it bewildered her how such an emptiness could be so full of pain. She would go from man to man, crying tell me, show me, teach me, help me to learn, help me to see and to perceive, help me to know! She was terrified that she would never discover what it was she needed to understand, what her heart and her mind and her soul starved to comprehend.

What must I know? she cried, as if her life depended upon it. She sensed, in fact, that her happiness did depend upon it, and that a woman, through the fault of knowing less than she needed to know, could lose her reason.

She soon knew all that there was to know in Jerusalem. And the Jews offered no lifeline to other places. Even her father, whose ships sailed into foreign harbors, denied her an escape. Rome was not a fit place for a Jewish woman, and Alexandria was becoming a disgrace. There was no mighty Temple in either of those cities, Joram of Magdala would say, only secondary synagogues, and where the place of worship is secondary, so are the worshipers. Foreign Jews were only a step above the riffraff, not a span higher than the gentiles, disrespected and scarcely worthy of respect. In Jerusalem, however, even though the city was occupied by the invader, the Romans paid a certain deference to the rights of Jewish men and their womenfolk; that is, if they were Sadducees. Even the Pharisees were treated with a measure of civility. We should be thankful for such tolerance, her father would say, and not go wandering off the rim of the Jewish earth. Beware of unknown perils.

There would be no help from him or from anybody in this Jewish city. Only from the foreigners. In some way she had to be accepted by them. She had to be noticed, she had to look beautiful in the eyes of a Roman or a Phoenician or—best of all—an Alexandrian Greek.

Thus, Herod's party. It was in honor of the Roman New Year, and Pilate, the newly designated procurator, was to be the guest of highest eminence. Except that he could not or would not come from his palace in Caesarea at the appointed time, so the feast was postponed a fortnight—until the Ides of Idiocy, her brother said. The truth was that the imperial Pontius Pilate, immediately on his arrival from Rome, had taken an instant dislike to what he called the Jewish sanctimoniousness of Jerusalem, and had vowed to go to the capital city of the land he governed only when he must—for example, to inspect his military fortress from time to time. The fortress, named Antonia, was on one high hill, and Herod's palace was high on another. It was on Herod's summit that the New Year of the Romans was to be celebrated, and where Mary—if fortune favored—would be one of the celebrants.

She had had a most alluring gown fashioned for the occasion, jade-green satin, in contrast to the reddish walnut of her hair. The gemstones at the border of the bodice were rose opals, which would capture, not accidentally, the flushed gleam of her skin. Yesterday, on the Sabbath, she had made off with her brother's key to the safe in the counting chamber and had borrowed her mother's necklace of fern-green tourmalines, the shadow mirrors of her eyes.

Thorns and thistles.

The phrase, a nagging nuisance. In and out of her sleep last night. Why did it keep coming back? She must not think of that damned Zealot boy again.

Necklace. See how it gleams, she thought, and in the looking glass her eyes gleamed too. Suddenly, like finding a golden coin, she had a feeling of attainment. She would be invited to Herod's palace tonight, her raiment and her jewels would make her beautiful, she would *feel* beautiful, she would walk in an aura of roses and myrrh, men would flock and hover, foreign men with swift minds and sharp instances, and she would be glorious in many languages. And tomorrow, or in a near autumn of tomorrow, she would be in a distant country. How her departure would come about she did not know. She might go as a friend, or as a lover. Or, in some well-considered expedient, as a wife. Some way . . .

She heard the bondman's bell in the corridor. It was the fullest tone, and signaled to the servants that her father was arriving. She hastened to the window and threw open the lattices.

He was hurrying. A good sign; her father was not a man who would hasten to impart bad tidings. She watched as Zabis, his personal servant, went to meet him. The chamber man carried a marble ewer and a goblet and some cloths. The stone terrace was at a distance from her window, and she could not hear their voices. They were standing between the fig trees. Zabis was bathing her father's face and offering him water to drink. They were laughing. That, too, was a good sign. Her father was handsome when he laughed; everything about him seemed more beautiful at such times; his Phoenician mantle took on more color, and his graying hair seemed more bristling, more alive. She wished he would shave his beard, the way some of the Sadducees were doing to the horror of the Pharisees, but his modernity stopped short of it. He would never take a knife to his face, he said; it was Roman butchery. This puzzled her. How could he resist the Roman custom in one thing, and adopt it in another: keeping slaves. Wasn't it a sin? Her father, mindful of the Jewish law, had indignantly denied that he kept slaves. Bondmen and bondwomen, he called them, as if there were a difference. There is a mighty difference, he retorted: My servants can go free. Anytime they like, at liberty. Whereupon she pointed out that the mark of the slave—the slit earlobe—was ineradicable, even when a slave was freed. Vexed, he answered irrationally that some people are *born* with slit earlobes, they *need* to be in bondage. I'll give freedom and paid employment to any servitor who asks for it, he said, but they don't want it, they want to be taken care of—and I care for them. . . . In truth, he was a benevolent man and practiced the Roman cruelty with kindness.

Presently, she heard a flurry of bondspeople in the corridor, and knew they were rushing to do him service, and she hoped he would not tend to business or bathing before telling her his news. It was not long, however, before Zabis came; she was summoned.

She flew down the corridor. Her brass sandal heels clacked on the stone floor. The tall portals of her father's chamber were open and she bolted across the threshold. His back was turned and he was facing the shelves, as if reading the titles of the books and cataloguing the silver bowls, the amphorae, the temple dogs of Cathay.

"What did he say?" she blurted. "What did he say?"

He turned slowly. "He said you could not come."

The belt of her peplum was too tight; she needed more air. "I don't believe it. What did he actually say?"

"That the guests were not his choosing. Pilate told him specifically those he wanted and those he didn't."

"Those he didn't?"

"Jews. As I warned you, Jews."

"But Herod himself—"

"His being a Jew doesn't matter. He is merely a slave, preparing a party for his master."

"He will be the king, you said."

"Even as the king—a slave."

She was frustrated and in a rout. "Then, you should have treated him as a slave—and *made* him invite me. You're stronger than he is, and you have more to bargain with."

"I had nothing to bargain with. He gave me everything I demanded for the two cargoes, and he commissioned another three. We were not in the business of entertaining a Jewish girl at a Roman festival."

"When you say Roman, you mean obscene."

"Roman parties are obscene, yes."

"I don't believe it."

"Ask your brother. They eat swine and eat like swine. The women's nipples are bare and the men disport themselves with animals. . . . Other things."

"You promised you would do your best to get me an invitation. But because you disapprove, you didn't even try."

"I did try. Not as persuasively as you would have wanted, perhaps, but to the limits of dignity."

"And you were glad that you failed."

"Yes, I admit it." He didn't raise his voice. "It deeply distresses me, Mary—this appetite of yours for Roman things."

"I have no appetite for 'Roman things'!" she cried. "I simply have to go away somewhere! Why don't you let me go away?"

"Go where? Alexandria?"

"Why not? You let Caleb go. I could leave with him when he returns. I wouldn't be alone. I would be safe. Why don't you let me go?"

"With him? He is even wilder than you are."

"Yet you trust him. Why not me?"

"I trust him only as a trader, not as a man."

"But as a man, you'd let him go anywhere."

"I do not make the Law."

"I hate the Jewish Law, I hate it!"

"You blaspheme."

"And I hate you for punishing me with it!"

He turned away, and she knew he was hiding his hurt. She loved him deeply, and admired him, and needed his affection. She wished they could live in the same dwelling without injuring each other, but as their differences loomed larger and larger, everything else seemed to be getting smaller, the city and the chambers they lived in, the corridors along which they walked, and in the closeness their thin skins were constantly abrading, the wounds remaining raw, with little chance to heal. Anomalously, she felt better fortified to endure the conflict than he was, and she pitied him. If she wept now, it was not for herself but because she had hurt him, and she knew that weeping made it worse: it took advantage of the man. She wished she could hide the tears.

"I'm sorry, Father," she said.

"Yes . . . I know." Still, he did not turn to face her. He seemed confused and, oddly, as if she had misled him in some way. "Why can't you be like other women?" he said plaintively. "Why have you set yourself so far apart?"

"It's you who have set me apart, Father."

"Me?" He was injured. "Me?"

"Yes. I remember, on my fifteenth birthday, you said, 'How singular you are!' And I was. You wanted me that way. You taught me to walk at my full height, you commanded me to be beautiful. You engaged heaven knows how many tutors to educate me. I have in my head the labels for so many things and thoughts and imaginings that I can summon almost anything I need. And I've learned nearly as many languages as I have fingers on my hands. But where do I speak them? Where do I use these wonders I have learned? What do I do with all this, Father? Do I simply get married and have children and bury it all with my baby teeth? Don't you think it's a terrible thing that a woman should be so equipped as I am, and have no use except as an animal has uses? What do I do, Father? Tell me what to do."

He raised his hands and dropped them, helplessly. She did not want to give him further pain; it was a heartless tyranny to make such a forceful man feel so ineffectual. But it was nothing compared to her own ineffectuality. Damnation, she thought, I'm weeping and he'll see it, and he'll try to comfort me, and be even more impotent than before, and I'll crumple and be a kitchen cloth. She hurried away.

In her own chamber, her eyes measured the distances. An immense room. Twenty ells, perhaps, from wall to wall, in both directions. To say nothing of the alcoves, one for her sunken bath, another for gowns and sandals and jubbahs from Araby and silks from Ceylon, and the recess room where she kept the paints and powders of her alterations, the hundred talcs and polishes and waxes that she called the merchandises of her beauty. And the gems and trinkets, the costly ones as blatant as a slap, and the sad, regretful ones like afterthoughts. All of them, all to adorn and decorate, to make her more comely, more pleasing, more tantalizing—to whom? For what?

Thorns and thistles.

She swept the bottles off the tables, flung an urn of unguent against a looking glass. She broke vials and smashed ewers. Talcs and powders blew a white smoke about the room. The shattered flasks of oils, so sensuous when discrete, made a noisome stench when mixed together. With each crash of destruction she uttered a cry—laughter and outrage, mirth and murder—kill it all, she shrieked, kill it all, kill it!

Afterward, appalled, alarmed, not believing she could have done such vandalism, she tried not to notice her heartbeats, and gazed at a sight she couldn't comprehend.

She had not heard her brother enter until she saw him standing there, at the doorway, quite still, neither grave nor smiling, a stranger. Someone a few years older than she was, tall and lean, clean-shaven in the Roman style, everything about him Roman—mantle, tunic, laced sandals, including, she knew, even his speech, Greco-Latin in the fashion of an educated Roman youth. Roman, traveled, free.

He waved a casual arm at the chaos. "What does this do for you?" he asked.

"Hades."

"You mean you're making Hades—or sending me there."

"Hades, Hades."

"Or perhaps you want to go there yourself."

"Anywhere."

"If Father would let me, I'd take you with me."

She drew an uneven breath, moved to the dimmest corner of the room, to be alone. With a little gasp she put her head into her hands, wanting to hide from her havoc. She was ashamed. It was new to her, this rage, and the fright was new as well. How could she be Mary of Magdala and be that rabid woman?

"What?" she said. "What did you say?"

"I said that I would take you to Alexandria if he would let me."

"Thank you. He won't."

"I know he won't. I asked him again."

He did not move any farther into the destruction. "Why did you do this?"

"I don't know. I think I'm losing my wits."

"Perhaps it's a good thing. What good are they to you?"

The irony, and his understanding, helped. She tried to smile.

He moved from the doorway at last, threading his way among the breakage, a young man fastidious about his delicate sandals, holding his mantle a bit more closely than necessary. In the tantrum, she had torn her dress, and her coiffure was disheveled. He reached to her forehead and brushed away a lock of hair.

"I wish I could take you with me," he said.

"Did you really ask him?"

"Like a beggar."

"What did he say?"

"What he always says. He used his favorite word."

"Obscene."

"Yes."

Caleb had a face that was made for mockery. His eyes did not exactly match in color, and one side of his countenance was different from the other. Half his mouth seemed to speak genuinely, with a touching concern for his listener, the other half ridiculed. She felt that he loved her, yet there was derision in it, and she was not certain whether he was deriding her—or himself for caring.

"He added a little something to the word 'obscene,'" the young man continued. "He said that *I* was obscene."

"He sees obscenity everywhere."

"But he may be right about me." A fractional smile. "Anyone who loves Alexandria as I do . . ."

"Is it so shocking?"

"That's the point—it never shocks me. On the day I landed there for the first time, they were eviscerating a man in the marketplace. Nobody seemed dismayed—hardly anyone even seemed curious about why it was being done. And I must say that curiosity was about all I could muster."

"You didn't think it an atrocity?"

"Yes, but atrocity seems only fitting to the times."

"I don't believe you mean that."

"I do—oh, I do."

She shivered. Caleb appeared disappointed that she, too, disapproved. "Don't be a Pharisee," he said.

"I'm not."

"You might not like Alexandria. You might miss the comforts of hypocrisy."

"I am not a hypocrite!"

"How would you feel in a city where men make love to men—without closing the lattices? Where wives go interchangeably between husbands, and husbands between wives? Where fathers lie with their daughters, and brothers with their sisters? Where certain dogs are bred because they have smooth tongues and a taste for women's parts?"

She let the soiling question dangle, not touching it.

Watching her, amused, he asked, "Well? How would that make you feel?"

He was up to his old tricks, she thought, mocking, trying to raise hackles. Perhaps part of what he related was true, perhaps all of it. She rather doubted his picture of Alexandrian depravity, but that was not the point. He was testing her, gauging her readiness for bizarre and unsettling experiences.

"I've been too sheltered," she said. "I need to be shaken up a little."

He did not seem to breathe. Only his eyes blinked, too frequently under the strain of gazing at her so fixedly. He continued to take the measure of his sister, as if appraising everything about her: her size, her resources, the textures of her clothes and skin.

Gently then he laid his hand on her cheek and held it there. There was no motion in his fingers, not a tremor. His eyes met hers. His gaze descended slowly to the ravage she had done to her bodice, the rent at her breast line. He moved his hand from her cheek. With both hands, he gathered the two pieces of torn cloth into his fingers. He brought them together for an instant, then drew them apart again, wider.

He is going to touch me, she thought, to test whether I will be shocked; to tease me; or worse. And what will I do? She dreaded that he might put his hands on her breasts, yet wanted him to do it. Her heart pounded and she tried not to flinch from his look. She couldn't stand the silence, the waiting. *Touch* me, she thought, or let me go.

He let her go. Removed his hands from the bodice. Drifted a step or two away.

His voice was steady. "You're not a virgin, are you?"

"No, I'm not."

He nodded and smiled, and did not smile at all.

"I think you will get to Alexandria sooner or later. But what will you do there?"

The question had been at the bitten quick of her yearnings to go away. It smarted.

"What can I do?"

"It doesn't matter where you are—a woman only has three choices: wife, queen or courtesan."

"I'm not of royal blood."

"That makes it easier. The problem with courtesans, however, is not that they sell themselves, but that they don't know what price to set. They either ask too much and are abandoned—or ask too little and abandon themselves. One way or another, they get the worst of the bargain. So take my advice—and Father's, too: find a well-appointed Sadducee and marry him."

It had the coolness of an insult. As if he had struck her, and not in a temper. He had relegated her to a kind of winter storage, some frigid place where small-spirited and unimpassioned women were to dwell.

When he turned and left the room, she was alone once more, and desperation seized her. The wreckage seemed all too fitting, like the untidy truth, and she felt that if she cleared the mess away she would restore a falsehood. She wondered: would she have gone through with it, allowed this man, her brother, to make love to her? Not the act, but the uncertainty, filled her with apprehension. What have I come to?

Escape.

Was her mother's means the only way? Was dying a real or an illusory choice between alternatives? Was dying more a matter of free will than Jews were prone to admit? Her mother had chosen to expire.

She remembered how alive the woman had been in Magdala. Find the zest in things, she had said, where zest meant not only piquancy but essence. Flowers at every turning place, larkspur and lupine and asphodel, everywhere, in and out of nooks and niches, flagging every season; laughter overflowing gourds and goblets; fat brown cakes bulging, bursting with dates and figs and sultanas; nonsense songs and outbursts of gaiety, tumbling out of the bedclothes and plaited into the hair; Passover wine, even for the children, and bosom loaves of Sabbath bread risen with the yeast of comfort. A woman with a smile so radiant that sunlight, moonlight, lamplight were unnecessary. She was a hosanna. Mamma, Mamma, come quickly, run, run, see how happy I am!

Her mother's name was Leah, and she wore her hair in two thick braids, which she wound together into a coronet that made her queenly. Though she was a head shorter than her husband, the woman was the tallest person Mary had ever known. And when, in the earliest spring, they walked together to the Lake of Gennesaret and encountered the first crocuses on the hillside, the eight-year-old girl felt nearly as tall as anyone. How long do crocuses stay alive? she asked one morning. They live forever, little gosling, didn't you know that? What does Galilee mean? she asked another time. It means how beautiful you are. No, Mamma, tell me. It means how I adore you.

Love, love, the mysterious essence of everything! What else *is* there, her mother said, go ask your father. He would laugh, and her mother would laugh with him, and Caleb would smile slyly and steal all the pomegranates or hide the kittens. Galilee, sweet Galilee, so small that it could be hidden in the heart, her mother said, where seeking was finding, and running was arriving, where nothing was too late or too early, nothing too much or too little, and the soft voices of angels could be heard whispering from the summit of the nearest hill. Mamma, run, run quickly, catch me being glad!

Then, one morning, an unknown person sat outside the smaller sitting room the door of which was always open. Today it was closed. Your mother is sleeping, she said, and will not awaken until sundown; go and play. Midday, before he was expected, her father came from Jerusalem with a beardless Roman who knew about chills and fever. He had a musty, unpleasant smell about him, like spices gone rotten, and he said the windows in the room where her mother lay must be boarded and sealed tight, and the children were to live in a hush on the other side of the house.

Sometimes, in the night, Mary would sneak past Chana, the nursing woman, to look at her mother sleeping. The face was someone else's. Her features, which had been beautifully assembled, no longer belonged with one another. One evening, the ailing one opened her eyes and they had no color and her once sweet voice made her words sound like hisses. Why are you doing that? Mary wanted to say; why can't you talk to me? She felt deserted.

Mamma, run!

Time passed, while her mother was ill, and extra bondwomen were bought to do the woman's work. Her father made Mary a present of a servant named Enna who knew wonderful things. She cut an apple in a way Mary had never seen before, and disclosed two perfect stars. She sang an Egyptian song that returned upon itself in a delightful curl, and Mary learned to sing it. She added sums by a foxy trick of subtracting other sums, and taught Mary how to do it, enjoining her to secrecy as if it were wicked. The child couldn't wait to see her every morning. Best of all, she knew that Enna loved her.

Her father was loved too, by another bondwoman, in a way Mary did not understand. This one was a stunning Parthian with skin that glowed like apricot and a head exquisitely turbaned in dusky silks. No one saw her hair. She prepared the meals for the household, wonderful mixtures unidentifiable and full of exotic herbs and condiments that nipped at the tongue and excited all the juices in the mouth. Mary had the feeling that the food might be like the woman, Kooris, and there was something a little eerie in the speculation. Sometimes Mary thought Kooris was not altogether human, but a sort of elegant specter who could disappear at will. Often, she did disappear. For hours. And it was a long while before Mary noticed that at such times her father disappeared as well.

Caleb had two tutors, one of whom he liked. Occasionally, carrying the largest slingshots Mary had ever seen, the two stamping males went hunting for partridge. Sometimes they came back with partridge, sometimes they came back with oblique glances and no partridge.

One day, Mary realized that she was forgetting that her mother was ill, and for days thereafter she spent hours and hours at the sick woman's side. She would sit and talk as though they were actually having a conversation, but after a while she couldn't bear not hearing any responses, so she stopped visiting and went back to forgetting again.

Until the day the wonder happened. Her mother began to improve. Color started to return to her cheeks and she could sit up, leaning against the pillows, talking softly and smiling a little. Week by week she became stronger. On a Sabbath evening, she arose from her bed and said she wanted to light the candles and say the Sabbath prayer.

The candles were already lit. Enna had lighted them.

Not many days later—it was at the beginning of spring—she told Mary she felt well enough to walk down the hillside and look for crocuses. They got ready a little after dawn. Even though it was going to be a lovely day with no winter chill in the air, the child made certain that her mother was warmly clothed. Starting down the hill together, they were both elated, and Mary's heart sang. It felt like earlier times, only different: They had traded places. The child was taking care of the woman. Don't walk too fast, she said, breathe deeply, heed the wetness on the stones. She took her mother's hand. It was so thin and wasted that she wanted to kiss it and kiss it again and make it strong. She clung too tightly and her mother made a slight moan, and the little girl released her hand, as if burned. Not many paces down the hill, the woman tired. Go on alone, she said, bring me a crocus. Mary did not know what to do. She wanted to go home, but her mother said, no, go on, I can return safely by myself. Bring me a crocus, I dearly want a crocus. So her mother turned back, and Mary continued downward.

She was not alone for long. Enna came running from the house to join her, and they went down the rest of the hill together. As they approached the turning toward the brook, Mary looked upward. Her mother had been watching them descend. Both hands covered her mouth, as if she wanted to cry out.

The first crocus Mary found she crumpled in her hand and tossed away. The others—since crocuses are not meant for picking—were wilted by the time she got home. Her mother professed to want them anyway, but later in the afternoon Mary did not see them in her mother's room.

In the middle of the night the child heard a wailing. She hurried through the hallway and down the stairs. Outside her mother's room, her father was pounding on the locked door, calling his wife's name, Leah, Leah, pitifully begging to be let in, crying that it was nothing, that he loved her, it was nothing, nothing. At a distance, in the dimness at the end of the corridor, Kooris stood alone, clutching a bright shawl to her nearly naked body.

Her mother never got out of bed again. There was no need to, she seemed to say. Nothing that she had used to do was being neglected; the cooking, the housekeeping, the tutoring of the children, the sweet remembrances of flowers around the house, the baking of luscious cakes and meat pies—all were attended to by slaves. Even the lovemaking. And it must have been borne in upon the woman, Mary later speculated, that she, too, had been a slave, an all-purpose bondwoman whose tasks could be divided up and delegated. Now she was not needed. She had lost not only her loveliness, but her ability to quicken loveliness in others. Love was no longer a definition of anything in her life. So she chose to die in the dusk of an autumn day.

Mary did not realize she was dead until she saw her father standing on the stairway, not knowing whether to go up or down, crying like a demented child, rending his clothes, beating his head against the wall. Ashes, he kept wailing, bring me ashes!

The following day he mourned in a more formal way, according to the Law. There was a decorum of lamentation, strictly dictated in written formularies—how many days were to be set aside for grief, what clothes must be worn, precisely how they were to be torn, in what way the mirrors should be blinded. And the prayers—the specific blessings and beseechings, the protestations of love and guilt, the invocations for forgiveness—all were ritually prescribed. It was also prescribed who could attend the prayers for the dead. Only males.

Mary envied them. How merciful to be told exactly how to grieve, and how much grief was permissible. It was said that the God of the Jews was cruel, but He was certainly compassionate to men. Lament, He said, then cease your lamentation.

Cease. Oh, if she could only cease! If only Someone would tell her: you have wept enough, you have long enough cried in vain, you have ached more than your share of aching. If only Someone would tell her to stop rending the clothes of her spirit, and let her bind herself again. Ashes, bring me ashes! Dear Lord in heaven, when may I cease weeping over my mother?

Her grief never ceased, nor did her anger. Her mother had perished because she was not needed. And finally the woman had had no need of herself.

Mary knew that to be unnecessary was rarely what it seemed. Were she to ask most Jewish women if they felt superfluous they would have pointed to their *kasher* homes and their well-tended husbands and children, and scorned such a question. But suppose she had asked other questions: whether, alone in the world, a woman would be enough for herself; whether a grown woman had learned what the child had longed to know; whether, without her parents' God to share, she would have been able to make one of her own? Or do without any god at all?

Where can I go to have my questions answered? Mary asked. To the sages and priests? To the mountain of Moses?

Three times, Herod's party had been postponed, once on the very eve of the event. Now, two months after the Roman New Year's Day, it was announced again. With their mantles over their mouths, people laughed. Had Herod no pride at all? Was he in such a frenzy to rule Judea that he would kiss Pilate's toenail for the crown?

Mary understood his yearning. She had one too. If Herod's party really took place tonight—even if it was mortally dangerous for a Jew to steal her way into a festivity where the most honored guest was a Roman procurator rumored to despise Hebrews—she needed to be there. Uninvited, she had to go. No matter that lesser invasions of Roman purlieus had resulted in cripplings and mutilations, no matter that a beggar woman's eyes were gouged out for peeping into a private Roman atrium. The woman was not quick-witted, Mary thought. I am cunning.

Cunning was good, but beautiful was better. It was not enough, however, to be beautiful in a Jewish way. She had to look like a woman of Rome.

Her hair, parted in the middle, hung down simply to below her shoulders—like a fall of autumn leaves, her mother had said—but it was in the fashion of Jewish maidenhood.

About to call her servant, Duna, she desisted. Do it alone, she decided. She took to her combs and brushes. For over an hour she combed and stroked and scratched at her hair and could not decide how to dress it. There were too many Roman coiffures to choose from, too many coils and braids and intertwinings, and she had no skill in the artifice.

When summoned for the evening repast, she sent an excuse and continued to study herself in the mirror. At Herod's palace, the first guests would be arriving soon, she supposed, and she must hurry. But should she hurry and steal her way in through the melee of the assembling crowd, or should she wait until after the First Vomit, as Caleb called it, and enter during the second dining? The second, perhaps, when the guests were well on their way to drunkenness, and she would not be noticed.

No, she couldn't wait. Go at once.

The evening was passing quickly now, and her hair, with all the torturing, was beginning to fly wild. Hurry.

From a small alabaster jar she took a finger of ointment. Spreading it on her palms, smelling the evanescence of thyme and lavender, she smoothed the unguent on her hair. There were really only two choices: ringlets or a coronet. If she made ringlets at her temples, she could look like a typical young Roman girl, unmarried; if she wore her hair in a finely twisted crown, as her mother had, she could be taken for a mature woman, the young wife of a consul, perhaps. Ringlets: Romans had a predilection for virgins. Then, at the last minute, she added the coronet as well, and the result delighted her.

Carefully she painted her eyelashes with kohl. Not too much, however, for the slightest moisture from the eyes made this sooty powder of antimony run, and she would look as though she were weeping black tears. Mature women do not weep in public. Was she indeed a mature and world-wisened woman, the Romans might ask, or a vestal of purity? For an instant, she herself addressed the question. She decided to give it further thought, when she had time.

Now for the gown. How exquisite she would look, how luminous! By the flicker of the candles and lamplight, the glow of the jade satin was golden on the hills and forest green in the valleys of the drapery, and the opals glimmered like sky light, or blazed like fire. The dress fit her to sublimity, hanging innocently from her shoulders, then wantonly embracing her breasts and hips. Beautiful, beautiful.

Something wrong.

She looked like a Jewess.

Even with the Roman coiffure, she looked like a Jewess.

She knew what she had to do. But she could not bring herself to do it. If she did, and her father caught a glimpse of her, he would suffer a wound that would never heal. Even Caleb might be shocked.

There was no choice. She undid the bodice of the dress. She took a knife to the drawstrings and the straps. Tying them another way, she hoped the drapery would not be ruined. Then she rearranged herself in the costume.

Her breasts were almost totally exposed. In her nervousness and excitement, her nipples stood erect, catching the candlelight. They were like glowing rubies above the jeweled neckline of her bodice.

She was ready to go now, ready to go to Herod's party, to open the door of her prison a little, to view a wider vista of the world, as if she were a woman of Rome. One last glance at herself in the looking glass, debating whether to wear a mantle or a scarf. Then, because the day had been hot and she wanted no encumbrances, she decided against both. Free-limbed, bare-bosomed, chin high, she slipped out into the corridor, down the back staircase and onto the upper terrace.

Below her were the narrow streets of crowded Jerusalem, and behind the farthest hill, on which stood the palace, there was an illimitable sky, aglow with the thousand lights of Herod's candles and torches. She had never seen a more enthralling heaven.

On a summer's evening, when Judas was twelve years old, he tried to kill his father. They were in the saddlery, standing beside the workbench where his brother Tubal was cutting calfskins and his father was counting the day's money. He seized one of the long-bladed harness awls and, in a fit of wildness, struck at his father's heart. But Tubal sprang from his stool, grappled with the smaller boy and deflected the blow. The awl plunged into their father's forearm, severing an artery, and the blood gushed over a newly made wineskin and a number of unfinished sandals.

Judas's mother wept for days over the boy's abominable offense. His brother's contempt for him deepened, and for many months his father pretended that the younger son did not exist. Through Eliachim, the leech of Kerioth who tended the saddler's wound, the shopkeepers on the main thoroughfare and the neighbors as far down as the river heard of the occurrence. Everyone was profoundly shocked.

Judas, however, was not shocked. For all that he had never raised his hand in violence to anyone, he had expected some hideousness would occur between him and his father; he had dreaded it.

Perhaps it came from having loved the man too much. The boy had adored him. His earliest, his sweetest memories were the tales told in the sandal-and-saddle shop, the father at work, talking with tacks in his mouth, recounting the stories of the Scripture as though they had occurred only yesterday at the village well or at the river crossing. How the infant Judas had been named for a great hero, the Maccabee, and how he, too, would wield a sword and carry banners for his people. The boy recalled the Sabbath mornings in the crowded synagogue, just room enough to sit between his father's legs, rocking back and forth in the obeisances demanded by the prayer, rocking in unison with his father's body. Sometimes the bending and the praying were in such concord that the boy would think: we have been bonded, my father and I; we are one person. Best of all was the exquisite sadness of Yom Kippur evenings when the dusk was beginning to darken the synagogue and the first prayers of penance were starting, and his father would beg forgiveness in a sad swaying motion, beating his breast, swaying the lad with him; it was as if the man were taking upon himself the sins of his beloved son. And the boy would tremble with a strange and aching bliss, not quite understanding, yet knowing there was a goodness here, in his love of God and his love of his father. In fact, loving his father had taught him how to love God.

There was, to Judas, no man so blessed as his parent, Amos of Kerioth. Never since Genesis was there a creation so pure and devout, so partial to decency, so full of regard for Jehovah and for man.

About a year ago, an incident occurred. A three-wheeled wagon pulled by a farm horse appeared at the back doorway of the saddlery. The wagon was laden with hides, a great mound of them, still smelling of the tannery, pungent and sour, an after-breath of many vinegars. The leathers were not uniform; some were cut squarely or in oblongs, but most were skins that still held the shape of the animal. As Tubal helped the carter unload, Amos studied the screed of lading. So many calfskins, he murmured, branding them with his fingernail, so many bull- and cow-hides, so many sheepskins . . . and the rest.

Judas asked what the rest might be. Tubal and Amos exchanged a glance, then shunted the younger boy away.

As he mounted the outside stairway to their living quarters above the saddlery, Judas had a vague misgiving. There was something wrong. He tried to dismiss it, but a dreadful suspicion was forming in his mind: the hides had been stolen.

Sundown, at the evening meal:

"Do not concern yourself," his mother said. She served the men quietly. She would eat later, after prayers had been spoken. Rochah was a woman who distanced herself from everything; she wanted Judas to do likewise. "You'll learn the trade when you are older."

"I'm not talking about 'the trade,'" Judas said. "Only about this afternoon—the hides."

"They're just like the other hides," Tubal said. "Just a little cheaper."

"What makes them cheaper?"

"They're slightly damaged. Nicks and water markings."

"I don't believe you, Tubal."

There was a silence. Amos at last filled it.

"They are swine skins."

"The skins of . . . swine?"

"Don't be so shocked, Judas," Tubal said. "We don't eat the animal, we merely work the skins."

"But we are forbidden to touch them."

"We are forbidden to touch the dead, too," his brother continued. "But we go to burials, and wash our hands afterward."

"It is not the same thing."

"Finish your meal," his mother said.

"Father, it is not the same—is it?"

Hesitant, Amos said, "No, it is not the same."

"Then, why do you handle them?"

"You will know when you are older."

"I want to know now! Why do you buy them?"

His father lost his temper. *"Nobody wants them*—it makes them cheaper in the marketplace."

The boy could not believe what he was hearing. Nor the way he was hearing it. His father's voice was harsh—as if Judas were committing the sin against the Law, and by raising the question was compounding his transgression.

Judas did not know what to say or do. The meat he was eating turned wooden in his mouth. He was unable to swallow, and too humiliated to spit it out. He started to gag. Fleeing, he ran down the back stairs, rushed to the field behind the house and spewed his food upon the ground. If he could disgorge the rest of the meal as well, he would have felt better; it was as if he had eaten pig.

That was the year during which Judas would have his Bar Mitzvah. All twelve months would be dedicated to his learning the rites of manhood, so that when the splendid day of celebration arrived, he could stand beside his father on the bema of the synagogue and read his portion with ease and fluency, to show that maturity had come gracefully to him. To prepare for the occasion, it was customary to place a boy in the tutelage of a man of piety and learning, a master of the Torah, or a respected rabbi. Prior to the incident of the hides, there was nobody Judas wanted as his Bar Mitzvah guardian other than his father. And the special training had already begun. But, for days after the occurrence, the boy missed many lessons, and made excuses for his absences. His father pretended an unusual busyness in the shop, and did not press him.

During that time, Judas became aware of a number of things he had never noticed before. For example, during conversations in the saddlery, his father was never the first to voice an opinion, but always waited to hear the customer's point of view, then expressed himself with words that were a subtle rewording of what he had just heard. He seemed to vary his beliefs according to his customers. Nobody appeared to discredit Amos for this practice; on the contrary, his patrons and neighbors viewed him as a man of broad sympathies who saw merit in everyone's opinion. But Judas's new view of his father filled the boy with disquiet. He had always thought of his father as being full of wisdom, but was it merely prudence? And the troubling thought: was the man whom he so deeply loved and respected a dissembler?

As Judas watched his father more closely, his dreads were realized. The man did worse than dissemble. He lied. With the Romans, particularly, he seemed to have no qualms. He would tell them precisely what they wanted to hear, flattering their egos, smiling at their anti-Jewish jokes, occasionally even cheating them. On one occasion, when Judas was witness to such a deception, he stayed away from the shop for days. Finally, one Sabbath, his father asked him the reason.

Judas hesitated. Then: "Why did you cheat the Roman Albius?"

"I was not cheating Albius. I was simply getting back what he has stolen from me."

"He stole something from you?"

"Every month the Romans steal from us. They send publicans for the taxes. When they have gone, we have nothing left."

"Why do you give it to them?"

"If we don't, they beat us or throw us into chains."

Something was not as his father described it. "What do they do with the money?"

"They pay for the soldiers who insult our women and throw stones in our synagogues and dig up our graves."

"Why do you allow it?" Judas cried. "Why don't you and the other Jews—"

His father interrupted. "Enough of that!"

But his son was not to be halted. "At least, you do not have to be nice to them—smiling on one side of your face—pretending to be their friend!"

"What shall I be to them?" he cried. "What shall I be?"

The man was suffering, and Judas could not stand to see it. There was no longer any question of rightness, only comfort and kindness. He wanted to lay warmth upon whatever chill his father was enduring . . . yet . . . how to follow his father's precepts of honor and goodness?

Tubal was no help at all; he simply refused to think. His mother's view was that Judas must try to live more safely on the surface of things, and not to dig too deeply; to burrow in the earth was to uncover vipers. It was a counsel of fear he knew he could not heed. He kept brooding over the question and did not know which way to turn. Increasingly, he felt a heaviness in his mind; many nights, he lay awake.

Late one afternoon, in the market square, the boy heard a Zealot haranguing a crowd, telling them that liberation would never come to the Jews until the Pharisees ceased being duplicitous with God and man. And as the radical described the typical Pharisee, Judas had the sickly feeling that the man was talking about Amos.

That evening, alone with his father in the saddlery, being tutored for his Bar Mitzvah, he was trying to learn the subtle inflection of a difficult incantation. His mind wandered, and he asked: "Are you a timeserver?"

His father took a moment to reply. "Where did you hear that expression?"

"A Zealot said it."

"You must not listen to Zealots. They are dangerous. Do you know what a timeserver is?"

"Someone who says anything that will bring him a profit."

"Do you think I am a timeserver?"

The boy evaded the question. "The Zealot said that usurers were the worst kind of timeservers."

"Do you know what usury is?"

"A man who lends money at a profit."

"Do you think that is a bad thing to do?"

The boy lost his temper. "Profit, profit! Is everything to be done for profit?"

"If you are so opposed to profit, then you are opposed to me, Judas. And you may call me a timeserver and a usurer."

The boy felt as if his father was being torn away from him. "But you're not a timeserver, you're not a usurer! You don't lend money for a profit, do you?"

"Yes, I do."

"Are you a different man than you pretend to be?"

"Sometimes that is necessary."

"Then, sometimes you are a liar."

"I . . . cannot deny it."

"Then, tell me how to keep from hating you!"

It was such an agonized outcry that Amos could not immediately respond. At last: "You can keep from hating me by remembering that I love you, Judas."

"How do I know that *that* is not a lie?"

His father started to reply, but faltered. "I cannot answer that," he said. "In any event, it doesn't matter what I say—you have to rely on what you know about me. I love you very truly . . . but that is only part of the truth of what I am. Even if I knew the whole truth, it might be too difficult to utter—or too terrible—or I wouldn't have the words. It will be the same with everyone, Judas. If you seek for someone who will never lie, you will find no one. You will be alone with your purity—and you will have no one to love."

"Must I go through life as you do, making bargains with lies?"

"With liars."

"That is not what you taught me."

"Let it be one of the lessons of the Bar Mitzvah."

"If that is one of the lessons, I don't want the Bar Mitzvah."

He started to tremble, and his father reached to comfort him. "Judas—beloved boy—don't make the world so beautiful and so terrible."

With a wildness: "I haven't made it so! You have done it—you!"

"Then, you must forgive me."

He laid his hand on the boy's cheek, and Judas struck it away. "Let me alone—don't touch me!"

"Judas—I love you—"

"I don't want you to love me!"

"Judas—please—"

"Tell me how to hate you! Tell me how to hate you!"

The boy began to cry.

The Bar Mitzvah sessions stopped entirely. For months there was not a single lesson. With little left of the year, and Judas's thirteenth birthday approaching, the boy was not readying himself, the family was not preparing, no arrangements were being made with the synagogue, and there was a silence in the house.

It was an afflicted silence for everyone. Judas knew that his mother was particularly tormented, because she kept baking extra breads and cakes and meat pies, all the delicacies that the men loved . . . and delivering them, stale and scarcely touched, to the poor. Everybody seemed to eat less than usual these days. Especially Judas.

He ate and slept very little. He could count his ribs, and the circles under his eyes looked as though he had painted them with his father's leather-blacking. Sometimes he consciously avoided saying his evening prayers. Hitherto, the ritual had been a blessing, a friendly concourse with the Almighty, gentling the boy into a peaceful slumber. But now the prayers agitated him, they made him question every word as if to find some double meaning, to discover some sly and evasive innuendo written between the lines by the double-dealing elders. Occasionally, because he felt guilty for repudiating prayers, he spoke them mechanically, avoiding their significance. But then he felt tainted by hypocrisy.

Pharisee, he called himself. Timeserver, speaking to God in the words He wishes to hear, believing none of them.

Believing none? Had he wandered such a vast distance from his childhood faith, from his family, from everyone and everything he loved? On the path to manhood, how had he lost his way?

He felt that he was becoming ill. His head ached often, and sometimes his hands would shake. He was too proud to mention these concerns to his family, for he knew that they all disapproved of him. But, alone with his aberrations, he started to become frightened. He lived in a state of dismay as if something horrible were occurring, as if he were being transformed into a devil or a wild beast.

One day, needing to reclaim the forfeited comfort of his childhood, he went to his father's shop, and sat there, on a stool, watching Amos and Tubal at work. His brother was an apprentice; in a year or so he would be a master saddler. Watching the older boy's capable hands, and observing the surety with which Tubal did everything, Judas envied him. His own hands, his eyes, his whole life trembled with uncertainties.

It was sunset. Tubal was cutting hides for tomorrow's work and his father was counting the coins he had received during the day. Judas saw Amos do a curious thing. He set one group of coins in a pile apart. Roman coins—with the likeness of Caesar incised upon them. Graven images—sinful for a Jew to look upon, much less to keep.

His father collected the Roman coins and put them, with care, into a small leather pouch.

Judas tightened.

"What are you going to do with them?"

"When I go to Jerusalem, I will trade them for Jewish ones."

"No."

"What do you say?"

"Throw them away."

"They are valuable."

"They are filthy—throw them away!" He reached for the leather pouch.

"Take your hands off, Judas!"

The boy tore open the pouch, ran to the window and threw the coins out upon the street.

Amos tried to stop him, but Judas kept flinging the coins away. His father struck him. With a cry of rage, the boy turned and whipped his hand across his father's face. Amos hit him again and again.

Judas fell across the workbench and his hands clutched at the awl. He raised it against his father.

In the weeks that followed, Judas was scarcely addressed by anyone in the family. It was as though he were not there. He was in no way engaged with the others, he did not even sit at meals with them. Food was left for the boy as if for an animal. And the Bar Mitzvah was no longer mentioned.

When his thirteenth birthday was less than a month away, his father summoned him to the saddlery. It was nighttime, the doors of the shop were barred. An oil lamp, its wick nearly spent, smoked on the workbench. His father sat on a high stool and, working, did not face the boy.

"On the first Sabbath of Av it will be your thirteenth birthday. I have arranged with the synagogue for you to ascend to the bema on that day and read the appropriate passages. To prepare you for it, I have asked Rabbi Gemaliel Bar David to teach you the phrasings and incantations. You will go to him tomorrow."

Judas waited to see if his father had anything further to say. That was all of it. Still the boy did not leave.

"I am sorry for everything, Father." His voice was altogether composed.

"Yes. I am sorry too."

They did not look at one another.

"I do not want the Bar Mitzvah," Judas said quietly.

The man turned and glanced briefly at his son. "It is not a matter of wanting or not wanting. You will be thirteen years old."

"I do not want to ascend to the bema—or say the prayers—or read the portion."

Amos moved the lamp so that he could have an unobstructed view.

"I do not understand. You wish to deny that you are a Jew?"

"No, not exactly."

"But you do not wish to affirm it."

Judas tried to maintain his steadiness. "I am . . . afraid . . . to make a pledge that I'm not sure I can keep."

"It's not a pledge, it's a ritual."

"Still . . . a responsibility . . ."

"Yes, a responsibility. While you're younger than thirteen, you are a child. When you reach the age of thirteen, if you do not accept your responsibility as a Jew, you are no longer a child, and you are not a man. You are nobody."

"Nobody is what I am, Father. If I ever feel that I am somebody, I will be ready to get up upon the bema."

"You are doing things the wrong way around."

"I do not know the right way."

"I am telling you the right way."

Judas did not say that his father's word no longer had persuasion with him. The man understood the boy's silence. The stillness fell upon him like a blow.

His father said, "I hope you will one day return to what you were."

"I hope not," the boy replied.

Their voices were evenly modulated, not a syllable was raised. Both were speaking reasonably, without any apparent grudge. Judas was relieved that this was so. He had dreaded that his resolve might weaken, that he would go soft and show how shaken he was. It was a bitter comfort to know that he had stood firm.

As he turned to leave the shop, his father whispered his name. When Judas looked back, Amos made a helpless gesture in the air, then toward his mouth, as if to retrieve the utterance. His eyes looked so wounded that the boy wanted to cry out in pity.

But he resisted, and swiftly departed from the place.

His father had said that he would be nobody, which was exactly what he became. He had no place in Kerioth. He belonged to nothing. Soon, because he was neither man nor child, he gave up going to the synagogue. He had been relegated, not by any decision or decree, to a lesser place than the women. They, at least, had their own entrance door; he had no portal through which he could enter with the certainty that he would be welcomed across the threshold.

He did go to Rabbi Gemaliel—not for Bar Mitzvah preparation—but to learn to be a *sopher.* There were two kinds of *sopherim,* but Judas had no hope of ever becoming the exalted kind: a scribe. It would take too much learning—and religious acceptance—to become an interpreter of the Word, a legal intercessor between laymen and the Temple, between the Temple and the Roman Government. He would have to be expert not only in the civil law but the sacred one, and Judas could not give himself to such pious dedication.

He would be the lesser *sopher,* not a scribe but a scrivener; not a theological dignitary with a chamber in the synagogue, but a civil servant with a stool and a makeshift table on some thoroughfare, where he would perform minor writing and copying services for a shekel or two.

After a time, Rabbi Gemaliel was not satisfied to teach him penmanship, the mere use of quills and brushes. Your lettering is good enough, the old man said; now let us look to your knowledge. He started the boy on simple things, the proper salutations of correspondence, the economical phrases for describing standard states of body and mind, typical requisitions and receipts, the usual warranties and disclaimers and depositions. Then, slyly, as the first year of training came to an end, the old man began to slip more profound considerations into their learning sessions: If a woman has no dowry, how can you word her letter to a man in a distant city so that her fine qualities will make him feel compensated for her lack of goods and chattels? If the Roman law is at variance with the Jewish law, how can you take advantage of both without infracting the rules of either? How do you state a grievance so that it will be remedied, even if neither the statutes nor the customs are on your side? He taught the boy that the law was concerned with accuracy, which was quite separate from truth; that the spoken insult might be a passing blow, but the written one could be mortal; that a writ of divorcement had to be indited without anger; that bile was bad ink.

These were worldly matters, and Judas was relieved not to be having disputations with Jehovah. During his second year of training under Gemaliel, he set up a table on the shady side of the main thoroughfare, about halfway between his father's saddlery and the synagogue. He was the youngest of the three street scriveners in Kerioth, scarcely fifteen. While his fees were the lowest, and it was commonly agreed that he was as skilled as the others, he had few customers. The Romans, even though Judas's Latin was nearly as good as his Hebrew and Aramaic, patronized their own amanuenses. And his own people would not give their custom to a Jew who had rejected Jewish manhood.

He was shunned. Not in an insolent way, not by any overt insults or the casting of stones. But by a silent complicity of disregard. It was as if the Jews of Kerioth had written him into the register of the Romans, whose presence they were at pains to ignore. Even his family went about their daily lives as if the younger child had gone away.

Two more years went by, and there were no grudges anymore. But, ironically, the absence of resentment brought little ease to the young man, for no other emotion came to fill the emptiness. It occurred to him that the remission from pain was a questionable comfort. At home, he hardly ever had an exchange of opinions or a meeting of glances. Nobody, except his mother, ever came close enough to lay a hand upon his person, to touch his shoulder or his arm; and when his mother—rarely—made a contact with her younger son, there was such reservation in it—and guilt—that Judas felt the touch as if it were a punishment.

The only person he could talk to was Gemaliel. He spent all his spare time with the rabbi's books, and the old man helped him to improve his Latin and assiduously taught him Greek. But Gemaliel was growing feeble now, forgetting more and more each day, repeating things the boy had heard a great many times, the wording of this formality or that, the double meaning of a psalm, the infallible signs that a Messiah would come, a Messiah was on his way to save the Jews from the Babylonians. The boy would patiently correct him: Not the Babylonians, Rabbi, that was a half millennium ago, you mean the Romans. Ah, the Romans, yes, thank you, Judas, the Romans.

Day by day, the rabbi weakened. He began to lose the last vestiges of his wits, and to go blind. His inability to read was, to the venerable scholar, the worst penalty of age. Loving his old benefactor, Judas read to him, took care of him, fed him, bathed him, disentangled his hair and beard, and often talked him into slumber. Then, the final ignominy: the old man became incontinent. Gemaliel could not stand the shame of it. Let me die, he said to the boy, let me wander away among the psalms. But Judas bathed him and embraced him and resumed the reading of the sweeter songs of Solomon.

On the fourteenth day of Tishri, the rabbi, like a man transfigured, arose from his bed and announced that tomorrow was Succoth, the holiday that celebrates the spirit of the Jews after Exodus, as they wandered homeless in the desert, living under makeshift tents and the naked sky. For this merry festival, the old man was going to build the traditional tabernacle out of palm fronds and purple flowers and tree branches, and Judas must go and fetch them. It was as if Gemaliel had seen the Messiah, such was his elation, and Judas hastened to bring him spring blossoms and palm branches. It was amazing to see how the ancient invalid, despite his infirmity and blindness, went about binding boughs together. Chanting a psalm of David, darting friskily about his dooryard, he suddenly came to a halt, clutched a palm branch to his breast, let out a little sigh, and fell.

Relatives who had paid no attention to Rabbi Gemaliel in his latter years arrived from Bethany to attend his funeral. And nearly every Jew of Kerioth was there, together with a few Romans. They all lamented with eloquence. But Judas was never asked to join any *minyan* of mourners. So he did not grieve as a Jew, but as an alien. It struck him that he had never learned the mourning prayer, the *kaddish*, and he was at a loss to find the words for his loneliness.

The old man's estate was pitiful. Most of his library and his meager family heirlooms were left to the Bethany relatives. To Judas he bequeathed a few books they had closely shared, and eighteen shekels.

With the passing of the rabbi, there was no longer anyone in Kerioth who needed the *sopher*. What he himself needed he did not know, except to take leave of the town. He decided, in a kind of default of choice, that he had to go to some place where he could be anonymous, where his failure to have performed the Jewish rituals of manhood would not be questioned. Only in a large city could he lose his identity.

Jerusalem.

On the day that he was to depart, his brother surprised him. He gave Judas a capacious leather pouch of the finest calfskin, onto which Tubal had tooled a lovely figure of a doe with eyes peering out of a thicket of acanthus leaves. His mother filled the pouch with food for the journey, a meat pie and a honey-and-almond cake.

And his father offered a handful of coins, a tiny silver one and a number of brasses and bronzes. This was the only present Judas refused.

Amos's smile was more like a wince. "Take it. Jerusalem is expensive."

"Thank you, Father, but I won't need it."

"Yes—believe me—you will." He added wryly, "Have no fear—they are not Roman coins."

He was asking for a reconciliation of sorts, and Judas could not withhold it. He took the coins.

"I will accept these as a loan," he said.

A miller, with a horse and cart, was leaving that afternoon for Medrias, a small town along the way to Jerusalem. As the sun was lowering, Judas mounted the wagon and sat beside the driver. He did not look back until they had come to the end of the thoroughfare. When he turned, the street was empty; his parents and his brother had gone indoors. And it occurred to him that he no longer had a family; and, except for Gemaliel, he had never had a friend.

Jerusalem was a din. Judas thought, at first, that he would never endure it. There was no other mode of living here except noise. Vendors shouted everywhere, dogs yawped and asses brayed, camels harrowed the ear with their deafening groans, horsemen clattered on cobblestones while shrieking for pedestrians to scatter, beggars whined and wheedled for alms, charioteers twirled their raucous rattleboxes, trumpets farted and fanfaraded, and Jews cursed at the backs of Romans and at one another.

One morning, six days after he arrived, the pandemonium seemed to have gone still. All at once he saw what a beautiful city it was. Built in the hot Judean hills, carved out of unwilling rock, it was the wrong place for a city to be, a defiance of nature. Arid and sandswept as it was, there was a law that forebade the planting of gardens and greenery, because the wind might blow manure dust into the Temple and taint the Holy of Holies. It was a law totally disregarded. Flowers, in fountains of color, burst forth in hideaways, and made oases everywhere. He might be walking in a narrow by-passage walled in by rigid masonry and suddenly it would open as if with welcoming arms upon a well-yard full of potted blooms and fig trees, medlars, carobs. Forbidding gates would unfold to reveal a loggia hung with vines and creepers, colonnaded by scarlet oleanders. And water, always, everywhere, to confound the arid wasteland, springs of water, little pools of it, tiny waterfalls, giggling like children. Everything enlivened Judas and gave him hope. The very air of the city was exciting to him—cool winds and desert winds, both at once, and the scent of myrtle and anise, and—here, there and gone—the tickle and taunt of erotic perfumes: sandalwood and heliotrope and myrrh.

He loved the city and made a game of getting lost, wandering into the heights among the richest houses and downward to study the crooked streets, the markets and the watering places, the stalls where anything at all could be bought or bartered, and the pavilions of craftsmen that lined the pathway to the Temple.

The Temple: That was the most awesome wonder of all. At the heart of a wide, sunbaked square, it was adorned in gold and porphyry, and gleamed like a mirage. For days after his arrival, while he was trying to find work, he did not dare to ascend the hill of steps that led to the edifice. He dreaded that his view of the most sacred synagogue would be painful, a punishing reminder of his defection as a Jew. But, on a Sabbath morning, as he stood at the foot of the mount, he heard, faintly, the lovely lyric voice of a *chazzan* in the opening notes of a psalm. He could not help himself. Slowly he ascended, step by measured step, yearning to be closer, yet more and more apprehensive with every footfall.

The cantor's voice was full of love and longing. And so was Judas. At last he reached the top. The terrace was like a meadow of majesty, the greenery as lush as Eden. The breeze was a caress, and he walked along the perimeter of aspen trees that whispered him onward to the great portal. How immense the Temple was, how sublimely it filled the whole field of his vision as if to say: This, this is all the world you need to see. The rest is heaven.

Heaven was inside the Temple. He had never seen so much light within an enclosed place. A million lamps were glowing; the white silk of the Torah, and the gems that adorned it, made such a brilliance as to bring a smarting to the eyes. How exquisite it all was!

Now, as he heard the congregation in unison prayer, and watched the men in their praying shawls, bending and rocking and swaying to the same holy, imploring music, each man became known to him, intimately known; each man became his father. And the boy, standing in the rear of the Temple, felt uplifted and cast down, needing to laugh and to cry. Exalted as if he might fly, and faint as if he might fall, he murmured the Sabbath prayer and began to rock and sway, and the tears rolled down his face.

Later, when the congregation had dispersed, he remained in the Temple. The smell of lamp oil and tallow from the candles was as thick as the burnt lavender and thyme. He gazed at the vastness of the holy place and thought: This is my Temple. This is where I belong. I may not have spoken my portion, I may be named an outcast by my priests, I may even be lost to my people, but . . .

I am a Jew!

Only . . . dear God . . . when will I ever find you again?

He needed work. His father had been right—Jerusalem was expensive, and even if he did not waste money on a lodging place, but slept in a recessed entryway or under a vendor's awning when the market was deserted, his small store of coins was rapidly diminishing.

He had offered his services to the scriveners whose stalls were on the pathway to the temple, but, We are too many, they said; one man vies with another; every Jew wants to be a scrivener.

One day, his worry deepening, a thought occurred: While he might never be a true scribe of the Temple, he could go to one of them and offer to be an apprentice, someone to do the menial lettering work—without pay, simply in exchange for food and, perhaps, a cot to sleep on.

The scribe he spoke to was a handsome elder with great white *peyot* that curled in ringlets at his temples. He was meticulously clean, his hands and fingernails immaculate, without a sign of the inks or tars of his profession. On his shelves, blank parchments were neatly rolled and ribboned, his papyri were fastidiously stacked with a stone weight at each of the four corners to keep them from curling, and every quill and brush seemed freshly cut. His name was Reb Avrum.

Because his immaculateness extended to his breath, he munched on rosemary leaves as he inspected the samples of Judas's penmanship. One papyrus, then another, making little hums of approval.

"You have a light hand," he said. "A bit too light on the *daleths* and *lamedhs*—too birdlike—they fly from the papyrus. But better light than heavy, yes?"

"Yes, Reb Avrum."

He liked the elder, and felt for a moment that he, too, might be liked. And he was enraptured by the scriptorium, large and airy, with wonderful parchments on the wall lettered in many colors and in many styles of script. Some seemed so ornate as to be miniature pictures, quite beautiful, and he marveled at how closely they approached human likenesses without incurring the charge of graven images.

"Where did you learn your penmanship?"

"At home, in Kerioth."

"Ah, you are an Iscariot."

Judas had spoken in Aramaic, the Reb had spoken in Hebrew. The lad shifted to Hebrew.

"Yes, Iscariot."

"How old are you?"

"With your blessing, I will be eighteen."

"Blessing." He bestowed it with a nod. "And what shall we call you?"

"My name is Yehudah," he replied. "I am called Judas."

"And do you know how to write all the forms?"

"Yes, I do."

"The bills of property and complaint, the writ of death, the contract of marriage—warrants, summonses—can you write everything?"

"Yes." He paused in order to be cautious. "All that I am allowed to write."

"Allowed? You will be allowed to write everything."

"I . . . think . . . you will not want me to write the papers on death and marriage."

"Why not? They are the easiest."

"They are religious."

"Well, what of that? You are a Jew, are you not?"

". . . Yes. I feel that I am, but in fact . . ."

"In fact what?"

"I have never been Bar Mitzvahed."

"Why not?"

Judas tightened his hands so that the scribe would not see that he was trembling. "I viewed it as a pledge. And I did not know what to pledge . . . or whom to pledge to."

Meticulously, the old man rolled up the papyri and bound them with the ribbon. He handed them to the boy. "We cannot engage you in the work of the Temple. You are not a Jew."

"But I am!"

"No. In your feelings you are a gentile, and you must not come to the Temple again."

For days the man's words stormed about in his brain. He had never been forbidden access to a holy place. Even when he had been shunned in Kerioth, the doors of the synagogue had never been locked to him. It made him ill to think he had now been totally exiled. He felt cast out into the wilderness, Ishmael.

As usual, when tormented, he did not eat, he starved himself. Nighttimes, he walked the streets, seeing nothing, sightless. One day, in the afternoon heat of the marketplace, he fainted.

How solitary it felt to come to consciousness and realize that nobody had offered to assist him, for nearly everyone was afraid of other people's devils. And he thought, with mirthless humor: I have certainly not been helped by an offended God . . . and I am foolish to hope for His succor.

I must be my own helpmate.

The following day, he salvaged the wide wooden tailboard of a broken, abandoned cart, and he bought from a wine merchant a leaky barrel and two splintering wooden table legs. He scrubbed the tailboard at one of the wells, covered it with lath and sackcloth, then carried everything to the Alley Passage, a narrow corridor that led to the Temple. He set the board on the barrel and two legs, and made himself a table. He spent his silver coin to buy inks, quills and brushes, and all the rest of his money to purchase papyri and a few small parchments. Opening his samples of work, he weighted them down with pebbles.

Then he tried to sell his skills. He called to the passersby on their way to the Temple or the countinghouses, he called to the vendors of fruits and grains and cottons and sandals, to the physicians and bloodletters, to the *shochet,* the ritual slaughterer of animals. Appealing for attention, he described his services, the letters he could compose, the writs that he could copy and amend, the lists he could compile.

There were no customers. For two days he was without money for food, and, sleeping under his table in the wintering nights of Jerusalem, he quaked with cold. On the third day, an old, old man came to dictate his will. He owned a tiny olive grove on the outskirts of the city, with only a patch of land, and nothing else than a donkey and two sheep. He did not wish to leave anything to either of his married daughters, both of whom were ingrates, but only to a distant cousin, a woman nearly as old as he was, whose whereabouts he did not know. Give her my whole fortune, the doddering man said. And when the will was drawn, he left three shekels for the scrivener.

Judas did not realize how hungry he had been. He bought bread and Cana plums and black walnuts. And all at once, after one customer and one meal, he felt well again.

His luck improved. There were a few other customers and then more: land descriptions, depositions, letters to distant relatives, translations from Aramaic into Latin, copies of inventories. Late one afternoon he received a flattering testimonial.

It was a visit from a competitor. The man was middle-aged, portly and winded from having ascended from a lower position on the hill.

"Your prices are too low," he said.

"My prices are only fair," Judas replied.

"They are fair for a boy who does not have a wife and three young children."

"I congratulate you. May they live in health."

"They will not, if they do not eat."

"I am not taking the food from their mouths."

"If my customers leave me and go to you—"

"My customers are, for the most part, poor people. I cannot charge them any more than I do," Judas said. "However, I hope—before long—to have more work than I can handle. If this occurs, I will be pleased to send you—"

Apoplectically the man interrupted. "I do not want your charity! I want you to leave—and go to Satan!"

He flung his hand across the table, upsetting inks and papyri, and smudging work that had not dried. Then, summarily, departed.

Two days later a publican arrived. He, like the scrivener, was a Jew, but of a leaner, finer stripe. He had a quiet voice and he spoke Hebrew, not Aramaic, as if he had learned it elsewhere than Judea, possibly in Alexandria, where the Jews spoke more measuredly, with a Grecian accent.

"Do you know me?" he asked. "My name is Heskel Bar Itschak. I am the tax collector."

I must take care, Judas told himself. I must not respect the man's appearance or his speech. He is a Jewish traitor, toadying to the Romans. He gets paid to do their dirty work, collect the extortionate tax levies, do a little spying and informing, and perhaps a bit of pimping on the side.

"How much do I owe in taxes?" Judas said.

"Nothing, so far as I know," Heskel replied. "In fact, I do not even know you're here."

So that was it: He wanted a bribe. In return for a sliver of silver, the man would not report Judas's business to the fiscal office of the prefecture.

Judas felt a wave of disgust. Here he was, in business as his father had always been, being offered the taint of a similar corruption. And what was he to do about it? Stiffening his resolve, he determined he would not fall into the ignominious trap, he would not pay a slimy tribute. But he was curious how many shekels he might command in the political jobbery.

"What is your price?" he said.

The man's lips thinned. "My price for what?"

"For whatever service you will perform."

"I have already performed my service. I've come to advise you that your business does not exist—until you get a license for it."

"License? What is that?"

"Come now, you're a scrivener—you know as well as I do what a license is."

"Where do I get it?"

"The Roman prefectory—second portico."

"How much does it cost?"

"Nine pieces of silver."

"Nine pieces of—?" He was appalled. "I will not earn nine pieces in a whole year!"

"Then, you will earn nothing."

The publican turned and disappeared among the passersby. It was broad daylight everywhere except at the scrivener's table. The young man was enveloped in hopelessness, in gloom. Only yesterday, it seemed to him, he had exorcised the curses of futility and hunger; and today, just as he was about to raise his head above his poverty, this cruel malice had occurred. He had an impulse to blame it all on the callousness of a big city where all men are strangers, enemies. But he realized, in an access of unwelcome maturity, that his father had had to deal with the same sort of victimization in a smaller town. And had no choice with the Romans but to curse and weep and compromise. Bitterly it came to the young man that the monster Romans, with their civilized demeanor, had vanquished his people in a more insidious way than by usurping their homeland. They had usurped their souls. They had corrupted them, making the proud Jews into a servile nation of timeservers and publicans.

With the same fierce temper that had prompted him once to nearly kill his father, he kicked a leg out from under his scrivening table. The inkpots rolled and spilled over the parchment on which he had been working. He kicked the other leg. Brushes, quills, papyri slid onto the ground, and the inks and paints sloshed over everything. As he started to kick at the barrel, someone grabbed him.

"Stop it—have you lost your wits?"

It was the publican again. The boy twisted to get free, but the man was strong and did not release him.

"Let me be!" Judas said.

"To do what? Splash the city with ink? Is this the way you write your signature?"

"It's none of your business—let me go!"

Heskel released the scrivener and lifted one of the table legs. As he reached for the other: "What a mad dog you are!"

Judas started to tremble. The man was right: mad dog. Fury was his natural state; violence came too easily. Would he never learn to control his frenzy? And now, right now, could he not control his shameful quivering?

Pointedly, as if to give the boy time to recover from his humiliating tremors, the publican averted his attention from Judas and directed it to the rolls of soiled papyri. With studied care, he started to sort the good ones from the damaged. He looked at the parchment, half-written and now ruined.

"What a pity," he murmured. "Such beautiful calligraphy. Sentences ending perfectly, margins as straight as if the quill had been gifted with foresight. And every letter with the same leftward, upward slant—the slope of expectation. How could you have destroyed a thing so beautiful?"

"Go away."

Seeing that the young man did not want to share his misery, the publican tossed the defaced parchment onto the table and stood apart as if to study a wasted bed of flowers. When he stole a glance at the scrivener and saw that he had collected himself, he turned to him once more.

"I have come back to ask you a question," the publican said.

"I have no answers to anything—go away."

"Can you do sums?"

"Sums?"

"Yes. I see that you can write gracefully. But there are other things. Can you add this to that, and find a factor or two, and force numbers to do as they are told?"

Resenting him, and resenting himself for allowing the question to engage him, he muttered, "Yes, but I have no need for such skills."

"I have a need for them."

"Then, go and get them, and be damned."

"I already have them." He seemed unruffled by the imprecation. "But I can use yours as well."

"Go to Gehenna."

"I am offering you a position, scrivener."

"Gehenna, Gehenna!"

Heskel stopped smiling. "Civility, boy." There was an admonition in his voice. "It is true I do the Roman's handiwork, but I do not beat my breast for doing it. I have never cheated them—and they do not cheat me. I perform my task diligently—and they pay me well, and promptly. If there is a state of order in Jerusalem, we publicans can take our share of credit for it. Keeping the peace is a feat not totally without honor."

"Go get your honor from the Romans."

"I do. And from the Jews as well, those who are sensible."

"I am not sensible."

"You will be."

Abruptly the man's manner loosened. It was as if he discarded a cold metal armor of authority and stood before the boy in the homespun clothes of a family friend.

"Look to me, boy," he said. "I have a need of you. I have no children to help me with my work, and it grows onerous. There are long lists to be copied. And to be rectified—people die or move or cheat or falsify their names. Rectified, rectified. And sums to be recorded, writs to be served. Doing it all myself—it is too wearisome—my head begins to ache, and my hair grows thin. Will you come to work for me?"

"I am not a publican."

"No—I am the publican. You can be what you are—a scrivener—using the same quills, the same ink."

"My ink will turn to pitch."

The man blinked. "You are not a child anymore. You have had a taste of hardship, and you have not seen the end of it. Learn to be gentler with yourself. Look at you. Your face is drawn and your skin is grimy. You have been sleeping under this table like an alley beast, and perhaps you have vermin in your clothes and hair. I am sure this is not the life you dreamed of for yourself. Come to work with me. I will give you a fine table to write at and a fine chamber to sleep in. You will dine with me, and my wife will serve us equally—or you may dine by yourself, if you cherish your churlishness. You will eat well and sleep well, and you will be clean."

"Outwardly."

"I have learned that inner cleanliness is soon contaminated by a disease of the purse."

"I will keep my purse clean."

"Poverty is hard to cleanse."

When Heskel departed, Judas was surprised by what he felt. His contempt for the man had been in some way mitigated. The publican's kindness to me was honest, he found himself saying, and it could not have been a mask for cunning or sharp practice. The man seemed more thin-skinned than a tax collector should be, as if he were hiding some sadness, perhaps a shame. Again Judas thought of his father, and had a longing to make amends for whatever offense he had committed, to be younger than he was and the more easily forgiven, to weep the past few years away. He had a sudden sickness for home. No, not for home, for childhood, for a happiness long gone. *You are not a child anymore.*

And he wasn't. Nor would he allow himself to be as frightened as a child. He did not need to be a hireling, certainly not to a publican. He would take his business and his fate into his own hands, and continue to do his work *without* a license. Let the Romans do their worst. They would probably never even notice his presence. There were businesses in Kerioth that had flourished for years without permission from the authorities. One of them, a wineshop, was patronized by soldiers and bawds and prostitutes, and by a tribune who beguiled himself with ten-year-old boys. If conspicuous enterprises could avoid licensing in such a small town as Kerioth, where everyone knew what everyone was doing, how much less attention would be paid to Judas's little scrivening table in the great metropolis of Jerusalem?

He went on with his trade. And it prospered. Sometimes, at first, he quailed every time he saw a soldier or heard a horse's hoofbeats. But it was exactly as he had hoped—they didn't notice. As his business flourished, he bought himself a new tunic, and, hating to soil it by sleeping on the ground, started to look for lodgings. Not with ardor, for he would rather put the money into his business, lay in a store of finer quills from

Athens and the new wax tablets, the hardened kind that were coming out of Egypt.

One day he had a customer whom he recognized, a young man from Kerioth. He was Elias, the son of the *shammash* of the synagogue. He had been a precocious child, a poet of exceptional talent, but had suddenly turned into an unruly boy, an irreligious troublemaker. Like Judas, he had left home at an early age, and there were rumors that he had joined the Zealots, or still worse, the *sicarii,* the dagger men who were paid to assassinate.

He said that the nearly scabbed-over wound on his leg was nothing, but to the scrivener it looked deep and raw, and had to be more painful than Elias was pretending. His copper-colored hair was as ablaze as ever, although his manner was more civil than Judas had recalled. They exchanged pleasantries that were not really pleasant, for they had little in common except the town where they were born, and neither had an inclination to sentimentalize.

Elias wanted a letter written. He could very well have written it himself, but he had not the equipment, he said, nor did he want his handwriting recognized. When asked whether he desired the missive to be inscribed on parchment, papyrus or wax, Elias chose wax, so that it would not be permanent. It must be read once, he declared, and forgotten.

"To whom will you address it?"

"No one. There will be no names."

As a business practice, Judas had learned to conceal surprise. "And what will it say?"

"You have saved my life and you are very beautiful. I am a poet, but have no words to tell you how I feel. One day I will find them."

"Go on."

"That is all."

"Shall I sign *Elias?"*

"I said no names."

Judas told him the price, collected the brass money, and handed him the wax tablet.

"I do not want it," Elias said. "I want you to deliver it. And I will pay you for that as well."

Judas had never delivered a letter before, and had no notion what the task might be worth.

"If it is not far, I will of course not charge you anything," he said.

"It is not far. The top of the northern hill. The villa of the Magdalas. It is meant for the daughter. Her name is Mary."

There was a stir of horsemen at the end of the street. Elias turned to lightning and was gone.

At sundown, Judas carried the wax tablet upward in the hills. This part of the city was unknown to him, and he was caught by the lushness of the greenery and the opulence of the houses. He wondered at the mammoth stones so meticulously cut that they needed no mortar, and at the cataracts of purple flowers cascading down from high, high parapets. It was awesome and strangely serene.

As he came upon a plateau, not far from his destination, he heard the screak of wheels and saw a sight to take his breath away. It was a black chariot drawn by a pair of black horses, like a splash of jet ink across the whole papyrus of his life. Black, everything black, except for the ornaments. The trappings of the elegant animals, all gold—golden bits and bridles, even the harness studdings, all the same glowing gold on sable. And the storm-black chariot itself—its crests and its wheels, glittering, golden.

But the spectacle—the breathtaking spectacle—the chariot driver. A woman. The most beautiful woman he had ever seen—no, a young girl, his own age perhaps, with auburn hair flying, darting behind her like a wild pennon, or a crazed bird.

How magnificent she was!—clutching the reins with one hand, snapping a long whip with the other, cracking it aloft, never flicking at the horses, slashing at the firmament, tearing a rent in the silken skin of the sky. Delirious with speed, it was as though she were at war with heaven for having ripped the wings off the shoulders of her black beasts.

He had never seen such a woman, never such horses frenzied by a girl, and had never felt such a turbulence. He shouted as the vision flew before him, shouted an idiotic cry to halt. He felt as if he were in a terrible nightmare and a wonderful dream, both at once, and could not stand the painful rapture of it. Halt, halt, he cried, so that he might awaken.

A hundred ells away he did awaken, and the reality was more beautiful than the dream. The young woman was there, standing beside her horses. A groom was wiping them down, and she was talking soothingly to the beasts, as if to beg their pardon for having pressed them so hard. Her voice was deep and rich and round, and it glowed like an altar light.

He called with quaking voice: "I am seeking Mary of Magdala."

She looked at him and beckoned. "You have found her."

Oh, found her indeed, he thought, and almost forgot his errand.

He approached. Unwrapping the wax tablet from the grape leaves meant to keep the letters shaded and sharp, he handed it to her.

She thanked him, glanced at the message, flushed, then turned her attention to the scrivener.

"Did you incise this?" she asked.

"Yes."

"It is well done. The man who told you what to write—what is his name?"

He evaded. "It is not written."

"I see that it is not written," she said. "But you know what it is?"

"Yes."

"Then, tell it."

"He does not want it told."

"Did he say that?"

"He said, 'There will be no names.' "

"But he did not actually forbid you to tell it."

"That is a cavil."

Her attention sharpened. She studied him more narrowly. "Are you a scholar?"

"A scrivener."

"What is your name?"

"Judas."

He was fascinated by the alteration in her manner. The instant she had suspected that he might be a young man with something of a mind, she had embarked upon a game. A contest of wits. He suspected almost at once that she no longer cared about the identity of the poet, but had engaged herself in a friendly duel with him, to see if she could trick him out of the name.

"May I ask you an ungracious question?" she said.

He nodded.

"How much did he pay you?"

"Forty shekels."

"If I give you eighty, will you tell me his name?"

"No."

"A hundred?"

"No."

"Two hundred? A piece of silver?"

"No."

"How much?"

"He is an old friend. I would not betray him."

"I was merely testing you," she said. "I would not bribe you with money—I hope you believe that."

He did believe it; he was certain that's what it was—a test. He was glad that she had not seriously meant the offer, and glad that he had rejected it. It gave him delicious pleasure to realize that it was only a game, and that neither of them was corruptible.

It occurred to him that she was aware of his thoughts, and that they might not be different from hers. Her friendliness was a summer day.

"I think we are doing well," she said.

He could have leapt for joy. "Yes. We are doing well."

She reached out and touched him gently on the arm. "Why not? We are two good people."

"It is not ordinary," he agreed. "And if we are also intelligent . . ."

"Both virtues at once—that is most unusual."

"Most."

Her eyes glowed at him as if to say they had known one another a long time. We have, he wanted to say; oh, we have! Suddenly, without good reason, they both began to laugh. It was refreshing and a little silly. Then, as if laughter without logic were unnatural, they both became embarrassed by it. He wondered whether her sudden bashfulness was as real as his, or whether she was pretending. Real, it had to be real.

"He is very lucky," she said, "the young man who asked you to inscribe the tablet. He is lucky to have a loyal friend like you."

He did not wish to take undue credit. "I am not really his friend. It's simply that I have known him many years. We come from the same town."

"What town is that?"

"Kerioth."

She stopped sparkling and her eyes became older. That instant, he knew she had bested him, she had won the game. He had given her Elias's identity. If she really cared to pursue it, she would encounter no difficulty. A young red-headed poet from the small town of Kerioth—how easy to track him down, to point her finger at him.

His joy was gone. While his vanity was piqued that she had beaten him, the distress went deeper. He had been unworthy of a trust, he had doltishly allowed himself to be cozened out of something valuable that had been placed in his safekeeping.

She saw his discomfiture and touched him again, this time with the urgency of both hands. "Please—don't be sorry about this. It was only a game. I won't do the man any harm."

"Will you please forget him?"

"That's a pointless request. If you tell me to forget him, I'll recall him all the more vividly. Besides, this tablet is his way of asking me not to forget him."

He nodded ruefully. "And I myself have written it."

"Please don't look so fallen," she said. "You have a lovely smile. Can you do it at will?"

Yes, he could smile for her, he could die for her. He started to laugh with such delight that he felt like a rattlehead. She watched him without joining his laughter, but joining his happiness.

She then performed a little act of gratitude in the manner of the Phoenician slaves. Quickly reaching for his sleeve, she bent and kissed the cuff.

He had heard of the gesture but never seen it. Nor had he realized that it could be so intimate. He felt a rush of blood to his cheeks. Unable to stand the private closeness of it, and dreading to show his intoxicated embarrassment, he nodded quickly and hastened away, hurtling down the hill.

For days thereafter, he had a bleariness of sight whenever he thought of her, as if he could not brush the dust of her chariot out of his vision. She became a tangible presence; he could feel her touching him, her hand on his arm. And he needed her closer. Everywhere he went, he asked guarded questions about this Mary and the house of Magdala. It was not enough to know her name, to have her visage constantly before him, he had to know every detail of her life. But hardly anyone could or would tell him anything. Often, at the break of dawn or at the end of day, he would go into the luxuriant upper terraces of the city, where the Magdalas dwelt, in the hope of getting another glimpse. However, in all his wanderings to the mount, he never caught a shadow. The more vividly he remembered the bewitching young woman, the more he felt he had fantasized her existence, and he was dismayed at the thought that he might never again see her in the flesh.

But why shouldn't he see her? he asked. Clearly they were taken by one another—why shouldn't he pay court to her? He knew the answer, of course: She was the daughter of a rich Sadducee family, notoriously snobbish, and he was an impecunious street scrivener, shabby and homeless. The barrier between them, like the iron stanchions around the soldiers' garrison, was untraversable, as if they were Jew and Roman.

But perhaps, he told himself, his fortunes might someday rise to a level from which he might reach for her. In recent weeks, he had been taking heart from his crescent prosperity. As his patronage grew, he developed a useful device: He made himself believe that all the good fortune in his life was bound to the good fortune of having found Mary, and at bedtime, when he counted his benedictions, she was the better part of all the graces.

One night, as he was lying a few feet from his scrivening table, gazing at a heaven so close that he imagined the stars were sewn into his mantle, he realized that he had at last made his peace with Jerusalem. After nightfall particularly, when the byway was deserted and silent, as it was now, he had the sense that one day soon, with the miracle of Mary, his time might be blessed. He had started months ago with very little, and now he thought with pride about his possessions. In the dark, he could not see them, but drew confidence from knowing they were there. His table had been newly covered with deep-tanned oxhide, which provided a smooth, hard surface to write upon. His pens and quills had multiplied, and he had five varieties of ink, including a new purple made of gentian, a liquid lampblack, and an ineradicable brown tincture of vinegar and burnt moss. He did not keep large stores of papyrus, for the slightest dampness made it curl, but he had a good selection of parchment, all kinds, even the finest eweskin. Most of his supplies were stored in old reed baskets; in the new wooden coffer, fitted with bronze hinges and locks from Ephesus, he safeguarded the books he had been buying recently. Faced with the choice of more books or better lodgings, he was compulsively purchasing one tome after another. In addition to the three he had inherited from Gemaliel, he had four others, beautiful leather-covered treatises on words and songs and laws, the precious rewards of his burgeoning prosperity.

He felt good; if he were Roman, he would say the omens were auspicious. Soon, if his success continued, he might think of enlarging his table and, perhaps, building an awning over it. One day, not too far off, he hoped, he might marry.

Mary of Magdala, always Mary. In his visions, she was right there, within the call of his voice, the touch of his hand. But he cautioned himself not to rush forward prematurely, for there would be only rejections and forbiddances. Hasten slowly, he told himself, until the time to dare. Meanwhile, count the quills and the good fortune; savor the dream in the darkness . . .

He heard a sound. It was a murmur so soft that he thought it was the voice of the night itself, speaking covertly to him, whispering a secret he was meant to understand.

Then he felt the blow. It smashed down on him, like the fall of mountains. It was thunder, lightning, splitting his skull. He arose and stumbled, tried to shout and couldn't, cried in pain, no, leave off, not again, who are you, not again. He saw them, then, three, four, a thousand, rushing, scrambling, tearing things, axes falling, parchments flying, ripping, burning, no, let me be, don't strike me again, no, please, blood and ink and fire, go away, let it be, don't, not my books, not my beautiful books, don't, oh *please,* let me be!

He arose and someone kicked him, and he fell. They must not hurt me again, not there, oh no, let me up, my books, oh help me, help my books, don't kick me, please don't kick me, someone help me.

His books were burning, bleeding, he must snatch them, bind their wounds, bind wounds, please go away. Then one of them was driving something down his throat, and blood came gushing forth, oh bleeding, oh my books.

He lay there and could not move, and did not even have the strength to feel the pain. The wind took to whispering to him again, the same covert message as before, and still he could not decipher what it tried to say.

Nor could he understand what anyone was saying, not for centuries. Sometimes, nearly always, he did not know where he was, or why he kept on walking. He wondered at such times why hardly anyone wanted to look at him, how they turned from his presence as if he made them ill. He had a gesture that he did not understand. His hand seemed always to be extended. Once in a while, people put something in it, a scrap of bread, a morsel of meat; now and then, a coin. It was never what he really wanted the hand to hold, but he was not certain what he hoped for. Perhaps the hand was not meant to touch anything; perhaps the palm, the fingers were not his own.

Everything he touched had an ache in it. The pain, he told himself, was not in him but in things. All objects had sorrows built in them, and an odor that made him ill. Sometimes the stench around him was so sickening that he tried to stop breathing, and he would fall, gasping for breath, and dogs would bark and people would run away from him. And the ache, the ache so terrible that it was in every breath, in every blinking of the eye. . . .

At last, late one afternoon, in a village somewhere, he was bent over a little pool and was licking the surface of the water, trying to lick away the setting sun. But the sun remained, and he knew it was a difficult enterprise. So he just lay there, belly downward, looking into the warmish water, staring at the man's face.

He was an ugly man with scars and scabs, wet discharges from his nose and eyes, blood matted in his hair, something about his mouth that seemed not as it should be. He stared at the repulsive creature, nauseated by him, hating the wet sickness, wanting to destroy it. His arm made a slash of disgust at the ugliness. The water roiled. The sun vanished and so did the sickly reflection, but in a while, they both returned, and Judas saw his image and he wept.

He washed himself and the creature in the pool, and wandered away, and all at once he was in another place, sleeping and waking, and it was cold, bitter cold, and someone was covering him, and there was a lamp glowing. For days and nights, it seemed to him, there was a hovering presence standing over him, bending to touch him, to clean him, to murmur and be murmured to. He did not know who it was, or what was being done or if it needed doing, but he heard two voices, and time by time the voices came closer, and one of them was his own.

Then abruptly everything was clear. Like a message on a parchment he himself had written, it was all legible to him. He knew who he was and how he had come here, through wanderings and sickness and lunacy. I have been hurt, I have been damaged, he said, and perhaps there is a part of my being that will never know what it once knew, but I am well enough to recall how I was brought to pain, and that I am Judas.

But I do not know this other one.

The other one was trimming the lamp. His face and beard are younger than mine, Judas thought, but I would guess him older by some years. And ordinary. A man from the countryside somewhere, or, from the look of his hands, a workman. And ordinary—why did the word keep asserting itself?

Because he was not ordinary. For all the commonplace in the young man's aspect, there was something singular about him. And Judas—still struggling with his chaos—could not, even though he came to see him more and more clearly, find that differential oneness that set the man apart. Was it a special lineament, a particularity of feature, a way the head was held, an oddness in the glance? Or was it nothing, only a trick of lamplight? Or was Judas's mind still wandering, and the difference, imaginary?

"What place is this?" Judas asked.

"We are in a foothill," the young man replied. "Down there is Jericho. Does it matter to know where you are?"

An odd question. "Yes, it matters."

"That is good, I think. . . . Do you know your name?"

"Judas."

"Better and better."

"What is yours?"

"They call me Jesus."

"Where do you come from?"

"It is uncertain. Bethlehem and Nazareth." He raised his shoulders slightly. "Galilee."

"I am from Kerioth."

"I know. You told me."

Judas did not recall telling him anything. It occurred to him that he might have told the man in an unconscious state.

"Did I tell you that they . . . ?"

"Hurt you. Yes."

"Did I tell you who they were?"

"No."

"Then, I do not know."

"You said at first it was the Jewish scriveners, but you could not bring yourself to believe it. Then you said it was the Roman soldiers."

"Yes, the soldiers," Judas said. "But why did they come by night?"

"Sometimes they are proud of their cruelty—sometimes, ashamed."

The answer came too easily to the man's lips. Judas recognized his kind. He was one of those country folk who had an easy symbol or a ready proverb for every phenomenon. Such people did not interest Judas; their minds wore thin.

The man seemed to know what Judas was thinking. "I make the world too simple," he said. "Pay no heed to me."

And he smiled.

That was the difference!

The smile. Judas had never seen a smile that bestowed everything. Whatever laughter he had noticed on men's lips had always reserved something to itself, some chariness of spirit. The good humor was never more than part of anything; something was always withheld, or falsified: I smile, the expression seemed to say, but some of my laughter is derision, and not a little is malice, and most is no smile at all, for I give nothing as truly as I seem to do. But this man's felicity was a gift of his whole being, of his mind and his heart. This, all of this is my offering, it seemed to say, it is my happiness that you and I are here together. I give this to you, this is my joy of life, my love of it, and it is yours. Take it.

Taking the smile as a gift, Judas felt its thawing warmth. It made a hope for him, and a healing.

"I *want* to heed you," he said softly. "Tell me why they hurt me."

The man was troubled. "I do not know."

"Why did they punish me?"

"Because you did not pay."

"Pay? Are we to pay forever? Are we never to be free of them?"

"Them?"

"Romans, Romans!"

"There have always been 'Romans.' "

"And always tribute?"

"If we live in the world, we must pay tribute."

"If we live in the world?—*if?* Is there an alternative?"

There was no reply from the man. He seemed troubled by the question. He continued to trim the lamp even while it was lighted, spreading the tallow away from the wick so that it would not burn wastefully. A faint breeze made the flame unsteady. It illuminated Jesus' face in an inconstant way so that he appeared young and old from glimmer to glimmer.

"Is there?" Judas insisted.

"An alternative to the world?"

"Yes—what?—where?"

Again the man was silent. When he did respond to the question, his words seemed to Judas to be a meaningless evasion.

"I live with . . . others."

"Who are the others?"

He took so long to reply that Judas assumed there would be no answer. Impatiently he pursued the question. "Where?"

"In the desert."

"If you mean the world is a desert, there's no denying it."

"The desert I speak of is not in a parable."

"You mean it exists."

"Yes."

"And yet is not in the world?"

"It is a place where there are no Romans, where men arise in the dawn and make their peace with our beloved Father and with one another, where they seek the truth in the light of what is written, and they labor in the vineyards of God's love."

There was paradise in the man's eyes. He wondered if the Galilean believed what he was saying, or if he was fabricating Eden.

Judas said, "I do not believe such a place exists."

"It exists."

"Where? You say the desert—where?"

"There are many such places. In the mountains. In the wilderness. By the sea of salt."

"You are talking of the Essenes."

"They have many names."

Evasion after evasion. The bubble burst. No paradise here. There were dozens of sects that offered heaven in a desert, or by a salt sea, or on a mountaintop. Some of them were honest, some were false. The Essenes were among the honest ones; more and more world-sick men were finding in their enclave a quiet alternative to a life of despair. But they were only a wayside cult seeking paradise in a separation from the realities, the paradox of the richness of spirit in a life of poverty. It was a simpleminded nostrum, but not shameful. No need for the man to be so cautious and say "perhaps." If he truly believed in the Essenes, why did he equivocate? There was something furtive about him.

Judas was disappointed in the Galilean. The good cheer of the man, his radiance, had given the scrivener an insubstantial hope of some kind, a hint of heaven. But now, hearing him espouse such a wary pathway to a guileful God, Judas turned away. It saddened him that his benefactor was so cryptic about God, when there was such open kindness in him. Judas owed his life to his kindness, owed him his sanity. As the tallow in the lamp burned low, the scrivener spoke his gratitude and was answered only by that ineffable smile, which warmed him deeply, yet increased his disquiet.

"You have been so good to me," he said. "I will be at a loss to repay you."

"You will repay—someone else."

It was true enough, Judas suspected, yet it was unaccountably irritating to hear it said. It was the man's appetite for homily, perhaps; or his need to do two contradictory things at the same time: oversimplify and mystify. Whatever, the scrivener felt impatient again and at odds.

When the tallow was exhausted and the lamp failed, he did not want to converse anymore, and pretended drowsiness.

He thought he was awake all through the night, but if he had been, he would have heard the Galilean depart. Yet, when dawn came, the man was gone—and Judas regretted not having said farewell to him.

Throughout the days thereafter, as he wandered from village to village, earning a scanty crust as an itinerant scrivener, the Galilean continued to puzzle Judas. He knew that the man had tended him and nursed him and had healed his illness. But how had he accomplished it? He could not recall a single medicine or tonic or poultice. In fact, more to the mystery, he could not recollect a single meal they had had together, no benediction or breaking of bread, no drinking of water or wine. The wayfarer wondered how many days or weeks or months the man had tended him, and whether it was possible that they had been together for but a single night. He knew how inconceivable this was; yet, he had conceived it, and the outlandish notion troubled him.

Why was he having these perverse illusions? Were they the leftover vapors of his clouded mind? Or were they a perplexity that the Galilean had purposely left for him to ponder? Troubled, he tried to dismiss the man from his thoughts. He did dismiss him, all except the smile, which remained with him like the afterglow of sunset. But that, too, began to fade, and he was glad. The man was a visionary, he suspected, and Judas was through with the life of the ineffable. One day he said: An end to wandering. I must now deal with actualities, with the bloody knuckle of bread and brass.

He would not fight the authorities anymore; there dwelt disaster. He would offer his services to the publican.

The heat of the day had passed; by nightfall a sharp wind had arisen, and her breasts were chilled. For a moment she regretted not having worn a scarf or mantle; but her bare bosom would be her badge of acceptance.

There would be three hazards tonight. The first, at the lower gate and archway, where the chariots arrived; the second, at the head of the staircase, where the torchbearers held the flare before each face so that the stewards could determine admissibility.

These first two obstacles were calculable, not particularly dangerous. The third was unpredictable and might be a peril. Someone might recognize her as the daughter of a Sadducee, a Jew. It was unlikely, for there would be no Jews present, and nearly all the Romans would be strangers, holiday visitors from Caesarea and Tiberias. Besides, she had dressed not only with a view to beauty but to disguise: her hair in a coronet, her eyes painted with an Oriental upward slant, the drapery of her gown slashed in the Roman mode to give the hint of discreet accessibility. And the most effective diversion from her face, the luscious bosom unadorned. Still, anything might happen, anyone might ask a damning question and raise an alarm.

Trusting nobody, neither charioteers nor chair bearers, she had left her chariot at an inn some distance away, and had arrived on foot. Mary was frightened and excited. Something good would come of this, or terrible; anyway, provocative. Her pulse raced and, as she approached, her senses began to tingle. My feet are ready to run in any direction, she thought, my hands are itching to grasp or fight. It was too frantic, there was too much to perceive. The flares of the torches, the rearing and neighing of the chariot horses, the whistling of the hostlers, the shouting and cursing at the slaves as they sweated under the weight of the carriage chairs, the clanking of shields, cries of recognition, screeches of delight, the mounted centurions in their silver armor swishing their swords through a sea of sky—what a thrilling chaos!

In the flaring, flashing torchlights, the colors were rampant—crimsons, purples, greenish yellows; young women with ears painted cerulean blue, eyelids of silver, mouths of jade; middle-aged matrons whose breasts had begun to sag, with vivid images daubed on their bosoms to disguise their pendulousness—rams' heads with tongues to hide the areolas, a blaze of sunsets, a pair of erupting volcanoes.

She had a sudden trepidation. Chariotless, she might be mistaken for one of the harlots. There were many of them—without servants or equipage—hawking their delectations to the sentries and chariot drivers who would be waiting out the night. Some of the prostitutes were young, a few were beautiful; all were Jewish women dressed in the Roman fashion. That someone might take her for a street whore was a possibility she had not considered; it made her skittish.

On impulse, she darted into the roadway, into the melee of moving chairs, chariots, horses. She slid like an eel through the crowd at the landing stage. Jostling her way to a chariot that had just discharged its passenger, she snatched at the bridle of the nearest horse, and railed at the driver: See that you return on time, you drunken lump, she said, and she slithered into the current of the guests.

At the staircase, she thought how easy the first obstacle had been. But the next one would be more slippery. Ascending the stairs, she was coming to it, step by step.

A Roman steward and two Nubians stood at the upper landing. The taller of the black men held his large cornucopian torch at the highest extent of his arm, to offer general illumination. The other torch, a smaller one, was held quite close to each guest's countenance. The steward wore a toga embroidered with flowers; a round man with a round voice that made circles of embrace and welcome. Dear Darolus, how good to see you again, and little Melia, fresh from Rome, and ah, the learned preceptor from Antioch, what a surprise, how good you are to come this long way from home, so well you look, so totally recuperated, sweet Cornelia, good Marcus, my friend, how delighted I am with the consul's news, greetings from my wife, oh, dear magistrate, cousin, welcome, is your sister with you, the newest bauble, is it not, and so becoming, Luculla, Cato, Rustus, well seen, well met, welcome.

"What is your name?"

Her heart stopped. "Lavinia."

"Which Lavinia? Of what family?"

She tried to be taller than her height. "I had not thought there would be need . . ." With languid annoyance, she allowed the sentence to die away. Then, with a burst of irritation: "The family is Decimus—Gaius Decimus—tribune from Tusculum. Daughter of his sister, Camilla."

The steward was daunted for only an instant. "I had not heard of such a tribune."

Her glance turned him upside down. "What is your name?"

It was not a question but a summons. He answered it. "Alberus Nassitus."

"We have not heard your name in Rome."

He smiled uncertainly. The guests were crowding on the stairs. Suddenly, past his shoulder, she waved to someone—no one—on the terrace. "Ah, Praetor—how splendid to see you here!"

Without waiting for the steward's permission, she hurried past him, into the swirl of people, as if en route to an embrace.

On the terrace there was instrumental music—lutes and psalteries and graded densities of cymbal—and singers, weaving among the visitors, serenading now one, now another, making each listener a special, honored personage. How gracious and cultivated it was! Except that there were too many people, too close. Cool as it had been below, here the guests teemed in the sticky, crowded heat, seeming to adhere to one another in a yielding linkage of their persons, melding flesh to flesh. She felt as though she, too, were dissolving into a trance, sensual and seductive.

But the smell of the perfumes, so pleasant at first, had become oppressively pungent, like the burning of skin and hair. She wondered about the Romans, how they were constantly bathing and scouring their bodies, yet disguising their cleanliness with the fetor of dead things; how the women would douse themselves with the essence of dead flowers, and the men would smear their armpits and genitals with the musk of dead animals; they must find a libidinous pleasure in mortality. As she felt herself catching some erotic enticement from the night, it disturbed her that part of its allure might be revulsion.

She began to feel a little faint.

And was dashed out of it.

The man was familiar to her, not because of the uniform, but the limp. Picking his way watchfully among the crowd—the centurion Tullius. She had seen him a number of times, and a few months ago he had noticed her. Where did he go? he had asked about the Zealot, and she had lied. He would remember her: the Jewess outside her father's counting chambers. He would give the lie to her Roman appearance and Roman name, and demand to know what she was doing here tonight. Was she, by mischance, a friend of the Zealots? Was she carrying a weapon for an attempt on a Roman life? Had she ever given comfort to the *sicarii?* Had she hidden a dagger somewhere?

Abruptly she realized the enormity of the risk she had taken. What a reckless fool!

In panic, she decided to flee. Rushing toward the stairs, she stopped. Wrong direction: a solitary guest going downward as the others were coming up. Too conspicuous.

A new thought struck her. If Tullius was here as a guard and not a guest, he was assigned to this station—on the terrace. He might not at any time tonight go indoors into the great ballroom. If she could make her way inside, without his seeing her . . .

She threaded a passage through the densest throng. Not for an instant did she take her eyes off him. No question that he was "in conduct" tonight, as the Roman soldiery called it; his attention was as vigilant as her own, his directions to the guards were delivered swiftly, with hardly more than a gesture or a glance.

Suddenly he disappeared. She felt like ice. Find him, she warned herself, *find him.*

Tullius reappeared. Closer now. Too close. It was as if he had dematerialized in one place and become palpable in another. He might do it again and suddenly be at her side, his hands arresting her. If she could only glide along the wall and slip over the threshold into the banqueting chamber—

There he was, standing before the very doorway through which she had to pass. She halted, frozen.

The throng on the terrace was thinning out. The last guests were entering the festival hall, and soon there would be no crowd into which she might disappear. She would be as detectable as her guilt.

Then, a camellia. The Roman matron was laughing and so was Tullius. She archly lifted a shoulder, and the lame centurion leaned into an uneven bow. Straightening, he touched the pink flower in the woman's hair. She gave it to him. He held it to his nose; he bit a petal . . . and Mary slipped past both of them, and into the banqueting chamber.

She gasped with relief, then wonder. She had never seen such a sumptuous ballroom. It was a celebration of the Roman arch. Arches above arches, one curve vaulting above another, and all conjoining into a single gilded dome. And the room itself, as if vying with the aspirations of the ceiling, was built on terraces of greenery. On the long balconies, tables were laden with immensities of fruits and flowers and nutmeats and sweetmeats in tumbling mounds; and roasting lambs on spits, and calves and fowl and a wild boar from the hills; wines, too, many and various, purple and red and golden, pouring out of silver faucets in the walls, running in rivulets into the sluiceways through the floors.

In the air, wild birds flew. Sparrows with gilded feathers, and doves painted blue and white and persimmon, and a thousand hummingbirds, and pigeons with tiny brass bells on the tips of their wings. Not that anyone heard the chiming of the bird bells, for the lyres vied with the citharas, and the citharas with the flutes, and they all vied with the jangling of cymbals.

The guests reclined on divans or on the pillowed steps. Some lay in couples, some in multiples. Because the lamps and torches were beginning to warm the hall excessively, the men were starting to remove their togas, the women their mantles, and to lie about in tunics and bodices. The dining had already begun preciously, with tongue-tip tasting: the epicures dipped the ends of their fingers into the broth of larks' wings and licked the liquid scarcely more than a drop at a time; they nibbled at white grapes with ginger sauce, to tease the palate; sniffed the mixture of flower pollens and fine pepper so that they would sneeze and start their juices flowing.

Mary was intrigued by the diners and their exotic foods, but she had even more fascinating things to gaze upon:

There were two of them, both magnificent, both made of teakwood from India with armrests of onyx, inlaid with opals and beryls and amethysts. The larger throne stood on a higher platform and was meant for the lofty surrogate of the Emperor Tiberius: Pontius Pilate, procurator of Judea, Galilee, Peraea and the inland provinces. This greater chair of state was separate from all else in the festival chamber—august in its solitariness—awaiting. Pilate, notoriously unreliable, notoriously unpunctual, might arrive when the festivities were dying; he might not arrive at all.

The smaller throne was occupied by Herod Antipas. He was a middling man who, somewhere between boyhood and adult years, had mislaid his identity. He wore a Roman toga but clung to his Jewish beard; yet, even the beard lacked definition, dyed black in the Phoenician manner and curled in the Syrian. He had neither the kindness nor the cruelty of his father, Herod the Great, neither the brilliance of mind nor the madness. He retained the uncouthness of the Idumaean savages from whom his family had sprung, yet cunningly imitated the civility of the Jewish race, to which his father had defected in order to be declared the sovereign of Galilee.

Herod was nothing but a hunger. He hungered for Judea. Calling himself the King of Galilee, which officially he was not, he yearned to be the king of all the Semites—Galileans, Samaritans, Peraeans, Judeans—all, everything.

And Pontius Pilate could make it possible. The procurator could plead his case with Tiberius in Rome. To the end that his dream might be fulfilled, Herod had modified the whole body of his life, almost to blood and bone. Long ago he had given up the hated Aramaic of the Idumaeans; then he had abandoned the Hebrew of the Jews. He spoke only Latin nowadays, and enough Greek to make him appear an erudite Roman. His Jewish tailors, dressers and bootmakers were in the past, and he had imported foreign craftsmen, notably a famous toga-and-tunic-maker from Alexandria. Most significantly, he had erected for himself a palace in Jerusalem, a fitting residence for the anticipant king of all the Semites. Shrewdly, he had built to the plans of a Roman architect, not with square lintels but with arches, not in the tradition by which his father had restored the Jewish Temple, but as a vast indoor forum of soaring arcs that might not be out of place on one of the seven hills above the Tiber.

And this ostentatious revel tonight was meant to demonstrate to Pontius Pilate that the Idumaean Jew had Roman friends in Jerusalem and that they loved him, and if he were made king of the Hebrews, Jerusalem would cease being a parochial Jewish city and become a lustrous Roman metropolis. How he would manage it financially was hard to tell, for Herod was always deeply in debt, owing vast sums of money to men of commerce everywhere, including Mary's father.

She had been presented to Herod years before, when she was not yet five. Her father had taken her to Tiberias, the summer capital Herod was building as a tribute to the emperor. She recalled nothing of the occasion except that the man had lifted her, held her in his lap and kissed her fully on the mouth. It was not the kiss she had minded so much, although it had been unpleasant. It was the odor. She had never been so close to a perfume-anointed male, and the slough of smells, the expiring of bad breath, the sweaty regalia of royalty and the spicy sweetness of his perfumery had made her break into a fit of sneezing, to the amusement of the court and the embarrassment of her father.

She wondered if Herod still had the same royal reek. Apparently not. He was greeting the guests—Romans all—lubricating them with a special unction: he remembered, or professed to remember, everyone. Some he embraced, some he fondled. He made mouths at them, kissing as many as he had time for, sucking at the air around them, as though he wished to imbibe people, like liquids.

She did not want to join the procession that led to Herod's throne. It would be easier—and safer—to disappear in the crowd. But what purpose would her disappearance serve, how would she widen her world by the breadth of a hair? She might as well not have come. People of high estate must deal with people of high estate, her father had once said, and had added: If I try to make a compact with a Roman of inferior rank, I fail. But with a Roman of my own status, it is easier to accord: we understand one another. It could be the same for Mary at Herod's feast. She would not find a common language with a retainer, but with a dignitary. There was really no alternative: she had to be acceptable to Herod—to Pilate, in fact—or not at all.

So she joined the procession to the smaller throne. The file of courtiers was long and, for all his warm demonstrations of regard and affection, Herod made short shrift of every meeting. This would do no good, Mary realized; he might listen to her false name, pretend to recognize it, smile regally, press his lips to her knuckles, and the moment would be over. She would get lost in the promenade.

I must not do it this way, she thought.

The procession was getting shorter. She could hear the greetings.

This is a *blunder*, she thought; I will be wasting my one chance. He will not notice me at all.

She was close enough now to see the oily rouge on his cheeks, the driplets of perspiration from his heavily pomaded hair.

Slip away, she told herself, get out of the line, don't waste the moment, run!

"And you, my little doe?" He was trying to remember her, and couldn't.

She was rigid in every muscle. Her tongue clove to the roof of her mouth. She attempted to say it—my name is Lavinia Decimus—but no sound came.

"Your name, gazelle?"

"Mary . . . of Magdala."

His eyelids flickered. ". . . Of Magdala?"

"Yes. My father is a Jew. And so am I."

For an instant, he said nothing. "You were told that Jews were not to be admitted?"

"Yes."

Quietly: "Then, why did you dare to come?"

"I wanted you to know that Jews can be as needful to you as Romans . . . and as beautiful."

He studied the thought as if it were profound; also studied her breasts. Without change of expression, he leaned forward and gently kissed one of them.

"You are quite right," he said.

And suddenly he laughed. A donkey's laugh, a bray. For a flash, it frightened her, but others were laughing too. Unaware of what had prompted the gaiety, the guests took his merriment and waved it about like a flutter of flags.

Disregarding the others, he made a sudden hubbub, snapping his fingers and clapping his hands, and a divan was brought for the Jewish guest, so that the exquisite young woman could sit beside him. All at once, trays of fruit appeared, and meats, and ewers of nectar and wine, and golden vessels of steaming lamb and fish and partridge, relishes, condiments, sweetmeats, one food bearer after another, a caravan of delicacies. Eat, Herod said, eat, my pretty, eat, my little moth, these pomegranates came from the hills of India, this honey bread is from a new strain of Galilean wheat, these are the Mesopotamian grapes, why do you not eat?

She could not eat, she could not swallow because of the pounding of her heart. Her first victory—how easy it had been! No pomegranate could be so delicious, no honey bread so sweet as this moment of swift triumph.

"It is all so beautiful to *look* at—it seems a sacrilege to destroy it."

He laughed and started to destroy it himself. And all around her, the destruction was in progress.

The guests were not, as she had first imagined them, precious epicures. They were gluttons. They gorged like ravening beasts on shanks of pig and calves' livers and the smoked entrails of spring-born fawns. They ate ambidextrously, shoving the juice-dripping meat into their mouths with one hand, and condiments or fish or mounds of bread with the other. No effort was made to compose complementary tastes; they clutched at whatever struck the eye and whetted the appetite. Delectable as the food might be, it was not its delectability that mattered; only the speed with which the provender might be consumed. And the quantity. To that end, the liquors from grape or grain and the amber meads were not meant as titillators, but flushes. Gorge, gorge, and when the food was a wadded obstruction in the throat, pump it down with a potation. Until the maw was so overfed and overfull that it was time to sicken.

Time for the First Vomit. The moment came to many of the guests simultaneously. They rushed to the *balnea* at the top of the aisles. Bursting with too much food, they bellied down over the marble basins, and spewed forth the undigested contents of their guts. In the center aisle, where there were too many guests waiting to use the same convenience, one was spewing into the folds of his tunic, another on the floor. These two fled from the banquet hall.

Herod looked annoyed, and she was puzzled. "The Vomit should be volitional," he explained. "When it is accidental, it is a vulgarity."

She wondered if he considered the rest of the behavior a gentility.

In any event, he did not overeat, nor did he vomit. His mind was not on food, but on the empty throne. She could not count the number of times he glanced at it. Her dislike of the man was tempered by pity. She did not want him to be humiliated; she hoped that Pilate would come. And she herself wanted urgently to take the next step along her successful path of the evening, and meet the procurator. But it was getting late. Alas.

Suddenly the trumpets bellowed. He was arriving! His chariot had appeared. There was a huzzah on the terrace. The horns blasted again and again as cymbals clanged and drums rolled.

He stood at the wide portal, in the midst of his entourage. She had not expected him to be so handsome. Vilification of his character had contaminated the image of the procurator. Nobody had ever mentioned that Pilate was a tall man or that he walked like a divinity. Nor that there was a wariness in his eyes, like a beast at bay, uncertain whether to flee or strike. She had never sensed in a human being a warning so attractive.

Without acknowledging Herod's presence, the Roman strode directly to the larger throne. As he was adjusting his gold and purple toga, he seemed to have an afterthought, and raised his arm to the Idumaean, more in the way that a military officer halts his troops than as a friendly greeting between rulers. This niggardly salutation seemed more than ample to the subordinate; Herod executed a deep and deferential bow.

The dining hall had become quite still. Now the Idumaean called for another fanfare. He could scarcely wait for it to die away before he delivered himself of an oration. Thrice welcome, he said to his guest, and thrice times thrice, enumerating the dozen reasons for his admiration and his homage. When he had concluded, he awaited a response.

Pilate rose to acknowledge Herod's welcome and the plaudits of the celebrants. Raising both arms, he opened and closed his hands one single time. That was all. He sat down. Not a word spoken, not a smile bestowed. He had offered as much thanks as he thought the gift was worth.

Mary looked at Herod. He was smiling as if he had received an accolade, but she knew the smile was false. She felt another surge of pity for the man, and contempt. And as she glanced at Pilate and saw the cool and impeccable grandeur of the procurator, the unpitying judgment of the eyes, and the distance he had placed between himself and all others, she felt a chill of dread—and challenge.

However humiliated Herod had felt, he now pretended gaiety. He raised both arms as if to touch the dome of the hall.

"Jugglers!" he shouted.

The jugglers came racing in, down all the vomitoria. They tossed baubles in the air and wine-filled goblets which they caught without spilling a drop. Immediately behind them came the magicians, to bring forth doves and violets and mangoes from the bodices of women, and eels and white mice and squawking roosters from the tunics of men.

Then came the lutists, a hundred of them, making such a heavenly music that the spectators lifted their voices and sang with them—and Mary did too—and the hall was afloat on a celestial cloud.

Suddenly, in the midst of the rhapsody, trumpeters came rushing down the aisles, blaring a horrendous blast, and behind them, cymbals and drums and men dressed as devils, beating on sheets of tin and bars of iron. The cacophony was so terrible that Mary clapped her hands to her ears—but she was the only one. The other guests were shrieking with the noisemakers, laughing hysterically, screaming at full voice, enjoying the violation more than the heavenly music.

Mary was amazed. She could not believe that such a childish insult to the mind and senses could bring forth such demented delight.

It happened again. This time, with dancers. There were fifty of them, all foreign women—slaves, Herod said—of many sizes and colors. Some were hairless, some had great pyramids of shiny blackness on their heads that scarcely looked like hair. All were, in some distinct way, beautiful, and all were nude. Their movements were a confusion, as if they had combined their various native rites and adapted them to the Roman taste for lubricity. They performed in a disorganized abandon; some scurried aimlessly from torch to torch, some glided or leaped, a few simply strutted and made lascivious gestures to call attention to the bodily features they were proudest to exhibit. Hardly any were graceful, but Mary's attention was engaged by a frail black woman, quite young and with a forlorn beauty, who remained rooted in one place, totally immobile except for her arms, which she moved in slow, sinuous motions before her face, as though she was trying to entrance herself into believing she was alone, not ogled in her nakedness. Arms drifting this way, that way, she was like a fragile newborn creature hiding her presence behind wind-stirred reeds.

Mary was touched by her, and—unexpectedly—touched by the other slaves, even those who were making ugly gestures and obscene gyrations. And she applauded.

Then came the Amazons—a score of them—mighty women taller than any of the spectators. They were not truly Amazons, Herod said, but the pick of the foreign slaves—from Africa and the East and from distant islands—the most mammoth women in the world, the most handsome. And their costumes were all different from one another, all splendiferous: extravagances of fur and feathers, fantasies of bone and straw and seaweed, silks that were heavy and rich while others were fragile, transparent, like the skin of the sky.

But if what they wore was a munificence of color, what they performed was a dreary embarrassment. They were neither singers nor dancers nor acrobats. The divertisement they enacted was a combination of everything, without being anything. They sang a song about gladiators, not in unison, lacking harmony. When they moved to what was meant to be a pattern, some were not sure of the steps; there were many collisions. Suddenly everything halted—the Amazons stopped moving, the musicians were silent. Everyone, it appeared, had forgotten the next step, the next note of music. Total arrest.

The stallion came roaring down upon the stage. Forelegs up, snorting, stamping. The Amazons and closest spectators fled to safer places:

The beast was wild, violent. He wheeled one direction, then another, bent on destruction, his outcries a madness.

Then came the Amazon of Amazons. She was the most monumental of them all, the most magnificent. Her hair was as black as the stallion. It was impossible to imagine her in any other garment than her glowing naked skin. Her belly, thighs, buttocks undulated in voluptuous curvatures, her enormous breasts were high, proud, with nipples like purple plums. She carried a whip in her right hand and a gleaming white leather saddle in her left, its girths streaming like ribbons. As the animal charged at her, she snapped the whip at his head, and flayed him with the thongs of the saddle. Again the lash—at the fetlock, at the flanks, at the haunches, maddening the horse into an imbalance that would give the saddle an advantage. But suddenly he kicked, the leather flew, and as she went to recover it, the beast's hooves came down upon her. In the very moment when it appeared she would be trampled, the saddle seemed to vanish, and miraculously appeared upon the stallion's back. She clung to the crupper and lashed with the whip, and as the animal wheeled, the girths were fastened tight—and she had done it!

But now, the formidable—to ride the wild one. The stallion charged and charged again, and she struck at his shanks, at his forelegs, challenging him to rear, to stand upright as she was upright. Lash! The horse twisted to elude her. Lash, lash on the haunches, lash! It happened: he arose on his hind legs, snorting fire, and as he did so, she reached to the ground for a long wooden prod, and with it she tantalized him, baited the underside of the animal, his phallus, already engorged with excitement, with rage. Once more his hooves came pounding down on her; once more she was not there. Behind him, she snapped the lash again. He twisted, a black wind, he stormed, he thundered, while she gave him the flail and the rod. With a great leap skyward, the creature tried to burst out of his swollen skin. Lash, bait, bray—and suddenly—! She tossed the whip away, and the rod. She was as naked as the animal. She was going to mount him—but no—not on his back, on his underside; going to seize the girths, hang on to them, and ride him, belly to belly, male and female. The woman was unarmed now, and the beast sensed it. Up—silently this time—and his forelegs came down. A hoof struck her. She fell. He had it all now, all his own! He reared and roared, and when his forelegs came down, she was underfoot, but had snatched one girth and was clinging to it. He dragged her a few meters, and then: the other girth—she had it now, she was under him, she had him in her embrace, her hands clutching to the leather thongs, her body pressed against his, her thighs wide to receive him.

The crowd, a clamor. As the Amazon was on the verge of the consummation, the torches were torn away. The arena was cast in darkness, the woman and the beast vanished. The guests rose to their feet, shouted, clapped their clatterboxes, yelled for satisfaction. The *act*, they screamed, we have been cheated of the act! *The act!*

As if on signal, they stopped shrieking, and started to rock with laughter—either at the demonstration they had watched, or at themselves for expecting to witness the improbable. And Mary also laughed. But there was a queasiness in it: she had been excited.

The next display was a buffoonery. The stage was suddenly crowded with a host of animal pretenders, actors dressed as bulls, stamping and locking horns in bloody battle, goats and ewes in the pawing shifts and shuffles of a rut, leopards, crocodiles, jackals, hyenas, a tiger waylaying a giraffe, two elephants with their trunks entwining, making love.

Into the midst of this menagerie, a middle-aged man came running. He was dressed like an ordinary citizen, a propertied merchant perhaps, except that his toga was tied behind his back. And extending from his groin, a three-foot appendage made of cloth and leather, a stupendous penis, dragging on the floor.

The so-called animals turned and saw him. The goats and ewes shook from side to side, as if giggling. They tried to touch him with their paws. A leopard and hyena scratched at him, to claw the thing. When he slipped away from his tormentors, they pointed and laughed; embracing one another, their bodies rocked with hilarity, they fell on the ground; the elephants raised their trunks and hooted in mockery.

The man, embarrassed, insulted, did not know what to do with his encumbrance. He tried to cover it with his arms, with his toga; he tried to pretend it wasn't there, and to walk like any casual citizen, head at a nice angle, with dignity; he tried to hide it behind his back, to sit upon it.

Everything changed. When the giraffe advanced and lowered his great neck so as to lick at the comical member, the man had had enough ridicule. He lifted the encumbrance off the floor, turned it into a weapon, and struck at the long legs of the giraffe. One limb, then another, slam with the penis, slam, slam, and the giraffe fell helpless. As the tiger entered the fray, the man cudgeled him with his weapon, one whomp after another, and the wild cat lay on its back, begging for mercy, paws waving in the air. The man was feeling the power of his phallus now, and laid about with it. Leopards, jackals, driving them back into their wilderness, flaying with his penis, thumping and walloping his scorners and mockers, conquering the wild beasts with his leather manhood. But on came one of the elephants. The duel, then, between trunk and truncheon. Backward, forward, leather against leather, the man shouting, the elephant thundering, and at last: the pachyderm, bested, raised his trunk, let out a frustrated bleat, and trundled out of the arena.

Snap! went the jaws of the crocodile. The man screamed with realistic agony. The combatants were locked with one another. Then—main force—the merchant tore himself away. His valiant weapon was gone.

But—miracle to behold!

Where his false penis had been, the real one stood. Vigilantly erect, a foot long!

Cheers, huzzahs. An accolade from the crowd.

"Ave, phallus!"

He bowed modestly and pointed to his member as if to say that the hero of the occasion was not the actor but the appurtenance.

The crowd, delighted with such a delicate deference, shouted even more deafeningly.

"Ave, phallus!"

He grabbed the accessory and made it dip, as if to take a bow.

"Ave! Ave! Ave!"

Delirium. Men whistled and shouted, women screamed as if to faint, and one of them, middle-aged, ran down to the stage, tore off her arm bracelet and hung it on the protruding bracket. The actor removed the golden bauble and waved it in a grand gesture of gratitude; but the woman's escort, her husband perhaps, came puffing and panting into the arena to retrieve the trinket. Outraged at such chariness, the woman tore a necklace off her throat and, with defiant largess, draped it on the object, now an emblem of glory. As the husband tried to snatch it, the actor, struggling to retain it, shoved it closer to his testicles. A struggle. The spectators shouted and rose to their feet. They took sides. Some were for the penis, and some for property. There was laughter in the voices, but also a cause to espouse. It became hot, hysterical. People ran to the melee, they grappled. Fists flew, clothes were torn. Riot.

But not for long. A blare of brass, a show of soldiery. As quickly as the fracas had begun, it was over. And everyone was laughing once again.

Better than laughing: feeding!

The Second Eating began quickly, with a sense of urgency. The food bearers were moving imperatively among the crowd, as if to prevent starvation.

Again, Herod prodded Mary toward food, but she had even less appetite than before. She was unnerved by the entertainment. Not only by its childishness, its ugliness, but that she had laughed as if the naïve vulgarity was something she had an appetite for, a hunger perhaps, as the Romans had a greed for victuals. She had clapped her hands, she had shouted; on a few occasions, she had risen from her seat. It was a view of Mary of Magdala she had never seen.

She wondered how Pontius Pilate had taken the entertainment.

Once or twice, while it was going on, she had caught glimpses of him. He seemed entrapped in boredom. As he appeared now.

"Would you like to meet Pilate?"

Herod was watching her. Both arms outstretched, he helped her to arise from the depth of her cushions.

"Come, we will go to him."

She tightened. This was what she had wanted, but now that it was happening, she dreaded it. The whole occasion was out of joint; she was going to be presented to the procurator by a subordinate for whom Pilate had contempt. A Jewess at a festival restricted exclusively to Romans, she was about to have her maiden *inductio*—under the wrong auspices—to a man of final authority who was cold and, inescapably, cruel. In flight, she started away from Herod, but he clutched at her.

Baiting was in the air. The Amazons had baited the stallion; the false animals had baited the man with the monstrosity. She, too, was to be baited. Part of the show. Or else, she would be offered as a morsel of food from Herod to his honored guest, a tidbit to titillate the palate.

As they walked, she could feel cold perspiration spreading in her undergarments. She hoped the wetness would not seep through to the outer silk.

"Pilatus, my friend," her escort said, garbling Greek and Latin, "this is a young beauty that has appeared as if by conjuration."

Pilate looked at her and scarcely nodded. He said nothing.

"She is exquisite."

It was a woman speaking, and Mary noticed her for the first time. She was of the nobility, no doubt of it, yet self-effacing, noticeable only upon second glance. Claudia Procula, Pilate's wife, the descendant of emperors, ten years older than her husband and two heads shorter, seemed to fade in his presence. She was not a pretty woman, her forehead too high and her mouth too wide, a countenance that seemed prodigal with feature and expression. But what it expressed was precisely what her brain thought and what her heart felt, so that it was a face to put one's trust in. Her hands, too, were trustworthy; she extended both of them to Mary.

The Jewess took them as a gift of comfort. "Thank you."

"By conjuration?"

Those were the first words Mary heard Pilate speak. His voice was in the low strings of the lute, plucked sharply, without tremolo.

Herod was laughing. "Yes, that's how she appeared—by esoteria—certainly not by invitation."

Pilate was appraising her. She felt his eyes, on a journey of her person, halting at way stations. The first was her mouth; she had never known a glance so concentrated that it could hold in focus a field as limited as the lips. Then her bosom: studying it intensively, one breast at a time, as if distinguishing discretely between the white skin and the rose. Finally at the folds of her gown, where the fall of the drapery altered to hint at the separation of her thighs. When his eyes returned to her face, she felt as though all her clothes lay in a mound at her feet.

"Why was she not invited?"

"I did not want to displease you, Pilatus. I promised you no Jews."

The mask of the Roman did not alter. But he took longer to respond than seemed necessary. When he did, his survey was solely of her breasts.

"You are uncovered."

"Yes."

"Are you not concerned that you will be taken for a harlot?"

"I meant to be taken for a Roman."

"Do you think it is the same?"

"I do not know what it is. That's why I am here."

"To see what it means to be a Roman?"

"A Roman woman, yes."

"Do you think bare breasts define a Roman woman?"

"They are a kind of definition."

He looked at his elderly wife, whose breasts were not exposed, and Mary flushed with embarrassment. For the first time, she saw an expression on the magnificent face. It was meant to be a smile, she was quite sure, but it suggested no pleasure, only irony.

"Being a Roman means many things," he said quietly. "Tonight it means amusement. I will introduce you to our form of it."

He made a sign to Herod, not much more than a flickering glance. But the Idumaean knew dismissal. He muttered a few more sycophancies and slipped away, toward his smaller throne. And ignominiously he left his tribute behind him, the Jewish girl.

More by the ministry of looks and glances than by overt commands, divans arrived for the comfort of the procurator and his wife and his courtiers and his special guest. Taborets were brought with Phoenician wines and Grecian nectars and fruit essences from Syria. Then the cithara players were summoned, and the food-bearing slaves, and a portable *balneum.*

"Have you ever eaten with Romans?" Pilate asked.

"No."

"You should therefore begin with the fruit elixirs, then slip into the wines."

Again that wild thumping of her heart: she was *here*—sitting with Pilate—she had succeeded for the second time! And this time an added wonder happened. Her throat was no longer constricted, her juices flowed, she was hungry!

Pilate was pouring elixirs into a series of golden goblets, indicating which she must drink first, and second and later. She had never tasted the extracts of such delicious fruits, sweet yet tart, with an assertive clarity that cleansed her tongue and palate and seemed to open all the passages to her brain. Delicious, delicious, she kept saying, but he would not allow her to loiter over them. Nothing must live long enough to pall, he said. It was time for more potent liquors.

Wine and more wine, and her head began to lighten.

"Let her be," Claudia said. But Pilate ignored his wife as if she weren't there.

Then the food came. Delectable compotes of cooked fruit and lamb, tiny morsels of veal in an acorn-colored dressing that smelled mouth-wateringly now of ginger, now of garlic, now of cloves and cubebs, with no real identity except its own luscious ambiguity.

There was more to eat, fish and fowl and exotic porridges, and as she was becoming sated, Pilate kept urging her to other pleasures.

Try this, the merest taste of it, he was saying, with Claudia protesting unheeded, and have a touch of the pheasant liver, a tidbit of the dove.

He's making me a game, she realized, stuffing a beast to the bursting point: he wants to watch me getting ill. It was obvious to her: this was his revenge for the Jewish trespass. And she had a deathly dread that if she resisted him in any way, the vengeance would be more disastrous.

The man who could not smile for pleasure, was seeming to do so at last. "Wash it down with wine," he urged.

"I have eaten too much. I cannot."

"A little liquor of thyme and mint, to settle any queasiness."

She had a sip. And indeed it helped a little. She had another sip.

"Thank you," she murmured. "I have had more than enough of everything."

"You must have a little emesis, then, and eat some more."

She had never vomited, not even as a child. The thought was not only disgusting to her, but acutely painful. She could see them bringing her the *balneum* and the feather, and could not endure the possibility that she might be forced to thrust the long quill down her throat. Much better, she thought, if she was being tortured by the man, to have the spewing occur naturally, through an excess of eating, not by the duress of a torturing object.

As if aware of her thoughts, he said, "You may use the feather or eat some more and allow yourself to vomit *sponte.*"

There was no third alternative—that she could depart. She must brave it out.

"I'm feeling a bit better," she murmured. "Perhaps I will eat a little more."

Now he was not hiding it: his pleasure was plain. "Good. Are you at last ready to eat like a Roman?"

"I thought I was eating like a Roman."

"Hardly, hardly." He leaned forward and brushed a crumb from the side of her mouth. He ran his forefinger along her eyelid as if to smooth away a fugitive lash. Then:

"Will you eat pig?"

She remained quite still.

His eyes narrowed. "If you steal into our midst and pretend to be a friend, you must behave as a friend—or you are an enemy. . . . Will you eat pig?"

She heard it as an ultimatum, and wondered whether her scruple was, after all, so profound. Even though she had known, in the suppressed margin of her mind, that nothing she had eaten would have a priestly sanction, since it had not been ritually prepared, she had given no thought to the uncleanliness of the food. She herself had occasionally cooked a meal without hewing slavishly to the Mosaic rules, and some of the household servants had been notoriously lax. Even her father, religious as he was, had made it a point of not asking too many questions.

But *pig* . . .

She must not shudder at the thought, she told herself. Tonight, she had willfully exposed herself, seeking experience, yearning for it, needing to comprehend it, telling herself she had to learn more about the Romans, for they were not only her captors but, perforce, the companions of her future life. And if she was to live an enlightened existence in their midst—and a dauntless one—she must understand who they were, how they were the same as Jews, and how they were different.

An end to this intellectual Jewish superiority over a nation that had exhibited itself as being, in many ways, far superior. Perhaps even in the province where Jews were most arrogantly proud—their theistic philosophy of life—the Romans might have reason to be prouder. Who was to say that the Jewish aesthetic was more beautiful? Who was to know for certain that the contemplation of the naked body was of a lower order than the contemplation of a naked thought? Or the pleasures of the palate, the felicities of food, even a surfeit—who was to determine that they were more demeaning than the fasting on Yom Kippur? Was one torture of the stomach more worthy than another? Why should an ascetic act that scourges the body be deemed of higher morality than a hedonistic one that pleasures it?

Were these not some of the questions she had come here to answer?

"Yes, I will eat pig."

There was a scurrying of slaves. The dish would be a special regalement, the procurator said, and she would be honored by it. Meanwhile, wine to drink and lyrists to sing of the sweet hills of Tuscany and the swift rivers of the Apennines and the yearnings for home.

Soon she saw Nubians carrying a great silver tray. They came from below, from level to level, until they approached Pilate and the divans around him.

She could see Pilate swallowing with anticipation.

"This will be the perfect introduction to the savors of pig. Auspiciously—with delicacies."

He nodded to the Nubians. The two men lowered the tray and settled it on the largest taboret.

"These are pigs' innards," Pilate said. "Kidneys—intestines—bladder—heart. They are so fresh, the life is still in them."

They were uncooked—raw and running with blood.

"Look at the heart," he cried delightedly. "It's still beating—a kiss of love in it! Look—look—it's beating!"

A pulse of life; she could have sworn she saw it.

Pilate took his dagger from the scabbard at his waist, plunged it into the heart, and blood broke from it in a gush. He put his hand in the red wetness and licked his fingers. Even after having been pierced, the organ seemed to tremble. With his blade he cut off a gory hunk, opened his mouth and sucked the dripping flesh off the point. Its juices ran onto his lower lip. He mouthed the heart flesh with slavering satisfaction. Once more he extended his dagger, cut off another piece, and held it across to her, almost at her lips. The blood dripped; it had a hot sweet smell.

Mary vomited and fled.

She had left her chariot and horses at the Inn of the Carobs, a half league away from Herod's palace. The walk should have taken her a quarter of an hour, but she had to stop a number of times. The first time, she vomited again. The second time, she washed at the traders' well, doused her face and hair and throat with the night-chilled water, and allowed the wind from the hills to dry her skin and cool her body.

She began to feel slightly better—purged. More than the riddance of the disgusting food, more even than the ablutions of the water, was the purification by the outdoors, the cleansing by the dry-washing wind, the cloudless sky, the glittering cold stars.

The evening had been a humiliating failure. None of the illumination, none of the opening of vistas she had hoped for, dressed for, dreamed of, had come to pass. It was bathos—all mockery, no moonlight.

Still, she did not regret it. Not one to pity herself over a punishment, even if it was unjust, she considered tonight's penalty deserved. She had done a wrongheaded thing; more accurately, she had done it in a wrongheaded way. In search of knowledge, adventure, the illumination of a new world, she had thought of herself as a pilgrim. Well, she was not a pilgrim, she was a spy. And if she had clear-mindedly seen herself as a spy—someone who trespasses in enemy country—she would have been better prepared against emergency. Better armed. With knowledge. So that nothing that had happened tonight would have shocked her or left her unprotected or made her vomit.

She had to learn more, know more. Ignorance was an unforgivable vulnerability.

Fatigued to the marrow, she was impatient to find her chariot and go home.

Her chariot was missing. There was no sign of it at the Inn of the Carobs, and no sign of her horses. As she approached the hostelry, there was something peculiar about the place itself. She had never known it to be totally dark. Always, even in the depth of night, there was at least one oil lamp aglow at the front door, and others in the stable yard. But now, blackness.

The innkeeper was well known to her. A cynic named Baleel who pretended to hate everyone, Romans, Sadducees, Pharisees, Zealots. Despite his misanthropic view of life, he was a friend of her father's, recommended by Joram to all his business guests from foreign places. Mary made a game of arguing with him from time to time, and he held no grudges, liking her, occasionally extending to the girl the privilege of his stables.

But there was no chariot in the stable yard tonight, nor were there horses in the stalls. No mounts of any kind, not even an animal belonging to a guest. And the largest of the stanchions lay clumsily athwart the central doorway, ripped from the ground.

She did not want to awaken Baleel, or anyone else at the inn, but she saw no alternative. Walking out of the stable and across the wide, cobbled yard, she felt isolated in the broad moonlight, an uneasiness.

She heard a sound.

It was the high wind, perhaps, lifting the loose stanchion, making it creak. But the stable yard was almost entirely enclosed by the stalls, and the wind here was not gusty enough to stir the heavy timbers.

Silence now. No wind, no noise of any kind.

Slowly she continued toward the inn. At the open gateway of the stable yard, when the front door of the hostelry was within sight, she heard the noise again. More clearly. An odd, unidentifiable little discord, like wood scraping on wood, or the tearing of cloth.

And it was coming from the inn.

She halted, dreading to draw nearer.

Why was she afraid? she asked herself. Was there any reason to expect that the inn would be silent? What weirdness put that notion in her mind?

Still, it was a foreboding sound, and it grew louder as she approached the entrance. She did not halt, this time, but continued toward the doorstep. Each footfall was more frightening.

Now she was at the door. And saw it moving. Here, in the open, there was indeed a wind, a teasing gust, pulling at the badly hung door, letting it go its way, pulling again, backward, forward, as the stiles complained against the floor, and the leaves of the iron hinges complained against each other.

Why was no one attending to it?

She entered the inn.

There was no illumination except shafts of moonlight pouring through the two narrow windows. But by the light she could see disorder. One of the trestles of the largest table had collapsed, and the lamp and candlesticks had slid down to the floor. The room reeked of spilled lamp oil and dead wine. A stool had been broken and a water amphora had been smashed.

And there was nobody.

"Baleel!" she called.

Nobody answered.

"Baleel! . . . Baleel!"

She heard a stirring at the door behind her. She turned. A man stood in the open doorway, silhouetted against the moonlit outdoors.

"Baleel?"

"It is not Baleel." The voice spoke in Latin.

Abruptly, she heard a rustle on the stairs, then a sound at the door of the serving room. Men, she could not at first tell how many, all around her.

"Who is it?" she said.

A light appeared at the top of the stairs. Slowly, the man carrying it descended the staircase—carefully, as if measuring one step at a time, giving meticulous attention to the crippled foot.

She saw his face. Tullius.

Not a word was spoken by anyone. It was as if they did not want to distract the impeded man, lest he fall. He came at last to the final step and advanced.

She tried not to show her fear. "Where is Baleel?"

"He has been arrested."

"Arrested? Why?"

"The Jew has given refuge to Zealots."

"Baleel? That's not true."

He did not respond for an instant. "How do you know it is not true?"

"He is against them. I've heard him many times—!"

"Are you against them too?"

"Yes, of course."

Someone made a low laughing sound.

"It's true!" she cried. "You know who my father is—Magdala. You know how Sadducees—! We all hate the Zealots—you know that."

"Then, why did you give refuge?"

"To whom?"

"We ask you the same question," Tullius said. "To whom? What is his name?"

"I don't know what you're talking about."

Slowly he moved, held the lamp close to her face so that he could see her, watch her eyes for falsehood.

She could see him more clearly too. It was not a vicious face, but it held such afflicted grievance that she sensed he might spend his whole life sharing it, divesting himself of it, consigning it to others.

"The Zealot—what is his name?"

She turned from the closeness of his visage.

He grabbed her arm and twisted her back again. "You lied to me," he said. "You told me he had gone across the roof, and I sent soldiers after him. But someone saw him coming out of the front door of your father's counting rooms."

"The someone who told you, told you wrong."

"The someone was a Jew."

"Jews can lie almost as well as Romans."

He slapped her. The lamp shook in his hand, the oil doused the wick, the light flickered, there was a small blaze, and the centurion handed the lantern to one of the soldiers. The room went to near blackness, then the wick righted itself, and the glow returned.

The eyes of Tullius surveyed her. He seemed to regret his roughness. He extended his arm and with careful fingers smoothed her hair where the wind had touseled it. With oddly gentle hands he turned her so that she faced the light, studied the bodice of her dress where spewing had left a soil. He wetted his fingertips with his tongue and rubbed at the soiled spot. If a lover had performed so intimate a gesture, it might have touched her; Tullius disgusted her.

His voice was conciliating. "You did not have an enjoyable time tonight, did you?"

"No, not enjoyable."

"Why did you go?"

"I wanted to know the Romans."

It was the wrong thing to say and she instantly regretted it. "You wanted to know what?"

"Know nothing in particular. Simply what they are like—how they live."

"Or die."

Better be still.

He continued. "Or how to make them die."

He made a gesture and suddenly it was as if an octopus had laid hold of her; tentacles, a thousand tentacles it seemed, were on her body, in her clothes, at the most intimate parts of her person. She kept shouting, begging, let me go, take your hands off me, I have no knife, no weapon, I'm hiding nothing, let me go.

The search was over. They had torn her dress; her skirt, her bodice were ripped where the garnets had covered the seams. She tried to clutch the materials together but had not hands enough.

"Did you have Zealot friends at the festival?"

"I had no friends."

"Enemies?"

"I did not consider the Romans my enemies."

"But you do now."

". . . No."

His voice lost its resonance. "What is the boy's name?"

"I do not know."

"Why are you holding your breasts?"

"My bodice is torn."

"You went breast-naked to the party. Why not now?"

"Because you make me feel dirty," she said.

With a curse, he snatched at her hands, tore them away from their purpose, took hold of one side of the bodice and ripped it, rent it downward, tearing. Then, as her hands reached him, scratching at his eyes, she felt others upon her, ripping her clothes as he had done, striking her, beating her with their fists and their mail-armored boots. She knew she was bleeding but did not know from where; all she saw was the blood and the bleeding that would not cease. The pain was everywhere, so that she could not support all of it in an upright position, she had to fall. But they would not let her fall, not yet. And when they did, they were all, it seemed, upon her. Holding her arms and her head, pulling her legs so far apart that the agony was unbearable, they were on her and in her and punishing every part of her being. She knew nothing except pain. Pain and counting. One, two, three, until all seven of them had killed her, maimed her, murdered her, killed her, killed her again and again and again. Tullius was the first and he was the last as well, and after him she could not keep track of anything, not of the stabs of pain, or the fury, or the light.

⁂

A bondwoman tended her. She was an elderly Greek whom Mary's father had purchased not because he needed her but because, even at sixty, she had a youthful elegance and was meticulously spoken. To Mary she brought remedies for the damage to the flesh, but no comfort for the soul. There is some secret corner in a woman's mind, the bondwoman said, where she is forever pure and chaste, in essence virginal. No physical act of love ever robs her of that precious purity—except rape.

Mary knew the woman was right. The spoliation was not in the loins alone, but in that onetime pure and peaceful place that would thenceforward be soiled and full of pain. And of hatred.

She hated the world and hated being alive. Some nights, lying in bed, she hated her body for the ugliness that had been perpetrated upon it. Touching herself, bathing herself, putting her clothes on in the morning, revolted her. The configuration of her limbs, the fullness of her breasts, the mounds of flesh that made her person, seemed vulgarly excessive to her; her femininity itself was an excess, an overindulgence, as if she had been caught in the unclean act of being a woman. Her female appendages and organs were an affront, an obscenity; she felt grotesque. It would have been better, she thought, if she had been born disembodied, or not born at all.

Her shame was a perversity. It was as if she had committed the heinousness upon herself; she—not those others—had torn and ravaged her. *She* was the abomination. So she tried to hide. She looked at no one. Her eyes saw nobody and nothing that did not remind her of her shame. And there was death and destruction in everything. The earth was only for burial, the wind was for desolation, the sky was for falling.

Her hatred became one of her vital functions; she breathed, she took daily nourishment, she slept, she purged herself, she hated. And she hated not only those others, but herself the worst, with the fierce irrationality of pain. Always the same indiscriminate agony, so that she could not distinguish her person from her torment. She no longer existed as a distinct and separate self; she was conjoined—physically, it seemed to her—with the monsters who had brutalized her. She lived with creatures who made her shriek; they were her enemies, but they were also her blood and being. She lived with demons.

⁂

"You do not understand—you are not a Roman citizen," her father said. "You have no rights."

"I have rage."

"It is not the same."

"Rage may be more effective than rights," she said.

It was strange, she thought, how the animus grew stronger every day, stronger as she herself grew stronger. In fact, it was the fury that had made her recover in three weeks instead of three months, as the physicians had prognosticated. Fury, the panacea.

"You will be better off without your angers," her father said, and her brother nodded.

"I will be nothing without my angers."

"It is all beside the point," Caleb said. "There is nothing you can do about anything."

"There is everything."

Her father looked frightened. "Please, Mary, put this behind you. It is dangerous to dwell on it. Tell yourself that it was a hideous atrocity, but that it is over—and it could have been worse."

"Worse? What could have been worse?"

"They could have killed you."

In despair: "Why didn't they!"

"Because they believe you will lead them to that boy," Joram said.

"In fact, I'm sure they feel they had a right to kill you," her brother added. "They know you helped the Zealot—why shouldn't they put you to death for such a treason?"

The words tore. "I wish they had!"

Her brother was sardonic. "If that is your wish, your fury may make it come true."

In grim quiet, she studied them. "I think you are both loathsome," she said in scarcely a whisper. "You want to turn your backs, you want to pretend it never happened. You want to live like rich cowards all your life."

Her father winced and turned away from the contempt. "We have gone as far as we can go."

As far as they could go consisted of Joram's appearing at the prefecture and lodging a complaint as a noncitizen, with no legal rights in the court. He had specified that on a certain instance his daughter had been assaulted, abused and raped by Tullius, the centurion, and by six soldiers of unknown identity. To everyone's astonishment, the six unknown men had voluntarily come forward and identified themselves. They altogether denied that any of them had sexually violated the girl or had employed other than commonly accepted tactics of interrogation to induce the complainant to divulge the name of the Zealot enemy to whom she had given refuge. There was a grim reversal in the making. Instead of being the plaintiff, Mary might suddenly turn into the defendant, with the charge of treason hanging over her head. . . . And the whole matter had, by tacit consent of all parties, been quietly dropped.

She had sensed, at the time, with what dim consciousness she could muster, that her father had little recourse in the courts. She did not blame him for having failed to achieve justice. But his refusal to discuss the subject in the last fortnight, his effort to hide all signs of the irremediable harm and shame and obscenity, meant only one thing: cowardice. She felt that a hideous sin was being condoned; in fact, that they were all becoming complicitors.

"If you can slip away from this without doing anything about it, you will sicken!" she said. "It will poison you, it will be a pus!"

Her father turned his stricken face to her. "What can we do? Dear God, Mary, what can we do?"

"Kill them all."

"There is a cursed devil in you."

"Seven."

"Cast them out, for heaven's sake, or they will do worse harm to you than the Romans have done!"

"I know only one way to cast them out."

"Jews are not murderers."

"Is it not written that a woman ravished must be avenged?"

"Yes, but it is not written that the revenge should be in our own hands. That is up to the Lord."

"So far, the Lord has been on the side of the Romans."

"That is sacrilege."

"And stupidity," her brother said. "Let us say we agreed that we should murder them—who is to do it? You? Father? Myself? You think we would be skilled at such an enterprise?"

"There are people we can pay."

"If you pay an assassin, you never stop paying him. Do you want to be in bond to a *sicarius* all your life?"

She knew that they were right, and she knew that they were unforgivably wrong. With their unarguable logic and their moral rectitude and their prudential caution they would achieve larger and larger houses, and smaller souls.

While her fury, her demon of demons, would grow and eat at her entrails and ultimately devour her. Unless it could be slain.

There was no one to turn to. As a child, she had had acquaintances but no friends, and as they had grown, even they had drifted away from her. They were the reputable daughters of the respectable rich; they hewed to custom and decorum with a dread that someone might think they had been tainted by the wanton soilure of the Romans. Mary's failure to conform, to dress in the guarded Jewish way, to marry early, her avidity for more learning than a protected Jewish woman might ever need, had branded her as wayward. Someone to be avoided, a breeder of trouble. In fact, Mary was quite sure, they were not as shocked by her tragedy as they professed themselves to be. Their private appraisal would be inevitable: she had brought it on herself.

She was abandoned by everyone, cast out to wreak a futile and lonely vengeance. Aching with fury, shame—and not a little fear—she wanted to destroy the world; she wanted to hide from it. She wanted to make a noise so terrible that it would tear the sky, she wanted to weep like a baby. She wanted, afflictedly she wanted a friend.

And she thought of Judas. She had recalled him often in the past few days, remembering his face as one of the kindest, his eyes the deepest. There was an abyss of longing in the young man; she had felt it immediately after he had gone; perhaps the same sort of hunger as her own, an anguish for knowing. Knowing what? Perhaps they might ask the question of each other. He could be a kindred soul; he might even be a friend.

One morning, when the assault which seemed to have happened yesterday was actually months before, she went in search of Judas. She asked for scriveners in the marketplace, found one and another and a third, and none of them was the young man she sought. Directed to what was called the Alley Passage, she came to where his stand had been. Hardly anything was left of it, a few splinters from what must have been his table, a number of broken baskets, and inkstains on the cobblestones.

He left in the middle of the night, someone said. A nearby potter told it somewhat differently: the Romans had come and crippled him for life. A woman who sold seeds and spices said she knew the truth of it: a *quadrum* of Roman soldiers had appeared; the boy had been beaten witless, and he had done damage to himself, and died.

Mary believed all of it; no matter how inconsistent the reports were, she believed them all. Oh, the bastards, she said, oh, the poor boy, the bastards, the poor beautiful boy with the look of goodness in him, and decency and sensibility, and the sweet eyes of kindness! Oh, the monsters!

Believing every tale of Roman atrocity, she collected them as a keeper might collect ferocious animals, kept them locked up in her cage against the day when she would loose them to do their ravage. Tales, all kinds of tales of Roman inhumanity, true ones and false, searches and seizures, outcries in the night, exiles and tortures, beheadings and defilements and castrations—she collected them, catalogued all the illustrations of the Roman gluttony and corruption and cruelty and rapaciousness. So that she saw no choice but to rid the world of Romans, brutalize them as she and Judas had been brutalized, slay them all. At the least, drive them from Judea. How?

How? She had no allies in Jerusalem. The Jews she knew lacked her persuasion, her daring and her wrath.

Only the Zealots had it, and they hid in the hills, in Galilee, in caves, in the desert. And how could she find them?

She thought of the red-haired boy, the poet of Kerioth.

The camel driver was crazy. So was his camel. And they despised each other. They kept perpetrating spites, the man on the animal and the animal on the man. The camel driver's malice was expressed by teasing the beast. To get an extra mile or two out of him at the end of day, he would unsaddle the feed bag and carry it a few yards ahead of the hungry brute, urging him onward, onward. The camel would protrude its floppy lower lip so that it quivered, let out a terrible, violent croak, and trudge hungrily after his demented master. For the camel's part, his spite against the tormentor was cruder but more effective. He would simply halt the march, then turn and lumber off in the wrong direction.

Perhaps her father had been right, Mary considered; it was an error to hire an unknown driver and an unknown beast. This was one of the Syrian camels, known to be eccentric and subject to fits. Her father's beasts were southern Arabian, of better quality, and their two drivers had been with the family since enslavement. They could be counted on to take her more swiftly and with greater comfort to their summer house near Magdala. But that was the crux of it: she had lied. She was not going to their summer house near Magdala, was not going to the green hills in search of quiet and peace and solace for her aching spirit, she was going to Kerioth for murder.

She would find him, the young Zealot. It would not be an impossible task to track him down—if not in Kerioth, somewhere else. In the town they would tell her where to go, for they would know him. It was not, after all, a major city. How many red-haired young poets could there be, approximately her own age, and acquainted with a scrivener named Judas?

They would be suspicious at first, until she told them her own story. And showed them what she had brought to help the Zealots' cause. Assassination, she knew, came at a high price, and there were seven of them to execute, but she would gladly pay whatever the custom demanded.

The jewels and silver money were not in the calfskin nightsack that she always carried at her side; they were strapped around her waist, hidden beneath her undergarments. They weighed a good deal and added to the discomfort of the desert heat.

The winter season: she had not imagined such a sun or landscape. It was a crouching menace of a country, striped by gullies and wadis like a tiger, parched and panting, ready to leap at the throat. She burned. The flaxseed unguent she had spread on her skin had not given her enough protection; the backs of her hands were blistered, the flesh on her cheekbones seemed too thin and stretched too tight, and her eyeballs felt as though pins were pricking at them. The worst part were the mirages. She had been delighted with the first of them. It was a lovely lake, a cool sweet mirror of the sky. But the next time, when she yearned to bathe in the wet refreshment and the illusion turned into a hot sea of sand, she hated the mockery, and felt scorched.

"You said we should be in Kerioth by nightfall."

"It will be tomorrow noon." The driver was surly. He pointed with his beating stick at the camel. "He loiters in the heat."

He whipped his stick at the camel's neck. The beast raised his head with a jerk, and lowered it.

"He goes slower when you beat him," she said.

"If I do not beat him, he does not go at all."

The camel poked along and dawdled to a stop. This time the driver lifted the stick and struck with all his might across the beast's head. The camel let out its awful sound and moved onward more quickly.

The driver laughed wetly. "Perhaps you are right—and so am I."

Toward nightfall, they halted and made camp. As she had done the evening before, she helped him imbed the poles and set up the tent. Inside it, there was room enough for both of them, but the camel man, with surprising nicety, said he preferred to sleep outdoors, where he could keep an eye on the wretched beast. Again he refused to share her figs and bread and cheese, but drank the gruel of wheat and sour goat's milk that he carried in his leather urn. He made a variety of digesting noises, got up and circled the tent a number of times. There was no wind tonight, and no need to choose a windless side, so he lay down on the side farthest from the moon, and before she was settled inside the tent, she heard him snore.

She thought she had just fallen asleep, although later she realized it was nearly dawn, when she heard the faint stirring at her side. She became taut with dread: it was a reptile, she was sure of it.

She felt at her side, and it was her nightsack moving. He was trying to slip it out from under the flap of the tent. For an instant she simply smiled grimly. He was, no doubt, reasoning that she had to have some valuables with her, and surmised they were in the calfskin bag. But he would be disappointed in the nightsack—

Except that she had a knife in it. She had determined that never again would she be without a weapon, and now she would be robbed of it. What's more, he would go off and leave her marooned in the desert.

The purse slipped through. It was gone. And she heard a soft slithering.

With a leap, she was out of the tent. He was scurrying toward his camel.

"Stop!"

The man was short and squat and not as fleet as she was. By the time he had hold of the camel reins she had caught up to him.

She snatched at her nightsack, she snatched at him. He turned and struck her. Reeling back, she recovered and went at him again. He was trying to mount the camel. She clutched at the fist that held the purse and as he whipped the sack across her face, she seized his wrist and sank her teeth into it. He groaned and kicked at her, kept on kicking. Now her hands—claws—scrabbling at his face, tearing, ripping with her fingernails, blood and blood, and he moaned and flung his arms wildly, and tore himself away. But as he once more tried to mount the beast—it may have been the scuffle that frightened the animal—or the smell of blood—or plain madness—it raised its forelegs not like a camel but like a frenzied stallion—raised them high and then down, stamping on the man—

—she thought of the stallion and the Amazon—beauty, grace—but this ugly animal, ugly man—!

—stamping—pounding the body into the sand, up and down with vengeance, the head a scarlet wetness, up and down—

Stillness then.

The camel, halting, wheeling, and away.

The man was a mass of blood, and lifeless.

It was curious how the sight of him did not frighten or disgust her. Dead, that was all. Only dead.

⁂

The camel was gone. When she had turned from the body of the driver, the beast was a hundred ells away and fleeing like the demented thing it was. She had run after it, shouting, shrieking, and realized that she was simply compounding absurdities.

Dawn then, and walking in the desert. Full sun and heat, and her throat constricting as though she were being garroted, her eyes like burning coals, her head full of mirages, falling into one lake and another, dry, dry, burning lakes of sand, and head full of flames, on fire, bursting, mirages, lakes of fire.

Get up, she said, do not die in the sand, get up, look for the mirage, seek the lake of fire.

She saw the whiteness in the distance, white and standing square, something other than sand, and something to go to. Falling, rising, bearing toward the whiteness only because it was neither sand nor false water, falling, rising to the whiteness.

Then she heard the sound somewhere, the call. She turned.

It was a donkey cart, moving toward her. A slow deliverance. Closer and closer, and the driver descended to support her so that she might not fall again. He was a shortish man of middle years, built like a cube, with a beard of lentil color. He seemed to have trouble talking, as though there were an obstruction in his throat. He asked:

"Where do you go?"

"To Kerioth."

"I cannot go so far. But I will take you to my people."

He led her to the back of the cart, made a space and helped her to get aboard. There was scarcely room. It was clearly a water cart, for the conveyance was crowded with great jars, some ceramic, some of leather, most of them covered with leaves and basketry to keep the contents cool. She yearned for water, and as he moved toward the front of the wagon to set forth, she was about to call to him when he halted.

Turning, he said, "Want to drink?"

Without awaiting a reply, he trundled to the rear again. Uncapping one of the huge jars, he tilted it forward, held the cap under the bottle mouth, and the remarkable liquid poured to overflowing.

How unexpected it was: the cool water burned her throat. Even with the pain, she wanted to drink all of it at once. But he took the cap away, and only let her have it sip by sip. When it was gone and she asked for more, he said: later.

A mile or so along their way, she was feeling somewhat relieved.

"You said your people," she called. "Who are they?"

"The Poor Ones."

She knew about the Poor Ones. Some gave themselves that name, not as a badge of their impoverishment but as a proud emblem of their renouncement of worldly goods. In Jerusalem they were called Essenes or Ascetics. She had heard them referred to as the Distant People, either because they lived far from the city in wilderness places—caves, deserts—or because they seemed to speak from a remoteness.

The white specter Mary had seen was not a specter. It was the high wall of the Essenes, and the wagon was approaching it. None too soon, she thought, for her head was spinning and her skin was ablaze.

As he helped her down, she thanked the waterman and told him her name.

He inclined his head. "My name is . . ." He was having a difficulty. Hesitating, he started anew. "I am called Eben."

He walked from the wagon to the gateway. She did not follow him. Giddy, afraid she might fall, she clung to a wheel of the wagon and closed her eyes to shut out the dizziness.

When she opened them, Eben was talking through the slats and iron bars of the great gate. On the other side, she could see a little gnarled person, old and wizened, a dried fig of a man, wearing a mantle far too big for his shriveled body.

"But she is a woman," the ancient said.

"And I am a man—open the gate."

The old man did not know what to do. His body quivered with the immensity of the decision demanded of him, and at last was unable to make it. Lifting the skirts of his mantle, he turned and trembled out of sight.

Eben beckoned. Unsteadily she moved to the gate and clung to the iron bars to steady herself. Again she closed her eyes, and when she opened them all she could see was men. Although they were all, except for Eben, on the other side of the gate, she felt as if she were surrounded. Men. Oh, God Almighty, she muttered to herself, must they be men? Need I always be ringed about by men, taken hostage by them? Is there not a solitary woman here to help me?

"We cannot take her in," one of them said. He was the tallest of them all, patriarchal, with a beard of snowy white, and a voice meant for mountaintops.

"But we must bring her out of the sun," another responded. He was perhaps the youngest. He seemed quieter, more diffident than the others. "She may have need. . . ."

The patriarch repeated. "But we cannot take her in. She is a woman. It is not allowed."

"Then, I will tend to her out there."

It was a kind of tabernacle made of reeds and rushes. She lay under a canopy of fronds and branches and was not uncomfortable. There were grasses beneath her that were just turning yellow, and they smelled fresh, like a well-kept haymow.

She was impatient to continue her journey to Kerioth the following day. But when, at dawn, Eben appeared in his water cart, she was not as strong as she had thought herself to be, and lay back on her bed of grass, gasping for breath.

She remained with the Essenes for three days. From time to time some of the brothers came. Whenever they did, they stood at the gate of the high wall, and waited there a moment as if to summon up the courage to do something naughty. Then they would come with smiles and little giggles and benedictions and a crust of bread, and they would ask how she was faring. Some seemed reluctant to go inside again.

The visitor who came most often was the one they called Jesus. It was he who had built her tabernacle, and it was he who mended her with his broths and smiles. His smile was different. Theirs, because the patriarch's injunction about women had in some clever way been circumvented, was filled with mischief. His had no mischief in it, only kindliness and healing.

At first she could not understand this constant good humor, this everlasting benignity in the man. Then she remembered a little boy who used to come to their family Passover *seder* when she was a child. Her mother had told Mary to be especially kind to him, because his smile and his timidity were part of his trouble. He will never harm anyone, her mother said, and you must not harm him. Be gentle with him, as he is gentle with everyone. He does not know any other way; he is a simpleton.

That must be the key to Jesus: he was a simpleton. He was as kind to everyone as he was to her, so she would be kind to him. On the second day, she learned that being kind to the man was not as easy as being kind to the little boy. What seemed to repay him for his attentions to her did not consist of telling him how grateful she was for his care and goodness, nor complimenting him on his patience and gentleness. He was repaid only when he saw that she was not in pain. And this was a repayment she could not easily make.

This did not conform to her picture of him as a simpleton. There was something about him she could not comprehend. Perhaps it was his loyalty to this simpleminded cult with its emphasis on poverty and prayer and meditation and its isolation from all worldly things, and its insistence on chastity.

"Have there never been any women here?" she asked him one day.

"Yes, there have been."

"Then, why . . . ?"

His eyes glinted a little. "Our Reader . . ."

And he paused. The Reader was the highest elder of the Essenes, the Teacher of Righteousness.

She pursued the question. "Is there a rule against women?"

"No. Only a rule of chastity."

"Then, why did he keep me out?"

Again the wrinkle of amusement. "Sometimes he reads the Law in one way, sometimes in another."

"Is he so capricious?"

"No. Mysterious."

"He looks like Moses," she said.

He teased her. "And Moses looks like God."

For an instant she was surprised, for it sounded sacrilegious. But it wasn't; he was merely summoning his childhood's image, much like her own, that combined the two almighty names into a single sanctity.

"Why is the Reader mysterious?" she asked. "Because he wants to be like God?"

"Perhaps."

"Do others here want to be like God?"

"Some, I think."

"And you?"

"No. I wish only to love Him as He loves me."

She kept on questioning him about the mysteries of the Reader and God and Moses, and the mystery of the Essenes that people always referred to with whispers and heavy glances.

"I do not know the mystery of the Essenes," he said. "I am still a novice here."

He had arrived over a year before, but there were still eleven months before he could take his vow, and learn the mystery.

She grinned. "Will you tell it to me then?"

"No."

Mary wished he did not smile so much. She no longer wanted to think of him as a simpleton.

At dusk of the second day, she asked Eben, "Does he ever lose his temper?"

"Temper?"

"Doesn't he ever get angry?"

"Sometimes."

"At whom?"

"Himself and . . . I think . . . God."

"Does he say so?"

"Oh, no."

"Why do you think he gets angry at God?"

"Because He . . . does not always let him heal."

"Can he heal?"

". . . Yes."

"Jesus can do that? How do you know?"

"He has healed me."

"How did he heal you? Of what?"

"I am a mute."

It was nonsense. "You're not a mute. You're speaking."

"I was a mute. I could say nothing."

"Come, now. Nothing?"

"A dog could bark better than I could speak. A cat could mew. I was dumb."

All at once, the discussion became too much for him, as if he were unequal to her interest, and might be struck dumb again. For an instant he was tongue-tied with gratitude and bewilderment and faith. His hands became unsteady, and to hide the weakness he made fists of them and held them tightly to his breast. "I love him," he said, and went away.

There was a full moon that night, and as she and Jesus sat in her tabernacle, his face was illuminated as if the whole sky were gazing upon him.

"Eben told me something strange."

He did not fill the silence.

She continued. "He says you caused him to speak again—that he was mute."

As if the moon had gone under a cloud, his whole manner seemed to darken. It was the first time she had seen him distressed; his face was filled with an anxiousness that his eyes could not hold.

"It is not true," he said.

"He says you healed him."

"I do not heal anyone. With God's help, we heal ourselves."

"Some say that with God's help, we can heal others. I do not believe it. Do you?"

He looked at her. The silence was difficult.

She continued. "Eben insists that he was mute—and you made him speak."

"He was not mute."

"He says he was."

"There is a difference between one who is mute, and one who does not speak. I merely asked him to speak to me, and I taught him how. I am still teaching him."

"How do you teach him?"

"By hearing what he says."

It was the night before her departure, and they were both saddened that she was leaving. She felt, for all the enigma of the man, for all his secrets left untold, for all the depth within him into which no light had shone, that she knew him well. One day she might come to love such a man as this, and rue it. Rue it for the goodness she would need—and lack—if she were ever truly to comprehend him. For, even now, knowing him as well as she thought she knew him, she did not understand him at all.

"Tomorrow—when you depart—I shall think of you."

"And I of you," she replied.

"Where do you go?"

She had an impulse to tell him the truth. But: "Magdala."

As if he had not heard her answer, he repeated:

"Where do you go?"

She had her story all made up, a trace of truth, and mostly falsehood. She did not tell him about the seven soldiers, nor that she was en route to Kerioth to find a Zealot boy and others like him, for revenge. She said only that she had tired of Jerusalem and wanted a bit of solitude, a place to contemplate. "I was on my way to my father's house in Magdala," she concluded. "It is pretty there, and tranquil. My hope was to lie back and find serenity. But the camel driver meant to cheat me, so he took me out of my way. When I leave here, I'll continue toward my destination."

He was just as cryptically quiet as he had been when she had related the death of the camel driver. He simply gazed at her now as if he knew she lied and the lie was unimportant; only she herself was important to him. His silence was unsettling. Then he spoke:

"Whom do you wish to slay?"

She was startled. In his concern for her, he had intruded upon her private person, had trespassed, had stripped bare her most secret thought. Unnerved, she tried to recover her composure: "Slay? No one—nobody."

Now that the covert lie was open, it seemed to hurt him. His eyes no longer smiled. He spoke with a sadness that made her feel gray.

"If you slay one enemy and another and another—and even if no new enemies arise to take their places—you will still not find what you seek."

"What do you think I seek?"

Again he did not answer, but murmured that it was time for prayers, and he went indoors.

In the early dawn, before her departure, the silence of the man continued. She had a desperation to know what he was pondering. She was wordless and helpless, with the few minutes passing, and Eben getting the water cart ready, and a sense that some vital message from Jesus was not yet conveyed.

"Tell me what you are thinking," she said.

He shook his head with a kind of distant sorrow, and that, too, was incomprehensible. Did it mean he did not know, or did it mean he could not, would not tell her?

"Please—tell me!"

He stepped away from the water cart, walked backward a little as if to keep her a bit longer in his gaze, then departed through the gateway.

She called after him: "Tell me!"

But he did not turn again.

She was nettled and hurt. She had managed him better in her mind when she had thought him a simpleton; she wished she could again think of him that way. But she must stop thinking of him as a wise man, for if he was truly so, why did he not share his wisdom with her? Perhaps he was one of those pretenders who derive their reputations for sagacity through their trick of silence. Silence and knowing glances. Stillness, without much motion in the mind. Yes, perhaps he was one of those.

But she knew this was the recourse of her pique; it was not so. The man was truly wise, and his wisdom was in his healing. He had healed her burning skin and her sun-craziness; he had made the mute to speak. This was a wisdom deeper than the mind. It was a profound knowing in the heart and soul. What was it that he knew?

Well, she would not be here to discover the secret of the man who had so mysteriously mended her.

But had he really mended her? Had he brought a lasting remedy for her ache? No, it was only temporary, only an illusion. He had given her an imaginary comfort, a momentary remission from an agonizing sickness that she, and only she, could heal.

And for which there was only a blood remedy.

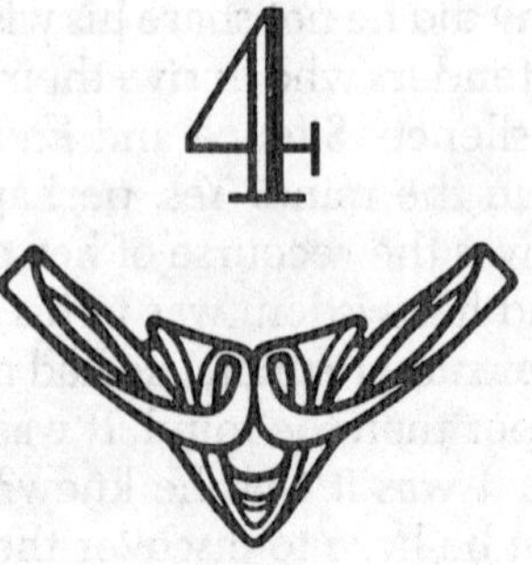

About four months after Judas went to work for Heskel the publican, his employer added another chore to his duties as accounts keeper. He deputized the young man as a tax collector. Heskel's work had been getting onerous and he wanted to use his own efforts in gathering the larger levies in the marketplace and at the Temple stalls, and be relieved of the pettier "donations," as he called them.

Judas disliked the word for its implication that there was willingness or gratuity on the part of the giver. There was only rancor. And soon he hated doing the Roman dirty work, gouging the street potters, the spice grinders, the alley vendors who made no more than a pittance from their skins of wine or jars of oil. He could barely stand their resentment.

It perplexed him. Why did he stand it? Having failed as a scrivener, why did he not offer himself for other work that had no disgrace in it, no matter how humble—as one of the trench laborers at the aqueduct, or as a cleaning man in the *kasher* slaughterhouse, or even as a beggar in the streets? Anything would be more dignified than such shameful employment. Certainly he didn't persist in it for the luxury of living in Heskel's house—wealth and prodigality made him uncomfortable. Nor was it the bounteous salary, for he gave nearly all of it to the poor. Then, why did he so compulsively cleave to this reviled vocation? He gave himself half answers that had to do with temporariness and expedience, but he knew there was some hidden reason he would not or could not seek. Obscurely it worried him. Then, one day, after a summer of tithe gathering, something took place that deepened his anxiety.

It was late in the month of Elul, a midday of heat and drought, that

Judas set forth toward the Sheep Gate to go in search of a man who was ten weeks delinquent in taxes. He was a drover named Achaz who was hired, when he was fortunate, to drive small herds of goats from the hills north of Jerusalem into the center of the city. The animals of perfect quality—sacrificial quality, that is—he would deliver to the Temple stalls; the others he would herd into the nearby abattoir. Achaz was paid very little, and rarely in coin. Sometimes he was given goat cheese or flesh; occasionally, a bag of salt which he had to sell in the marketplace.

Always, the drover entered the city through the Sheep Gate, and today it was Judas's intention to stop him there. If the man settled his arrears, which he would be allowed to do by paying either in coin or in salt, Judas would instruct the praetorian sentry at the gate to allow the herdsman and his flock to enter Jerusalem. If not, Achaz would have to return the goats to their owner, and until he paid the Roman levy he would be barred from earning a livelihood in the Roman dominion. Judas dreaded the encounter. Achaz was a brutish creature, a Peraean Jew from beyond Jordan, and, as the saying went, a man beyond Jordan was beyond Jewry.

Toward noon, in the heat, through a veil of ocher dust, Judas saw the drover's herd approaching. The tax gatherer passed through the gateway and walked out a little distance to meet him. Seeing Judas, the herdsman came forward, reached down to the bellwether goat, took hold of the thong around the animal's neck and stilled the tinkling noise. The other goats, with no sound or leader to follow, slowed down but did not stop moving; they milled in a lazy stupor, colliding with one another, complaining. There weren't many of them, fifty at most, but their nagging nasal noises made them a multitude.

"Ho-hah! Publican!" the drover called.

"Hail." In Latin.

Achaz let out a brawling laugh that scared the animals. The merriment mocked and made an unpleasant sound. Besides, unsightly. The man's teeth were like broken bits of walnut shell, jagged and sparse. His middle-aged shoulders shook in a way that suggested spasm more than amusement, and his clenched fists pummeled the air.

"Today I fool you," he shouted, between convulsions. "Today I pay your heathen tax! And may you lie in a Roman grave!"

In a rush, in a flurry, shouting, laughing, waving his arms in the air, he pushed a path through the huddle of goats, shoving them this way and that, rushing to get to his destination, which was a black ewe at the rear of the herd. On her back was strapped a dirty goatskin with, perhaps, a few pounds of salt in it. He untied the strips of hide that secured the pouch, pulled it off the animal's back, held it by the thong that secured it and waved the sack around his head. He made an outcry of victory.

"I pay my tax, you dirty publican! I pay my tax, you Roman pig, you pig of Rome—I pay, I pay!"

With a shriek of contempt, he threw the bag at Judas's feet.

For a moment Judas did not stoop for it. When at last he did, he muttered, "Thank you, Achaz."

"Go thank your Roman pimp."

The pouch itself was slimy on the outside, unpresentable, and, before selling the salt, Judas would have to put it into a respectable container. He hefted it.

"What is its weight?" he asked.

"Just what I owe. Go and weigh it yourself."

It did not seem heavy enough. Judas knew not to be cheated with light weight. And there were other ruses Heskel had warned him about: the adding of fillers to make up extra bulk, like the ground-up chaff of wheat or husks of millet.

He untied the thong around the neck of the pouch. He opened the sack. A stench assailed him. He looked inside. The bag was full of goat dung.

He barely glanced at Achaz, who stood there in silence but with a maniacal smile on his face. Without a word, and without violence, Judas placed the pouch on the ground.

Quietly: "I will instruct the sentry to bar you from the city."

Judas turned to reenter the gateway.

The sound he heard behind him was neither a laugh nor a cry; it was the noise of a rabid animal. Judas felt the man's hand wrenching his arm, felt himself being twisted.

The drover's face was contorted. "Take your tax," he shouted. "Take your tax!"

The herdsman shoved his hand into the bag, brought forth a handful of dung, and cast it into Judas's face.

"Take it—take your tax!"

Another handful of the vile stuff.

Judas turned to retreat. The drover pursued him, grasped him once more, threw him to the ground.

"Take your tax!"

Handful after handful of manure onto the tax-collector's face, onto his robe, into his hair. The stench, the mucky dampness.

A crowd was gathering. Guards came from the gate, with the praetorian sentry hurrying, shouting.

The herdsman's shrieks were no longer violent, but despairing. "I have no money! How can I pay? How can a Jew treat a Jew like this? I have no money! I have nothing! I have nothing!"

It was over. The herdsman left the empty pouch on the ground, struck with the back of his hand at the neck of the bellwether goat, and turned the flock in the opposite direction, away from Jerusalem, back toward the hills whence he had come.

Judas arose from the ground, wiped his countenance, but did not even try to clean his clothes. Nobody came near him; he was too repulsive and he reeked.

At last, someone did approach, the sentry. He pointed to the departing drover. "What is your wish, publican?" he asked. "Do you want us to arrest him?"

"What?"

"The drover. He's your charge, not mine. You want us to arrest him?"

Judas's head reeled, as if the heat had stricken him. The man had asked a simple question, yet he could not understand it. "What do you say?"

The sentry, puzzled by the publican's obtuseness, looked at the guard. Then, more slowly, to Judas: "The herdsman—shall we go after him?"

"Yes . . . after him . . . and . . . tell him he may go through."

The sentry was confused. "Go through the gateway?"

"Yes."

"Without paying the tax?"

"Yes."

"Is it what you mean to do?"

"Yes . . . I think so . . . yes."

"It is your responsibility, of course, but . . ." The man was inarticulate with puzzlement. "What of the tax? What of the—" He pointed to the ground "—the shit?"

"Nothing . . . it will go away . . . nothing."

Without comprehending, the sentry and the guards looked at him and at one another, baffled by his decision. Well, he thought, his head still spinning, I'm as baffled as you are. As he started for the gateway, he saw one of the guards point his thumb at his own forehead: demented. Judas smiled ruefully. Perhaps the man was right.

⁂

As Judas was bathing, he decided he would not try to understand why he had done the deed; he was, in some knotted way, apprehensive that he might understand too well. His position in life was tenable only if he did not think too deeply. Besides, any energetic churning of the whys and wherefores of his mind and conscience had lately begun to upset his innards, put his stomach in a gnarl.

He must learn to appreciate the pleasures of his status. For example, the self-indulgence of this luxurious bath. These gurgling and gushing fountains, one with warm water flowing through pipes barely under the sun-baked surface of the earth, the other with water so chilled it took his breath away, cool water drawn through lead tubing buried a hundred feet and tapping the well at its frostiest depth. And the sweet shallow pools the waters flowed into, with lush lotuses and lilies and hyacinths floating on their surfaces, one pool lower than another, five of them, their runoffs slipping, gliding down the easy hillside, from one *lacuna* to the next. The Romans knew about *lacunae* better than Jews had ever dreamed; they knew their prosy usefulness and their poetry. Heskel had bought all of this from a Roman customs officer—house, waters, land on the nearly highest hill—lusting, as he said, for the pools and the garden. Especially the garden, as precise and formal as Latin verse, all alignments measured and predictable with a kind of military precision, the oleanders marching in a tight file of conformity, the grassplots laid out in legions, the flowers massed in strict battalions, one color per column. Beautiful, overwhelming and painfully perfect.

No, he must not find fault with its faultlessness. Enjoy it, Judas told himself, pleasure your senses in the fountains, in the warm wetness of your skin, your hair, your beard, rub the moist luxury onto your breast and belly, play it on your groin, drink it, plash in it, expire in it, let the water and sunlight console your heart.

In a little while, he wished he could take a more prolonged delight in the fountains, but they palled. He did not know, as the Romans and Sadducees did, how to bathe for hours at a time, how to dine a whole evening away. So he stepped out of the shallow pond and onto the warm mosaic of glazed stone.

Erratically, for a moment, he had no inkling what the next step might be, as if he had not performed this ritual a countless number of times.

Why did I let the man go through the gateway?

You are clean now, he said, and still wet. You must dry yourself. There were drying cloths on the marble table. Deborah, Heskel's wife, always personally provided them for him. These are special cloths, she said, coarser than my husband uses. He likes the finer weaves because he is older than we are, and while the skin of his hands and face has roughened, his body skin has grown more sensitive. I like the rougher textures, as you do.

The cloths were warm from the sun, and their coarseness brought a salutary heat that was different from the heat of water or weather. The rubbing chafed not only his skin but his mood.

The drover . . .

He spread one cloth, sopping wet, on the table edge, and took another. He wondered if it was true that the body skin becomes more sensitive with age.

He stopped drying himself.

She was looking at him again.

He could feel her staring down from the upper peristyle, watching him in his nakedness. With a flare of annoyance, he thought: I must catch her at it this time. Carefully, without moving too much, he turned his head a little, and glanced upward.

There was nobody there. That did not mean she had not been there. Again he had been too late; again he had failed to embarrass her. Damn the woman and her gazing, gaping eyes.

But what if he was wrong? What if it had never occurred, and he had simply imagined that she had stared at him? Or what if it had occurred only once—by accident—and he had been hoping it would happen again, and by design?

Abruptly, a strangely pleasing confusion . . . he thought of her as Mary of Magdala, and he had a vision of himself going to court her, as though he had earned the right. He could almost justify such reveries now that he was not impoverished anymore, and had good clothes to wear, and pieces of silver saved.

Except . . . a publican. Could he imagine himself telling her, "I'm a tax collector for the Romans"? But how long need that be true? He would go and find her at a later time, he told himself, when he no longer plied a trade that shamed him. Later. He would not be a publican for the rest of his days. . . . How clearly she shone in his daydream, how brightly.

He finished with the second cloth and laid it next to the first one on the table, got into a clean linen robe, walked along the tiled paths through the greenery and up the wide marble stairway, crossed the lower peristyle and entered the quiet of his well-appointed chamber.

It was still only midafternoon. He had not completed even half of his day's collections. Nor had he done any of the accounting work toward the tax report, imminently due on the calends of September.

Fatigue; he suddenly felt as if he were dying of fatigue. Yet he did not wish to sleep. He had a longing, he could not tell for what. A notion: I will go down to the Temple. I will not try to be admitted, simply stand at the open door and watch the men with their shawls, and listen to them pray.

What a nonsensical thought. He had been nowhere near a Temple portal in more years than he wanted to count. He had no need for it anymore, nor was he a hypocrite who would pretend a need.

Tired, so tired . . .

He lay down on the bed and closed his eyes but did not sleep. In the distance he heard a song, a woman singing sweetly, somewhat sadly, a Grecian melody. It was so soft that it drifted in and out of his mind like a delicate, exquisite gliding fish that broke the surface, caught the sunlight, then submerged again.

Deborah. What a lovely voice she had! He wondered if she was simply singing, or singing for him.

The drover . . .

"It was reported by a Sheep's Gate sentry," Heskel said.

"To whom?"

"To the civil guard."

"Which one?"

"The legionary at the Antonia."

Judas was apprehensive. It was a civil matter, not military, and certainly not important enough to be taken to the fortress. "Why did he report it to the soldiery?"

"Because he is a soldier. He does not report to the tax chamber, he reports to his officers."

"But there was no military provocation."

"There was a breach of order, apparently. And the drover refused to pay his tax."

"He did not refuse."

"There was some obscurity on that point . . . the implication that you had waived the tax."

"I merely said he could go through. I did not waive the tax."

"Good. Then, we are all right. Just so you did not waive any tax, we have not infracted any rule. Excellent. Let us forget it, then."

It was not excellent, Judas knew, and Heskel would not forget it. It was simply his employer's reluctance to pursue an unpleasantness. Sooner or later, because he was a tidy man who insisted on the exact balances of all accounts, he would return to the matter.

Meanwhile, the evening repast must not be spoiled. It was an almost soundless meal, just the two of them. The table was too long for quiet voices. And speech this evening had no presence in it, only an echo of presentiment.

Women did not eat with men, and Deborah entered only to bring each course, serve it, then silently vanish. There were enough servants in the house, male as well as female, and that Deborah should be allowed in the dining chamber when men were feeding was a laxity in custom. But Heskel had a contempt for custom and a love of Deborah. She makes me relish every bite I take, he had once said; when I watch her walk it makes my juices flow. Judas had agreed that she did, in fact, excite the appetite, and was sorry he had said it: Heskel had looked vigilant. It was the extra vigilance of a man twenty years older than his wife.

"You do not eat," Heskel said.

"Yes, I am eating."

"You're too thin, Judas. And I suspect you don't sleep soundly at night."

"But I feel quite well."

"I don't believe you do," he said.

He knew that Heskel's concern was genuine. The man was good-hearted. And he seemed to find it easier to reveal his feelings to his employee than to his wife. Judas could only guess at all the blank spaces they had between them.

"There is a new doctor from Alexandria," Heskel continued. "It might be wise for him to see you."

"No, please, Heskel, it is not necessary."

"They say he is not an ordinary leech—"

"You're very kind—and I do thank you." Then, overcome, impulsively: "I thank you for everything, Heskel, for everything!"

The older man was touched by the younger one's emotion, and looked down at his plate. "You must try the skin of the goose. It has been encrusted with ground dates and figs and walnuts. I think Deborah herself made it."

"I've tried it. It's excellent."

Everything, in fact, was excellent. It always was. Unlike the meals of the Romans, there was never a superfluity of food. But a generous variety. There was always a choice of fish or lamb or poultry, and the table was routinely decorated with exotic fruits—bittersweet carobs from Cyprus, figs of every color, red and purple and white, blood oranges from Egypt; breads of many kinds, including the unleavened, saltless ones in or out of season; and special sauces made with currants and mulled wine, with hickory nuts in a persimmon jelly, with plump raisins in horseradish so strong it could make him cry.

The odd thing was that it was *kasher*. There was never a sign of pig, nor a mixture of milk and meat, there was never a suspicion that any Mosaic finicality had been breached. Odd, yes, because Heskel was a nonbeliever. Born into a family of rigidly orthodox Levites who had, as he put it, spent half their lives in the Temple, he never prayed anymore and had no belief in the Lord. He claimed it was painless for him to be a publican, because he was totally indifferent to the disdain of Jews. Let them all be contemptuous of me, he said, even the contemptible priests. I would rather deal with the Romans. So he collected taxes for them, and took a goodly share, and ignored the insults and brickbats, and did not let the religionists harden his heart, and was charitable by stealth, and paid no tithe to God.

Then, why did he keep a *kasher* house? It was only when Judas understood the man—and became attached to him—that he discovered the reason. Simple, and it should have been obvious. The man was deeply in love with his wife—and she was devout. If she wanted a *kasher* life, she could have it.

Her name was not really Deborah, it was Althea. She was a Cypriot who had been taken into slavery. Heskel had bought her right off a ship near Askalon, and, at the age of fifteen, she had become his bed companion. It never occurred to him that she had any qualms. The Greek mind, he said as he recounted the experience, has easier standards of morality than we do; it does not see perversity under every coverlet.

But one evening, in a tiny storage room that he hardly ever entered, he discovered his wife in the midst of an extraordinary activity. Her hands covered her face and she was murmuring a prayer over the Sabbath candles.

He was appalled that she had converted to Judaism. It did not matter to him that she loved him and wanted to be one of his people. It made no sense to the publican, for *he* was not one of his people. What a stupid thing to do—to barter her Greek emancipation for a willing enslavement to a jealous, bad-tempered, vengeful Deity! And a prudish one who would not look kindly on her carnality. How God-gulled she was to exchange her healthy sensual pleasures for a sickly moral guilt!

And he realized how painful it must be to Althea every time he touched her. So he freed her of slavery, called her Deborah, and married her in the Temple.

Thereupon, their love had flowered, Heskel had said with a twinkle. But his twinkle had been enigmatic, and Judas suspected that the flower had withered.

The dinner was over. Deborah brought the marble bowls with lime juice. As the men washed their hands she gave Heskel a cloth and brought another to Judas. The young man spilled a little of the liquid and the woman deftly took the cloth from him and wiped his robe and his hand. Then she did an unaccustomed thing: she lifted her own hand to her face and breathed in the scent of the lime.

"So lovely, so fresh," she said. "I could bathe in it."

It was an untoward thing to say and she flushed, looking quickly at Heskel. But he simply nodded agreeably, without reproof, and, as if she had escaped a punishment, she hurried from the room.

The larger part of Judas's fondness for Heskel was compassion. He felt deeply sorry for the publican. For all his worldly goods, for all his strength, his freedom from pious sham, he seemed a creature of sadness. It was as if he lived with an aching emptiness, a void that even Deborah had not filled. He was lonely. He had turned his life away from the only Companion who might have given him the love he wanted. Once, when Judas had hinted at the thought, the older man had scoffed it away: the Creator is mighty in jealousy and justice, the publican said; but He cannot be omnipotent if He is incapable of love.

Sometimes Judas dreaded he might turn into Heskel. But I am different, he reassured himself, I still believe in the Lord. It is one thing to refuse to worship God as the hypocrites do, but quite another to refuse to worship Him at all. The possibility that this might ever happen to him chilled Judas to the marrow. But it would not happen to him, it could not, ever.

Yet, he too felt an ache, an emptiness . . . .

Heskel had said something and Judas had only half heard it. "You said . . . ?"

"I asked a question." The older man was silent for a long while, as if wondering whether it was indeed true that his employee had not heard. Then he repeated: "Why did you let the drover through?"

"He had herded the animals a long distance—and it was a long distance back."

"Did you think of that at the time?"

". . . No."

"Then, why?"

"He was shouting, 'I have no money! I have nothing!' . . . It was too pitiful."

"Did you pity him?"

"I was . . . not aware of pity, no."

"Even when you have—in the past—been aware of pity, you have insisted on the tax. Yes?"

"Yes." He did not look at Heskel. He shifted the position of the bowl of lime juice. He did not spill it. "But if a man has nothing, there is little we can do."

"We can put a stop to his trading. Which you have been known to do."

"Yes, I have."

"Then, why did you not do so today? Why did you let him through?"

". . . I don't know."

"You must think about it," Heskel said quietly. "What was different about today from other times?"

"Nothing was different."

"Yes, something was vastly different. He threw dung at you."

"Yes."

"Has anyone ever done that to you?"

"No."

Heskel smiled wryly. "Why was dung so persuasive?"

Judas felt a quiver of panic. "I don't know."

The older man pursued it. "Why did you reward him for assailing you with turds?"

Judas felt a need to get away. He started to rise from his chair. "Will you excuse me?"

"No, I will not," the man said. "Answer my question. It was as if you *wanted* him to throw filth upon you, to revile you, to shame you! *Why?"*

"Because I am a failure!"

"No. You are not a failure."

"I have failed my family, I have failed at being a scrivener, I have failed at everything I have done!"

"No! You have only failed in the ritual of being a Jew. Only the ritual. Is that everything?"

"It has seemed so to me."

"Hateful heaven, how morbid we Jews are! Religion is everything! It is how we eat and how we make love, it is how we pay tribute to nature and to our priests! We are constantly measuring ourselves against God and finding ourselves unworthy!"

"We are unworthy!"

"No!" he shouted. "Why are you unworthy? What are you ashamed of? Why is every day a Day of Atonement for you? What are you so guilty about? Why do you want to cover yourself in shit?"

Judas got up from the table and hurried from the room.

Outdoors, he walked downward toward the gardens. The moon was too bright, the stars too glittering, and he felt too visible. He realized that, of late, he was always in search of hiding places.

He wanted, here, to be still, not to move overmuch, not to think. Even the slight breeze was excessive procedure.

Heskel was wrong. Religion is not everything to me; God is everything. And I am not special in this regard. God is everything to everyone among the Jews. We are a people who order our thoughts, who judge our rights and wrongs, who tell our tales of wonder according to Him, only according to Him. Our heroes have obeyed Him, our villains have violated Him, our teachers have taught us that He is the root of everything, our prophets have read futures only in His Being. He was our Genesis, He was our Exodus from slavery, He was our Law in the desert. Without Him, there can be nothing.

And that is true for me, Judas Iscariot. Without God, I am nothing. I have lost my way to worship Him, and have not found another.

Nothing. Only guiltiness.

He wished the wind were a bit less bothersome. And as if the night had listened, the zephyrs obeyed and went to other places. The trees no longer stirred. Their shadows lay dark like sleepers on the grass. The flow gate at the upper well had been lowered; even the fountains were now still. If he could only stop the motion of his mind . . .

He heard another motion, elsewhere. It might be a carp breaking the surface of a pool, or a frog water-flopping. But it continued, a footstep at a time. Then he saw her, up above, crossing the peristyle, silhouetted against the light of the flaring oil lamps.

She started down the stairway. He had an impulse to slip away, but was held by the look of her. No wonder Heskel loved to watch her walk; she moved to music. Even her clothes seemed attuned to melody. Silken, they flowed to the rhythms of her body.

He thought about her age. Perhaps a half dozen years older than he, maybe even more. Could she be thirty? Her eyes looked prematurely old, but her mouth was young. He wondered what kept a mouth looking youthful. Appetite?

She stood before him, as close as perfume, and was silent. Smiling, but unsure. There were strings of gems coiled into the braids of her sable hair; some were hidden, like secrets, others glinted.

He was too uncertain to speak, and if she held the silence any longer he would have to walk away.

"You must not listen to my husband."

"Must you?"

She gleamed with amusement. "Is it so wrong to eavesdrop?"

"I don't know about . . . wrong."

"If I don't eavesdrop, I never know anything. I'm not permitted into a room, only on the threshold. So I spend my life at keyholes."

She had a wayward mouth, and her breasts were large.

"Why are you always so dejected?" she asked.

Wincing, he made a helpless gesture, as vast as the question.

"And why do you let my husband make you feel so guilty?"

"I don't 'let' him. It happens."

"I think you invite it."

"I'm afraid I can't do anything else."

"Oh, but you can. Heskel says that guilt is a moral indolence. And people in this country are sloths. Everyone lazes in guilt."

"Not Heskel."

She laughed. "How silly that is! He feels more guilty than anybody."

"About what?"

As her laughter was disappearing, she said, "About not giving me a child."

"Do you want one?"

"Yes—he does too. And it's impossible to make him believe that the fault can be in my body, rather than his. The point is, he *wants* to take the blame. It's the way Jews are. They need to take the blame for everything."

"You are also a Jew."

"By choice, not by curse." Her smile was rueful now. "It's dreadful to be *born* that way."

"Yes . . . it is dreadful."

He felt that he sounded lugubrious, and it embarrassed him. He wanted to appear more cheerful, and did not know how.

As if she divined his thought, she said, "There is a saying in Greek, 'One man, one life, one sorrow.' "

She talked in figures of speech: thresholds, keyholes, sorrows. It was Greek. A Jew talked in litanies, a Roman in numbers, a Greek in metaphors. He wondered which she was.

She was studying him carefully. "You did not smile when I said that silliness about sorrow."

"Wasn't it serious?"

"Not everything that is serious should be taken seriously," she said. "Do you know how to smile?"

"I'm afraid not."

"Your body smiles."

The stillness returned. But now he could not deal with it. He wanted the breeze to start up again, to make the shadows move.

"Perhaps my body hasn't caught up with my mind," he said.

"It is fully grown."

"You . . . watch me."

" . . . Yes, I do."

"I know you do."

"I know that you know it."

"How?"

"Once—about a week ago—you looked up at the peristyle to catch me looking at you. And I saw your body . . . change."

He flushed with embarrassment and turned away.

"It's not shameful," she said.

When he made no response, she asked, "Have you ever had a woman?"

"No."

"You are too old not to have had one."

He was discomfited, he was stirred. "Perhaps there was no urgency."

"I'm sure there was . . . and is."

"When it happens for the first time, I'll send you word of it."

"Send me word now."

He could feel himself changing, as she put it, and was grateful for the darkness. "I have no word for you," he said.

He started to move away, but her voice stopped him:

"Wait."

She looked up at the peristyle to see if anyone was there.

"If we stay here, we will be seen from the house," she said. "But at the bower below the bottom pool . . ."

"No."

She seemed at a loss, afraid to lose the momentum of her impulse. "Please." She took a step forward. "Touch me. The folds of this robe will separate. Touch me."

"No," he replied. "I cannot."

"Do you not want to?"

He made a vague gesture for her to go away, and knew she saw that he wanted her closer.

"Then, please—" She halted. "Are you really so fond of Heskel?"

"Yes."

"As fond as you pretend to be?"

"Please—let me alone. My feeling for him is the only goodness in my life right now."

"Then, do him a service! Give him a child!"

He was stunned. He must not let himself believe she wanted him for such a reason. No, only for an insanity of other reasons, for a momentary pleasure or forgetfulness, or the rarity of a woman's triumph. For a reprisal, perhaps, against her husband, or against life. But not for a child, not for someone she and Heskel would have forever—not for Heskel's sake.

He moved to leave her.

She gripped his arm. "Touch me!" She pulled her robe apart, and showed him how she was. "Touch me!"

"Cover yourself," he said, and hurried away.

Returning to his bedchamber, he began to tremble. The oil in his lamp was nearly exhausted and the flame guttered, but there was still too much light. He extinguished it. He went to the window and looked down toward the garden where they had stood together. She was still there. He could see her clearly in the moonlight. Her hands covered her face, and he recalled Heskel's description of her before the Sabbath candles. He wondered what candlelight she saw right now. Was it Jewish or Greek? He wished he had not blown out his lamp; he wanted a light for a blessing.

Hours later, lying in bed, sleepless, he still felt the oppression of the darkness. For all the moonglow that spilled through the window, there was no light to see by. He felt blind and bereft; his loneliness was a shroud.

Then it was taken away.

The door of his chamber opened and she appeared silhouetted

against the dim light of the hallway. Slowly she closed the door, approached him where he lay, slipped off her robe, and slid into bed beside him.

Vaguely, in what felt like a drugged sleep, he had heard her stirring in the night, and in the morning she was gone. He was glad of it. He could not have talked; his feelings were too tangled in puzzlement and pleasure and wonder and remorse. And each one of the emotions was itself a disorder. The pleasure, for example, had been at first a mortification. She had so excited him with her mouth and her movements—her tongue was an adder's—that he had made his wetness on her arm, of all places, and she had lain there, laughing. The second time, although he had arrived like a warrior ahead of his herald, he had at least been inside her, and she had professed to be pleasured. You will be better the next time, she had said. There had been no next time. And he vowed to himself that there would not be.

He dreaded seeing Heskel. But as the publican sat at the end of the table and broke his first hot bread of the morning, Judas could see that he was without suspicion. While the younger one's spirit pitched and tossed on a roiled sea, the older one floated in serenity, as if on a boat becalmed. Judas had an urge to churn things up, but the publican anticipated him.

"Arrears today," he said quietly.

Judas tightened. No need to remind him. He had been doing arrears for two days and there were at least two more to go. He detested them. Yesterday, with the drover, had been unfortunate; today would be worse. There was a curt retort on his lips, but he did not make it.

No need to. Heskel said shamefacedly, "I don't know why I remind you of such things—or why you suffer it. It's not as though we feel differently about the hateful chore." He smiled dryly at himself. "I suppose I need to share the misery."

How considerate the man was, how generously he redressed any wrong he had committed. He was trying to make amends, not for the petty comment about arrears, but for his candor of last evening.

Judas had to meet him in kind. "I wasted four hours yesterday. But I promise to make them up by nightfall."

"No need, no need."

Deborah entered with goat's milk and ripe melons and with the steaming porridge of mixed grains. She looked exactly as she had looked yesterday morning. He wondered at it. He knew that he must appear different to her; he certainly felt different. How could she seem so unaffected?

She lifted the wooden bowl off the tray and set his gruel before him. But then, as she dealt with the bread and melon, he saw that she was indeed altered. In the way she glanced at him, as if she were whispering.

He felt a flush and looked down at his bowl of porridge. It was the porridge she was whispering about. It was not as usual. On the surface of the nut-colored cereal something floated. It was a red rose petal.

With a dart of pleasure, he sensed that she had lightly touched him in a secret place. But the excitement smarted: she was teasing him.

Out of the corner of his eye he could see her behind Heskel, looking at him. She wants me to notice the presence of the petal; wants it to be a token between us, the promise of another assignation. She wants me to lift it with my spoon, take it in my fingertips, kiss it, put it in my mouth, let it lie there, on my tongue.

With the tip of his spoon—not touching the petal with his fingers—he lifted the thing out of the porridge. Then, as if it were an insect, he flicked it away.

She left the room.

Heskel put bits of figs onto his melon and ate the two fruits together. When he had swallowed his final mouthful, he said, without looking at Judas:

"Insignia."

The younger man hated the discussion as much as he hated the object. The insigne was the silver Star of David into which the Roman fasces had been incised. He was meant to wear it as a badge of his tax-collecting authority. He rarely did.

"I have it in my pocket," he responded.

"It is not meant for your pocket."

"I will not wear it."

"It is the law."

"It is an insulting law. It makes me into a Roman."

"You work for the Romans."

"I work for you."

Heskel paused a moment. His grimace was a hopeless one. "Why do you make things difficult for yourself? You are trying to take the sins of the whole world upon your shoulders. But you refuse to take the blame for a small trespass of your own. If you go about collecting taxes, you cannot say you do it at my bidding, you do it at your own. You work for the Romans."

"I work for you!" Hotly, he sprang from the table. "I work for you!"

"That is only a half-truth."

Judas reached into the pouch of his tunic and brought forth the silver emblem.

"Here—take it back! I will not wear it!"

Violently, he threw the insigne on the floor and started toward the door.

"Judas!"

As he hurried through the corridor he could hear the echo of Heskel's voice. There had been no recrimination in it, only shock. The publican could not believe that Judas could perpetrate such an injury to their relationship.

Such an injury . . . if the man only knew what a deeper violation he had suffered. It was when Judas had reached the peristyle that he realized it was because of the deeper violation that he had vented his rage against his friend. Compared to the betrayal of last night, the insigne was nothing.

He returned to the dining chamber, contritely apologized for his blaze of temper, retrieved the insigne, and affixed it upon himself.

Judas had to collect arrears in three sections of the city: the Court of the Gentiles, the marketplace, and Gehinnom.

Only Jews were allowed inside the Temple, and only a *minyan,* of ten Jewish men all past the age of Bar Mitzvah, were considered a quorum eligible to worship. Alongside the Temple, however, at the Court of the Gentiles, everyone was welcome, even the uncircumcised. Travelers came from everywhere, and, in the motley of costumes and coiffures and skin colors, it was difficult to tell the faithful from the heathen. There were Jews and gentiles in Roman togas made from the cottons of Cairo, there were Ceylonese in silks, and Parthians in wool, nomads in camel hides, Africans in leopard furs; there were Temple priests in white satin, Mount Hermonites in sheepskin, Galileans in sackcloth.

And things, things, every quality and variety of things to buy and sell. Fruits and baskets, weavings and sweetmeats, jellies and jewels, dyes of all colors, playthings of wonder that inflated and exploded and ran and tickled and teased; and musical instruments that sang and twanged and whistled and wept on strings.

Animals, too, and slaves for sale: turtledoves and cattle, pygmies and giants from Africa, pigeons and poultry and grown people of both sexes and children from the Taurus Mountains and the Cappadocian Steppes, and wonderful birds in myriad sizes and colors, ostriches and macaws and parakeets.

Even money for sale: Persian dinars for Judean shekels; Cypriot copper for Jewish gold; the gentile-contaminated coins taken by the moneychangers in barter for the only clean specie acceptable in the sacred Temple. Every kind of money.

And every kind of tribute, Judas the publican always noted. There was hardly anything that was not taxed by the Romans: head tax and street-cobble tax and water tax, excises on meat and bread and salt and wine, levies proportionate to the depth of a well and the height of a wall. There was scarcely an object, a transaction, a service, a bodily function that was not assessed. In one of the wine taverns there was a legend scribbled on the wall: "Be grave. There is a levy on laughter."

Nor were the Romans singular in exacting their imposts; the Jews did it as well. There was a difference, however. The Romans called it a levy; the Jews called it an offering. It was a gift to God, and to His sanctuary, to be administered by His priests. Never, in anything a Jew could do, was oblation to the Almighty neglected. Birth, Bar Mitzvah, marriage, death, rejoicing and sorrowing, working and playing, blessing and cursing were all occasions for paying tribute. If a man went to pray, he brought a coin; if a woman wanted a husband, she brought a turtledove. A young girl impatient for the starting of her flux brought salt; an infant male, at his circumcision, felt the blade at his penis at the same moment that the votive ram felt the knife at its throat.

As a gift, as a benison, as a prayer, as a prepayment for divine consideration, there was always gold to be given, and blood to be drawn. The gold, in leaf, was applied to the exquisite dome of the Temple; in ornament it decorated the crowns and gowns of the High Priest, the scrolls of the choristers, the letters of the Deuteronomy; in ingots and garlands it was stored in a great repository adjacent to the Holy of Holies.

As to the blood, it was not wasted. Nothing was. When the animal was slaughtered, only its spirit reached the King of Heaven; its flesh remained on earth. Very choice flesh too; only the finest animals were acceptable for sacrifice. And when the spirit had flown, the carcass was ritually bled and ritually butchered—for the tables of the priests and the Levites, and for sale in the Temple-licensed stall where the dedicated meats were sold at a premium. From the sacrificial altar, the blood ran through sluiceways to the gardens of the High Priest, some hundred ells away. There it was used to fertilize his orchard, which, blessed by prayer and sacred blood, brought forth large and bountiful fruits.

In the Temple area, Judas collected back tax money from a trader in sacrificial turtledoves and from an incense grinder. Another delinquent, Asa Bar Samuel, the owner of a licensed butchery, was a besetting puzzle to Judas. He was always the most in arrears, with the least justification. It was ironic to Judas that Asa, who was a man of comfortable means, with the privileges of special franchise from the priests and the Romans, should constantly be laggard in paying his tax to the civil authorities. He seemed forever to be testing the Romans, challenging the multitudinous foreign idols—which he habitually insulted—with the might of his one and only God. It was an empty defiance, for Asa knew in his heart—as all sensible Jews knew—that they existed not by the franchises of the Temple but at the sufferance of the Romans. Half a cohort of legionaries could have ground all of them into the earth.

Judas wondered at his hubristic people, how they nurtured their false pride, their delusion that they were not altogether helpless and enslaved. Some talked about total freedom as if it were bound to happen, and imminent. A great leader would come, like a Maccabee, and then . . .

When? He will come, they would answer, he will come. Look to the sky and a star will brighten; open the door on the first evening of Passover and he will arrive to drink the ceremonial wine. They secretly listened to soothsayers who said he would arrive on the first day of Tishri, or the eve of Yom Kippur, or the tenth of tomorrow. He will come.

He was the Messiah, and he would come. Nearly every Jew believed in him, the one who would free them not only from the Roman yoke but from the tyrannies of poverty and sickness and sin. He was not a figment, he was a tenet of belief. He had been promised by the prophets. It was predicted how he would materialize, bringing gifts of peace and amity and salvation, how he would burst upon them in a mantle of glory.

Nearly everybody knew this to be true, for they knew him almost personally; he was the national familiar. The splendor of his spirit was described in unmistakable terms by the learned men in the Temple. His magnanimity was invoked by impoverished roving rabbis who called him the lord of goodness and mercy as they murmured in alcoves and alleyways, asking only a crust of bread to feed their emaciated bodies. White-robed men of purity stood out of the sun or in the shelter of colonnades and described in definitive detail what celestial raiment he would wear and how he would be trailing clouds of beauty.

There was a discrepancy that puzzled Judas. All who prophesied the advent of the Messiah loved him; all knew that he would bring eternal life and love and felicity; all knew that his arrival was inevitable, *he would come.* But there was no agreement as to who he would be. The stormy ones said he would be a heroic warrior, like the Maccabees, that he would wield a sword and lay waste the Romans. The ascetic ones said he would be a stark and abstemious spirit, exacting repentance. The ignominious ones who yearned for glory said he would be a sublime king who would restore the Jews to their radiance. The wronged said he would be a terrible judge upon those who had wronged them. The lonely saw him as a father of love and mercy.

Judas knew that if the Messiah could be all those disparate things, he could be none of them. In fact, that is exactly what he believed: that he was none of them. He did not exist, and would not. He was a dream, a delusion.

⇄

Toward noon, Judas went to the second section of the city, the marketplace. Here was where he made most of his collections; and here, among the edge-of-survival merchants of Jerusalem, was where the taxes were most onerous. For these were the marginal tradesmen, the moilers and tinkerers, eking out a narrow living between buying and selling, carefully counting their meager fortunes in stale morsels and bits of string.

Yet, anomalously, collecting arrearages was never any trouble here. The tradesmen always meant to pay; they simply needed extra time to catch up, to catch their breath. One of them was particularly disheartening to Judas. It was not merely that the taxpayer was a saddler, like his father. The resemblance was more hurtful. The man pretended to admire the publican, and he toadied a little. When Judas said a wryness, he giggled too merrily, he agreed too eagerly with comments on the dry weather or the sandy wind. So that Judas found it distressing to speak to the saddler. Sometimes he wanted to strike the man for his servility, but sometimes he wanted to hold and hearten him. This is my father, he told himself, the man I have not seen in many years, the man of dignity who has lost his pride, the father whom I loved and cast away. Now I am the tax collector to whom he bows and scrapes—and I cannot bear it.

⇄

Judas had only one more collection to make. It was in the Valley of Hinnom, called Gehinnom, for it was like a hell of punishment. Approached through the Dung Gate, it was on the other side of the wall, south of Jerusalem, where the city dumped its rubbish and offal. Like the inferno it was named for, perpetual fires were kept burning, to subdue the sickening smell and to prevent pestilence.

It was a place of flies and rats and roaches, an abomination, and here lived the poorest of the poor. Here lived the sick as well, the blind who begged in the streets, the lame, the lepers, the mad. There was much madness.

The tax delinquent whom Judas was seeking was a seller of ointments. It was a grim jest, the young man thought: salves for sores that would never heal, lotions for lepers. But even if the dealer in medicaments did not pay his tithes on time, he apparently did well enough; there was profit in hope for the hopeless.

It had been a long day and Judas had walked through all of it. His feet were weary and he still had far to go—across the whole width of Gehinnom, eastward to the Kidron River, where the so-called apothecary had his stall. It meant trudging through the worst slough, through the leper band. He tried to deaden his senses, to close his eyes, his ears, his nostrils. But he could not help seeing the festering faces, the limbless ones dragging their bodies on the ground, the eyeless; he could not help smelling the rot or hearing the whimper of their warnings that they were unclean. *"Tameh!"* they cried. *"Tameh!"*

There was an even worse stench on the River of Kidron. Northward, near the river, stood a tannery belonging to the family of Caiaphas, the High Priest. In it, all the hides from the Temple sacrifices were brought and cleansed of hair and blood, which filth floated downstream to the wadi of Hinnom, where the water expended itself and left only the putrefaction.

His trip across Gehinnom was a waste. The seller of ointments was dead. Merchants at neighboring stalls reported that he had never had a sick day, but he was old, and had died peacefully in the night.

Judas returned toward Jerusalem. Choosing another pathway in the hope of avoiding the lepers, he had to go through the busiest marketplace. And there he saw Jesus.

That is, he thought the man was Jesus. Often, in the last few months he had thought he saw him. And now again.

This man, at any rate, was the image of the Galilean. The same stature, wearing the same homespun, a beard of a similar color and cut, the loftiness of forehead. And there was that lovely way that he tilted his head upward and sideways as if heeding other voices.

But there was a vast difference. The man was shrieking at the crowd, and Jesus would not have shrieked. The man seemed to hate everyone, most of all the Romans, and Jesus would have hated no one. And the man was urging violence.

No Messiah talk from this one. Do not wait for saviors or miracles, he shouted, do not put your hope in dreams, but in daggers. As the Zealot raised his blade, the paupers cheered and lifted their shriveled arms, and the cripples lifted their canes.

Suddenly, from what quarter Judas could not tell, the soldiers appeared. They were on horseback, five or six of them, and they quickly laid about them with their swords. People fell. Some were trampled and some died in blood. The Zealot ran for his life, and horsemen pursued him.

But one of the horses went berserk. A wild one, perhaps younger than the rest and panicked by the blood, he pitched and bared his teeth, he shrilled in terror, lifted his forelegs into the sky, then pounded downward into the earth. The legionary was thrown but quickly gathered the horse's bridle, yanked at him, and beat the beast's head with his iron helmet. He pulled him up tight at last, but the horse was still restive, snorting and stamping, and not to be trusted. The soldier looked to the mob. The crowd was fighting back, and his comrades were slashing bloodily with their swords.

The legionary cursed and shouted. He did not know what to do. His eyes fell on Judas, on his Roman insignia.

"Publican!" he cried. "Hold the rein!"

Before Judas knew what he was doing, he had the leather strap in his hand.

The legionary, sword drawn, charged into the crowd. His blade flashed and whacked and went red with blood. Crying and bleeding, the people took to flight or fell. And still the sword of the soldier kept on slashing.

While Judas held his horse.

While I held his horse, Judas said for hours and into the night, while I held the legionary's horse.

He thought of the dead and wounded. He thought of the Zealot who looked like Jesus and wondered if he had been slain.

While I . . .

He wanted to weep and could not; he was not, he told himself, worth weeping for.

Walking to the window of his bedchamber, he looked out at the quiet night. He could see only the uppermost pool from here. There was not a ripple on it; so still that the stars lay on the surface, separate and motionless as if waiting to be gathered and put away.

The pool was shallow, he knew, only a foot or two; he wondered if it was deep enough to drown in. He smiled bitterly at the ridiculousness of it; drown in your self-contempt, he said.

The crowd was mostly beggars, he thought, the blind and the lame and the hopeless. There was little life left in them, and perhaps the deaths were not unwelcome. But the Zealot was young and bold, and he had the strength of his rage. O Lord, let him be alive!

But he knew it was not likely.

The horse had been wilder than he had realized at the time. The rein had cut his hand. There was blood on it that water would never wash.

The pool was full, so full of stars.

He heard a sound behind him.

Deborah was there. She carried something; he could not see what it was.

"You didn't come to the table," she said. "I've brought you some food."

"Thank you. I don't want it."

She placed the dish on the low taboret. "Heskel told me what occurred. It was not your fault."

"Go away," he said.

She started to unbraid her hair.

"Please do not . . ." he started. "I want you to go away."

But she continued. First one comb, then another; she placed them on the taboret beside the dish. Then the long slivers of amber.

He wanted to make love to her. But he could not do it and go on hating himself. I need to hate myself, he said; if I can only hate enough—! He had thought, once, how much love he had in him; and now, if he had as much hatred . . . for himself . . . it would still not be enough.

Her hair was down.

"Please," he said. "I need you to leave me alone. *Please.*"

She started to untie her bodice.

"I can't—I can't!" he cried. "Please—if I think of what I did today—and didn't do—! If I think of Heskel—"

"Don't think of him."

"I can't go on betraying and betraying!"

He started to weep.

She was naked now and moving to him.

"No!" he cried. "No!"

When she laid her hand upon him, he did not know what possessed him. He struck at her, then struck at her again. She started to cry out, and he grappled with her. With his cut hand he reached for her throat—and with the other hand, he tightened and tightened.

Suddenly, when she started to go limp, he knew what he was doing, and let her go.

She slipped to the floor and he thought she might be dead. But in a moment he could hear her gasping for breath, wheezing, making hideous sounds, not human.

He did nothing. Simply watched her, horrified at what she looked like, and what he himself had done.

Then, when he saw her struggle to arise, he helped her. He said nothing, made no sound of contrition, nothing. Nor did she.

For a long while she stood there, quaking, uncertain what to do. Still he did not help her. At last she gathered her clothes, all of them, with the utmost meticulousness gathered everything, down to the final bit of amber. And went away.

He did not try to sleep; he did not lie down.

He thought of the heinousness of what he had done, of the murder he might have perpetrated. He thought, too, how much he had changed, how the sense of life's goodness that had warmed him as a child had now chilled almost to extinction.

As he recalled the Zealot who looked like Jesus, the man became Jesus.

It was as if the eyes were gazing at him, and the mouth speaking.

You are not a murderer, it said. You are not a betrayer of your friends and of your people. You are a devout man in search of a devotion. Go and find it.

The following day he said farewell to Heskel and his wife, and went walking toward the desert.

Twice she had gone in the wrong direction. She had assumed, because the red-haired one had come from Judas's town of Kerioth, that other Zealots would be there, she would find an encampment of them. But when she came to Judas's birthplace, although the people remembered him and Elias, they said that both had drifted far from home, and there was no rebel company.

Westward, then, through the cities of Judea, the large, the small, the living habitations, the dead ruins, Hebron and Gaza and Gath and Emmaus. Another camel to hire, a succession of donkeys, and many times she trudged afoot, across the arid plains, through mud villages, over the savage barren hills. How could a country so small be so vast a wasteland? . . . And no sign of Zealots.

Though there was no turning back, she was afraid her courage would not equal her resolution. A woman traveling alone, she was constantly apprehensive. No matter how ready and sharp her weapon, she was afraid that, any day, any night, she might have to wield it. Well, had she thought it would be easy to find a nest of rebels that the Romans were straining to root out and exterminate?

One evening, at an inn near Machaerus, there was a rumor of a Zealot raid on the prison. A detachment of Roman soldiers, twelve of them, with only one Zealot dead. As the innkeeper was relating the story to her, she thought she detected some covert pride, a suggestion of a closer affiliation with the Zealots than the man's mere Jewishness would account for. She sat up later than the other guests, and the more the landlord spoke the more she suspected he was a secret Zealot. So she told him a story—a totally hypothetical tale—of a rich Jew who had been brutalized by Romans and was offering a wealth of gold to anyone who would avenge him. But at the hint of genuine involvement, the proprietor blanched, said that in all his twelve years as an innkeeper he had never really met a Zealot in person, and skittered off to the safety of his bed.

Zealots—where? Northward, people whispered, the rebels are all up there, up there in Galilee. It finally made sense—the saying was that only trouble comes from Galilee—that was where she would find troublemakers. She went northward, north of Samaria, north of Mount Tabor, north of Tiberias. How ironic it was that she passed within an hour's walk of Magdala, and the lie she had told her father—that she was going to their onetime home—had nearly turned out to be true. All that afternoon, she yearned to turn back to the haunts of her childhood, to see the wildflowers on the hills once again, and put a crocus on her mother's grave. But it was the wrong season, too late for crocuses.

When she had passed the Lake of Gennesaret, she knew by the misleading directions the Galileans gave her, by their inconsistencies and shifty glances, that she must be close.

On a night of unseasonable rain, a downpour, she entered the town of Chorazin. She asked questions and received no answers. Her spirits fell. Her clothes were worn from weeks of travel, and wringing wet. The purse in which she kept her knife and money and jewels was frayed, and its roughness, next to her body, chafed her skin. She felt dirty, had not had a proper bath since an inn at Scythopolis, long days before, and the downpour did not make her feel cleaner. Chorazin was about as far north in Galilee as she could go, and there was nothing here but a quiet, respectable town with not a sign of rebels or cutthroats. She was on the edge of despair.

Soon, on the northern outskirts of the town, she knew she had to find immediate lodging for the night: she was shivering with cold.

She went in search of light, and there was none. Passing the entrance to an alleyway, she thought she saw a figure move. Her pace quickened. Diagonally across the muddy roadway, in the shadow of a horseless cart, she saw a man. Clearly, he did not mean to be seen, and hung back, silent.

Mary loosened her mantle, reached into the pouch at her waist. Her fingers closed on the handle of her knife. But even with the weapon—would she ever get over her feeling of defenselessness?

She stopped walking, anxious. She dreaded going forward into the less populated section, and if she turned back toward the populated center of the town, it would be a great distance in the deluge. She shuddered, freezing and afraid.

She decided to turn back.

Passing the alleyway once more, she saw that the man was closer now, and ready to emerge.

She began to run.

Suddenly, ahead of her, two more.

In terror, she bolted across the path.

Another one. Then another.

All at once, as if by signal, they were upon her. She raised her knife. A hand of iron was at her wrist, and she felt a wrench of such pain that she thought she would sink with it. Her knife was gone, and she struck at them until someone pinioned her arms. In the wetness, she broke free, but only for an instant. When they seized her once more, she clawed and bit.

As quickly as it had begun, it was over, and she was indoors in a wide room, low-ceilinged, with lamps hardly aglow, a tiny fire on a hearth, and the smell of burning paraffin and oil.

She had not noticed until this moment that her hands were tied and her face was bleeding. Someone was giving her a cloth, and showing her how, with wrists bound, she could still hold the compress to her cheek.

He was older than the other five or six, and apparently their leader. His eyes were the brightest objects in the room, brighter than the lamps; restless yet gentle, with mitigation in them; but his jaws were hewn of rock. There was a mark on the back of the leader's right hand. It was a *P.* Mary had heard of the sign, but had never seen it. The letter stood for *perfidus.* Usually, when the Romans applied the brand of traitor, it was only a preliminary stage in a torture; those so marked were soon killed. This one had escaped.

"Who are you?" he said.

She hesitated.

"What is your name?"

"Mary."

"Everyone's name is Mary."

The others smiled, but he did not.

"What are you doing here?"

"I am looking for a boy from Kerioth."

"Kerioth? You are a long way."

"Nevertheless."

"There is no one here from Kerioth."

"His name is Elias. He is a . . ." She must take her chances. ". . . a Zealot."

The man looked genuinely puzzled. So did the others. "I do not know that word," he said.

"Everybody knows that word. Like Mary."

"What does it mean?"

This would be her opportunity. "The Zealots are brave fighters. They will free us from the Romans."

"Why should you want to be free of them?"

Was he not a Jew, as she had supposed him to be, or was it a trick?

"Why?" he persisted. "The Romans keep the peace, they encourage business, they build viaducts and bring fresh water, they make well-ordered governments."

"They are loathsome."

"If you loathe them, why do you wear their clothes?"

"I do not."

Without discourtesy, he lifted a corner of her wet mantle. "This seems to me of foreign cloth, and it is certainly the Roman cut."

"It was made for me by Jews—in Jerusalem."

"To the Roman pattern."

She felt herself flushing. "Would you unbind my hands, please?"

With her own knife, he cut the bond, then looked down at the weapon. "The dagger, too, is Roman."

"Not Roman, meant for Romans."

"We are not Romans."

"I know what you are—I hear it in your speech—I used to live not far from here. You are Galileans—and Zealots."

He raised the knife to her lips. "If you say that word again, I will cut your tongue out."

The warning was cold-blooded. Still, she took the risk: "You are a Zealot—which is what I want to be."

He did nothing. Silence. Then:

"You are Mary of Magdala—the daughter of a Sadducee. You do not wish to be a Zealot. You wish only to be revenged on a number of men who did you violence."

She was shaken. "You asked my name when you already knew all about me."

"Much about you, yes."

"How do you know so much?"

He gestured to someone in the corner, barely visible out of the firelight. The man stepped forward. Even in the brighter illumination, she scarcely recognized him. He seemed much older, and his beard was fully grown.

"Elias . . . ?"

"Yes."

As if all her trials were over, she felt relief, like the breaking of a fever.

"I am sorry we had to treat you with roughness," he said quietly.

She turned quickly to the leader. "You see?—he knows me. I helped him once—the Romans—I'm sure he has told you—I have come here as a friend!"

The man did not immediately respond. He took a long time, appraising her. "I don't know what you mean by friend. If you simply want us to assassinate a few Romans for you, does that make you a friend?"

It unnerved her. Only her father and brother could have been aware of it. Certainly not Elias, nor the frightened innkeeper at Machaerus, across the Dead Sea, a hundred miles away.

"How did you find that out?" she asked.

"It is hay, not horses." A Galilean expression: do not belittle me.

"If you know that I have come for a service," she said, "you must also know that I am willing to pay."

It was premature—crass—to talk immediately about money.

His smile was sardonic. "We are not paid assassins."

"I'm sorry I said that," she replied quickly. "But my willingness to pay does not make me an enemy."

"Nor an ally."

"But I am! We all have different reasons for hating the Romans—all of us—him and him—and you! Should we reject those whose reasons are not our own?"

He seemed to look at her in another light. She had the sense that he eased.

The room was warm, but she shivered again in the chill of her wet clothes.

"You will be ill," he said. "I'll see that you have a warm robe and some food. You may sleep in here by the fire."

She was on edge. "You're right—I've come here for one purpose alone—to pay you for avenging me. Will you do it?"

"I do not think so."

His eyes narrowed. Again, the appraising look. And she could see that he was deferring judgment. "Tomorrow one of our number will be on trial. I will allow you to be a spectator. There will be a matter not entirely unrelated to your own."

He gave orders to two of the men.

"I'll keep your knife," he said. "You'll be alone here, and no one will harm you."

"I'm grateful," she said. "What is your name?"

"Simon Zelotes." As he left the room, he beckoned to Elias.

❖

The single-roomed building in which she slept, the meeting place of the Zealots, was made of baked clay and had been a granary. As

Simon Zelotes had promised, she spent the night alone and nobody harmed her.

In the morning when Elias came to awaken her with warm milk and raisin cakes, he said that the men, when they came there for meetings that lasted more than a day, were billeted in private homes. Many lived nearby and were employed in Chorazin or Bethsaida or Capernaum; a few were farmers or herders of small flocks, goats mostly, and sheep. Elias himself was a cooper, who repaired barrels and casks; there was scarcely any time for poetry these days.

"We must earn a livelihood," he said. Then, as if to show he had not lost his poetic nature: "Nobody can make a living as a Zealot, only a dying."

"Do many die?"

"In the winter, eleven were caught in Caesarea. One of them was my cousin. Pilate ordered them all killed. They were buried in an unblessed grave. Last week they caught a man in Gehinnom. The horsemen ran him down and drowned him in the River of Kidron." He smiled grimly. "Some say he died at the smell of the water."

He took a piece of one of her cakes, dipped it in her milk, and ate it. Looking around, he leaned toward her conspiratorially. "We have even killed our own."

"For what reason?"

"In one case, cowardice; in another, treachery."

"What sort of treachery?"

"He was seen going through a gateway of the Antonia."

"Was that so conclusive?"

"Why would a Zealot—willingly—without being arrested—enter a Roman fortress?"

"This trial today— is it for treachery?"

"No. I don't know how they will describe the charge." His bright face clouded. "It has been a trouble—it worries all of us. I'm glad my name was not drawn from the lottery. It would plague me to be one of the judges."

The judges, when the court was assembling, were five men of varying ages. The oldest seemed about the age of Simon Zelotes, perhaps forty; the youngest could not have been any older than fifteen. (If he has read his Bar Mitzvah portion, Elias said, he is man enough to be a judge.) There were about fifty spectators. Except for Mary, no women. And the men so pointedly paid no attention to her that she knew they had received instructions.

The defendant was the tallest in the room, and the most defiant-looking. His eyes were the blackest, and his hair, his beard, were as black as if spun from tar. He did not seem to be sitting on a chair, but on a throne, and was treated not as a prisoner, but as a king. Although he could not be any older than thirty, the men with whom he conversed seemed to vie for his attention, and even the gray-bearded ones said his name, Barabbas, with an unbegrudging deference.

There was a stir as Simon Zelotes entered. He was followed by a scrivener who carried a small roll of parchment. The *ezer*, a busily officious helper, blew two notes on a ram's horn, the spectators started taking their seats, and the scrivener placed the parchment, a quill and a small ceramic vessel of ink upon a table. The judges, who had been standing in murmured conversation, turned about and seated themselves on a long wooden bench, separate from the others.

Everyone was seated now, except for Simon. He held his right hand up, extended it outward to his side, then moved his arm forward toward the judges in an unspoken courtesy. He directed the same gesture toward Barabbas, and the latter slightly inclined his head.

The leader, having officially opened the trial, reached to the table and raised the parchment.

"This is a writing of the particulars against Barabbas. At sundown yesterday he agreed he would not contest any of them. We may therefore proceed today with but a single question: are these acts that this man has perpetrated good or evil—do they help or harm us?"

Simon crossed toward the judges. As he extended the parchment to the oldest of them, he said, "We all know, in one detail or another, what is written here. This is only for the archive, and for those in our band who wish to peruse it."

The judge accepted it with a nod, and the Canaanite returned to the table. He resumed:

"I am not the enemy of Barabbas. I bear no malice against him. Nobody can say that he is not brave. Nobody can say that he is traitorous. He has gone on many raids against the Romans. He has maimed a large number of them, and killed more than his share. On some occasions, he has been the leader, and none of us has ever found fault with his cunning or his courage. On several occasions he has come to the rescue of Zealots who have fallen. Two springs ago, the time I suffered a wound at the hand of a centurion, he carried me four miles to safety, when he himself was bleeding. As a man—even as a friend—I make no complaint against him."

It had been, apparently, easy for him up to this time. Now he hesitated, proceeding with difficulty. "But as a Zealot, I find him gravely at fault. A Zealot is a patriot. A Zealot burns with passion for the freedom of the Jews. Freedom from the Romans—that is his only zeal, his agony. Now, I don't say that Barabbas is wanting in this fervor. But he has other furies as well. He robs, he pillages. Mostly, he is a marauder among Romans—and that is to our benefit; but sometimes it does not matter to Barabbas whether his victim is a Roman or a Jew, just so the spoils are worth the plundering. Last year, on the fifth day of Heshvan, he robbed a Jewish minter and left him dying in his counting room. This did not come to light until quite recently, and he denies he meant to harm the man. But, two days ago, he robbed and killed another Jew."

There was no interruption, no outcry of denial from Barabbas. Silence.

When Simon resumed, his voice was harder, colder. "We are not a court of law here, except as our own Zealot laws are concerned. We would be hardly justified to punish murderers, for our hands are none too clean. But when we kill, we do so in a common cause, a conscionable one. And when Barabbas kills, it is too often for selfish purposes, and shameful ones. For this we don't punish him—let him be punished as the Almighty wills. But now we Zealots are also being punished—for the sins of Barabbas. We are being tarred by his pitch. People have begun to say that we are not patriots, we are thieves, we are robbers, we are brigands. It is rumored that, behind the shields of our rebellion, we hide our spoils and pilferage and plunder. There are worse rumors—that we are vandalous with blood, that we cut the throats of Jews as well as Romans. Last week, my sister locked her house against me. She said I was another Barabbas. And she called me . . . *sicarius.*"

The murmuring in the room was scarcely audible, and Simon did not have to raise his voice. "I am not a dagger man, a cutthroat, a paid assassin. Nor are any of us. But if Barabbas remains in our midst, we will not be called Zealots, but *sicarii.* We will lose what following we have among the people, and they will come to despise us. We will be dishonored. Our passion will become an ignominy. And each of us will be Barabbas. No matter what his prowess has been, no matter how well he has served our cause, Barabbas has become our curse and our affliction. I call for his expulsion."

He sat down. The silence lasted until it became doubtful whether Barabbas would rise to his own defense. He sat there, massive as a mountain, lost in abstraction, as though the proceedings were merely bad weather, and would pass.

At length, when he became aware that all eyes were upon him, he stirred a little. Still he did not rise. Even when he finally spoke, he remained seated.

"I do not deny anything," he said. He pointed to the parchment. "What's written there is written. Perhaps, if I could write, I would inscribe it all myself. But what is not written is that I am one of you. I have always been one of you. I was born a Jew, circumcised a Jew, confirmed by vows a Jew, and have fought as a Zealot and a Jew. This was not mentioned by Simon Zelotes. He did not mention that I love the Jews and hate the Romans just as he does. He did not say that I always choose the most dangerous missions. He did not say that there is hardly anyone in our company who would not follow wheresoever I might lead, into fire, into flood, into the grave. You who are hearing me are some of these men. Because you know I am cunning in protecting you and that I value your lives as I value my own, you are not afraid. However I lead you, I am your courage. Simon Zelotes did not say that.

"He did refer to the day when I saved his life. He did not dwell upon it much. Why should he?—it's a commonplace. Look there—to the ten or twelve men from Bethsaida—do you recall how I rescued them from half a cohort of legionaries? You—Ephraim—sitting among my judges—do you remember how I saved your brother from the sentries at the Tower of Siloam? Manasseh!—is Manasseh here? Tell them about the swords of the praetorians! . . . Does nobody speak for me? . . . So much for gratitude.

"Well, then, the common good—the Zealots—what is good for the Zealots? I don't know the answer to that. But what is good for the Jews? Me—Barabbas—I am good for the Jews. Yes, I rob and I pillage and I kill—and I strike fear into the hearts of the Roman soldiery. I am the scourge that will drive them out of Jerusalem and off our Jewish earth! I am the terror and the blood and the disorder that will send them quaking back to Rome. I am their panic! . . . Do you think you will scare them by tossing an insult, by denting a shield, by bloodying the nose of a sentry? No! Havoc—it will take havoc! It will take robbing and raping and murdering and burning! Chaos! We must make chaos! And chaos is my name!

"Understand, I don't want to be called by that name. I want to be called Barabbas the Jew. I want to be called a man with a noble passion. I want to be Barabbas the Zealot. If I am not one of you, I am a petty troublemaker in the street, I am a robber and a pickpocket, I am at best a *sicarius.* I beg you not to reduce me to this. If you do, you will break my spirit and I will die of it."

He was finished. He had not risen from his chair, nor did he rise now. He simply turned his attention away from the judges and, seeming to seek a nullity to gaze upon, his eyes fixed upon the wall.

The *ezer* arose. He reached into the pouch at his waist and brought forth five squares of papyrus, each the size of his palm. Going to the scrivener's table, he took up the quill. He dipped it into the container of ink and, walking to the first of the judges, handed him the quill and a square of papyrus, and reminded them: All that was required was a single stroke or a double stroke. If the judge meant Barabbas to be acquitted, he was to draw a line from one corner of the papyrus, diagonally to another. If he meant the man to be expelled, then he must add a second diagonal which would cross the first. When the judge signified his comprehension, the *ezer* turned his back on him so that neither he nor any of the spectators could watch the marking of the judgment.

Four times the process was repeated. There was no haste to have it done; it was as though the deliberateness itself was part of the indicted man's ordeal. At last, when all the lines had been drawn, the *ezer* collected the papyri. Silently, he read each of the five judgments. Without a hint of expression, he returned the papyri to the eldest judge, so he could add these records to the parchment. Then the *ezer* raised the ram's horn and blew a long, thin note.

"The judgments are all one, with no dissenting marks." An instant. "It has been decreed that Barabbas will depart from us, and never again be permitted to call himself a Zealot."

There was a faint stir in the room. Nobody departed. It was as if, by some custom or decree, or by some spontaneous grace, the spectators were allowing Barabbas to depart without having to make his way through any milling crowd: the dignity of being alone.

But, for a moment, he seemed too dazed to move. At last he took a deep breath, and, like a stuporous giant, made his solitary way out of the room.

When he was gone, the others also departed, in twos, in threes, their voices muted. No one, apparently, seemed gratified by the decree. Not even Simon Zelotes, who had himself brought the action. He simply remained in his chair by the table.

Mary also remained, and so did Elias. As she arose, the young man beckoned her to stay, as he himself slipped outdoors.

She did not speak. She knew that the leader was perturbed, and by tacit courtesy, waited for a sign from him. His head was lowered; when he raised it, he seemed surprised that she was there. He pretended to smile.

"What did you think of the verdict?" he asked.

"I was very moved . . . that it had to happen."

"But you do agree it had to happen?"

"It was . . . I think . . . just."

"You 'think.' You are not certain?"

"Yes—it was just. But . . ."

"But?"

She demurred a moment. "It may not have been altogether prudent."

"How was it imprudent?"

"Now that he has departed, you have no control over him. He will still go forth, marauding and plundering—probably more wantonly than before."

"It will no longer be our concern."

"But it may be. The crowd may still call him a Zealot, and still blame you for his crimes. And meanwhile, you will have lost one of your best leaders."

"What was our alternative?"

"You are rebels. No matter how you justify yourselves, the Romans will call you criminals. So why try to cut such fine points in the law?"

"If we don't reserve some tenet of morality . . ."

"Not a tenet, an illusion."

She could see that she had added to his disturbance. His response was agitated. "Are you pleading Barabbas's case or your own?"

"I don't consider that Barabbas's case throws any light upon my own."

"We don't kill for money. I say that to you as I have said it to Barabbas."

"There's a difference. Barabbas received the money—he profited by it. I will *give* the money."

"By giving it—and by my receiving it—you make me into a paid assassin. I am Barabbas."

"That depends."

"On what?"

"On what you do with the money. If you keep it for yourself, you are a *sicarius.* If you use it for the Zealot cause, you are a hero."

For the first time, she saw him smile. It was reluctant, and she knew he reluctantly respected her. She had won a point, but she had not as yet won everything. He was still far from ready to accept her proposition.

"Suppose you do lay my moral qualms to rest," he said. "What about your own?"

"I have no qualms about killing seven monsters who violated my existence."

"Listen to what you say. 'I have no qualms about killing seven'—and so forth. . . . It suggests that you yourself would do the killing."

"Why is it important who does it, so long as it is done?"

"We were talking about morality—which is a kind of responsibility. Who will carry it? Who will take the blame?"

"I hope no one will have to."

"I'm not talking about getting caught, but about catching one's self."

"I'll always gladly tell myself that I did it. I won't consider it a sin, but an act of justice."

"At first, yes. But you have a good mind. And as your mind matures, so—unfortunately—may your morals. One bad night you may awaken to the fact that you are a murderer. What do you think you will do about that?"

"I will deny it."

"Exactly. And do you know how? By extenuating. You will say, 'I didn't wield the knife, I didn't tighten the garrote. It was those others. I wasn't even there.' Non mea culpa, as the Romans put it, and your soul will be free of it."

"We've come around in a circle. My soul would be free of it now—this minute—now."

"But it should not be—that's my whole point. The murders must cost you something."

"I will pay a great deal of money."

"That is nothing to you."

"God in heaven, what should it cost?"

"If the crime is a great crime, it is worth a great risk."

"What must I risk?"

"Body. Soul."

"How?"

He gazed at her steadily, then reached beneath his robe, to his tunic. What he brought forth was Mary's knife. He handed it to her.

She felt a chill. "No."

"You have already carried it."

"For self-protection."

"You must do this also in an act of self-protection. It is the morality of revolt. If you kill seven men out of vengeance, what human decency does it serve? But if you rid the earth of monsters who brutalize it—kill them in self-defense—in defense of the world you live in—there is a considerable justice in that."

He confused her. The leader was clearly a man who sought an honest principle, struggled to find it, and suffered in the search. Yet, what he seemed to discover were moral reasons for doing immoral things. She had had a teacher once, a Sophist, who had boasted that he could always make the worse reason appear the better one. And, unsettled, she felt Simon Zelotes was giving her reasons inferior to her own. She had a simple motive in wanting to kill seven ogres: revenge. But now he was entangling it with complicated moral reasons. Troubled, she distrusted them. Her own imperative was more honest, she understood it better, it was hotter and more potent: a bellyful of rage.

But she knew intuitively that in one regard he was right. Wielding the knife—with her own hand—would more satisfyingly assuage the fury than having someone else do it for her.

"I have never killed anyone."

"You are still young."

"I would not know how."

"You can be taught."

She took the knife.

She was trained as a Zealot. And was made to feel honored by being accepted as one of the men. Not that women were lacking in the company. But because they were not trained as fighters, they were not admitted to the cabals of conspiracy.

Nor might Mary have been if she had not, almost immediately, turned over to the company nearly all her money and jewels, leaving just enough to live on until her mission was completed. She donated the valuables without any urging from Simon. He did not need to be persuaded of her ardor, but, she suspected, the others did. And, as the leader had said, the golden substance meant nothing to her.

Hardly anything of substance mattered to her. She no longer cared what she wore, what she ate, where she lived. Her dwelling was a lean-to on the field side of the granary. It had been a shepherd's lambing hut and, although it was entirely enclosed against the elements, it was little more than a shed. The floor was pounded earth, the bed was straw sewn into hempen sacking. If it was uncomfortable, she scarcely noticed.

An anomaly: she could not feel what she felt. It was as if the ravishment she had suffered had made her insensate, had robbed her of physical awareness. Her food, for which she paid a modicum, always tasted exactly the same, although the old widow who brought it asked if she liked this dish better than that, and Mary fabricated distinctions. She shortened her mantle to the same manageable length that the fighters wore, and took in her tunic, for she had gotten thinner; but they were the same garments every day—washed in the brook when necessary—and she no longer had any interest in variety.

This indifference to her senses made her indifferent to pain. Through weeks of training, although not as strong as the men, she could endure more. In fighting, she would never win a bout, but in trials of endurance, in the simulations of torture, she was always the last one to fall or cry out.

One sundown, she and Elias were walking across a meadow. He was teaching her how to drop as if she had been killed, and how to control respiration. It was one of many such instructions. At the beginning of her training, he had helped her in everything, had shown her how to run long distances on an economy of breath, how to kick at vulnerable places, how to stifle a sneeze or a hiccup so as not to be heard, how to gouge an eyeball, how to drive a dagger with the power of the whole arm. And this lesson too—on disguised animation—she had already learned. From him.

"How many times will you teach me that?" she said.

"It bears repetition."

"Only to numskulls."

"You think you know everything."

She knew she did not know everything. However, she had learned a good deal and, while lacking his experience and strength, knew as much as he did. But it frustrated him to be unnecessary to her; he could not stop teaching.

He was patient but persistent. "Let me explain one of the details of this procedure."

"No!"

He flinched and she was remorseful. Speaking softly, she touched his arm. "I've been hinting for days, Elias, and you don't want to hear. . . . I no longer need your help."

He was vexed, and hurt. "Why do you have to be so independent?"

She tried to be calm. "Because I cannot go on being dependent . . . on anyone."

"You mean men."

". . . Yes."

"Then, why are you one of us? Why do you drive yourself more fanatically than anyone else? Why do you have to be superior to all of us?"

"I have to be superior . . . in order to be equal."

"In order to be a man, you mean."

"I do not want to be a man."

"Then what, then what?"

"A demon."

"I wager it would be harder for you to be a woman."

"I have no interest in being such a thing."

"But you are one."

"No."

"Let me prove that you are!"

It burst from him, what she had been expecting for weeks. He was in love with her. Any moment he would use those very words, and she would have no answer for him. He was her dearest friend, in fact her only one, and precious. But she had a madness in her, a memory that rioted against men, and the thought of making love was a fear and a revulsion.

"Let it be," she said.

"I love you."

"Let it be—please—let it be."

"I would give my life for you."

Let it be! Let things be as they are while we are friends; let us not lose one another. Let me hold on to what is so dear, so needful to me, the only remnant of what I was.

She did not know what she would do if, by loving him in the only way she could, he would think it too little and she lost him altogether. She did *not* love him too little. She had a deep need for him as a friend, a need for him to be exactly what he was. For what he was—a man of equilibrium, more Greek than Jew, a believer in moderation and the golden mean—helped to stabilize her life. Even his poetry, his sense of perfection, was comforting; it made her feel that balance was beauty. Elegance is counterpoise, he said. The ugly and the beautiful weigh exactly the same. And there is always something of one in the other. The purest, whitest lamb is the first one to the sacrifice. Is that not sad and beautiful and ugly? Or think of murder. Is there anything more hideous? Yet, think of the murder of Pontius Pilate. Is that not exquisite?

It was his dream to assassinate Pilate. He talked of it in ideal, Platonic terms, without passion, with an aesthetic sense of fitness and equanimity. Everything would be done according to immaculate plan, in a chastity of order. Force would balance force; weight, weight. There would be no excesses, not of cruelty or of gore. There must be just enough pain to cause a single moment of elation, the moment of *ah* that happens in a poem. Ideally it should be felt by the murdered as well as the murderer. And when the victim was given his quietus, he must have *his* ecstatic instant as well.

The instant of *ah.* For Elias it was the climax of the beautiful, in death as in life.

For all that he was a Zealot, and had spilled blood, she had never seen any cruel wrath in him. One day she asked, "Is Pilate your single hatred?"

"Oh, I don't hate him," he said quickly.

"Of course you do."

"No. From what I hear, he's a man I could admire. He reads Vergil, they say, and Ovid. And there are verses he has written—after Catullus—that are said to be touching. I'm quite sure that if I knew him, we would be good friends."

"Yet you would kill him."

"I kill not for hatred but for love."

"What a hypocrisy."

"No! For love! For love of my people. How long can I go on aching for them? How long can I endure their slavery?"

"We are not in slavery. Some of us do very well with the Romans."

"We are enslaved!"

"Willingly."

"That's it—exactly! We have allowed ourselves to think that we—that they—" Overwrought, he stopped and started. "Our *minds* are enslaved! Our minds—which we were once so proud of—look what the Romans have forced us to do with them. They've made us agree to what our intellects tell us is a lie. They've made us say 'sanity' when our logic has said 'sickness.' They've made us speak with their leaden words and count with their inflexible numbers. They've made us *measure* objects of beauty when all we wanted was to love and admire them. They've made us applaud their ornamentations and excesses as if they were admirable, when we perceive them as vulgar. They've taken levies on our souls and taxed them almost out of existence. They have forced us to say yes, when everything we are cries no, no, no!"

It was a frenzy. When he subsided, his voice became calm, he seemed in more pain than before. "Do you know how the Romans enjoy eating the hearts of animals?" he asked. "They are eating ours."

"I hope you kill him."

His mood suddenly lightened. "Oh, I will," he said airily. "I surely will."

Whenever he had an audience and had leave to expound his dream of killing Pilate, he was at his poetic best. The spectators listened enrapt. Every detail was wonderful to them, for it was a vision they wanted to come true, although they did not dare imagine it for themselves. But whenever the telling was concluded, they all laughed at him for being too whimsical, moonstruck.

Mary did not call him moonstruck. Nor did Simon Zelotes. Each believed his dream could come true. The Jewish destiny was built on dreams come true. The death of Pilate, the death of Mary's seven demons, the Messiah. All would come to pass.

The question was, When?

"When?" she asked Simon. "When?"

"Be patient," the leader said. "There are seven of them, and it is difficult. We have barely started on a plan. We do not even know whether we must think of them all at once, or severally. Difficult, difficult."

"May I help in the planning?"

"No. Only in the waiting."

The waiting was terrible. It made her think too much, it made her remember. She remembered Magdala. Not more than six miles away from her childhood home, she could have walked there in an afternoon. The house and the gardens and the two chariots were still there, still belonging to the family, still the same bondspeople, two of them near the grave, she imagined, still looking after things. With too much time on her hands, she wanted to go and see the old place again, but some inexplicable dread kept her from doing so. Preoccupied with Magdala, her childhood there seemed more recent than her latter days in Jerusalem, and her dead mother seemed more alive than her father and brother. She wondered why this was, and it finally occurred to her that the reason was simple and complex: because she was a woman, more closely related, through pain.

Life had betrayed them both, she felt, and when she envisioned her vengeance, it was a score she would be settling not only with Romans, but with life itself. With eight men—her seven and her mother's one. Strange, how she had never—until the assault upon her—thought of wreaking her mother's vengeance on her father.

She had spent nearly a decade of her growing years scarcely remembering his infidelity to his wife. Her mind and her heart had had no time to nurture a grudge, for they had been occupied with loving him. She still loved him. Then, why was she reopening that wound, inciting this resentment, coupling it with her other, more awesome need for retribution?

It alarmed Mary. She felt there was a sickness growing in her. She must have her vengeance finished and done with—quickly—so that she could return to health. The word for health in Latin also stood for sanity.

The Romans had contaminated her; their death would heal her.

With God's help, we heal ourselves.

Someone had said such words to her, she could not remember who. . . .

That Essene, Jesus.

She had not thought of him in all these months, and wondered why he had come alive at this time. She had been feverish then, with thirst and exhaustion and desert heat. Was she feverish now? Was this obsession with vengeance a canker, infecting her whole being, fomenting a rancor against her father, whom she had never stopped loving, poisoning her against loving such an attractive man as Elias, turning her emotions about all men into a virulence? The Latin words again, *vir* and *virus,* man and venom.

A Roman morbidity. Cure it.

With God's help, we heal ourselves.

What if she no longer believed in God?

Retribution, then. Her only remedy. It could not come quickly enough. Delay was an abrasion; it tore at her skin.

She had gone to the limit of a woman's action. Now she had to wait for them, the men.

Waiting. Suspension. Passivity, until one of them—Simon, particularly—would sound the call to arms.

Meanwhile, inertness . . . tension, tension. If no call came soon . . .

One day, alone, under a motionless sky, with hardly a blade of grass stirring, she felt as if her blood were slowing in her veins, stiffening, and she took to flailing at the air, striking, cursing, stabbing, killing all the nothingness.

Six days later, Simon Zelotes spoke. We are ready now, he said.

There was a man named Paktonos, who came from one of the ten Greek cities in the northeastern province of Palestine known as Decapolis. Paktonos worked in the Antonia fortress. A learned man, he taught Greek to the tribune and Aramaic to the centurions, and, because he was better versed in the Roman deities than the Romans were themselves, he taught the soldiers their religion, how to decipher auguries and oracles, how to petition their gods, how to worship and outwit them.

It was well known: Paktonos hated Jews. Particularly, he hated the Jewish religion, which he considered dogmatic, and the Jewish god, whom he called humorless and spiteful.

Paktonos was a Jew. He was a spy for the Zealots. And it was with information supplied by the pseudo Greek that Simon Zelotes prepared his plan.

The garrison at Antonia, like installations throughout the Roman Empire, fed off the conquered land. Twice a year, however, a ship would arrive from Rome with special supplies and provisions not available in Palestine. Delicacies like the smoked pork of Tuscany and dried *amarasca* cherries and a sweetmeat called *melmamilla,* or honeytit, but for the most part they were the condiments and spices of home, finocchio and oregano and the pungent anise of the Po Valley.

The ships from Rome would stop at Rhodes and Cyprus, then sail onward to Palestine, to Caesarea and Joppa. This last year, however, a landing was made only in the more northern city, for Joppa was suffering an epidemic of the green sickness, and although there was some concern about an infection of the galley slaves, the greater worry was spoilage of the valuable cargo.

From the uninfected port, therefore, caravans of camels would carry these precious imports to Tiberias and Scythopolis and to the Roman fortress in Jerusalem. Each of the caravans would be escorted by a small squad of cavalry. In the *equitum,* of ten horsemen, who would protect the lading bound for Antonia, three were to be Mary's prey.

"What about the other four?" she asked Simon.

"They are not in this detachment. And even if we could destroy all of them at once, would it be advisable? Would it not unmistakably point you out as their slayer?"

She could not, at this moment, be as circumspect as he was. Her brain whirled.

"In fact," he continued, "to make it less suspicious, we will also kill one of the innocents."

"A Roman soldier is never an innocent."

He nodded grimly. "That is a lesson we did not have to teach you."

"How many do we send against them?"

"Four men and one woman."

"Five against an *equitum?*"

"One of us against two of them seems ample—in the way that we will do it."

"How?"

"The caravan will break its journey at an inn near Arimathea. We will be guests at the inn."

The inn was an ancient one and in the days before the occupation it had been called The Safehold; now, to attract the Roman trade, it was more grandly called The Castellum. With none of the grandeur of a castle—no towers or battlements, no position on an eminence—it was large, with many chambers. And ugly.

The Roman caravan was going to break its journey at the inn. The camels and horses would be fed and rested there, and the *equitum* would take lodging for the night.

So would the Zealots.

Simon's instructions were for three of the five to arrive separately, at different times, from late afternoon until early evening, before the caravan. Mary was not to appear alone, for this would invite curiosity; her companion would be Elias. They would come as husband and wife. Not as lovers, Simon had cautioned, for that might be too interest-provoking.

Elias had asked, "How do we indicate that we are married?"

"By bickering," the leader had said. (Simon had been married once; his wife had decamped to Athens.) "Do not actually quarrel, for that attracts attention. Only a dreary little squabble—say, about the suitability of the chamber."

The so-called married pair were the first to arrive. Double-mounted on an old, spavined mare lame of hock, they dustily entered the inn. Almost at once they voiced different preferences as to their lodging: He wanted a roadway room, and she, the side to the stables, where the wind would be less chilly. The innkeeper, his hostelry nearly empty, suggested separate rooms, but when they confessed to a shortness of funds, he pointed out that the stable-yard side, somewhat noisier, was somewhat less expensive. The wife seemingly won the argument; actually, its conclusion had been prearranged: they needed a view of the stable yard.

Not a glimmer of recognition passed between the innkeeper and Elias. Although the owner was a Jew and a friend, he could be counted on to recognize none of them, and to say nothing about any disorderly occurrences that might occur this evening.

Neither Mary nor Elias was hungry. Her throat was so tight that a mouthful of food might throttle her. But it would have been unusual for travelers to arrive and take no sustenance, so again they professed poverty and asked for the least and the cheapest, and their host brought them some unidentifiable leftovers, "mysteries from the midday meal," Elias said. There was time to spare, so they toyed with the scullery slops and went on quibbling with one another in voices so low that the few others in the common room soon gave up listening.

About an hour later the third Zealot arrived. Manasseh was eleven years older than Elias, but by nature roisterous; he could not hold still, his typical state was hubbub. When he sat, he jiggled; when he walked, he sprang. In his thirties, he was still a young colt laying waste to a meadow. Now, however, as he entered the inn, he was a twisted cripple, as hobbled as the spavined beast they had ridden, his right shoulder a foot lower than the left, his right leg almost useless. It would be hard to recognize him as Manasseh, the jumping rabbit of Chorazin. The pretense was persuasive.

It occurred to her, with misgiving, that she, too, should have had a disguise. And so should Elias.

"No," he murmured. "The color of my hair always gives me away—and everything looks false. As to you—you're a woman—that's your disguise. Nobody would believe that a woman . . ." His voice drifted. She could see he was uncertain. Then he buoyed himself up. "Besides, it will all be done in the dark."

Reuben was the fourth. Ordinarily a sloven of a man with a soiled mantle, unwashed skin and unkempt hair, he was now as shiny as a copper urn. Impersonating a typical Syrian merchant who peddled wares from town to village, he wore a cloak of striped Akka cloth and sandals dyed in brilliant Antioch blue. But it was his hair that so completely transformed him. His beard was divided into two halves, in the Syrian mode, each half made of a million tight little curls, while his head was covered with silly ringlets giggling down to his shoulders. All these tresses, whiskers and braids glistened with grease and were so heavily scented that the pungency smothered the aromas of cooking and woodsmoke from the hearth.

It was nightfall when the last Zealot arrived. Simon Zelotes seemed ill. He wiped his forehead with the sleeve of his cloak as if he were perspiring, and in embarrassment made fitful little clutches at his belly. Murmuring, the indisposed man arranged with the landlord for his bedchamber, and was about to go up the stairs to inspect it when his breath came short, he let out a little moan and raced outdoors.

"My God, what a time to be ill," she whispered. "Shall we go to him?"

"He is not ill," Elias muttered. "He is pretending a looseness of the bowels."

"But why?"

"An excuse to run outdoors as often as he needs to."

"For what purpose?"

"The horses."

The Roman horses, when they arrived, would have to be dispersed, and it could not be done all at once. Several trips would be necessary.

But need Zelotes have chosen so noticeable a ruse? His behavior and the disguises of the other two made Mary nervous. If the leader had instructed them to be inconspicuous, why were he and Manasseh and Reuben playing parts that were so ostentatious? Was it true, as people whispered, that Zealots were bold to the point of arrogance, that they flagrantly exhibited themselves in feats of rash heroics, that they performed outrageously to prove how quick and cunning their wits were, compared with the plodding, systematic slowness of the Roman mind? Or was it because their religion forbade them to be actors, to have theaters and circuses and graven images, so that they played out their pretenses in the perils of reality?

"It is simpler than you make it," Elias said. "Look at us. We are five people who seemingly have nothing in common. We are incongruities. But the Romans need congruence in everything. They must count their military units in hundreds—precisely. If they build a bridge it must start on two sides of the river and meet in the center—perfectly. All their gods must have discrete and separate functions—punctiliously. They cannot stand it when things get mixed up. Incongruities are threatening."

"But should we *want* to appear threatening?" she asked.

"I think incongruity serves a better purpose—it causes confusion."

He made the generality like a graybeard; then, hearing the pedantry, he grinned like an oaf. He was unsure of himself again, embarrassed, like a child caught in the citron jelly. She loved this quality in him, his impetuous flirtation with an idea, then his sheepishness at finding it superficial. It was comic and it was sad, the way his mind ran from home to nowhere. He might have made a good poet, she thought, but he needed more than a verse to write, he needed one to live by. It was this unfound man in him that touched her the most. She longed, when she saw him in a maze, to lead him somewhere, anywhere in safety, to comfort him, to embrace him. If only he could be satisfied with an embrace of affection, how sweetly she could love him.

It was becoming dark. The caravan was expected a few hours after nightfall. Across the room, they saw Simon looking at them. Elias raised his head a little and the leader nodded. The signal.

The married pair were meant to retire, and make themselves invisible. Elias, who had made forays into Caesarea and Jerusalem, might be recognized by one of the soldiers; Mary, by three of them. Better to disappear.

By the light of a tiny oil receptacle, they made their way up the steep stairway. In the bedroom they did not remove their clothes, did not loosen so much as a sandal strap. To the tension of their enterprise was now added their abashment at being, for the first time, so intimately alone together. They stirred about the room like dogs making a place to lie upon; and while the bed usurped most of the space, they pointedly ignored its presence.

Half sentences and discomfiture . . . testing, straws in the wind of conversation as if they were meeting for the first time . . .

"On such a night as this," he said, "we could beguile the time . . ."

She used the same plea as before. "Let it be."

Gratefully, she saw that he was going to make light of it. He pointed to the bed. "Go ahead—it's as safe as a cradle. Lie down—I won't—"

He stopped and even in the dimness she could see him turn crimson.

She wanted to comfort him. "Never mind. The word is not so terrible if it's you who say it."

"I am a lummox," he said.

"No, you're not. Lie down—I won't rape you."

They laughed and lay together and he held her hand and recited Catullus and begged her not to expose him as a Jew who quoted Roman poets. He spoke the words with a touching perception, making himself susceptible to every intimation of love. His voice was more mellow than she recalled, and the southern inflections of Judea seemed to caress the sensual rhythms. Some of the poems she had never read; those few with which she was familiar were lovelier to the ear than they had been to the eye, and she wondered aloud if love poems were written in darkness.

The thought pleased him and he laughed. "Does that mean you're feeling something you haven't felt before?"

She must not mislead him. "Yes." She smiled. "Awe at your memory."

Playfully he slapped at her and they both giggled. For the briefest sigh of time, they had forgotten why they were there.

Then, hearing the sound, they remembered. They hurried to the window. The croaking of one of the camels was the loudest noise. The rest was horses' hooves, and the shouting of commands, to men and animals.

The caravan entered the stable yard. It was smaller than she had expected, only three camels, heavy-laden; the ten mounted soldiers seemed more protection than they required. At this distance, she could not recognize any of the men, and it would be her task to identify the three.

The door of the bedroom opened and Simon Zelotes entered.

"Can you see them from here?" he asked.

"Yes, but they're not close enough for me to point them out."

The leader nodded. "They will lead their horses to the innkeeper. He knows to draw them to the light. Watch carefully."

It was a swift process. The innkeeper and his hostler were taking the horses two by two, leading them into the stable, where the boy would tie, feed and water them. On the other side of the yard, the three camel drivers were not unburdening their beasts, merely fettering them to outdoor stanchions.

Four of the horsemen passed under the flaming light; Mary recognized none of them. On the fifth she tensed.

"Gaius Cassianus."

Zelotes leaned closer to the window.

The sixth and seventh horsemen went by, both unknown to her. Soon two more.

"The tall one—Olus Bactrianus. And the one with the skittish horse—they call him Antaeus of Syracusae."

"That's it, then. Paktonos was right—three of them." He turned to the door. "I'll see where they are billeted."

Mary caught her breath. The tenth horseman had just dismounted. And he limped.

At the window—looking down—she trembled.

"Him—!" she said. "I thought only three—!"

Elias looked out the window. "Simon!"

Zelotes closed the door and returned. In silence he gazed out the window.

"Tullius?"

"Yes."

"It can't be. That one is not a centurion—there's no insignia."

"The trappings on his horse. And the man limps! It's Tullius, I tell you!"

"Calm yourself."

She felt Elias gripping her arm, but it did not steady her. A tremor, like lightning. Then, on fire: "I hate him the worst—I will be the one to kill him!"

"We will see how to do it."

She felt that this exultant moment might get away from her. She might be cheated. "No—Simon—please—I must. He was the first of them—and the last. I want to be the last thing he sees."

He stared at her.

Abruptly she became ashamed of her emotion. He thinks I have lost control, she said to herself. I must hide my feeling, I must remember my training. Stop being a woman.

"I will do whatever you order, Simon."

But she could see he was not convinced.

"Look to her," he said to Elias. And he departed.

Ignominy. Look to her, the female. Take care of her tantrum. Put cold water on her wrists, see that she does not faint.

Unfair. She had shown more feeling than Elias, but not less courage. In fact, she had volunteered for an extra danger. Not fair. Well, she would add her vexation to her other furies.

She slipped her hand under her mantle. The hilt of the dagger was cold; she needed her vengeance to be as cold as the metal. She ran her finger down the blade. Close as it had been to her flesh, it was like ice. Ice, yes . . . Admirable.

Elias was watching her go frigid.

"Good," he said.

She walked to the window. The camel drivers were squatting on the ground, under the stable's overhang, not far from their beasts. Samaritans, she guessed them to be; the Romans hired them because their hostility to Judeans could be trusted. Two of them were eating. One was already stretched out and snoring; soon the others would be doing the same.

There was another man under the overhang. He was wide awake. One of the soldiers, of course, left to keep the watch. She wondered which one.

An hour passed before they heard from Simon once more. He was followed presently by Reuben. There would be a need, the leader said, for a rearrangement of the plan. Two elements had changed. With Tullius part of the *equitum,* the number of soldiers to be dispatched tonight would be four instead of three—and possibly a fifth. As Manasseh entered, Simon looked at him questioningly and the sham Syrian pointed to the window and said, "Antaeus."

This was the second change. It was rarely the custom for a senior officer to stand watch, and Antaeus was second in rank to the centurion. But his horse was unsettled and had been ailing, and the officer wanted to be close to the stall. Instead of sleeping in the hostel, he would spend the night at the barn.

"Inside the barn, or out?"

"It is a warm night and the stable stinks. Probably outdoors."

Reuben said, "What if he cries out?"

Manasseh spoke confidently. "He will not cry out."

Reuben pursued it. "There won't be much light. If your knife misses its mark by so much as an inch—"

"He will not use his knife," Simon said.

Manasseh opened his pouch and withdrew a sinew. It was a goat's tendon, long and thin but as strong as iron. He carefully wound it about his wrist.

"When?" he asked.

"After I am through with the tethers," Simon replied.

"You will have to slip by Antaeus."

"I will not slip by him. I will pass him openly."

Reuben and Manasseh looked at one another. The latter said, "I think you should go around the back, Simon."

The leader considered. His task was to convert the tetherings of the Roman horses from a firm hitch to a hook hitch, easily broken. There were two ways to get into the stalls: through the stable yard and by way of the privy, literally a backhouse attached to the horse barn. Similarly, the backhouse could be approached from two directions. The long path was to go around the stables, outdoors. The more customary way was to go directly through the stables; it was not only the shorter distance, but gave protection against the elements.

"I will go through the stable," he said. "And I will try to do them all in one trip."

"Ten horses? How will you account for the time?"

"My loose bowels will have tightened."

Reuben laughed; the others did not.

Manasseh worried. "At least wait until the Roman is asleep."

Simon smiled. "On the contrary. It is safer to have him see me."

Mary wondered whether this was prudence or arrogance.

"Now," he continued, "as to the others. They are all sleeping two by two. Gaius and the Bactrian are in the chamber at the head of the stairs. Reuben and I will attend to them. Tullius and his serving man are in the room immediately beyond, on the same side of the corridor." He looked only at Mary, as though bestowing a gift. "They are for you and Elias. . . . The doors will be barred, of course, but the trammels and the pivot nails have been loosened. One sharp blow and the bar will fall. But it will make a clatter and awaken them. That will give you only a little time to strike. You must strike at once. . . . The rest is as we planned."

The leader ended the meeting. It would be hours before the final action—when the soldiers were asleep. He would summon them, he said, not by entering their rooms, but simply by raising the latch of each door. A low sound—they must listen for it.

When Simon and the others had gone, Mary and Elias scarcely

looked at one another; glances might betray their edginess. While she paced each foot-worn floorboard, he lay on the bed gazing at the ceiling. The oil in the lamp was running out and the light flickered, casting gusty shadows across the walls. Better to snuff out the flame, she thought, for it might catch Antaeus's attention and make him wonder why they were awake.

As the room went black, they heard a shuffling sound. She ran to the window; so did he. Simon. He looked like an old man, bent double, clutching at his belly, scurrying for relief. They saw Antaeus rise in vigilance, then heard Zelotes mutter something they could not apprehend. But the Roman caught it and gurgled with laughter: the embarrassment of an old Jew was always good for a snicker.

For the longest time, it seemed, Simon did not reappear. It made them nervous. More nervous still when they heard one of the horses whinny, at which sound Antaeus roused himself, listened for another equine report, and, hearing none, rested his head against the post once more.

The old Jew came out of the stable. He was standing quite upright now, and seemed much alleviated. With more dignity than before, he muttered again; it was apparently another quip against himself, so the Roman laughed even louder than the first time. Only one of the Samaritans stirred at the disturbance, uttered a vague insult at Judeans and Romans—the Samaritans hated everybody—and went back to sleep.

Then blackness, stillness. There was no further activity and, since Simon did not make another sally across the stable yard, they assumed he had loosened all ten hitches.

Outdoors, below, a meager light from the entrance lamp. Indoors, the darkness seemed to grow blacker, the silence more still.

Within the hostel, there was not the faintest hint that anyone was awake. No sound at all, not even the creaking of old wood.

Nothing.

Standing at the window, Mary saw no motion from the Samaritans, but the Roman was slapping at stable flies.

Nothing.

Then she saw the shadow. Briefly—an instant—it remained within the circle of the lamp. It moved quickly. All she could see were the bright stripes of the Syrian mantle; the rest was lost. The stripes, moving swiftly like the signal of a flag.

Then the man appeared, but only his head and hands. He was behind the post against which the Roman was resting. Suddenly the hands with the sinew made a quick, flicking motion. The Roman's arms flew out. They convulsed discrepantly, as if they were not a pair. The head twitched one way, then another, hung oddly, and was still. The swiftest glimpse, then, of the tendon flipping free like a kite tail in the air.

Not a sound had been made. Nothing had seemed to change, not even the Roman's posture. He still leaned back against the post, as if asleep.

The head and hands had disappeared. He must be in the stable, she thought, seeing to the horses.

The latch. Elias was the first to respond to the sound; he started for the door. Mary felt for her dagger, to see how easily it would slip out of the sheath, and followed.

The corridor was lighted only by the spill from the lamp over the stairway. She could see Simon and Reuben at the nearer doorway, across from the steps, suspending action, waiting for the two others to go beyond them. They passed so close that she could feel their breathing.

Reuben stood sideways, his shoulder poised and ready against one door, while Elias was ready against the other. They waited for a sign from Simon.

Simon nodded.

A clatter of breaking, of falling wood. But only one door flew open —Reuben's. The other bar, while loosened, had not fallen, and the door was jammed.

Reuben, strictly to plan, rushed into the room. There was an outcry. An outcry, too, from Tullius's chamber.

Simon, concerned not for himself but for the whole effort, did not enter the bedroom, but started toward Elias. It was a blunder. He was seized by someone, the Bactrian, who twisted him and grabbed his knife hand, held him in a vise, trying to break his arm. Mary was the closest, and as she started to Simon's aid, something struck her from behind, and she fell. She was dazed, and her knife was gone.

"Get up!"

It was Simon's voice. He was still struggling with the soldier. She had to help him somehow. But she could not rise. Suddenly the Roman was within her reach. From the floor, she raised her fist, once, twice, smashing upward between his legs. The moan was hardly more than a whisper. Then she saw the knife in his belly, and when Simon drew it forth, the blood came gushing and flowed upon her, on her hair, her face, her breast.

Simon was gone, she did not know where, and the blood was in her eyes, she could hardly see. But she heard noises behind her and she turned.

A Roman lay on the floor, writhing, and Elias was struggling with another one: Tullius. The centurion's head was wounded but he still held the dagger, still waged battle, and the Jew was losing it. She started toward them, then saw the glitter on the floor. Her knife. She stooped and seized it.

She felt everything now, all excitement and terror.

"Strike!" Elias cried.

She struck. The Roman twisted and her knife rent his tunic, nothing more.

She struck again, and there was blood this time, the Roman's body blood. As Tullius pulled backward, his arm shot forth. Elias did not seem to see the Roman's weapon, nor did he feel it. Only the woman before him—he stared at her—she was all his eyes could hold.

Then he fell.

The centurion, wounded, bleeding, turned to deal with the woman. But he, too, fell, thrashing about, cursing, trying to get up. Then suddenly he was still.

She sank to her knees beside Elias.

"Elias," she cried. "Elias . . . ?"

The question in the outcry was not answered.

The original purpose of the raid had been fulfilled. As specifically planned, three soldiers had been slain. To an extent, Mary had been avenged. Four swift Roman horses had been substituted for four slower Zealot beasts, and the other animals had been stampeded so that pursuit of the raiders had been impossible—exactly according to the tactical scheme.

There had been only two mishaps. According to a message from the innkeeper, they had been mistaken about Tullius: he had been wounded, but was not dead. And Elias was.

Such was the report that Simon delivered to the company of Zealots, who approved the raid as a successful one. Not that they were callous about the death of one of their number, they were all fond of Elias, and they mourned him. But they had taught one another that there was an acceptable way to mourn: briefly.

It was a lesson Mary tried to learn, but could not. No matter how she endeavored to create vacuums of forgetfulness, Elias returned to fill them. The way he walked, his hands, his voice in the cadences of a love poem, his kindness—she would mourn Elias as long as she could remember him. As long as she remembered that his death had been her fault. . . .

"Try not to think that way," Simon told her. "You struck—you wounded the man. You did as any of us would have done—your misfortune was not exceptional. We have all had them in our time."

"But Elias— I failed him!"

"You must stop weeping," he said.

"I am afraid to stop."

It was true. It was as if the tears were bedimming her mind, misting over a truth that she dared not see in all its clarity. My fault, she said, as if confessing to an offense of lesser magnitude. But another, more terrible accusation was there, behind the tears, and sooner or later she would have to stop weeping and aridly face the full horror of her sin. She had killed him. By not plunging the dagger once more into Tullius, she had plunged it into Elias. The Roman blood spilled on her she had washed away; the blood of her precious friend would be there always.

Simon continued to console her. "You must think of yourself as a Zealot. Death is not a new thing to us."

"It is new to him."

"It is nothing to him. But to you it is guilt," he said sharply. "And you must stop it. Guilt only gives longevity to grief."

A few days later he told her she would have to leave. She had been expecting it, but not for the reason he gave. It appeared that Tullius, who had been unconscious all this time, was now recovering. He was still in delirium, however, telling feverish tales of what had happened, full of inconsistencies. One story accused the Samaritans, another said he had been attacked by a whole cohort, another said women. . . .

"If he should come to his senses . . ."

"Yes, I understand."

"Your presence is a danger." Then, quickly, to soften it: "Unsafe for all of us, yourself as well."

She smiled grimly. She had expected to leave because she had failed. This reason—safety for everyone—was an easier one to bear, if less true. Well, she must accept whatever mercies others made for her; she could not make her own.

"Where shall I go?"

"The boldest choice is often the wisest."

"Jerusalem?"

"Yes. Home."

What an odd, old-fashioned word.

She would leave in the morning.

Your presence is a danger. Indeed, mostly to myself. She had no urgency to live. The only passion that kept her alive was for vengeance; her need had not perished with the three soldiers. On the contrary, the death of Elias had whipped up the flame. What a painful irony that she had seen the boy for the first time when Tullius was hunting him, and for the last time when Tullius had slain him. Tullius always, Tullius who had raped her and killed her precious friend. If there was a prayer left in her, and if there was a God, she prayed that Tullius would die. Or, better still, she pleaded, let him live, so that I can kill him! How hapless it was: the man she loathed was the only one who kept the blood flowing in her veins. Was an obsession to murder a sufficient reason for staying alive? Somehow, someplace, sometime . . .

That night, she walked in the meadow and tried to dispel the vision of Elias, but the more she tried, the more she wept. Fragments of the poems, phrases that had lilted on his voice, now lamented in the night air. Only a few of the words connected, and none made sense. After a while, she lost them altogether. Where, she cried, where did they go?

Then, with a pang, she knew what grieved her most. There was no ecstasy in his dying. No *ah.* Only shadows in a narrow hallway, only the meanness of her lack of skill and thoroughness. Then a spill of blood and a breath that could not be summoned.

No great public funeral, no multitudinous outcry at the death of a hero, only her small and secret tears. No *ah.*

Perhaps the man did not exist. Perhaps he had dreamed the encounter, a phantom of fever in the desert. Surely he would have come upon him by now, Judas thought, somewhere in these foothills, or someone would have heard of him. Jesus, the searcher had said a hundred times; Jesus, a Galilean.

The place was in this area, according to his clouded memory; Jericho is down there, the Essene had said. In vain he had asked a score of people in the city, and they had been niggardly with information. This is a place without responses, an old sexton told him; Jericho no longer answers to the trumpets.

In any event, there was no such Jew there. Nor in any of the smaller towns and villages, nobody answering the description.

The description might be faulty. Yet the details were so lucid to Judas. The commonplace features that had lighted and become strikingly singular, the smile that had been a gift of warmth against the chill of night. And the vision of a haven:

A place where there were no Romans, the strange one had said, where men made peace with a beloved Father and one another, where they seek the truth by labor—how did he say it?—in the vineyards of God's love.

No wonder Judas could not find the place. It was, as he had originally thought, a fabricated Eden. But it had to have been *told* to him for it to recur in such a convincing way, even if blurred by doubt.

Well, that was all that was left of it, the doubt. And he might as well go back. Go back to what, go where?

There.

The mirage, where the man was waiting.

He was standing before the high wall with the sun so burning white upon the clay and so fiery on his face that it was all part of the figment, Judas thought.

But the man waved, and did not disappear.

Judas ran. He ran through the scorching heat of the desert, he ran and fell and arose and ran again through the lie of the mirage, to the truth of the figure that beckoned to him.

Come, it said, come here.

For many months Judas was confused. He did not know how to be part of the Essenes, or if he belonged here at all. He lived in a low clay building, in a tiny cell, and not a single demand was made upon him. He could work in the grainfields or in the orchard or vegetable gardens if he liked, or he could simply spend the day in prayer. Or in nothing. His food was brought to him, and he ate alone; he was not permitted to break bread with the elders or even with the novitiates, for he was in that group of nonexistent ones known as "wayfarers," which signified that he could go and come as he pleased. He was a traveler.

He rarely saw Jesus. The man had presented him to the Teacher of Righteousness, who was the head of the community, and to the Twelve Elders, and had virtually disappeared. Judas did not know where he slept. Only a few followers lodged in the clay house; some were temporary people, nameless, almost faceless like himself. For the most part, the Essenes lived elsewhere, in the wilderness, in tents or in the foothill caves, and came in only for evening meals, or for holiday prayers in the small synagogue, or for the Sabbath.

They were quiet men of all ages, who spoke little, in low voices and half sentences. They always seemed to be withholding something, as if they had secrets not only from the world but from one another. He did not understand them at all. He had heard of Essenes nearly all his life, but never knew precisely what they were. Perhaps because they were many things; they lived in many places. Some groups had even ceased to call themselves Essenes; at least they had severed their association with the center of the cult, near En-gedi, where the Law was a stringency. Unlike Jesus' community, where the Law was interpreted without severity, in the En-gedi enclave expressions of joy were forbidden, fasting was often protracted to the edge of starvation, it was a mortal sin to bring a flower indoors or to illuminate the holy manuscripts in color, for the world was black and white. The several communities had other differences; they even found different names to call themselves: Evionim, for example: The Poor, because they had forfeited their worldly goods and made a vow of poverty; Covenanters, signifying that Moses' covenant with God had been neglected or corrupted, and somehow was going to be cleansed again; The Many, suggesting they were a multitude bonded together into one people. But they were not a multitude—only a few thousand of them—and they were not one people. They did not even have one name; some used *all* the names—as Jesus' community did—and still said that they were Essenes.

With as many differences, the groups had much in common. All believed in the Mosaic Law and kept it holy; they had faith in their exorcists and healers; they were children of light against the children of darkness. And darkness was what they had fled from: the sins of Jerusalem, the contamination of the priests and the Temple; the commerce of the Sadducees, the hypocrisy of the Pharisees. The cruelty of the Romans.

To dispel those darknesses, they prayed for the angel of light. He would bring them forgiveness for their sins, he would reinstate the Law, he would cleanse the Temple or build them a new one; he would do battle with their enemies, he would rid the land of the oppressor, he would bring them peace. With one accord they agreed that he would create the Kingdom of Heaven. And with one accord they knew who that angel would be: the Messiah.

These beliefs were fervent, and in his first weeks, Judas felt that his spirit was still ailing, not vigorous enough to engage in the fervors of the Essenes. He had all he could do to come to quiescence here, and accept this place.

As time went on, however, he wanted also to be acceptable. For something good was happening to him in the presence of the Covenanters. He began to feel safe. He could feel a lightening of heart. At first, he questioned every felicity. Any day, he warned himself, adversity would fall upon him; a thunderbolt would strike or an arm would wither, his brain would cease functioning or someone would catch him in a reprehensible act.

But no catastrophes. The quiet in his mind continued, and he began to feel a gentle pleasure in his hushed life. Through the summer he worked silently in the vineyard, and he might, in the fall, be asked to assist the vintner. He slept soundly at night, he took well to the simple provender, he prayed not only when he was idle but when he was occupied. He began to trust his own tranquillity.

Except for a lingering apprehension: He was there only on sufferance, temporary, still a wayfarer, and without lasting status; at any moment, he might be requested to leave. And on each occasion when he had asked one of the elders what he must do to become a novitiate, he had been put off with mumblings and excuses.

His dread grew and grew. There was some terrible reason they did not want him there, something they were keeping from him.

"It is not what they are keeping from you," Jesus said. "It is what you keep from yourself."

"I keep nothing."

"Are you ashamed to be a Jew?"

"Oh, no!"

"Afraid, then?"

Judas felt a tremor. "I am neither."

"You are many years past thirteen. Have you ever stood on the bema?"

"No."

"And you had no Bar Mitzvah."

"How did you know that?"

"You told me—when you were ill."

He did not recall it. Ill, yes, and haunted, and here he was, haunted again.

"What must I do, then?"

"You must do nothing."

It was ambiguous, Judas thought, but then he realized that Jesus had meant no double meaning, but was merely echoing Judas's own. "Must" was the wrong word.

He felt a sudden tingle, an excitement.

"I want . . ."

Jesus nodded. "Yes?"

"I know there is no such thing as a Bar Mitzvah for someone of my age, but . . ."

"It is only a ritual, and it has its own time. But reading the Scripture on the bema is a time that never passes."

"But if one loses a special moment . . ."

"I think—His moment is never lost."

Again Judas felt the stir of excitement. His smile was as broad as he had ever felt it. "How long will 'now' take?"

"I will see to it. A month or two."

"Thank you. You are a friend. Thank you."

"Shall we send word to your father?"

Judas had tried, in recent years, to avoid thinking about his home in Kerioth, to avoid the ache. But now, would it at last be possible to heal the wound? He would have liked his parents there—his father alongside him on the bema, introducing his son as Judas Bar Amos—but it would not do. Here was one occasion when a time had come and passed. Amos of Kerioth was a world-accommodated man and the Essenes were otherworldly spirits; there would be disapproval on both sides—and Judas was now as little related to his father as he felt close to his new-found companions. Amos's presence would cause father and son an inevitable distress. All that would ever be remembered of the occasion would be its sorrow.

"No," he said. "I will not have my father here."

"May I present you for your first time?"

It had not occurred to Judas that such a young man could act as his guardian. But, all at once, it seemed to him that this was why he had delayed for so many years. He had waited for this moment and this man. He had waited to find a new friend and a new father.

For the rest of the summer and into the early weeks of autumn, Jesus prepared Judas for the reading of his first portion. The student had forgotten much; there were vacancies to fill. Judas loved to learn and Jesus loved to teach. Like the good rabbi, he looked for the light in the listener's eyes. The days were all for learning, days of benison.

"Teach me everything," Judas said. "Teach me as if I were a child of twelve again."

Jesus replied that the young man was not twelve again, and must discover maturer meanings in "Bar Mitzvah," a term that implied he was the "son of the commandments". But there was duress in the interpretation, and Jesus said that if the commandments were graven in tablets of stone, their significance was not only in God's written law, but also in man's intention. "Bind them upon thine heart," said the exhortation in the Shema. It was one's heart that told the intention, and was therefore held accountable, even more than mind and will.

There were tales to be related about other Bar Mitzvahs, Jesus said, about how Abraham, at the age of thirteen, was called by the Almighty to go forth from the home of his father and turn his face against the worship of idols, and how he had done as he was bidden and had found the one and only God. And how, at the age of thirteen, the twin brothers, Jacob and Esau, had gone their separate ways, Esau to bow down before idols and graven images, and Jacob to give reverence only to the one God and to found the house of Israel. *Midrash,* tales of tradition, tales of children becoming men. . . .

They read the Torah, the Law of Moses, the five books that the Greek Jews were calling the *pentateuchos,* and they debated the meanings. What does this question ask and what does that statement signify? Was the Flood an allegory or did it actually occur? This prophecy, that one, is it a wish or a warning? How much must I follow my reason, and how much my conscience? "Behold I set before you this day a blessing and a curse." Can such opposites abide together? Is He a God of puzzles and perversity; do these books tell adages to clarify, or enigmas to mystify? Does the Lord truly *want* us to understand?—there is much to suggest that He is the preceptor of puzzlement.

The ceremonial day was approaching when Judas would go to the synagogue, mount the steps to the bema, and, for the first time in his life, before the entire congregation, read aloud from the Torah. Jesus had taught him how to pray while wearing the phylacteries, the little boxes which contained minuscule parchments inscribed with passages from Scripture; how to tie the leather laces gracefully and affix one box upon his arm and the other on his forehead. He had also taught him how to chant in melodic notation, in trope, for the recitation of his portion of the Torah. And more rapidly than a twelve-year-old boy could have managed, he was getting ready.

As his test drew nearer and nearer, Judas knew that he had read well, had prayed devoutly, had prepared for the occasion in every way except one.

He was not prepared to terminate his lessons with Jesus. These had been such weeks of happiness as Judas had never known. Because the man from Galilee was a blessed teacher, Judas began to feel that he was a blessed student. Each day of enlightenment in the glow of his rabbi, each day with the security that it was real and it would be real again tomorrow, had been a gift from God. The sweet sessions of learning, like a balm, were restoring his mind and mending his ailing soul. And he dreaded the termination of this enchanted interlude, dreaded going back to those empty times when he saw Jesus rarely and in fleeting glances.

Judas himself had chosen the day on which he would be, as he told himself, Bar Mitzvah. While at En-Gedi the Torah was read every day, in this community the readings were held each week. Three times a year, whenever a third of the enscrolled story had been narrated, there was always a celebration. The most jubilant of these holidays took place at the end of the year's readings; it was a festive time, a rejoicing in the triumph of the Torah. And Judas wanted, when that day of gladness would arrive, to read the concluding portion of the scroll.

In the synagogue, on the eve of the festival—and the eve of his reading day—the extra lamps had been lighted. Children appeared from the nearby villages, and the wives of those few Essenes who were married came in bright dresses with pure white shawls upon their heads. The older boys carried banners, and others held long branches on the ends of which were affixed scooped-out oranges or pomegranates in which lighted candles had been inserted. Some people clapped their hands, not in unison but haphazardly, whenever they felt merry; some sang to an inner music. There was much chattering and embracing and laughter. And kissing. Judas had never seen so much innocent and friendly kissing. Everyone kissed; even men kissed one another, on the forehead and cheeks and, occasionally, in times of great holiness, upon the lips.

There was disorder, too, until the procession started. Then, as the scrolls of the Torah were taken from the sanctuary, a hush descended. The Teacher of Righteousness shouldered the precious burden and carried it about the synagogue, so that those who wished to feel its texture might touch it with their fingertips. In his seventies, the Teacher was tall, taller than anyone, with a white beard and white hair flowing to his shoulders. The silken cover of the scrolls was white as well, and since he held the Torah on his shoulder so that much of it was higher than his head, it seemed to Judas as if he were bringing it down from the mountain in the desert, white and pure and beautiful. . . .

The following morning, there were only men in the synagogue. Since today's was the final Torah reading of the year, the worshipers who stood on the bema were the most celebrated. Three of them would do the reading. The first was the precentor, Rabbi Tobias, chosen by the Elders for the beauty of his incantations. As he started to read the First Portion, it was in the pure tone of a great *chazzan,* yet a cavernous voice, all echoes. He read of the last days of Moses, how the revered leader, full of years, went once again to the mountaintop, to gaze down on the land of Canaan, the haven to which he had hoped to bring his people. He read how the patriarch looked upon the tribes of Israel and blessed them.

The second was Jesus, who stood upon the bema, spoke his own full name, Jesus Bar Joseph, and identified himself as the surrogate father of Judas Bar Amos, who stood beside him. He chanted a prayer and closed his white prayer shawl across his breast; then he recited the benediction, *Baruch shepetarani me'onsho shel zeh,* Blessed is He who has freed me from being the conscience of this child.

Another prayer then, and he turned to the third one on the bema.

Judas's mouth was dry. He started to chant the last portion. The words held fast to his tongue and would not come forth. His lips opened and closed, and he began to tremble. But he felt the hand of his teacher on his arm, and strength and spirit flowed through him.

He told of the last days of Moses, of the old man looking upon the land of his dream: Gilead as far as Dan, Naphtali and the earth of Ephraim and Manasseh, and Judah as far as the western sea, and the palm trees of Jericho. This was the promised land, the land of his heart's hope and his years of yearning. Yet: "I will give it to your descendants," the Lord said. "I have caused you to see it with your eyes, but you shall not cross over there."

And Judas, sorrowing for the patriarch's blighted dream, chanted how Moses, the servant of the Lord, died there in the land of Moab, and how the Lord buried him in a valley somewhere, and no one has known his grave unto this very day, and how the children of Israel wept for him.

Suddenly, as he finished the reading, Judas knew how glorious it was to be a Jew and how aching. What a cry of lamentation he made, what a cry of joy, and he could not stand how happy he was. And he felt someone comforting him and giving him praise and kissing him, and it was his teacher, Jesus.

"You are now a novitiate."

The Teacher of Righteousness raised his white head and opened his arms in a wide gesture of welcome. He complimented the young man, who had yesterday read the Torah with such elevating grace, and complimented Jesus, who had taught him. Then, as if Judas had never set eyes on the Twelve Elders, the Teacher led him around the council chamber and presented him to each of the dignitaries. Not all of the Elders were elderly. Two of them were only slightly older than Judas, possibly about Jesus' age, in the late twenties or early thirties; only Enoch, who was eighty, doddered a little.

It surprised and gratified the novice, how differently they behaved today. Formerly, they had never seemed to notice he was there; if he was working in the fields with one of their number, or passing on a pathway, none of them ever greeted him, not so much as a nod. Now the younger ones were taking his hand, and the older ones were enfolding him in embraces, and Enoch, the venerable Master Scribe, was patting him on the head as if he were indeed a thirteen-year-old Bar Mitzvah boy. Judas found himself grinning, giggling, and Jesus was smiling, while the Teacher, laughing, was trying to dismiss the Elders so that he could get on with his guidance of the novitiate.

When the Elders had gone, the Teacher turned to Jesus. "You will be the preceptor to your friend."

Judas's heart leaped up. The sessions with Jesus would continue; they would not be separated.

The white-haired man gave all his attention to Judas. "This is a place of God. Some of our older followers call it The Place. Whether it is one or one of many, it belongs to the Lord. We are here to learn His ways. And you are now in the novitiate." He smiled. "Do you know what the novitiate is?"

"It is a time of trial."

"Yes, you are on trial—and so are we."

He went on then to say that it was a two-year period during which Judas could leave willingly, without hindrance, or be expelled. A time, for everyone, of searching and discovering. He would consecrate himself to God and the Jewish people. He would work, he would learn, he would pray. He would obey to the letter the Manual of Discipline.

During the first year, he would be taught by his preceptor, and apprenticed to one of the Elders in the work to which he had been assigned, and he would have no privileges or comforts. For a twelve-month period, he must sleep on bare boards; he must eat alone, not with any of the members of the community; he must draw water, for drinking and bathing, from the wells that had not been declared the ritual ones. At the end of his initial year, he would be permitted the use of the ritual waters, but not allowed to sup with God's elect, in the refectory.

It was not that the refectory was a sacred place, but that supper was a sacred occasion. Only those who had passed through two years of novitiate and who had been allowed to take their hallowed vows would be admitted to its secret. That was at the heart of their sanctity: The Secret. It was the heart of their safety as well, the Teacher said; it was the shield that God had given them against their enemies. And they dared not impart it to anyone who was not yet in the bosom of the holy order.

As the Teacher spoke about the mystery, Judas sensed that the hardest task of his novitiate would not be the lack of comforts or the stern discipline, but his prickling anxiety to know the secret of the supper.

"Now," said the Teacher, "tell me who you are and who you have been."

In a few moments, Judas could hardly believe how easy it was to confide the most intimate details about himself. Oddly, the presence of Jesus, rather than making things more difficult, gave him the sense that everything he told was understood, and he was receiving a quittance for debts and disgraces.

"You started as a scrivener," the old man said. "Would you like to return?"

"Yes, I would."

The Teacher nodded and said to Jesus, "Take him to the scriptorium." And the meeting was over.

When Jesus opened the door of the scriptorium, Judas gasped. It was the most beautiful, the friendliest room he had ever seen. Hundreds of scrolls were stacked upon the shelves. Leathers, tanned and tooled, hung upon the walls, with the songs of David and Solomon written upon them. In color! Vivid illuminations, crimsons and golds and blues, so many blues, cerulean and azure and indigo and lapis lazuli. Ceramic jars, too, large urns and narrow cylinders, some of raw terra cotta and some painted and glazed, shining like burnished copper.

Around the table, the scriveners sat, their heads only inches away from their work, inscribing their leathers and parchments and papyri.

Some wrote with trimmed feathers, which they dipped into inkwells; others painted with the finest-haired brushes, drawing droplets of dye from ceramic vessels.

Enoch, the Chief Scribe, was supervising one of the scriveners, who was sealing a finished parchment into a tall jar.

"Against time and weather," the young scrivener explained.

The old man grimaced. "Against Romans."

It would be buried where the barbarians would never find it. He said testily, "In a cave by the sea." Then he grinned like an imp. "As if there are any caves by the Dead Sea."

Finished now, Enoch gave his regard to the apprentice. He showed the Deuteronomy that was being copied, and the Exodus and the Leviticus. His favorites were the shorter things, a psalm, the Song of Miriam, a eulogy written by one of the Elders.

He was especially proud of the illuminations on the wall, one of which he himself had painted. Waggling a finger at it, his arm trembled; he had a bit of palsy now, he said, and no longer had a hand for quills or brushes.

Admiring, Enoch pointed to an illumination of one of the Songs of Solomon, a work of art vibrating with color. He touched it gently, as if it were alive. Then he winked. "The Elders hate it. Aaron Bar Tsvi says he would never have left En-Gedi if he had known we would decorate our books in shameful colors. Ebenezer calls them graven images. But I won my point. 'Graven,' I said, 'but not images.' Not a single image—am I right—can you find one?"

Judas and Jesus admitted that they could not. Enoch shook with glee.

"Tomorrow—you will start at dawn tomorrow," he said to Judas. "You will copy something beautiful for me, yes?" Giddily he corrected himself. "For the Almighty, I mean. For the Almighty—yes?"

Judas promised he would try.

Jesus showed him the other common rooms in the building, the study chambers and the scullery and the pottery and the rooms of private prayer. Last of all, he led him toward the refectory.

Judas's curiosity quickened. "Am I permitted to see it?"

"To see it, not to sup in it."

Jesus opened the double doors and revealed . . . a disappointment. There was nothing awesome or mystical or sublime about the chamber. On the contrary, it seemed like a vacant place, sparsely furnished, too meagerly appointed for its size. Walls of unpainted clay and benches and tables of rough-hewn planking. It was too poor and barren for the august tone they used—"The Refectory!"—as if it were an anteroom to heaven. Certainly no enigma could be hidden here. What secret could be concealed in such an open void?

Suddenly, chilled, it occurred to him that it had to be something so directly sent from God that its starkness would make it unknowable to the uninitiated.

"The secret," he said to Jesus. "You know it, do you not?"

His preceptor did not answer.

Judas realized what an indiscretion he was committing, but he could not control himself. "When did you take your vow?"

Again no answer.

Driven, Judas continued. "You've been here three years, did you say?"

"Yes."

"Then, you took your vow a year ago?"

"No."

Judas was puzzled. "When, then?"

"I have not taken it."

"Not taken it?"

"No."

"But why?"

"When I know the answer, I will tell you," Jesus said.

Judas loved The Place. As his world grew smaller, he could feel himself grow larger. He felt a deepening and a broadening in every aspect of his life. Although he was merely a scrivener and not a scribe, he could see his work getting finer with each papyrus or parchment he was called upon to do; his hand was resolute, Enoch said, and his colors were starting to purify. Color, yes; Judas had lived, it seemed to the young man, in a world of gray and shadow. Now it was alight with sun-showers of color. What a blaze!

When his mornings were over, he would hurry to the scullery and help himself to his midday meal, which might be a stew of some sort into which he would dip hot bread, or raw vegetables freshly picked from the gardens, and fruits—cherries, often—still warm from the sun. Then, on the run before his last mouthful was swallowed because he did not want to miss a minute with Jesus, he would go charging into one of the study cubicles where he and his preceptor would pore over one of the Five Books of Moses, ferreting like moles into the lore and the Law.

Day after day, each session more absorbing than the one before, and he did not want any changes. However, Judas did not mind the few hours a week he spent with one Elder or another, a specialist in a separate study. Nehemiah the apothecary, for example, who had an extensive store of dried herbs, seeds, pods, grasses, remedies for a hundred ailments: headache, sleeplessness, a variety of itches, excess of wind, emotional indisposition. Some people call us the Therapeutae, he would say. Especially about water. It was the greatest nostrum of all, he said with his forefinger in the air; water, taken internally or applied externally, water, water. Bathe, he would reiterate, bathe as often as we all do here, wear well-washed white clothes, always white, and *bathe.*

If Nehemiah was the healer of bone and blood, Elon was the healer of spirit. He taught exorcism, really, although he preferred less mystical allusions to his art. Just as the grower of wheat must expel rats from his granary, so the grower of goodness must expel the rodents of the soul. Black vermin, gray vermin, brown vermin, even the pretty, seducing white ones, they are all demons, Elon would warn, we must drive them out! Not by incantation—his voice would get thunderous—not by astrology or wizardry or necromancy, for those are the deceits of Belial, but by honest, forthright prayer and direct faith in the one and only King of Heaven. Prayer is not mystical, he would say; pure common sense.

Judas spent an occasional hour with Moshe, the teacher of Tongues, who taught the subtleties and pitfalls of language; with Ebenezer, who specialized in Seers and Sages, interpreting dreams and visions as the auguries of Final Revelation; with Aaron Bar Tsvi, who claimed that he only taught *against*—against lies and evil, and particularly against the idols that the heathen worshiped like the toys of children who needed more than one.

However interesting he found his other teachers, Judas soon started to begrudge every minute away from his preceptor, precious time forever unrecoverable.

And he knew that Jesus loved to teach him. You have the mind of a scholar, the Galilean had said, and the probity of a prophet. But sometimes, when they studied the Law together—which gave Judas an almost rapturous pleasure—the student was at a loss between reason and righteousness, between thought and feeling. If the brain is the organ of thought, he asked, and the heart is the organ of feeling, what is the organ of conscience?

Jesus rarely gave him ready answers, but replied with the words of Isaiah or Malachi, or with a parable. Occasionally it seemed to Judas that Jesus' replies were not consistent, as, for example, when he cited the commandment against murder, yet said a man must at some time sell his coat and buy a dagger. He said this more than once, and it bothered Judas that it was so much on his friend's mind.

One day, a field horse went lame and lay in agony, writhing in the hot sun. Someone called the Teacher of Righteousness. The old man stood over the mare and seemed so tall, so physically strong, that Judas believed that by the sheer might of his presence, the animal would cast out the demon of her pain. But the beast's agony went on, and her twistings and whinnyings grew more and more pitiful. The Teacher knelt beside the stricken creature and talked quietly to her. Then, in the most loving way, he put his arm around the mare's neck and held her in an embrace of such devotion and such sadness that the old man's eyes were filled with tears. Abruptly, in one sharp spasm, the Teacher yanked his arm and broke the creature's neck.

Was it a blessing or a sin? Judas asked; what did the Law relate about killing and kindness? What if the animal had been a human being?

Often, such questions were like the blowing of dust. Sometimes asking them and getting no answer was nettlesome: scratching the mind when the itch was elsewhere. But there was one inquiry which, when he asked it, always gave him pleasure, even if there was no ready answer.

Where is the Messiah?

If this was the most frequently posed question among Jews everywhere, it always seemed like a new one to Judas and Jesus. They never tired of asking. It was their daily study, their game, the burden of their labor, their dreaming. The Messiah, always the Messiah.

"Do you truly believe that he will come?" Judas asked.

"Yes, I believe it."

"When?"

"On the very day that he arrives."

Judas would laugh, as he was meant to do, and proceed soberly. "What will he be?"

They scoured the Scriptures for answers. They studied every book of Moses, chapter, verse, the intervals between the words, the meanings between the lines. In Deuteronomy it was written that God had promised a prophet who would speak with His words. Isaiah had foretold that a king would appear, another David, "a rod from the stem of Jesse." Malachi had said, Behold, the Lord will send a messenger.

Prophet, king, lawgiver, priest, messenger. Which will he be? Can he be all of these?

What if he is none? What if he is beyond the Books of Moses, beyond the story of man, beyond the mind's imagining? What if he is both good *and* terrible?

An agony, a joy.

What will he be? Will he be an angel, wreathed in light? Will he make a heaven on earth, or transport earth to heaven? Will he bring an end to sin and heartache and Romans? Will he be an ordinary man? And if he is, how will we know that he is the Messiah?

"He will tell us."

"But what if he does not?"

"He will."

"What if he tells us and we do not believe him?"

"It will be a pity."

"What if there is no Messiah?" Judas asked. "What if there will never be? What if we are deluding ourselves?"

Jesus looked at him with such a sadness that Judas ached. And it suddenly occurred to him that Jesus was certain about some aspects of the Messiah and uncertain of others. And he wondered if the Nazarene's own uncertainty was at the heart of his distress.

Some days, when the closeness of the lettering caused Judas's eyes to become inflamed, Enoch would send him away from the writing table and tell him to walk a while in the fresh air. Judas would thereupon go in search of Jesus. The scrivener loved to watch the carpenter at work, because the man took such pleasure in his tools. And he was so strong. Once, when he was building a sheepcote, he carried a timber three times his own height. It rested on his shoulder and he walked, not touching it with either hand, and the beam rode evenly, drifting neither upward nor downward, as steady as the horizon. It is no great thing, he said, if the beam is in balance.

Another time, he had constructed a cistern. When the rains came, it leaked. It will leak for six days, the carpenter said, and on the seventh it will not. It came about just as Jesus had predicted, and Judas was reminded of the Lord laboring, then resting on the Sabbath. That was a week of miracles, Jesus replied; this is merely the swelling of the boards. Something in the Galilean made him renounce the thought of miracles, as if it frightened him.

It was on that seventh day that the Zealot appeared. He was a nondescript, middle-aged man named Uzziah who came stumbling off the desert, wounded and bleeding. He said he was a fugitive from the Romans and there was some concern among the Elders about taking him in. The last time a rebel had been sheltered, the Romans had stormed the gate, broken a kiln and a wall of the pottery, and burned a wing of the common building. The worst damage had been to scrolls and parchments. Enoch had become ill over it, and the Elders were certain that the old scribe would be dismayed if they gave sanctuary to another Zealot.

But it was Enoch who insisted that they open the gate to the new refugee.

Jesus, of course, agreed with Enoch, and so did Judas. The latter, however, in his heart, resented the breach of serenity that the Zealot's presence would cause; the scrivener prized the repose of The Place. But the Zealot was admitted. Judas did not take a deep breath until the wounded man was mended and gone.

All the time the Zealot was a wayfaring guest, Judas was aware of Jesus' silence. At last, the day before the man departed, the carpenter spoke.

"He is one of us."

"No, he is not. We are people of peace. He is at war."

"He is in revolt. So are we."

Judas knew it was the truth, and inescapable. All Jews, except for the wealthiest of Sadducees and a few cowardly Pharisees, longed for a revolt. What the Zealots hoped to accomplish by havoc and bloodshed, the Essenes sought through holiness and prayer. Prayer, faith, religion were in everything. There was no distinction between the sacred and the secular, for God was the totality of their being. He was their history and their politics, their art and amusement, their thinking and their loving, and—yes—their sword. The revolt, whether it was happening in The Place or in other places, was always there, because God was.

Except: what were the Essenes contributing to the insurrection? How did their holiness and their escape from the world help to rid the land of Romans? Judas thought that this, to Jesus, was the most disturbing question.

It was more than that, Jesus said. There were other ways in which the Essenes seemed just as benighted as the Pharisees. They prayed for the Kingdom of Heaven, but not for all the nations, only for the Jews. They petitioned for salvation, but only for the pure in heart, not for sinners. They lifted their latches to refugees, but normally their gates were locked. They meted out their charities, but only in accordance with the Law.

When he heard his teacher being so critical of The Place, Judas was disturbed. The comment marred the serene perfection of their life here, and, obliquely, cast a shadow on their friendship. It said not only that something in Jesus' life was less than it should be, but that Judas was not making up the difference. And if he could not redress such a discrepancy, he was in some way insufficient, failing Jesus as a friend.

But his preceptor gently chided him for having such a thought. Judas was not at fault; it was the others. Because they feared the Divinity, they feared their own humanity; because they did not trust their love, their love was not to be trusted.

The depth of devotion in the man Jesus had not as yet found a home here. But where else could he find it?

"Where?" Judas asked.

Jesus was deep in thought.

"I beg you," Judas said. "Take your vow."

"Yes . . . I will take it."

"When?"

"In a little time," Jesus answered. "Before the Passover."

"Do you promise?"

Jesus reached out and gently touched his friend's arm. He did not promise.

With a surge of desperation: "Promise me you will! Make me a vow!"

"A vow to take a vow?"

Jesus' mouth smiled, but his eyes did not. And still he did not promise.

⁂

Overnight, Enoch turned into a tyrant. He had been the cheeriest, the most compassionate Elder of all the twelve, he had made the scriptorium a world of adventure where any daring was permitted, where every scrivener's papyrus was limited only by the range of his vision. Every stroke of quill or brush that Enoch laid his eyes upon was beautiful or showed good auspices or was on the verge of creating an elegance. If he ever saw a fault, he never called it such, only an escaped opportunity which could always be recaptured.

And suddenly he had become a monster. Baruch's quill point was always blunted, he said, Elisha's yellows were made with urine, Hanam always illuminated the least important letter, Ezekiel had not covered his paint pots and his bronze had dried like turds in the pasture. Nothing was pleasing to the Chief Scribe anymore, not even the vividly colored illuminations of Judas.

Late one evening, long after work was over, Judas passed the scriptorium, where, under the closed door, on the threshold, he saw a thin line of light. Someone had neglected to extinguish one of the lamps. Enoch would excoriate them in the morning for the waste of oil.

He quietly opened the door and was astonished. The old man sat at the table with a single lamp flickering. A beautifully tanned hide lay spread out before him, and Enoch was decorating it. But the quill quaked in his hand, and as he was setting it down to take up one of the brushes, some of the paint dripped off the tip. The scribe, muttering wretchedly, snatched at a wiping cloth and tried to dry the wet damage, but the color smeared, he inadvertently dropped the rag on the floor, and when he went to stoop for it his back would not bend to the task. Then he could not move, he just sat there, cursing at the cloth and at his dotage.

To avoid adding to the old man's humiliation, Judas turned to slip away, but the door creaked and Enoch turned.

"What?" The old man was startled. "Are you spying on me?"

"No."

"Go away—go away!"

"Enoch—"

"Go away!"

And he began to weep.

Softly, Judas departed.

The following morning, Enoch did not come to the scriptorium. He was ill, the message came, confined to his cell.

"He is dying," Judas said to Jesus that afternoon.

"Has Nehemiah seen him?"

Judas smiled wanly. "It is beyond an apothecary, I'm afraid. And the physician from Jericho has come and gone. They say there is nothing to be done—old age. But it is not—it is a broken heart."

"You think his heart broke only yesterday?"

"No—years ago," Judas replied. "When he laid down his quill."

"Why, then . . . ?" Jesus did not finish the question.

"His last dream. What a spiteful thing, that he cannot have his last dream."

Jesus turned away. For the rest of the afternoon, they were both abstracted, and well before sunset, they gave up trying to work.

Toward dusk, Judas debated whether to visit Enoch once again. The last time he had done so, this morning, his presence had not seemed to bring comfort to the old man. On the contrary, he had turned his face to the wall.

The scrivener decided, however, that he would simply take the sick man a little food, and depart. In the scullery, he poured some broth in a bowl, added a few morsels of bread, and started for Enoch's cell.

Except for a weak, flickering candle, the corridor was lightless. But not altogether silent. There was a murmuring. Judas took it to be someone in evening prayer, perhaps the old scribe. No, the voice was stronger. As Judas approached the door, he thought he heard a second voice. Clearly now, two of them. Enoch and Jesus.

His impulse was to join them. Reaching for the latch, Judas hesitated; something deterred him. He could not tell what it was, a special quietude in their tones, a note of communion perhaps, too private or too secret to be interrupted. Or overheard.

Slipping outdoors again, he thought of eating the bread and broth himself, but he was unaccountably not hungry, and went to bed earlier than usual, without his nightly meal. He lay awake thinking, trying to understand why he was so perturbed.

Having been restive in the night, he overslept. It was broad daylight when he scrambled out of bed and hurried along the path toward the scriptorium. Approaching the little terrace of cobbles and grass outside the doorway, Judas saw a sight to gladden his heart.

A table had been placed outdoors in the morning sun. Sitting at it,

Enoch. Before him, papyri, parchment, an inkwell, quills, brushes, paints. And the old man was working away.

As Judas drew closer, the Elder raised his head. He smiled. His face was as if he were well again, and had shed ten years of his age.

"The trouble was," he said cheerily, "it was too dim in there. I cannot see to write, to paint, to do anything. But out here in the sunlight—"

He giggled, his old self again.

And his hand was steady.

Enoch worked outdoors for a few hours. At midmorning, he entered the scriptorium, made a few advisory comments about the work of the scriveners, then asked Judas if he would come outdoors to help him. The old man needed no help, really; he simply wanted the company of Judas. In a little while the scrivener was working on one side of the table while the scribe was working on the other.

An amazement within an amazement. Not only was Enoch painting with steady hands again, but with astonishing speed. It was as if he had been granted a specific allotment of hours and must complete his work before time ran out.

Already, well before noon, his illumination had taken form, and it was clearly going to be a work of great beauty. He was emblazoning the first few lines of Genesis. The background for the lettering was finished and dry. At the bottom, and mostly in the lower left-hand corner, he had painted the colors of chaos. Blacks and browns and purples, with slashes of bloody red—darkness on the face of the deep. Then, moving upward, the brightening into luminous hues, the Spirit of God hovering over the waters, and the earth, which had been without form and void, was being found in a radiance. Then the glory, "Let there be light."

It was forbidding and terrible, and dazzling.

As the old man started to inscribe the first letters of the first words of Genesis, Judas could feel his exaltation spreading across the table and out onto the fields.

He had already imprinted the first words:

"In the beginning . . ."

As he finished the symbol for the Forbidden Name, he looked up and smiled. He seemed a man who had been irradiated with divine love.

That afternoon, with Jesus: "You did it for him," Judas said.

"I helped him."

"You healed him."

"He healed himself."

"You made him young again."

"That part of him was never old."

"It was a miracle."

"No!"

The word stunned Judas—a cry of wrath. It was vehemence of which he had not thought Jesus capable.

"It was not a miracle! I cannot perform miracles! No miracles, no miracles!"

And Jesus departed.

They had no session in the afternoon. Hurt, perplexed, not knowing why Jesus should have been so infuriated with him, Judas did not know what to do with himself. He returned to the outdoor table and went back to working on his parchment. The sun was hot and Enoch had withdrawn for an hour's respite, taking his Genesis with him. Judas worked listlessly, his mind with Jesus.

In the broiling heat of the afternoon, he saw his preceptor coming toward him. When he was close enough to touch the table, Jesus said:

"I hope you have not as yet forgiven me."

Judas was puzzled. "Why do you say that?"

"There will be more to forgive."

The scrivener tried to smile. "How does the saying go? 'If there is more life, there is more fault. If there is more fault—' "

"I am going away."

"Going away? What does that mean?"

"I am leaving here."

"Leaving The Place?"

"Yes."

The quill trembled. He set it down. "To go where?"

"There . . . the wilderness."

"To do what?"

"To ask . . ." He stopped. "To find . . . ." Again he stopped speaking, as though there was no sentence that he could finish.

"How long will you be gone?"

"I will not return here, Judas."

I must remain still, Judas thought. If I rise, I will tremble to pieces.

"But you said—your *vow*—you said—"

"I cannot take my vow."

"But you promised!"

"I did not promise, Judas. I said—"

He arose and his body shook. "You promised—you cannot betray me—you promised—"

"Judas, I did not!"

"You promised. You cannot leave me!"

I am losing my wits, he thought, I am beyond my will. The inkwell was in his hand and he was throwing blackness all over the parchment, splotches of stain and blackness—

"You promised! You promised!"

That same afternoon, Jesus departed and Judas did not go to the gate to see him off, nor did he say goodbye to him. Only in his mind's eye did he watch him go, as if he were witness to the darkening of his sight. The following day, when he returned to his work in the scriptorium, all the colors had faded, and whatever he painted turned to dun.

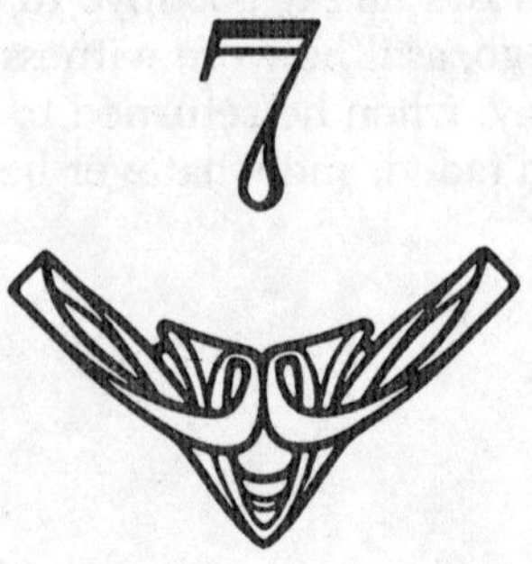

On the surface, nothing had changed in Jerusalem. Her father's villa on the hill was just as classical and courtly as ever, the marble of its peristyle just as polished and cold. Her servant, Duna, a portly bondwoman from Ephesus, was as avid to be summoned, and Mary's clothes were as meticulously tended. None of the servants treated her as if she had been away, none asked where she had gone. Only Zabis, her father's personal servitor, who had known her since she was a child in Magdala, gave her a warmer greeting than if she had merely come back from an afternoon in the marketplace.

At first, because remembering was unbearable, she tried to tell herself that her existence here in Jerusalem not only seemed unchanged but *was* unchanged. She had only imagined that evil era in her life, that passage through Sheol, seven beasts shrieking forth from a cave, three slain and one wounded, and the death of a young man who had loved her. None of it had happened. Only this was true: this bodice of silver lace, the amethysts that traced their way in and out of the eyelets of embroidery, the sweetish perfume that cloyed like flattery. This was Mary, the rich Sadducean woman of Jerusalem and Magdala. Unchanged.

But nighttimes, when she could not sleep, she knew that the alteration was deep. Fire was in her now, knives, corrosive acids. Ice.

Tullius, it was whispered, recovered or unrecovered, had been sent to Rome. Or Gaul or Macedonia. Speculations. In any event, he was gone. . . . She would find him somehow.

The one puzzling difference in her father was that he asked no questions. He seemed so relieved to have his daughter home that he wanted nothing to mar the perfection. He fondled his contentment as if it were a tiny lamb that would always remain near and loving. Surely, she thought, he must sense the sickness at the heart of it. And how unlike Joram of Magdala this was, not trying to dig it out, not asking questions, not dismantling deceits. He should be badgering: Where have you been? You lied about going to Magdala; where did you go, what are you guilty of?

Now only honeyed smiles and adulation—how beautiful my daughter is!—and gratitude for her presence. Where was the righteous father? What was happening to the stern old Sadducee? How had he come to terms?

One day she had a partial answer.

A *quaestor* arrived from the Civil Order Office of the Antonia. A small, apologetic man, his shiny Roman trappings seemed too large for him, and his task—to pose official questions—was so burdensome that he stuttered over the heavy, insinuating words and could barely manage the lightweight, innocent ones.

"About your daughter," he started diffidently, "I have a query or two."

The advent of the man had come as a surprise, and she was unprepared. She envied her father's composure.

"My daughter has not been well," Joram said.

Instantly she caught the signal. She must play a recessive role, the ailing one.

The official looked from one to the other. "I'm glad to see that she appears to have recovered."

"One day she is splendid, the next day . . ."

"Only a question or two."

"I wouldn't count on the usefulness of her replies. Her memory is unreliable—the aftermath of such a violent disturbance—you must understand that she was brutishly assaulted."

"Yes, of course. Deplorable."

Her father affected gratitude. "I personally will answer whatever questions I can. I probably remember more than my daughter does."

A false atmosphere of good fellowship had been created. The *quaestor* expanded a little. "No difficult questions, understand—nothing complicated. Only her whereabouts."

Joram looked puzzled. "Her whereabouts?"

"Yes—the past few months." He turned to Mary. "Where have you been?"

She took her cue from her father, stared with unfocused eyes to indicate she did not know the answer.

Joram knew the answer: "She has been here."

"Here in Jerusalem?"

"Here in this very house."

"For all these months?"

"For all these months."

"And nobody has laid eyes on her?"

"We have."

"But others . . . in the city."

The Sadducee pretended to be disappointed. The Roman was not as sensitive as he had suggested he might be. "Do you know the shame that clings to a young girl when she—! Do you expect her to parade herself in a city where everyone knows that she has been disgraced?"

"Not parade, no. But not a soul has seen her."

"She has hardly seen herself."

Ingenious, she thought, this portrait of a woman beside herself, her senses scattered. And perhaps not altogether untrue. Her father's picture of a damaged girl who had hidden behind the window shutters, too mortified to step into the sunlight, was, in all probability, exactly as he would have liked her to behave. No wonder he could make it so credible.

But the *quaestor* was not altogether credulous. "May I speak to your servants?"

Her heart sank. She wondered what evasion her father would think of, and if he might resort to bluster.

Instead, he was equable. "Of course you may."

He took the wooden clacker from the table, carried it to the doorway, made a grating sound.

Zabis stood on the threshold and, at a gesture, entered the room. He was beardless, and his hair was fluffy, a gray cloud. The old man's eyes were so glowing black that they gave a youthful vitality to his face; and, except for the solemnity of his walk, he did not look his sixty years.

One question, then another, and Zabis's forehead wrinkled. "I do not understand," he said.

The *quaestor* was more irritable with the servant than with the master. "I think you understand me very well."

"But if you ask me where the young woman was—" At a loss, he fingered his slit earlobe, and turned to his master. "Am I permitted?"

"You are permitted."

Zabis turned to the questioner. "The poor child was ill unto death. She lay in her bed, and could scarcely move. She did not eat, did not sleep, and if anyone approached her, she wept like a pitiful infant, or she screamed. Oh, she screamed a good deal. For weeks, for months, there was nothing we could do for her. Nobody could tend to her—she would not allow it—not a physician, not a nursing woman, no one. We thought she had taken leave of her mind. Perhaps she had. And then—

little by little—without help from anyone—she began to be herself again."

"In all this time, she has been here?"

"This is her home. Where else would she be?"

The Roman cleared his throat with a throttled sound, and muttered that he had no further questions for him. Zabis looked to Joram to confirm that he was being dismissed, and his master nodded.

When the bondman had left the chamber, the *quaestor* said to Mary, "Do you concur with what the servant said?"

"I can hardly remember anything."

A canny answer; the man smiled wryly. "What should I expect you to say?"

"What indeed?"

"You have nothing to add?"

"I do not know how to help you," Mary said. "Am I accused of anything?"

She had not thought it such a risky question, and was surprised to see her father tense. After what he had handled so adroitly, this seemed little enough for him to handle now. Why should it so unsettle him?

"No," the *quaestor* replied. "You are not accused of anything."

She expected the word "yet," but did not hear it. And the official departed.

Fragments in the air—scraps of questions—debris in the wind before a storm.

"Should I not have asked him whether I was accused of anything?"

His manner was surprisingly bland. "Not important . . . although it might have suggested a certain . . . guiltiness." Abruptly his equanimity was gone, he was edgy. "Forget it. You did well. We both did."

He was shying away, trying to erase the experience. "Would all the servants have replied as Zabis did?" she asked.

"Yes."

"Will they do it as skillfully as he did?"

He did not face her. "I told them precisely what to say. And I warned them that if any harm comes to you, they will all be sold to Gaul."

She wished he would meet her glance. His manner is guiltier than my own, she thought; he is behaving like a fugitive. She wanted to free him of the worry, but did not know how. Certainly his refusal to know where she had been and what she had perpetrated would not, ultimately, make things easier. Moreover, she *needed* him to know, needed to confide in him.

"Perhaps I should not have asked him that question." She watched him closely. "But if he had responded, what do you think he would have said?"

"I would rather not talk about it."

"But we'll have to, won't we?"

"I hope not."

"I'm sure we will—and we may as well do it now. What do you think they will accuse me of?"

"I do not know."

"What do you imagine?"

Confronted, he faced her angrily. "I don't want to know and I don't want to imagine!"

"But we're bound to be questioned again, and sooner or later—"

"Sooner or later the Romans will destroy everybody! Sooner or later the world will come to an end! Sooner or later we will all be blessedly dead and our—!"

He stopped in the midst of the outburst. She had never seen him so irrational. He shook, unable to quell the riot within him.

Then everything seemed all right. For the next few days there was not even a hint of worry or vexation. The incident had never occurred. He was affable and good-natured, even making witticisms about the ironies of the new tax assessment on ink and papyrus, the proliferation of false Messiahs, the flight of intellectuals to Alexandria.

She had never gotten on so cordially with her father. He seemed almost pathetically grateful that she had come home. It was as if he had dreaded she would never return again, and here she was, his only daughter, more beloved to him than Caleb had ever been. While he was often querulous about why his son was lax in sending business reports from Alexandria, and worried whether his unruliness was getting him into trouble, the young man's absence had never made Joram suffer as Mary's had. And now that she was home, he rejoiced because he loved her.

Mary knew he loved her with the blind and mindless devotion of a parent who would do anything to make her happy. Of course, he had not done what she had most wanted of him: help her avenge herself. But she felt that he had refused to do so for no selfish reason beyond his obsessive worries about her safety. If anything should happen to her . . . His love was desperation.

So was hers. He was the only man left, the only male whose affection she could trust. He was her single bond to the young girl who had thought life beautiful and exciting and full of mysteries she would one day comprehend; he was her last tenuous tie to herself as a woman of some worth.

At one time, when she was nine or ten, their love for one another had been wholehearted, tender, innocent. The impairments she had counted as the wages of growing up. And in those days it struck her as cruelly ironic that something as enduring as love was said to be, must be tossed away with outgrown clothes. But now, a few weeks after she came home, something happened that restored their devotion, and she loved him again.

Her father became ill. Nobody knew what was wrong with him. He languished. At first, it did not seem serious that this man who was dedicated to his business affairs should leave the marketplace and his counting chambers in the middle of the morning and go indolently home. The physicians pacified his complaints and debilities with tonics and physic-laden elixirs. They brought him metal-and-mineral waters, they thinned his blood with vinegars, they applied any number of leeches.

He grew worse. The twinges became torments. Midday, he went to bed with excruciating headaches; midnight, he walked the corridors, or wandered onto the peristyle, where he would lie on a cold marble bench to chill his feverish body.

His only comfort was his daughter. Mary took care of him. She brought him compresses, hot or cold, she bathed his hands and feet, placed little gauzes on his eyes. For a while—daily—she brought him lotus water to drink, and turned herself into an apothecary on the search for camphors and calomels, for ointments that would soothe his skin, and balsams that would make zephyrs in his nostrils.

In the first few weeks, he had arisen from time to time, taking short walks, even—infrequently—appearing at meals. Then he gave up and became bedfast. And suddenly an odd thing occurred: he turned into a cheery, lighthearted man.

Joram of Magdala became an eccentric. It was as though seeking the logic of life had been at the heart of his malady, and all at once he had been released from the search. He no longer needed to make sense of anything. He was free to indulge his whims and caprices. He allowed his mind to wander, he made no effort to think of time as being sequential, he dreamed awake, he called servants by whatever names occurred to him, he sang little songs out of his childhood, he laughed at the most dreadful disasters as if they were absurdities. Not that he was becoming brainsick, nothing of the sort; he was simply, as he once put it, "letting my wits out on long tethers."

In Mary's company, the tethers were the longest. He no longer tried to be rational with her, nor did he demand rationality in return. Their conversations had no rules. One day, imagining they were back in Magdala, he said:

"Shall we walk down the hill today? It's time for crocuses."

The allusion was close enough to Mary's memories to arrest her mind. But there was something askew. He was confusing a recollection. She had never, not once in her remembrance, gone walking for crocuses with her father—only with her mother. He was imagining that he was Leah, his wife.

But there were no precise precedents to follow, not in this game, so she took her turn.

"Here's a purple one with a white center," she said. "I've never seen a crocus like this. Have you?"

"Yes. You showed me one yesterday."

"I did?"

"You even told me its name. But I've forgotten. Tell me again."

Something was still wrong. If he was playing her mother, he would have known the name, for her mother knew the identity of every flower that grew. Yet, Joram could not have Leah's knowledge, could he?

Abruptly, she saw the whole thing. He was playing himself—and was pretending that she, Mary, was her mother. He was remembering—what?—when?—a walk he and his wife had taken together? Perhaps a number of such idyllic promenades on the hillsides of Magdala, when they were young and in love and in crocuses.

"This is a Bethany crocus," she said. "They grow in the foothills near Jerusalem. They make a crown on a hilltop."

"And this one?"

"It is not truly a crocus. A little iris, I think."

"I thought we were all in the iris family." He was changing the rules.

"Yes. We are."

"What color are you?"

"White. Pure white. And you?"

"Purple."

"Yes. It becomes you. You are made for purple."

"Thank you, Leah. I am glad you think so."

Glad of everything. Gladdest when he pretended his wife was alive. And it was the playing of that game that mended him the most. Of all the balms and potions and medical futilities tried on the patient, it was the pretense that he was young again and his love young again that miraculously began to restore him to good health. Mary could see, day by day, how his memories of happiness were healing him, how after each deep draft of the wine of recollection he was able to deal with a new measure of sobering reality.

One evening, as if asking for a bedtime tale, he said, "What shall we play tonight?"

"Let's play the game that you are getting well."

He seemed alarmed. He tried to smile, and couldn't. "I will think about that," he said.

The next morning, when she awakened and looked out her window, her father was walking in the garden.

⁂

She thought that she, too, might be getting well. If "wellness" meant that Tullius was not in her mind all the time. But whenever she thought of Elias, the visage of Tullius followed quickly, and she needed to kill the centurion. Kill all centurions, all Romans.

One day, walking near the marketplace, her passion for reprisal burst aflame. She did not know what had set it off. Something about this neighborhood. It was a side street she rarely came upon, and she wondered why her feet had led her there. Some misfortune had befallen her in this place; she could not recall what it had been, or how it had occurred.

The Alley Passage, the street of the scriveners. That boy, that scrivener . . . how did he call himself? She remembered the kindness of his face, and something else—something special. Some singular hurt or longing like her own. An anguish for knowing—that was the way she recalled the phrase she had applied to him, and what a kindred soul he had been, and how he might have become her friend.

Clearly now—an image—a presence—the remnants of a writing table smashed by Romans, inkstains on cobblestones. The boy—crippled, someone said, beaten witless. He had done a damage to himself, and died . . . as if that were a damage.

Romans.

Judas. That was the young man's name. If he had lived, what good things might have come of him and his yearning curiosity? He might have written himself to glory, become a scribe in the Temple or a venerated sage; or, in one of those antic turns of destiny, with a name like Judas, he could have become the counterpart of a Maccabee, a leader of Zealots. It only *he* had lived, and not his Roman murderers.

Tullius first. Then Pilate—Pilate himself—to fulfill the dream of Elias. She alone must succeed where they had both failed. Knives. She must make a new companionship with knives.

⁂

It was only when her father was well again that Mary allowed herself to understand his illness. He had been sick with terror.

She had unconsciously known it all along but had pushed the notion into the recesses of her mind; what cure could she have offered him? The reassurance that her rages had been exorcised, that she would not commit murder, that no harm would come to them, and that he could sleep peacefully at night? She could give no such assurances of safety; he would have to find them for himself.

Which he did. He saw that no *quaestores* came calling again, the house was not watched by the soldiery, no threats were made—and best of all, his daughter seemed to have settled down to a quiet domesticity. So his sickness was over, erased from memory; he was a man restored. He went about his affairs with his former vigor and concentration, he bustled and hustled, he counted his cargoes, he counted his money. He put all oppressiveness out of his mind—his spell of illness, the violation of his daughter, her long and frightening absence . . . and danger. It seemed to him that all danger was in the past.

To Mary, danger was always present. So was the image of the centurion.

One bright afternoon, a beggar approached her in the street. As she was giving him a few coppers, he whispered the name "Paktonos" and beckoned her to follow him. Confused, she demurred for an instant, not immediately remembering that Paktonos was the Greek Jew who worked as a Zealot spy in the Antonia fortress. She hurried after the man.

His clothes were filthier than necessary, she thought, to make the almsman's costume seem real, and she wished he would not speak with such a froth of spittle. The rumors about Tullius had been untrue, he said. The centurion had not been sent home to Rome. Nor to Macedonia or Gaul.

"Where is he?"

"We do not know. But somewhere in Palestine."

"It is said that he is crazed—and does not remember anything."

"That also is not true."

He did not continue for a moment, but stared at her steadily, and she knew what he was telling her. She had been identified.

"Why have I not been arrested?"

"You are their *fatuus.*"

The *homo fatuus*—the brainless soldier, the unsuspecting dupe sent forward to draw the enemy's fire. In this case, more accurately, the brainless woman who would lead the Romans to the nest of rebels.

"You must not be foolish," he said.

"How do I avoid being foolish?" she said.

Her instructions then: Forget the name of every Zealot she had ever met. Talk to no one about her experiences, neither friend nor enemy. Make herself as invisible as possible.

"Wouldn't it be better if I did not exist?"

"We do not kill our friends."

When the mendicant had slid off into an alleyway, she wondered in what way the rebels could still consider her a friend. She was a danger to them now, and had never been a credit to their zealotry. And now the austere warning: she could no longer make common cause with them.

Only her own, private cause. Tullius was still in Palestine.

The following day she went to an apothecary who several times had brought medicaments to her father. He was a skilled old Jew whom even the Romans patronized. Suppose there were a Roman officer who was ill or wounded, she asked, where would he go to convalesce?

"Rome."

"Where in Palestine?"

"Caesarea, by the sea. Or the new place."

"What is the new place?"

"They call it Refectio. It is a refuge for convalescents."

"Where is it?"

"Up there—the northern foothills—beyond the Pool of Bethesda."

An hour later, she knocked on the door of Itschak Bar Haruz, a dealer in precious metals. He was a craftsman in his own right, a skilled silversmith, but latterly had become almost exclusively an importer of finished work. Much in debt to her father, Itschak was anxious to please.

"A silver wristlet, you say?"

She nodded. "For a man."

"I have a number of them."

"It must be from Rome."

"This one is Roman."

"And it must be enclosed in Roman packings."

"Here are Roman packings. Choose."

She chose and he carefully packed the handsome bracelet in the wool-padded wooden box.

"You must be certain to send it anonymously," she warned him, "as a gift from an unknown admirer in Rome. Only your own name and address must appear on the parcel, in case it has to be returned."

"Why should it be returned?"

"If the man is not there."

He asked to whom and where the gift was to be sent. She gave the information. Tullius Cato Nisus, Centurion. Refectio.

"Send it immediately," she said. "I will return tomorrow to see if it was delivered—and accepted. And I will want some sign that he received it."

"What sign?"

"His seal will do."

The following day she returned to the silversmith. The bracelet had been delivered and accepted. The centurion had no seal, the merchant reported as he handed her a *tessera* no larger than her thumbnail. In the glaze of the tile were Tullius's initials.

She walked out onto the street. She did not know what time of day it was, whether it rained or the sun shone, or whether to walk east on the cobbled hill, or west. None of it mattered. Knives.

She had hardly begun to formulate her plan when she was arrested. A *quadrum* of soldiers surrounded her in their square, and led her, walking, to the Antonia fortress. As the four legionaries marched her through the city streets, she stared straight ahead, scarcely blinking.

In an airless, stone-walled room, she was confronted by a subcenturion with bad breath and carious teeth and by the *quaestor,* who, in the dankness of this hole, turned into a reptile. He kept clawing at her with his questions, lashing as if with a tail. Lies, he kept saying, when you cannot name a single doctor who attended you, a single nurse, when it is known that you once helped a Zealot to escape, when you are still one of them; who is Simon Zelotes? where is the man called Manasseh of Chorazin, and where is Barabbas?

I do not know any of them, she said, you are making my head spin, I will say anything to please you, will it help you if I make up stories that are untrue?

For two days they withheld food and questioned her. On the third day, a tribune appeared. He looked exasperated, not by her, but by them. They went away and she heard them whispering in the corridor, but could not make out their words. Someone has made an error, she thought: it was not meant for me to be arrested.

That afternoon, they released her.

"Why did they let you go?" her father asked.

His face was white with worry. As he held the burning taper to the wick of the second lamp, his hand shook. She wondered how much to tell him, how much he wanted to hear, how much he could stand.

"They let me go because they want me to lead them to . . . my friends."

He did not ask who her friends were. He blew out the taper.

"Is that all you want to know?" she asked.

"Your friends are Zealots. That much I assumed."

"That is right."

"The months you were away . . ."

"I was with them."

"A Zealot?"

"Yes."

"The Zealots are murderers."

"They are rebels."

"There is a rumor that you . . . killed."

"I never killed anyone."

"Oh, thank God!"

"But I must tell you—"

He was not listening. "Thank God, thank God!" He held his hands against his breast and he was swaying backward and forward, as if in prayer, in thanksgiving. Thank God, he kept repeating, thank God.

She waited for him to be still again. Then she said: "I did not kill anyone. But I caused the death of four people. Three Romans and a Jew."

"I do not want to hear it!" But suddenly he seemed to realize there was no escaping anymore. He dealt with it as best he could, by temporizing. "You say you 'caused' the death. It is not the same as killing. Who knows who causes what?"

"Papa—"

"We think we make things happen—but we delude ourselves! Nothing! We cause nothing! We are helpless, we cannot stir a leaf!"

Stay gentle, she told herself, stay calm, don't let him hear how frantic you are.

"Papa . . . it will be better—believe me, it will be better for both of us if you know the truth. I *did* cause those deaths to happen. I paid for those Romans to be killed."

She could see him making a desperate effort to face whatever horror she would tell him next. "Very well," he murmured. "Let us say that you had something to do with the death of those three Romans—"

"—and one Jew."

"Let us say that. Admitted—between the two of us. But that does not mean you are a Zealot. And all of that—everything—it has passed. It's over now, finished. It has to be forgotten, you understand—it is all in the past!"

"And in the future as well."

"No! Mary!"

"There were seven of them. Three soldiers are still alive—and the centurion."

"Forget them. Mary, I said forget them!"

"I will never forget them."

"Mary—please—no! You will not lay a hand—"

"I will kill every one of them. And Tullius, the first."

"I said no! You will kill yourself—and all of us—all of us!"

He started to quake, his whole body in spasms, as if with palsy. And suddenly it was as though the sick terror had afflicted him again. He was in a paroxysm, his limbs convulsed, his eyes rolled back in his head.

"Father . . ."

No, he kept yelling, no. He was trying to fight his seizure and fight her as well. As she tried to put comforting hands upon him—go away, he cried, go away!

Driven off, she stood at a distance, not daring to approach him again, not knowing what to do or how to help him.

For a long time he stood in the middle of the room, quaking, trembling to pieces, too unstrung to sit down, and refusing to fall. At last, when he was somewhat recovered from his throes, he subsided into the large chair which he had always completely filled; now he was too small for it. He moved to the left side of the seat, occupying only part of the space, and he clung with both hands to a single armrest. He was gripping it hard, forcing the return of his control. At last he spoke with surprising evenness:

"I cannot let you kill yourself. Or kill me. If you do not give me your word that there will be no more acts of revenge, you may not live here anymore. Do you understand me?"

"Yes."

"You will promise to give it up?"

"No."

"Mary, please—!" He started to tremble again, then seemed to tighten every muscle. "It isn't only that your presence is a danger. I can't bear the thought of you destroying yourself. I can't bear it! I can't be a witness to your death!"

"I understand, Father. I'll go away for a while."

"Forever!" He started to weep in helplessness and heartbreak.

She could not endure his outcries. The man was in agony, as she was. She yearned to take him in her arms and console him as she had done through all his illness, but she knew that those times were over. Now, however, she realized that it was she who needed the embraces, needed arms around her, needed a loving word, at least a word of forgiveness. But those times, too, were over, and it made her ache.

The following day Joram told her that he had paid for her passage on the *Naias,* which would set sail for Alexandria on Tuesday, at sunrise. He also arranged for her transport to the harbor in Caesarea, and extended to her a white woolen pouch which, he said, contained a hundred golden shekels.

She did not take it. A trip to Alexandria had not been in her immediate plans. Her mission was here: Tullius. But her father pointed out to her that Roman surveillance would become tighter. And implicit between them now was the fact that she was no longer welcome at home. In fact, her father himself, without meaning to do so, might in some perverse way cause her capture.

The best thing now would be a tactical retreat, a temporary one, until the hue and cry subsided.

Alexandria. She did not want to go. And she recalled with a pang of irony how she had once longed for an Alexandrian adventure.

She changed her mind and accepted her father's gift of the pouch of shekels. It was the last money Mary ever had from him.

⁂

The ship was still far out at sea, it appeared to her, when she caught her first glimpse of the Pharos. There it was, beaming a pathway on the waters, the lighthouse of Alexandria. What a pride of loftiness, the tallest structure in the world, built for but a single purpose, to lighten the darkness of the sea. The darkness of her soul as well, she thought, as if it shined upon her alone, offering a refuge, welcoming her to the city of wonders.

When they put into the harbor it was early dawn and the embers in the beacon fires were still aglow. I have the best of both lusters, she thought: sunrise and the Pharos.

The wharves, as she disembarked, were as busy as broad daylight. There was never a minute, the captain had said, when a ship was not loading or unloading, and every corner of the world was accounted for in arrival or departure. The people: from everywhere, the sailors in leather or sackcloth or even silk, the slaves with shaven pates or turbans or colored markings on their skin, the slit ears and the numbered foreheads, the ones with ringlets in their noses. Shouts, bickerings, a quarrel about parcelment, a theft of saddlery, a crate of pigeons broken and the birds in flight, the Roman customs officers making levies and taking bribes, the Jewish peddlers and importers with lists on chits of paper, the soldiers and centurions waving their swords and slashing through sunbeams, the Greek interpreters shouting in Syriac and Celtic and Aramaic and Phoenician. And passengers from everywhere, Crete, Parthia, Cathay . . . Caesarea.

By messenger, an Egyptian boy, she sent word to Caleb that she was here. Then she waited.

In less than an hour, she recognized her brother's carriage, although she had never seen it before. It was in the Magdala style, exactly like her father's and her own, black and gold. Except: four horses instead of two. And her handsome brother, looking like an Alexandrian Greek, hair oiled and curled, white tunic with flickers of gold, jeweled rings on fingers and toes.

They embraced. What a warming, engaging smile he had; she had forgotten how much blandishment was in it. You are always the same, she told him admiringly, except for the gilt and the gloss, and the tighter crimping of your beard. He replied that she, too, was the same, but she saw that he lied.

"There are only two of us," she said as they were riding away from the harbor. "Why do you need four horses?"

"Two to pull and two to bluster." He grinned. It was the old Caleb, all right, every minute of his life a strut, every passage a parade, while he aped and competed with an image, the Greek god. What a bitter battle he was waging with the Apollo he impersonated.

And winning it right now. He drove recklessly, showing off and showing off the city. Proud of Alexandria, he displayed the great metropolis as if he owned and had created it. Light of the world, he called it, bigger and better and older and younger and brighter and blacker and prettier and uglier and more of everything than any city ever created. And he was right. The Jewish quarter, where he did not live, had more Jews than in all of Palestine; the Greek section, where he did live, had more poets and artists and philosophers than Greece had known in all its golden ages; the Egyptian quarter, he said, where never, not even in the rein of the pharaohs, had death been rendered such a rite of beauty; the Aphrodition, the lovers' market, where could be procured such delights and diseases of the flesh as had never been written in the annals of pleasure and pain. And best of all—best especially for his sister—

"Do you still have a rage for books?"

No. Other rages. "Yes, I do," she said.

"The Library—we have such a library—! You will sprout a hundred heads on your shoulders!"

They drove through the Brucheum section, the magnificent royal area of the city, then out of their way to gaze at the museum that housed the Library. Something about the edifice was beyond her understanding: how it could be so awesomely majestic yet so exquisitely dainty. It was the riddle of its contents, perhaps: some said there were more than a million books, so many that a great number had to be housed elsewhere, in the Serapeum, so many that they had never been counted.

The Street of Canopus then, regally colonnaded and broader than any thoroughfare she had ever seen, wide enough for twenty chariots abreast. Trees dressed in royal purple, flowers along every walkway, urns of greenery, and flower boxes dripping roses. Flags and pennants flying, flapping in the seaborne breeze, slashing and splashing their colors into the sky. She asked him why the banners, what was the festival?

"Alexandria."

A city celebrating itself, it lifted her spirits. I will make a pleasant, temporary life here, she thought.

In the Greek section, the avenue Caleb lived on was called the Flight of Hermes. The dwellings were built like Grecian temples, with columns and pediments and statuary on the porches. Caleb's house was a smaller version of the real thing, too pretentious for its diminutive size.

Indoors, it was more comfortable than its pompous pillars had suggested. The rooms were commodious although not large, with panels on the walls painted in rich reds and blues, and a wealth of softness on the floors and benches—rugs and cushions of wool and silk—and flowers in amphorae. And the surprising thing: the sculpture. Statues, miniatures for the most part, everywhere, on tables and in niches and on pedestals. A tiger's head made of terra cotta, a low relief in marble of gods and goddesses, a sea nymph in clay, a cedarwood carving of two children asleep, a marble bust of Athena which had been broken and mended. Mary ran her finger along the hairline crack that crossed the goddess's cheekbone.

"What a pity," she said.

"Fathers and graven images."

"Was he here?"

"Yes. I hid all the statues, but that one was too heavy—so I covered it. He took the cover off, pushed it off the plinth, and called me an apostate."

"Are you an apostate?"

"No."

"Are you still a Jew?"

". . . No."

"If you are not a Jew, then aren't you an apostate?"

He tried to smile, but she could see that he was off balance. And irritated. "Are there only two choices?"

"Probably not." She made an effort to be affable. "Would you like to call yourself a Greek?"

"Do I have to call myself anything?" His annoyance sharpened. "Do I have to be something with a name?"

She hesitated. "I think . . . yes. Something."

"What are you?"

"I am . . . I think I am a Jew. I cannot imagine being anything else."

"You mean God? All of it?"

"I don't know about all of it."

She had, of course, brooded over the extent of her Jewishness. But had never set any limits, certainly not aloud. Hearing herself, she was distressed. She needed a different subject. "When he comes to Alexandria, where do you meet? Not here, surely."

"No, he wants to imagine this house doesn't exist. I meet him at an inn near the Brucheum."

There was someone at the threshold. Caleb beckoned her into the room. She was a young woman, perhaps eighteen, tall and blond, small-breasted but broad-hipped, with a warm, moist mouth that seemed to be made for only small movements, for murmuring.

Caleb presented her to his sister. "This is Elva—she and her brother do the tasks."

The girl nodded and smiled a bit more than necessary, then said something Mary could barely understand. It was the Alexandrian street talk—Greek, with Egyptian slurs and contractions, not like the Attic she had learned.

"You will get used to it," Caleb said with fond amusement. "She wants to know if you're hungry. It's early for 'the midday,' but the meal is ready, if we want it."

She wanted first to bathe. The ship had been frugal with water, she said; her last bath had been in the sea, near Caesarea, five days ago; it seemed a century. Elva giggled over this and so did Caleb, and her brother explained that to Alexandrians nearly everything is funny: the lack of money or water, slips of the tongue, breaking wind at table, sneezing, hiccuping, rips in clothing, the heaviness of Latin, drunkards, the clumsy bluster of Roman soldiers, premature emissions in the bed, the mispronunciation of a name.

They summoned her brother, Thars, a few years younger than his sister and just as blondly beautiful. In a bustle, the two servants started to draw Mary's bath. The bathing area was in a corner of the garden, quite private, enclosed by vine-covered trellises. The tub was a large ceramic swan, pale blue, its wings spread wide to serve as trays. From the nearby well, just outside the enclosure, the two young servants carried water in large amphorae and in a huge jar that they trundled together. Mary could scarcely take her eyes off the blond water-bearers; they were as perfect as garden sculpture.

"Where do they come from?"

"They're Celts, the northern kind. They say they're from Jutland, but I don't believe they really know."

"Are they slaves?"

"Yes, I bought them two for one. They were very cheap."

"How so?"

"The boy was sickly—at fourteen he looked ten. You wouldn't know to look at him now, but at the time—two years ago—he didn't seem worth keeping."

"Would you have bought him if they weren't brother and sister?"

"That's not why I bought him."

"Why, then?"

"Because they are married."

"Married?"

"Yes."

"But isn't there a law against a brother and sister—?"

"Who obeys the law in Alexandria? Anyway, they came as a parcel—I had to buy them as a pair."

"Are married slaves not separated?"

"Not generally. They are more valuable as a unit. They procreate."

"Will these two . . . procreate?"

"Well, they occupy the same bedroom."

She wondered why it did not shock her, and if it was a sign some moral fiber was weakening or strengthening. Or nonexistent.

Left alone, she found the bath was wonderful. The well water was cool and the sun was hot. She turned her face to the sky and stretched her arms onto the outspread wings of the blue swan. She lay there, splashing, lying still, splashing again, luxuriating.

Someone was coming. She looked for something to cover herself with. There was nothing within reach. Unnecessary, however, for it was Elva with a vial of cleansing oil. Without a word, as casually as if she had done it every day, the blond servant pulled the ceramic stopper out of the bottom of the tub, bade Mary stand up, and began to rub her with the oil, which, she said, she would wash off in the second rinsing.

As the first water gurgled out upon the grass, the Celtic girl smoothed the unguent over Mary's body, cleansing her, massaging her, smoothing the soft pleasure of oil over her back, her belly, arms, breasts, and into all the most private places. The visitor's tension eased, she gave herself to every stroke, she voluptuated, as if her skin and flesh were hungry for these fondlings.

Again she heard footsteps on the gravel, and she tightened. The boy was at the archway of the arbor, carrying an amphora of water in each hand. His sister scarcely seemed to notice his presence, but continued applying the oil. The young man looked unashamedly at Mary's body and nodded soberly as if every mound and curvature were exactly as he had imagined. Setting one of the amphorae on the ground, he started to pour the contents of the other into the tub.

"It will be a little cold," he said.

"Yes," Elva agreed, "it will be a little cold."

Then they both giggled.

Mary felt gooseflesh. The boy noticed it and gently reached out his hand and smoothed the skin of her arm.

It was not the cold that had made her shiver.

Mary felt as if she had been born in Alexandria. There was no area of the city that seemed alien to her; she was a native everywhere. It was easy, of course, to feel at home in the Jewish quarter, for the Hebrews had tried to make another Jerusalem of it and had, in large part, succeeded, except that its numerous synagogues did not substitute for the one great Temple. Nowhere did she feel she was in a foreign country. In the Brucheum she was a Greek; in the Rhacotis, an Egyptian; almost overnight she learned to inflect the street talk in one dialect or another;

she ate the different foods with a variety of pleasures, and moment by moment she lost her Jewish qualms about living among the forbidden statuary. How potent her sensuous enjoyments were in mitigating guilt.

She was puzzled—and somewhat disquieted—by what she experienced in the Library. Not that she felt any disappointment in the place itself; it was more than she had ever imagined. The edifice was exquisite, walls of stone warmer than stone should be, perfect in the proportion of its spaces. The room with the collection of Babylonian clay tablets was diminutive because the tablets were diminutive, many of them no larger than a single joint of her little finger; then there were the moderate-sized rooms of the *membranae*—the leathers and parchments, skins of a hundred kinds on which men had registered the chronicles of their beings. Last of all, the great magnificence, the hall of the papyri. Long, seemingly endless scrolls, thirty, forty feet tall, hanging on the farthest wall, lighted through high, balcony windows—a blaze of color. Illuminations in the richest hues she had ever seen, some pigments so radiant that they shimmered, some so subtle that they seemed like the afterthoughts of shadows. At one of them, an old man stood on a lofty scaffold, simply reading what was written. Every half hour or so, he would loosen the sennit ropes so he could descend a little from his aerial heaven. She wondered if he really wanted to come to earth.

One of Mary's particular pleasures in the Library was the use of the *pitakes,* the catalogue of books. She had never heard of such a thing. Imagine, she said, just imagine: a million books, and the *bibliothecarios* will bring you whatever you ask for.

Whatever you ask for: That was the crux of her disquiet. She could not decide what to read, what to study. She no longer knew what she wanted to know. Not that she didn't have a thousand questions. But they were a gnarl of knots in her mind. Her brain felt like a clenched fist. What had happened to all those vibrant curiosities? How could she reach them again, how could she reawaken her hunger for knowing?

The biblio boy stood waiting. *The Iliad,* she said.

She did not read all of *The Iliad.* Only the section where Achilles avenges the death of Patroclus.

The biblio boy again. *The Medea.*

She did not read all of *The Medea.* Only the section where Medea avenges her betrayal by her husband.

The day she realized that vengeance was all she wanted to read about, she stopped going to the Library. And the Forum took its place in her affection.

There were many things to magnetize her to it. The smell of exotic foods from everywhere, the taste of wines from Athens and Persepolis, the Celtic meads, the tree-sap liquors from Macedonia; the sensual, sinful pleasure of eating and drinking outdoors, in public places, without the disapproving glances of the Jerusalem Pharisees. And the charlatans, the gleeful and the sly ones, the Chaldean soothsayers and Babylonian astrologers, the metalsmith from Cappadocia who could turn lead to gold, the Parthian with love potions.

Her favorite section of the Forum was a cool and shady byway made intimate by a grove of carob trees. To it came the oldest Jews of Alexandria, and once in a while their company was graced by the presence of Philo, the sage. He was known the world over, wherever Hebrews spoke of wisdom. And Mary loved to sit a bit apart from them and eavesdrop on the rabbi's counsel. The questions ranged from the divine to the preposterous.

"Rabbi, my wife and my son are constantly in quarrel. Whose part should I take?" . . . "Neither the woman's nor the man's. Only the part of justice."

"My son will be Bar Mitzvah. Yesterday he asked me, 'Is there truly only one God?' I know the answer, but what *reason* can I give him?" . . . "He said 'truly.' He has not asked for reason, but truth. Reason is at the service of anything, even of falsity. But truth serves only itself. One God is the one truth."

"Rabbi, I have two sons. They are both unkind to me, and I do not know to which of them I should leave my wealth. They both insult me, they hurt me—like my rectal trouble: whichever buttock I sit on gives me pain. What shall I do?" . . . "Give your wealth to the poor, and leave your sons your rectal trouble."

Mary especially loved the Forum in the early evening. With the oil lamps alight and the distant glow of the Pharos, and the sea so close, it was a terrace of enchantment. Zithers and lyres played, and lovers promenaded. Always, from somewhere and nowhere, a voice was singing, sweet and distant and plaintive.

What she liked best of all was the presence of unescorted women. In Judea, her father had frequently reprimanded her for daring to walk alone at night. He said it was unsafe; she felt that he meant not respectable. But in Alexandria, the most respectable women—young and middle-aged and old, punctiliously dressed—walked the cobbles of the Forum and the planking of the harbor walkways, and even the long causeway to the lighthouse—without danger or shame. To see women so free and so safe and so respected was, to Mary, the essence of Alexandria's enlightenment. How humane it was, how civilized!

"They are all harlots," Caleb said.

She was shocked, she was angry. "You have an evil mind," she retorted. "If you see a woman alone at night, she is a harlot. I walk alone there at night—and I am not a harlot. I see old women there—well dressed—with soft voices and quiet smiles—do you dare to call them harlots?"

"They are procuresses."

"I don't believe it."

"What do you think they are, walking the Forum at night all by themselves? Famous philosophers? Ministers of state?"

"They are women!"

"Which means that they are nothing! If they are not harlots or procuresses, they have no work! I've told you this before—do you remember? A woman is a queen or a wife or a harlot. And that is as true in Alexandria as it is in Jerusalem."

"It will not be true of me!"

"Of every woman! You had better marry quickly."

"I will never marry."

"Well, you will certainly not be a queen."

"Are you so odious as to think I have only the third alternative?"

He did not answer. They had been sitting outdoors on the peristyle at the garden side of the house. He arose and walked to the stairway; she also arose and went indoors. She stayed in her room during the evening meal. On first seeing this bedchamber, she had thought how restfully spare and uncluttered it was; now it seemed barren.

Alternatives. None that her brother had suggested was even remotely thinkable. One was a mockery, the other two were aversions she could never overcome. Then, what could she do for a livelihood? She had not even thought in terms of a vocation. Being a daughter had been her vocation, and now she was without employment. Disinherited. For the moment, she was her brother's guest, but tomorrow or next week she would be an unwelcome appurtenance, dependent upon him for food and lodging and an occasional trinket reluctantly bestowed. It made her blood run cold.

At dawn the following day she went down to the Forum and looked at it with new eyes. From being a place of divertissement it became—overnight—a battleground of occupations. In her mind she took the field against every task she saw performed as if it were an adversary, and pondered whether she could vanquish it. And whether she would be given a *chance* to vanquish it. The answers she confronted were dispiriting. There was nothing she was trained to do, nothing she wanted to do. She had, of late, been training herself for another pursuit.

The pursuit of revenge. It was her calling, her cause, but not, strictly speaking, an enterprise designed to pay for place and provender. Yet it was a mission she could never give up. If vengeance was her first principle, survival would have to be secondary.

But how to survive? She thought of playing a musical instrument in the Forum, but she had had only a few lessons on the psaltery, without notable promise; she thought of singing for coppers, but melody was only in her mind, not in her vocal cords; she thought of going to the theater in the Brucheum and offering her services as an apprentice actress, but she had no gift for pretense; honesty was her greatest talent and her besetting vice.

Having given up the Library, she now returned to it, but modified her reading habits. She did not ask for books that dealt with retribution, but took to reading whatever seemed apposite on vocations. Everything, however, was written for men. And one day she forced herself to notice what she had tried to ignore: in the main reading chamber of the Library, she was the only woman. It depressed her deeply.

Her low spirits were not elevated by the widening distance between herself and her brother. She knew that part of his alienation was a paradox: he felt ineffectual in being unable to help someone he loved, so he started—pointedly, it seemed to her—to ignore her presence. When he did acknowledge it, he could barely conceal his disapproval—of her Jerusalem clothes, her Judean accent. She thought he was growing contemptuous, and she did not know what to do with the hurt, or with herself.

One evening, before dinner, everything reversed. He came rushing indoors, took hold of her, whirled her around the room and shouted:

"We're going to a party!"

No ordinary party would have put the man in such a transport, for he was always larking about with one woman or another, at festivities that were only occasionally respectable. But this celebration would be better than respectable, it was to be given by Egyptian nobility.

"Is there still an Egyptian nobility?"

"Well, no—but there's Entemia."

"Entemia? It sounds like an infection. What is it?"

"Not what—who. She is the closest thing to royalty that we have here. If there's a drop of pharaoh's blood left in any Egyptian, it's in her veins. The rest of her is Ptolemaic."

"Which part of her gives parties?"

"The influential part. She knows every diplomat in Alexandria, every money merchant—and Roman generals, Greek philosophers, Arabian astronomers, artists from everywhere."

He restrained the rush of gaiety and looked at her with a quieter pleasure. "And if there's a creditable vocation for you anywhere in this city, Entemia will introduce you to it."

With a surge of hope, she embraced him, made noises of delight—and went white. "I have nothing to wear."

The following day he brought her a present, a gown so extravagant that it made her tingle.

"These spangles—are they real gold?"

"Gold-dipped. Jupiter, if they were solid gold they would have cost a ransom."

"A ransom anyway. Please don't tell me how much it cost. How beautiful, how marvelously vulgarly beautiful!"

But she had an apprehension. When she hurried off to her bedroom to try it on, her dread was justified. The gown was designed to expose one breast. With a catch in her throat, she realized how much she had altered from the girl who had willfully, wantonly cut down the bodice of another dress in order to go nearly naked to Pilate's party. It worried her: What was the essence of the change in her? Was it that she had lost her courage, her recklessness? Yes, it was that. The rape had robbed her of a precious self-confidence. Or was it pride of body? She no longer was proud of her breasts; they were shameful things to her. It was not merely that she could not wear the beautiful dress; it was that she could never again wear her own beauty. And she had a forlorn sense of a lost loveliness, forever gone and irretrievable.

She heard a knock on the door. With a start, she folded her arms, covering herself.

Caleb took only a step or two into the room. He saw his sister flushed with shame and did not advance upon her.

"Dear God, what's the matter?" he said.

"Nothing—this dress—"

"What about it? It fits you perfectly—you'll be dazzling."

"I—no—I can't wear it."

"Of course you can. It was made for your face, it was made for your body!"

"I'm naked."

"Mary—"

"I'm naked, I'm naked!"

Slowly, step by gentle step, he crossed the room. She cringed at his closeness. He spoke to her tenderly, as to a child:

"You must listen to me, my sweetness. You have worn a dress even more revealing than this. You were beautiful then, and you are beautiful now. You must forget whatever has happened in your life to make you think otherwise. You are beautiful—remember that—always remember it. Now . . . take your arms away."

"No."

Softly: "Take your arms down, sweetness."

"No—please. Go away—no."

Slowly, with the utmost tenderness, he reached to her, laid his hands on her arms, and for a moment held them there. When he saw that she did not withdraw, he delicately drew her arms apart and let them drift downward away from her bosom. But one of his hands was still there, almost touching her breast. And his eyes were upon her in a caress.

"How beautiful you are."

❖

Caleb's carriage took them through the swarm of the Egyptian quarter. Unlike the commodious avenues of the Greek and Jewish sections, the streets of the Rhacotis were narrow and stingy, without a tree or blade of grass, the gutters running with waste, the pathway pitted, mucky. The carriage stopped a dozen times, changing its route to avoid the living obstructions in the thoroughfare, dogs and children, adults as well, who loitered and chattered and dozed outdoors to avoid the heat and the humid infestations in their wretched little rooms.

Although Entemia's villa was also in the Rhacotis, it seemed a different country, park and woodland, the air now as fresh as it had been putrid, and, except for the sounds of the wheels and the horses, they were enveloped in the quiet of a soft summer's night.

There were no houses in public view. Once in a while, out of hidden places, there would be a glint of armor—one of the *custodia privata*, Caleb said, a retired Roman soldier, now a mercenary guard.

Suddenly there were many of them, eight or ten, then a glimmering of lamps lighting the sky and faint strains of music.

Villa was a modest word for Entemia's domicile. It was a mansion, a temple, a palace; all of these, and none. Whatever the edifice purported to be, it was Egyptian. And old. No matter that Caleb said it had been built within the past decade, in the flicker of the oil lamps there was an ancient cast upon the place, suggesting the departed centuries of Gizeh or Karnak. Bordered by carved columns in the hypostyle fashion, it was massively erected out of rusty granite and the white limestone of Sinai. The exterior walls were painted in the classical archaic colors, ochers and reds, and the varying shades of cuprous blue-and-green—life scenes of pharaohs, priests, lovers, hunters, masons, farmers; and everywhere the gods, Osiris and Isis and Horus, and the beasts of death and divinity, apes and jackals and hawks. All quite terrifying in their grim simplicity, all meticulously aged, the vivid-hued distempers now faded and worn, abraded away by artful hands, so that they seemed painted not by pigments but by time. What an exquisite gloom!

But not indoors. Lamps on walls and hanging from the ceilings, candelabra in the hands of slaves, and music from lyres and citharas and reeded pipes, with men dancing in the new Greek fashion of the theater while their ladies watched and clapped their hands and swayed. And the colors: mantles and dresses so vivid that they gave back all the glints they took from the lamps. Every kind of raiment, imaginable and unimaginable, from places she had read about but never believed existed, caftans and kirtles, peplums and burnooses, habiliments of silk and wool and fur and feathers, headdresses in shocks and manes and tresses, and everything glittering in gold, glittering in jewels, glittering. Even the music seemed to glitter.

Out of all this brilliance, coming toward them, was the most shimmering star in the firmament—a black star. Except for the stark whiteness of her face, everything about her was jet—a mantle of onyxes, black hair and black combs, and a line of kohl around her almond-shaped black eyes. She could be forty perhaps, Mary thought, but there was a timelessness, a beauty that spoke of perpetuity.

She extended both hands to Mary. "I am Entemia," she said. "Welcome to Egypt."

Not merely to her house, nor to Alexandria, but welcome to all of Egypt, as though she were its empress. And Mary felt that, until this moment, she had not officially arrived.

Entemia looked at Caleb. "Your sister is even more exquisite than you described."

In a flutter of self-consciousness, Mary's hand went to her breast. The Egyptian, except for her bare countenance, was totally covered, down to her gloved fingertips. Although Mary's dress was by no means the most revealing in the room, Entemia's decorousness made her feel nude.

But the woman's warmth was easing away all her discomfiture. In a glow of cordiality, she dismissed Caleb. "Go and dance. I want to speak with your sister."

And she knew exactly what to talk about, the only subject they had in common, Caleb. "The women of Alexandria will dismantle him with their love."

She said it with affectionate good humor, and Mary smiled. "I don't think Caleb will dismantle so easily."

Entemia looked at her more directly. "Do you see him always in one piece?"

There was something ambiguous in the question. Unsettling. "Do you mean do I see him as one person?"

"No. I think we would both agree he is more than one person. I meant: will he fall apart?"

Unsettled by the woman's directness, Mary retorted, "Caleb? Never."

She could see that Entemia was not being unkind. The woman touched her arm in a friendly way. "I want you to know—I have been married twice, and have had enough of it. Enough of everything. I have no interest in your brother beyond my deep fondness for him. And he concerns me. I have never known a man so in love with beauty—yet he buys and sells money, which he considers ugly. I think he is a spiritual man who was born into an unspiritual religion. What can we do for him?"

"Do you suppose we could make him a new God?"

The instant she said it she was sorry. Sarcasm, like the woman's headlong engagement of her, was premature. Entemia was genuine—and caring. She was certainly more knowledgeable about her brother than Mary was; she had been a whole sea closer to him, and was more sensitive to whatever distresses he was going through. She was Caleb's friend, and had worried about him. Mary's arrival had given her an opportunity to give expression to her misgiving.

Entemia, watching her, said gently: "You needn't say that you're sorry. I know you are."

Mary suddenly felt warm, she felt fortunate. Caleb's friend was going to be her friend as well. "Thank you," she said.

"Come with me."

Furtively, beckoning her guest to follow, the hostess stole away from her party. She opened a path, through one lavish room after another, some with guests and some without, onto a deserted corridor. It was dimly lighted only by wax tapers in sconces. Then up a stairway much narrower than the two main staircases of the house. At last into a huge dressing chamber. Hanging from iron bars and wooden racks, hundreds of cloaks, tunics, chitons, garments of every kind, and a myriad of shoes, sandals, underwear, waistbands. And scarves. It was the cupboard full of scarves that Entemia pointed to.

"Choose one."

Mary was puzzled.

"Choose the most beautiful one you can find—and cover yourself."

As the younger woman felt a flush of mortification, the older one touched her reassuringly. "Enough of that—stop being embarrassed. Three times, as we were talking, I saw you try to hide your breast with your hand. I say enough."

"I was stupid."

"Only a little," Entemia said with a smile. "Many women are beautiful on the surface. Their surfaces, therefore, have to be exhibited. Very few are beautiful to the depth—they need not expose their skins. You and I—we are deeply beautiful women."

They both began to laugh. In a flight of hilarity, they plucked at the pile of scarves, flinging the discarded ones into the air so that they seemed to float on the peals of laughter. No, not this one, it's too radishy red, laughter, how about this spangled idiocy, no, it makes your eyes look crossed, laughter, now here's a tawdry bawdry for you, laughter, laughter.

They found one that was as filmy and silvery as smoke, and Entemia draped it carefully around Mary's throat, then spread it downward across her breast, and hid the ends in the silken bodice of her gown. When it was finished, they started to laugh again, for it was clear to both of them that they had made Mary even more sexually tantalizing than before.

They descended one of the main stairways this time, and Entemia led the way through the dining hall, where tables were laden with great platters of food—meats, cakes, baskets of fruit, compotes of honeyed nuts, dates, raisins, the wild plums of the desert cactus.

Entemia put a glass in her hand and out of a ewer poured a liquid of clear crimson. It was *elixirion,* the Egyptian said, made of pomegranate juice, white wine and a spice or two. Pure nectar. Mary's head grew lighter. The world lighter too, easier to hold.

"Now you must meet the worthies," her new friend whispered.

The worthies were manifold and multiform. She met a metaphysician from Corinth, a poet from Mesopotamia, a geographer who had drunk too much *elixirion* and said the seas were full of burning islands, the devil's embers. She met a general from hither and an emir from thither; and a khan and a negus and a grand vizier from hereat and thereabouts and thence.

And their women, all their attractive women. That was what puzzled her. How was it possible to assemble in one evening in one place so many charming, tasteful, well-begotten people? It was all a reflection of Entemia.

She recalled the only other party of grandeur she had ever attended. Herod's party for Pilate. How the tastefulness of this one—people eating daintily, speaking in well-modulated voices, deferring to one another—contrasted with the vulgarity of the Roman debauch. Everything was so gracious here, so unstrained, so easy to enjoy . . .

Entemia murmured in her ear. "He has arrived."

For the first time, Mary saw a note of tension in the woman.

"Who has arrived?"

"Sejanus."

No wonder the tension. She felt it too. Nobody in the Roman Empire generated more loathing and cringing than Lucius Aelius Sejanus. He was the minion and minister of the Emperor Tiberius. If cruelty was commissioned by the Roman monarch, Sejanus executed it. And he had perpetrated enough in his own behalf. It was said that he hoped to be emperor one day, and had already poisoned Tiberius's son, Drusus. He had killed the wife of Rome's greatest general, Germanicus, and their two sons, so it was rumored, and had his cutthroats ready for

Germanicus himself. A Latin poem about him began: "Hemlock, gore and nightshade . . ."

He stood at the wide portal of the dining hall, surveying his audience. It seemed unjust that the man was not ugly. On the contrary, magnetic. Not that his appearance gave him any right to be; he was not tall, he was not slim, his features were not well-sculptured. But he had the reckless look of the wild, outcast animal, the quickness, the cunning, the predacity—and the deviltry.

Retainers behind him, he advanced toward his hostess. Apprehensive, Mary started to slip away. But Entemia reached for her. "Stay," she said.

When the minister was close enough to touch them, he wasted no time on salutations, nor did he seem to notice Mary's presence.

"I have not seen your house since the laying of the foundations," he said. "Why did you have them paint those beautiful pictures, then lay them all to waste?"

"Age, Sejanus."

"You Egyptians—you are always making love to your mummies."

She smiled. "It's a futility, isn't it?"

"I wish you had spent your money on a good Roman villa, with nice round arches."

"You don't like my house?"

"I don't like Egyptian architecture. Weight is not strength. And decay is not beauty."

"As if you Romans know about beauty."

"But we do."

Which was his cue for looking at Mary. "We certainly do. What is your name?"

Entemia said quickly, "Maria."

"Egyptian?"

"Greek," Entemia said.

"Has she no tongue? . . . Have you no tongue?"

"It is a bitter one," Mary said.

"Even before I have insulted you?"

"You have already insulted me."

"Have I? How?"

She was about to say that his very existence . . . but Entemia forestalled her. "Maria," she said in a hushed voice. "Maria, please."

"My name is Mary."

He looked from Mary to Entemia, then back to Mary again. He did not seem in the least put off by Entemia's lie. Rather, he seemed to be enjoying himself.

"Your dress is modish and it suits you," he said. "But this dreadful thing—" and he fingered the scarf "—it is a mischief of color. An afterthought, was it not?"

"This moment, I think it was a forethought."

Though his eyes narrowed at the indignity, he did not lose his composure. "You have just met me, girl. You may find me a man of some excellence when we are better acquainted. Why do you prejudge me?"

"I do not judge you at all. Your history does it."

"History?" Now he lost his equanimity. "History, do you say, *history?* Don't you know, girl, history is a liar?—don't you know that? Don't you know it is a cheat? Don't you know what history will say of me? It will spread rumors—false and despicable rumors!"

He was in a storm. His voice clamored and his arms sawed at the air. People turned to look, moved in closer, watched, listened.

Abruptly he was aware of his enlarged audience, and as quickly as his rampage had begun, he put an end to it—with a new inflection. In a show of oratory, converting his outrage into a declamation, he turned from one to another in the audience, as if to invite them into his mockery.

"Rumors, rumors! Can we believe the rumors that are spread about us? Dear friends and citizens, if we believe all the tattle and prattle—!"

Mischievously he stopped. With deviltry in his eyes, he challenged them. "I will tell you a rumor that is being spread about me. Let me see if you believe it. Listen, now—take heed."

He paused. It was as though he had stepped upon a stage. He looked at everyone as he told his story, he engaged one person, then another and another, and allowed no eye to wander.

"On an evening—years ago—when my father was the governor of Egypt—there came to me an Egyptian wizard from the desert west of Asyut. His name was Dazra and he was the wisest man I have ever known. He knew about embalming and he could decipher messages from the grave. He taught me to tell the future from the stars, how to read my signs and auspices, how to descry the different shades of white. I was in love with the man, with the stirrings of his brain, the darting surprises of his mind. And best of all, he was my friend—remember that, Dazra was my friend. . . . One day he came to me in great excitement. 'Tell nobody,' he said, 'tell nobody, but I have found the secret of the scarab.' He had discovered why the ancient Egyptians venerated the *scarabaeus,* a dirty little dung beetle that spent a lifetime rolling a little ball of manure into which it could lay its eggs. Why did they venerate this repugnant little vermin? Dazra, all by himself, had sniffed out the reason. The secret was in the word *khopri,* which means a god in the form of a beetle. And *khopri* is related to *khope,* which means 'transformation.' The beetle was the deity of the phenomenal transformation. What Dazra was talking about was too abstruse for me to understand. But then he added something that had an implicit meaning for me. 'There were Egyptians who were able to turn their mortal bodies into eternal souls.'

"Without entirely comprehending him, I was filled with eagerness. 'How?' I said. 'How did they make their souls eternal?'

"To which he replied that the mere possession of a golden scarab . . ."

" 'Can you get me one?' I asked him.

"It was almost impossible, he informed me. There were only a few sanctified scarabs left in the world, and they had all been stolen from the crypts of pyramids. Difficult to find, and exorbitant to purchase. Well, I lay awake nights dreaming of golden scarabs, I burned to own one. So at last I gave my wizard friend ten thousand golden denarii to buy me a scarab—and my eternity."

Sejanus paused and smiled grimly. "And you, of course, all know that he vanished with my money."

Again he halted. "However, that was not the end of him. I sent men out on searches, they sailed the waters, they swept the deserts. And we found him hiding in an Etruscan catacomb. The perfect place. I had him constrained and spread out upon a little gallery. Even though he was tightly bound in every limb, two strong men held his head as in a vise. Then I summoned sawyers, two of them. This is my friend, I said to them, and the wisest man I have ever known. Now, I would like you to saw off the cap of his skull. But do it neatly, so that the man may live. No, I said, do not bind his mouth—let the wizard scream.

"The screaming and the sawing sounds went on for quite a while. The blood pulsed in a rhythm so that it appeared the brain was beating like a heart. It was the part of him I loved and admired, the part that had betrayed me. So, while he was still alive, I took my knife and cut small pieces of his brain, all of which I ate. I ate his follies and his wisdom, I ate his lies and his auguries, and I ate the golden scarab he had promised me."

He paused and his eyes swept his audience. The spectators were struck with awe and horror. He smiled and, in the most cordial way, spread his arms wide. "Now—here I am—and that rumor has been noised abroad about me. Do you believe it?" Nobody seemed to breathe. "I ask you—do you believe that calumny?"

"No!" someone cried. Then others, no, no, false, untrue, it cannot be so, never, no.

He made a broad, imperious gesture of appreciation. Then he turned to Mary.

"How about you, my beautiful Jewess? Do you believe that rumor?"

"Every word."

He could not contain himself, he howled with laughter. At last, when his merriment had subsided, he studied her more intimately than before. Again he fingered the scarf about her throat. Quietly he turned to Entemia.

He pointed to Mary. "I will take this one," he said.

Without waiting for Entemia's response—or Mary's—he referred to one of his retainers. "Antenor—arrange the charges."

Mary felt faint. She could not believe what she was hearing. Frightened, angry, in a turmoil, she ran from the dining hall.

"Mary!"

It was Caleb's voice.

Running, running through the main corridor, through the crowds of people.

"Mary! Mary!"

Caleb did not catch up with her until they were outdoors. He tried to pacify her, to reason with her, but she broke away. She would have vanished altogether if she had had a conveyance of her own. As he was summoning his carriage, and while the grooms were bringing it, she walked away from him, escaping like a frantic creature from the flare of the lamps.

The carriage arrived, and when they were enroute:

"Why didn't you tell me you were selling me at a brothel?"

"I was not selling you."

"Why didn't you tell me!"

"Because you would not have come."

"You lied to me."

"I did not lie. Everything I told you about Entemia was the truth."

"Except what you omitted."

"What I omitted is not as reprehensible as you think."

"Not as reprehensible—? She is a harlot!"

"No. She sells harlots."

"That makes her the nobility you called her."

"That does not debase her any more than what we sell debases us."

"We do not sell whores!"

"You say that as if those women were dirty merchandise."

"They are."

"Well, we have sold dirtier merchandise in our day."

"Not wittingly."

"Winkingly."

"People, Caleb! She sells *people!*"

"And we buy! All our lives we have been served by people we have bought! Enna and Zabis and Duna—white people and black people—men as well as women—even children. Dear God—right now—in my own house—you are being served by slaves who were children when I bought them! Is it any worse that we buy slaves to clean our shit than it is that we buy them to lie down with us?"

"Yes, it is worse."

"Jupiter!"

"It is worse because lying down is our last privacy. We dare not sell it or buy it—or let it be invaded."

"Invaded! When will you ever forget those monsters?"

"Never! Certainly not while I see them all around me—in the same beautiful house—listening to the same music—drinking the same *elixirion.* Certainly not when a man who has boasted about eating a human brain reaches for the covering of my breast."

"There were other men there. I have been there many times."

"A plague on all of you!"

"You are the plague—you! You hypocrites, you are the plague."

"I am not a hypocrite!"

"Pharisee! Hypocrite!"

"I am not, I am not!"

"Pharisee, Sadducee, hypocrite! Sell the lamb for the sacred sacrifice, then steal the carcass! Marry in holiness in the Temple, then rut with the slave in a closet! But come to a city where the lovemaking is open and paid for and played in a clean bed—and you soil it with your lies and self-righteousness."

"I did not soil what was already soiled."

They drove on in silence. She could see that he was even more overwrought than she was. For all his defense of the Alexandrian custom, for all his self-justification, he was in no way a complacent man and he was shamefully facing his blunder, his guilt. Roiled, hurt by her and himself, he took his agitation out on the horses. She had never seen him cruel, not with slaves or inferiors of any station, never with animals, but now he cracked the whip, not in the air, but on their backs, and he cursed at them.

Hours later, when she was in her bedchamber and in her nightdress, she looked at the exquisite gown he had bought her. It lay on the floor in a heap. Undamaged and scarcely wrinkled, it seemed foul to her, contaminated. She did not know what to do with it.

Stooping, she picked up the garment. Carefully, as if it were untainted, she smoothed and folded it. Then, taking the silken thing with her, she left her bedroom.

Only a small lamp flickered on a wall of the corridor. She could hear her brother's voice downstairs—outdoors, likely—on the peristyle. He was drunk, and throwing things. Something ceramic perhaps, a drinking cup. And profaning everything and everyone. She heard Elva calling out, then Thars, and Caleb louder than the others, then the woman whimpering, then silence.

She had meant to return the gown to him, but this was not the time. So, passing his bedroom door, she meticulously laid the garment on the floor, just this side of the threshold.

It seemed hours later, and she was not asleep, when she heard a sound outside her room. Suddenly her door was flung open. He carried a lighted lamp in one hand and her dress in the other. His face was inflamed not only with drunkenness; she thought he might have been weeping.

"How do you dare to return this?" he shouted. "How do you dare to return my gift as if it were kitchen waste!"

"I do not want it anymore."

"It was a gift of love!"

"I was grateful—but I do not want it."

"What will I do with it?" His voice was a shriek.

She was frightened. "Caleb—go away."

"What good is it to me?"

Pulling her nightdress closer to herself, she got out of bed. "Caleb—please—I beg you—go away."

Dementedly, he shook the dress. "It is no good to me, no good!"

Suddenly, in a spasm, he held the dress over the flame, and it started to blaze.

"Caleb—Caleb!"

He dropped the lamp. The dress was blazing and he was still holding it.

She rushed across the room, and grappled with him for the flaming thing.

When the blaze was upon him, he stopped resisting and let the burning dress drift to the floor. She stamped on it and stamped. The sparks flew and her feet burned and she was afraid her nightdress would catch fire. He did nothing, he watched her.

"Help me—help me!"

And suddenly, when the fire was out, he grabbed her, he held her close.

"No—Caleb—let me go!"

He tried to kiss her, and as she broke away he clutched at her and at her nightdress, and it tore. Free, she started for the robe on her chair, and he reached for her, and stumbled. As he did, she began to struggle into her robe. But he pulled it away from her.

"Not more clothes—less!"

He threw the robe across the room and tore at the neck of her night thing.

"Caleb—! Please—"

He tore and tore and she was naked.

"Caleb, let me go!"

His hand was between her thighs. All varieties of pain came back to her, surging within her, and abruptly—her knee—as expertly as she had learned—the groin—once, and then again.

He moaned. He doubled over, moaned again, and knelt. But then he rose and reached for her again and her fist struck out, once and again and again, and he was no match for her.

Suddenly, as if he had been blinded, he stumbled from one place to another, making desperate little noises. She grabbed him and pushed him toward the door. The resistance had gone out of him. She reached for the latch, pulled the door open. There was no need to treat him roughly now. And all her anger was suddenly spent. Almost gently she nudged him over the threshold and into the hallway.

Alone in the bedroom, she took deep breaths and would not let herself surrender to the tremors. There was a smell of burning. She poured a ewer of water on the charred remains.

She tried not to tremble, breathed deeply again. How maniacal it all was. Her brother, however sick, however incestuous, loved her; and when he had tried to assault her she had done to him what she had been unable to do to those men of hatred. Ah well, the Zealots had taught her what to do. And she had learned her lessons well. Not well enough to kill the monster Tullius, but well enough to have killed her loving brother.

Love. No, love was a prating word. The blab of idiots.

She left Caleb's house in the early dawn, and never went back. Somehow, she would have to do life on her own. Do life, as if it were a task to be dispatched as quickly as possible, do it, and have it over with.

She had to find lodging, and she had little money. There were only two respectable inns in the city, and both were expensive. Nor could she afford a room in the luxurious Greek quarter. She wanted to live in the Jewish section, but for all her adherence to her heritage, she had a dread that if she could not meet the demands of Jewishness she might turn apostate, like her brother. Her only choice was the Rhacotis, because she could find cheap lodgings among the Egyptians, and anonymity.

Prices were higher than in Jerusalem, higher than she had expected. She had to settle for a smaller room than she wanted, in a less attractive place. It was a *hospitium* but inhospitable, a small building, a warren of rooms at the end of a twisting alleyway. Leaking in the rain, it welcomed waterbugs and beetles, none of them golden. Food, luckily, was inexpensive, for there was a market, where the cobblestones began, which called itself the Bazaar for the Empty-Handed, and she could buy low-priced goat milk and dates and cooked grains.

But there was no work. She offered herself as an apprentice to a score of tradesmen and craftsmen; there were always young boys who took precedence. When half of her money was gone, she tried to get chore work in sculleries or taverns, she offered to be a "slops" for the produce men in the harbor; more and more she heard the same replies: we have slaves who do this work—are you willing to subject yourself? Although she might agree to subject herself for a month or two, or even for a year, it appalled her how many workless people were willing to enslave themselves forever. They had no faith that life would ever improve; aliens, lonely, slavery meant belonging to someone. And many—the old and the sick—were not accepted, not even as slaves.

One day she came home to her room and found it ransacked. She felt a catch of dread that her money had been stolen. With bare hands, she rooted down below the cold coals in her cooking brazier. The shekels were all there. Subsequently, however, uncomfortable as it may have been, she wore her money in a sheepskin purse tied by a thong around her waist. It chafed her skin, but she was afraid . . .

Later, one evening just after sundown, she returned home after another disheartening day. She had seen a man slit his own throat in the marketplace, and it had not seemed altogether horrible; in fact, she had had a glimpse of logic. Perhaps the time might soon come, somewhere at the end of this dirty alleyway . . .

Someone struck her from behind. Then another pushed her to the wall and clutched her by the throat. The third was in her clothes, tearing, searching. He had the purse in his hand and was tugging at the thong. She kicked and scratched and tried to scream. The thong was tearing at her flesh. As she struck out, she felt a smashing blow in her face, and another. Something sharp, like burning ice. Another blow and another, and as she continued to fight back—

The memory of other beatings she had suffered—and the terrible realization: this is my lot with men, to be beaten.

Despair engulfed her. She stopped fighting.

Then, nothing. A long time, nothing.

At last she heard the voices, and someone offering things she did not want. Then thirsty, thirsty.

The liquid ran onto her lips and down her chin. She did not, for certain, know how to deal with it. Then she swallowed, and it was good. More, she said, give me more. Delicious. She remembered it from somewhere. More. It could have been the juice of pomegranates. What was the name of it? *Elixirion?* It was sweet and it was sour, it was cool and it burned. It was all opposites. More, more.

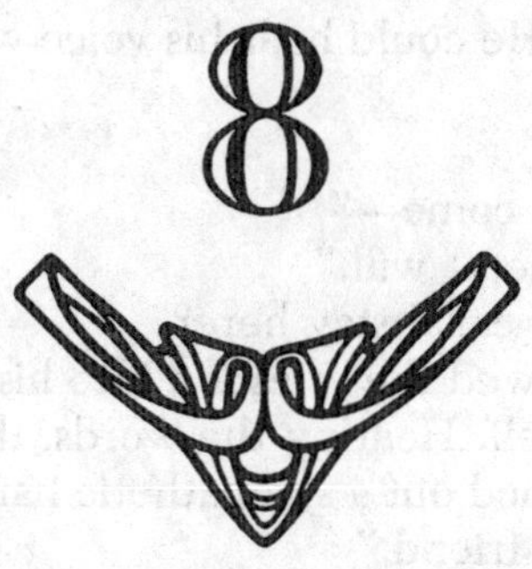

Tomorrow, Judas told himself, I will take my vow. Next week I will take it. On the evening of the new moon I will go to the Teacher of Righteousness and say, "I am ready."

New moons became old, Adar followed Shebat followed Tebet, and he did not take his vow. Nobody questioned him. Sometimes, in the scriptorium, Enoch would allude, with studied casualness, to other novitiates who had made their final pledges to the order. And on one occasion, old Ezriel, who was the keeper of the moneys and almoner to the poor, noted Judas's skill with sums and suggested that the young man should hasten and take his vow so that he might be entrusted with the office of cofferer. But no urgings, no importunities by anyone. Until Ezriel died.

Toward dusk one evening, in the room of contemplation, the Teacher of Righteousness said to Judas: "You have been here now—how long?"

"Two years, two months."

"It is a good time."

"Yes, it has been a good time."

"But you have hesitations."

"Yes."

"Doubts?"

"No, Teacher—I have no doubts."

"Then, do you not think that you are ready?"

"I . . . don't know. . . . How is one to know?"

"It is a question I should not have to answer."

"Please—how can I tell?"

"Some simply know. Others hear a voice—or find a meaning—or have a revelation. But all—I think all—are filled with a spirit of light."

"A spirit of . . ." He could hear his voice weakening. "I have not had it."

"You will."

"But if it does not come—"

"It will, believe me, it will."

"If it doesn't, how can I stay here?"

He had never allowed the question into his consciousness. Now it had simply uttered itself. Hearing the words, they frightened him.

The Teacher reached out a sympathetic hand. "You must not take your verses from your friend."

"He is no longer my friend."

"Whatever he is to you, he has left you an unfortunate precedent. Do not follow it—or you will go in misery to your grave."

He heard a lurking complacency; it provoked him. "Is everybody miserable who does not take the vow?"

"You are accusing me of pride."

"Yes, I am."

The possibility disquieted the old man. "Do you not—truly, I ask you—do you not see a difference between those of us who have taken the vow—and all the others?"

". . . Yes, I do."

"What is the difference?"

"You are at peace."

"Is that not precious? And all the rest, of little worth?"

"Yes . . . perhaps."

"Do you not want it?"

"Oh, dear God, I do!" he cried. "How do I get it? Please tell me how."

"That is the mystery." He spoke simply and with softness. "And when you take your vow, you will learn the secret."

The secret of the mystery, he thought as he walked in twilight toward his cell—that was what Jesus had forfeited. What a pity that he had come so close, had spent two years of his life to cast a light on the darkest enigma, and then, on the eve of revelation, had turned his back.

But perhaps he hadn't. Perhaps he did not need to be told the secret—*because he already possessed it.* Perhaps that explained why he was such an inspired teacher, why his hands held the gift of healing, why Judas loved him.

It was a lie that Jesus was no longer his friend. No matter how persuasively he told the old man—and himself—that his devotion to the Nazarene was over, he knew that he would love him unto death.

Sometimes he pretended that they were still together, that he had never shouted in anger at the man, that they were still walking the same pathways, asking one another the same conundrums in the Law, tossing pebbles into the same brook of learning. It was as if their conversations had never ceased, as if they continued endlessly and would go on forever. One discourse—which he had never had with Jesus—took form again and again:

"Tell me who you are," Judas would say. "You know all there is to know about me; now tell me who you are."

"I am what you see."

"No, you are not. Look at me, Jesus; is there a word of me that I haven't told? Is there any language that I speak—the touch of my hand, the caress of my eyes—my impatience—the enormity of my rancor—the pettiness of my petulance—the reckless haste of my conclusions—is there anything I say or do or try to conceal that you don't understand about me?"

"I believe what you tell me about yourself."

"Then, why don't you tell me who you are?"

"Because you see who I am."

"No, I do not. There is a mystery, there is a secret."

. . . On the second day of Pentecost, when females were admitted into the synagogue, one of the women loitered after the services were over and asked for Jesus. She was told that he had not been seen for many months. She seemed crestfallen. She had been seeking word of him from everyone, she said, and now, trying not to give in to her weariness, did not know where to turn.

Enoch, whom she was questioning, turned her to Judas. He was alone in the scriptorium when the woman entered. She was in her fifties, he would judge, and had once been round and pretty. Now her face was drawn and her eyes had sorrows in them. But she smiled. It seemed to Judas that the smiling mouth was sadder than the sorrowing eyes.

"My name is Mary," she said. "I come from Nazareth. They told me that you are a good friend to my son. His name is Jesus."

Her voice was like a coverlet against the cold. If she had not said "my son," Judas would have known.

"Yes, I am his friend."

That smile again. As if to a child who had offered her a precious keepsake.

"Do you know where I may find him?"

"No . . . I regret . . . no."

She looked away, not wanting to reveal her disappointment. She seemed confused, even embarrassed, like one who has asked an impolite question and has been rebuked. Then, more tangentially, she resumed:

"There is a man named Eben. He has a water cart. My husband, when he was alive, used to fashion wooden casks for him. He said—that is, my *husband* said—that oaken staves were far superior to . . ." She heard herself meandering and stopped. "There is another man in Nazareth who builds his casks these days. And when Eben came last winter, he said that Jesus was living here."

"Last winter, yes." He smiled in a friendly way. "Has it taken you so many months to come?"

"I did not want to come at all." Again the glance away from him. He thought: she is too diffident, poor woman, too easily abashed.

"Merely a visit . . . ?"

Her face took on a sadly knowing look. "Oh, it could never be 'merely a visit' . . . not to Jesus."

"What would it be?"

"Meddling."

"Really? No."

She did not answer, but this time did not look away. He might be wrong, he thought, about her diffidence. He must not mistake her sensitivity for weakness. Nor must he misunderstand her apparel, which was peasant's cloth, muslin and homespun, softened in many waters. Simple clothing, but not a simpleminded woman.

"You have a question," she said, "which you are much too kind to ask."

"Yes."

"If I did not meddle in the winter, why do it in the spring?"

He liked her. "Why, then?"

"It is said that he will come to misfortune."

"Jesus? Why?"

"He is offending people."

"I have never heard him utter an offensive word."

"The Pharisees—"

"The Pharisees commit so many offenses that they are easy to offend."

She smiled. "My son is full of things like that."

He had been guilty of a tricky little paradox, and she had caught him at it. She was wrong about her son, however; Jesus would have said it more simply. If she did not see that difference, was it a difficulty between them?

"You must not worry about Jesus," he said. "He is wiser than all of them—Pharisees, Sadducees, Romans—he knows who they are, and where they hide, and with how many tongues they speak."

"I know how wise he is. And brave. He has all the virtues. Only . . . he is a little deaf."

"Deaf?"

"He never hears the tidings."

"What tidings?"

"The worldly ones."

"If he hears the tidings of heaven—"

"It is not enough. He has no need to defend himself against heaven—God is his friend. But enemies . . ."

"Who are his enemies?"

She had seemed strong. Now utterly defenseless. And afraid. "I don't know. The trouble is, he doesn't know either. He never knows his enemies. He thinks everyone is his friend."

"You are making him a fool."

"No. His brother—when they were boys—James struck Jesus with a branch. Three times, four times, until Jesus snatched the whip away. And he held fast to the arm that had offended him. Held it. When at last James was no longer in his temper, Jesus took the offending hand and kissed it. A fortnight later, James struck him again, even more severely, and ran away . . . still unpunished."

"That says something of his parents as well as of Jesus."

"That says something of the world he lives in. And does not understand."

He could see the depth of her distress. "Do you think—at his age—you can help him understand?"

"I must not give up trying."

There was a latent moment when there was too much to say, and choosing was difficult. So they simply nodded.

"When you last saw him, how did he look?" she asked.

"It was a while ago . . . but he was well."

"Sometimes he's careless with himself. When he left home, he forgot his purse."

"Perhaps he did not forget."

She winked as if she shared a secret. "I had that very thought." Then: "But he does forget things. He forgets to eat."

"When he is hungry . . ."

She was embarrassed again. "I think about his meals because—what else could I give him now? If I could keep him from harm . . ."

It would be a mistake, Judas thought, to misconstrue the tears in her eyes. They had nothing to do with any failure of courage, nor did they stem from confusion of purpose. They merely bespoke the heartache of a woman who loved her son, no longer understood him or his nightmares, yet yearned to go to him in the dark.

"Enoch tells me that you love my son."

"Yes, I do."

"He thinks that Jesus is a little mad. Do you?"

"Jesus mad? Of course not."

"One of my daughters thinks he is insane, the other thinks he is blessed. My sons are equally divided. . . . Do you think he is blessed?"

"Who can tell about blessings? I pray that he is."

"If you love him—in that much he is blessed."

"Thank you."

"Do you love him enough to help him?"

"How?"

"Find him. Watch over him. Keep him from making enemies. I am so afraid—!"

"You must not be."

"Will you help me find him?"

"I cannot leave this place." Suddenly his heartache, like fire in the earth, erupted. "I want to help him! Believe me, I don't want him to come to any harm, and I would do anything—I would do anything! . . . But I can't. It's a bad time for me now. I'm about to take my vow—or not take it—I don't know where I am—and I can't leave. But I would help him if I could. Please believe me—I would."

"I do believe you." She touched him gently on the cheek. "You are so much like him—I can see why you are friends. I do believe you . . . Yes."

Two days later he went in search of Jesus.

He looked for him at random—Ramah, Shiloh, Jericho—wherever there might be a new rabbi teaching or a new thought stirring. Then, as a wave of tidings came out of Tiberias, he suspected that Jesus might be there, and if that was so, his mother could very well be right: Jesus was in danger—from Herod.

Tiberias was about to have a great festival. The city, named for the emperor by the sycophantic Herod, was about to be visited by Tiberius himself. It would be a time to curry favor with the old Roman, and to wheedle out of him the gift Herod so achingly wanted: to enlarge his tetrarchy to include Judea so that at last he would be the king, not only of the north, but of all the Semitic lands from Dan to Beersheba. The consummation of his dreams.

But he was afraid of trouble in Tiberias; there had always been trouble in Tiberias. The artificial capital had been built on unconsecrated ground; rather, on ground too consecrated—a Jewish graveyard. The Jews had pleaded with Herod not to erect his courts and palaces in such a holy place, not to violate the sacred dead. He was Jewish himself, they reminded him, even if his lineage was mixed; how would he be able to cleanse himself of such a sin? Still, the excavations proceeded, the graves and sepulchers were desecrated, and the new vulgarity of clay and stone was erected amid the profanation of Jewish bones. As a consequence there was always rioting in the city, often bloodshed. Herod was callous to it. It was as if the gentile side of him so hated his Jewish side that he could not find enough cruelty in himself to express it.

He expressed it upon all the Jews. Jesus, whose town of Nazareth was not far from Tiberias, had recalled to Judas how, when he was in his early teens and the city was being built, the Roman soldiers would come and round up the local craftsmen. Masons, coopers, stone carvers, carpenters would be torn from their tasks, forced into wagons and driven to the Tiberian building sites. Herod said they were being conscripted for the worthy cause of their Jewish tetrarch; Joseph, Jesus' father, who was taken with the others, said he was enslaved by a gentile tyrant. Jesus had told the tale with unaccustomed bitterness.

Now, a decade after the capital buildings were finished, after many importunities by the fawning Herod, and after many imperial promises had been made and broken, the emperor had again agreed to pay his first visit to the municipality bearing his name.

Once more there was the conscription of craftsmen—this time to decorate the city, to remove the scurrilities that had been scrawled on its walls, to repair the vandalism of Zealots, to cleanse the streets of offal and insult. Nothing will cleanse Tiberias, Judas could hear Jesus saying, it will perish in its filth.

That is where Jesus is, Judas told himself. He was sure of it. And if Jesus was in the Tiberian marketplace at this critical time for Herod, if he was speaking out against the sinful existence of the city, he would feel the cinch of iron. Romans were bad captors; Herod was worse.

On a broiling afternoon, Judas arrived in Tiberias. It stupefied him how a city by the beautiful waterside of Galilee could be so ugly. But there, on the shore of a sea that gave back all the glory of the sky, was the site of Herod's summer palace, vaunting its hideousness, the buildings huge and heavy and vulgar, a confusion of design, Greek, Jewish, Roman. Stingy little portals were overpowered by ponderous acanthus-leaved columns; windows wandered without pattern, all astray; there was too much gilt and too much paint in places that did not want color and needed space. The workmanship of oppressed craftsmen had been spitefully shoddy in ways that could be hidden—mortars badly mixed, joints unevenly assembled—so that stiles were out of plumb and fundaments were settling. A bad city, badly made.

But decorated—unholy word, how the town was decorated! With every profanity imaginable—signs and symbols of the Roman soldiery and coinage, pictures of Tiberius on silken banners draped from windows, frescos in plaster still wet and sagging, and busts, friezes, full-form statues of the emperor at every age of his existence. And the flags of the imperial conquests—Greece, Gaul, Illyricum, Egypt—flying from post and pedestal.

Much of the work had been done prematurely; Tiberius was not due for another fortnight. But Herod was anxious. For example, he wanted to test the strength of the wooden platforms that would line the avenue of the grand parade. Such vast seating stages for a single celebration had never been built before, not even in Rome, and what if they were to collapse while the trumpets were sounding Tiberius's processional?

Judas walked the public places looking for his friend. He went from the market stalls to the inns to the wineshops, asking discreet questions and getting no answers. There was no sign of Jesus, and no one knew him.

Toward nightfall, the street of the platforms became deserted. The buildings on both sides of the thoroughfare were civic structures; the officials and administrative workers had gone home. But, in the lamplight, the carpenters still hammered at the structures while uniformed Roman overseers kept watch. Judas inquired whether one of the workmen had been a carpenter named Jesus, but there had been no sign of him.

An altercation occurred. Just after dusk, the Jewish jointers, who were supposed to work until midnight, decided to cease for the night. The overseers reminded them that no such interruption had ever been allowed; the orders were that work was to proceed, in shifts, without cessation until the platforms were finished. They are finished so far as our hammers are concerned, the Jews replied. Angry words, then a scramble of fists, but there were only three overseers against a score of Jews, so the latter departed.

Hardly had the Jews disappeared when, from both ends of the long avenue, there was a clatter of horses. Judas's first thought: Roman cavalry; bloodshed. But no uniforms; they were not soldiers. Jews.

He took cover in an alcove of one of the buildings. At this distance, he could not see what the horsemen were doing. Something strange. Then he smelled it. Oil. They were pouring oil on all the wooden platforms.

Quickly, deftly, as though every movement had been drilled, the four horsemen from one end rode to meet the four horsemen from the other.

Suddenly, from nowhere it seemed, a lighted torch appeared. Another and another. Someone shouted and the torches were thrown. The platforms burst aflame—a small fire here, another there—then a roaring conflagration.

Judas ran. He must get to the end of the avenue or be caught in the inferno. The flames on this side were already impassable. He raced into the break between the platforms. No, the other side was equally ablaze.

The horsemen were gone.

The center of the avenue then, running, running.

Flare, heat, the crack of fire.

Fire, people yelling fire! The voices were not frightened but exultant. Fire!

Judas, safe now, at the far end of the avenue, hunched into a passageway. He could not take his eyes off the roaring tempest of flame. It was now one single enormous fiery furnace, and it shouted like thunder, as much a great voice as a great blaze, a birth-giving outcry. How terrible, how beautiful it was!

Someone else saw it, perhaps, as beautiful. The man stood at the end of the avenue, not far from Judas and unaware that anyone was watching him. The torch in his hand had not been thrown; it was unnecessary. The conflagration, like a blazing sun, illuminated the pleasure in the torchbearer's face. As the man gazed at the fire, Judas gazed at the man. He was middle-aged, with a beard already a little grizzled. On the hand that held the torch, Judas saw a scar. It was a *P,* the Roman mark of treachery, awesome and chilling.

The man watched a little longer, tossed his torch into the flames, coughed against the smoke, turned and disappeared.

About a fortnight later, in an inn on the outskirts of Tiberias, Judas heard the aftermath. The emperor, hearing about the fire, had sent word that he was postponing his visit to Herod's tributary city. Until the disturbances were well over, he said. Herod was reported to have been convulsed with fury. "The jackals! Until the disturbances are over! When will that ever be? Jackals!"

The man who related this to Judas went on gleefully: "I can tell Herod when it will be! Never! Not as long as Simon Zelotes is alive! Never!"

"How do you now it was Zelotes?"

"You saw the letter branded on his hand."

"Yes . . . but others . . ."

"It has to be Zelotes. Who could think of such a thing besides Zelotes?"

Judas replied that he was glad not to think of such a thing. He was not a Zealot, and did not believe in violence.

The man agreed with him. Despite my calling, he said, I am a peaceable man. He was an itinerant cutler who sold knives all over Palestine. He lifted the chain he wore around his neck and pointed to the leaden coin at the end of it. It had his name, Isaac Bar Shebna, with a number on it, indicating he had paid his tax to the authorities at the Antonia fortress and was therefore a certified cutler who had taken the vow not to make illegal knives. An illegal knife was a dagger small enough to be concealed, or a specially made iron nail which could be tipped with enough poison to kill a man with a single scratch—invaluable for murder in a marketplace, or wherever crowds gathered.

He winked. "For the *sicarii,*" he said. "Barabbas always carries a pocketful." Then he added quickly, "But I do not supply them, understand. I do nothing and say nothing to get myself in trouble. I do not even speak ill of Herod."

"You will die in a soft bed."

"But there are others . . ." Again he winked.

"Yes? Who?"

"The preacher of Jordan."

"Which preacher?"

"The one who says Herod sleeps with a whore."

Judas was hearing it everywhere, these days. Herod had become enamored of his brother Philip's wife, Herodias. It did not weigh enough with him that Philip and Herodias had a child, or that he himself was already married. He had broken a number of commandments and married Herodias.

"There are many who think he sleeps with a whore," Judas said.

"Think, yes, but do not *say.* This preacher *says.* He *shouts.* . . . He will be fed to sand rats."

They were sitting in the entry hall of the inn, drinking spiced wine. The cutler crumbled almond cake into his drink, waited for it to fall apart, then sucked the liquor past the crumbs.

"I think the man is sunstruck," he said.

"Herod?"

"No, the baptist."

Judas felt a heightening of interest. "In what way, sunstruck?"

"He speaks of a kingdom of heaven as if it were tomorrow."

"What is his name?"

"John."

"Are you sure it is John?"

"John."

"Might it not be Jesus?"

"I don't know about names. The Romans confuse me—even about my own. My mother says my name is Isaac, which means laughing, but the Romans wrote me down as Issaicus, which means an island in the sea. The innkeeper's name is Gabriel, which means man of God—the Romans call him Gallus, a priest of idols. The preacher says his name is John, but the Romans may have confused him—it may be Jesus."

"What does he look like?"

"He looks like what he is: a Jew. About your size. Beard of a lighter color than yours. And—if you will excuse me—better eyes."

"Beautiful eyes?"

"He is not a woman."

In fact, Judas thought, the man would not have been wrong to say he had the eyes of a woman, the gentleness. . . . It had to be Jesus.

The following morning, Judas turned southward again, through the valley of the Jordan.

The preacher was indeed, as the cutler had said, John. Not Jesus. He did not even look like Jesus. He was taller and leaner—almost cadaverous—and unkempt. Jesus was neat and orderly in appearance, and cleanliness came naturally to him; yet John, who was always wet, it seemed, always baptizing people in the Jordan, never appeared to have bathed. Not that he was unclean; he simply looked that way.

And not that he was bereft of reason, although the cutler and many others said he was. While the preacher's eyes burned with the fires of insanity, he was no madder than Jesus, who was the sanest man Judas had ever encountered. But he *looked* deranged.

He stood knee-deep in the River Jordan. His hair, sopping in ropes that hung down to his waist, was like the weedy river-wrack that grew among the rushes. And as he baptized one believer after another, he shouted to the spectators on the shore:

"Repent, for the kingdom of heaven is at hand!"

There were hundreds of people on the riverbank. Some beat their breasts when he fulminated against sin, some stood with their hands clasped, some knelt and prayed. To one side were the scoffers. They were young Pharisees, for the most part, better dressed than the believers. The beards of a few of them had scarcely grown, but their skill in mockery was well matured. They shouted taunts at the baptist, and he tried not to hear them. Until at last his patience cracked.

"You generation of vipers!"

He kept clamoring so furiously and so fast that Judas, at a distance, could not understand his words. The derision by the Pharisees did not stop. The preacher yelled at them that they were misbegotten, and who was their father?

"Abraham!"

John scoffed at this pride in their heritage. Even the stones—if God willed it—could boast that they were born of Abraham. He raised a fist to his tormentors, forewarning that since they were not wellborn, they would not bear well, and that the ax was laid to the root of the trees; every tree that did not bear good fruit would be cut down and thrown into the flames.

Judas drew closer but did not actually join the throng. When John's preachment was over, and he had come out of the water, his followers sat on the riverbank for their evening meal. Those who had brought food shared it with the others. A young man—not one of the Pharisees, for they had departed—offered Judas some bread and a handful of dates. In Tiberias the scrivener had earned a few shekels for writing an old man's will, but the money had been spent at the inn, and he was now hungry. Still, Judas was reluctant to accept the generosity in the guise of being one of John's adherents.

"I am not a follower," he said.

"Eat, and let follow whatever will."

Judas thanked him, yet did not accept the offering. "My name is Judas. What is yours?"

"Bartholemew." He offered the food again. "We are now friends, and there is always a sufficiency of bread. Please take it."

Judas accepted the gift, and afterward thought of the sweet boy as Bartholomew of the Bread.

The scrivener walked side by side with Bartholemew for the next few days, following John the Baptist without actually being a follower. And of everyone he met, he asked:

"Do you know a man named Jesus?"

One day, when he asked the same question of John the Baptist, the latter hesitated. "I am thinking of a kinsman . . . but who knows?"

He would add nothing more to his eccentric reply. There was much about the preacher that seemed eccentric. He often disappeared. He dressed primitively in a garment of camel's hair and a leather girdle around his waist. He never ate with the others; some said he subsisted on locusts and wild honey which he procured in the wilderness, and indeed his lamentation was, as Isaiah had foretold, "the voice of one crying in the wilderness."

But, for all his prophecies of doom and final judgment, he also predicted the heaven of Isaiah, where the crooked would be made straight, the rough ways smooth, and all flesh would feel the salvation of God. Judas believed that behind the man's mask of fury was a face of kindness. He who has two coats, the baptist said, let him share with him who has none; and he who has food, let him do likewise. He baptized everyone who came to him, even tax collectors, whom he cautioned not to collect more than was appointed to them. Once, three Roman soldiers came to ask him for advice. "Rob no one by violence or by false accusation," he said, "and be content with your wages." When he spoke those words, everyone nodded in deep seriousness, but Judas could not keep from smiling. Glancing at the baptist, Judas suspected that the preacher, too, was smiling.

If Herod hated John for condemning his marriage, he hated him more as the holy man's name became more widely known. The Pharisees also began to get angrier, calling him a false prophet. But John's followers said he was a true prophet, Elijah come to life again, and a few even thought he might be the Messiah. Judas hated such speculation. There was not the faintest sign upon the man, no symbol of the Messiah, he had not performed a single miracle; he was peculiar, yes, but peculiarity did not make divinity.

One day, a woman in the throng asked the preacher if he was the Messiah, and he answered: "I baptize you with water, but he who is coming is mightier. I am not worthy to tie the latchets of his sandals. He will baptize you with fire."

It was a vast relief to hear the baptist's response. Curiously, it drew Judas closer to the preacher. In fact, he considered acknowledging himself as one of the followers, and even entering the water of the river to have himself baptized.

But something occurred . . .

A brilliant spring afternoon. The sun was dazzling, and every object it shone upon gave back a blinding light. On the riverbank there were at the least a thousand followers. Scores had been baptized and scores more waited to be similarly dedicated.

Today the baptist, as he blessed one and another and another, was filled with rapture, and he rejoiced in heaven as if it had already happened.

Suddenly, as he finished the immersion of a child and handed the little boy back to his parents, he stopped and became totally still. The ceremony ceased. His eyes were fixed to the westward, onto the hill beyond the crowd. Walking slowly down the incline, out of the westering sun, came a tall figure in a pure white mantle. As the baptist saw the man approaching, it was as if he had been waiting for him since the beginning of prayer. Slowly he raised his arms to the white figure, raised them wide in the most embracing sign of welcome.

The crowd, watching this unaccustomed cessation of the ritual, turned to see what the preacher was gazing upon. When the people also saw him, they grew as silent as the baptist. Hardly seeming to move of their own volition, they separated and made a pathway for the new arrival. Step by slow step, he descended the hillside, passed through the avenue the people had made for him, and walked gently through the reeds and rushes, into the water of the Jordan.

Coming closer to the baptist, the preacher kissed him, then brought his arms together and let his hands enfold themselves as if in prayer.

Jesus stopped now and murmured something.

The baptist's voice was barely audible. He was saying that he had need to be baptized by Jesus, not Jesus by him. What the Nazarene's reply was Judas could not hear.

Thereupon, Jesus submersed himself as the others had done, and as the baptist's lips moved in prayer, Judas thought he heard a great sigh. Jesus arose from the water and turned back toward the shore. And Judas imagined, as the crowds opened to make a path for Jesus and then to envelop him, that it was as if all things were opening, as though men were opening their arms to one another, and as if the spirit of God were descending upon Jesus, like a dove.

⁂

How perverse it was! Now that he had found Jesus, after so many weeks of exasperating search, Judas was overcome with such shyness that he could not bring himself to make his presence known. He hung back among the crowd, hiding, trembling with gladness and vaporous apprehensions. The man might not be as happy to see me, Judas worried, as I am overjoyed to see him; he might be distant because of the angry way we parted. Or he might have changed in some manner that made him unable or unwilling to be a friend.

Certainly he *looked* changed. Not only because he seemed leaner and older, but because of something nameless, a recession in the eyes, yet a fervor. . . . Perhaps it was merely that this afternoon Judas had seen him at a distance, in an unearthly light; perhaps it was the baptism that had altered him.

In any event, the man was not the Jesus he remembered, there was something unapproachable about him, and it hurt Judas to think that this was so. At last, he was so shaken by the sight of the friend who was now a stranger, that the thought of approaching Jesus was too painful to him. And he knew he could not remain here, among John's followers. So, as inconspicuously as possible, he slipped out of the crowd and started away, northward along the river.

"Judas!"

Dear God, Judas thought, it is his voice.

"Judas! Oh, my friend! Oh, Judas!"

Judas turned and saw the man hurrying, his arms outstretched. For an instant Judas could not move; then he ran toward Jesus, ran to be embraced, and to weep. And Jesus held him.

⁂

Though the celebration had no precedent and no name, the evening was jubilant. There were bonfires on the riverside, and the music of psalteries and lyres; the women sang and the children ran and played games, and people told old tales and new dreams. Someday, they said, all the bells of heaven would be pealing, all the angels would be as merry as children, and the Messiah would come.

Meanwhile, this was the night of the day of baptism, the time of the cleansing. The people rejoiced and they danced, and made circles around the fires on the bank of the river. River and flame, fire and water, the blaze to burn the soul clean, the water to purify. They gave thanks to the God who had purged them of sin and envy and hatred, who had given them new skins and new souls, who had reaffirmed his promise of a hereafter and had restored the clean wonder of their childhood.

Through the evening, Jesus and Judas embraced a dozen times, and dined, and talked. Judas told how he had spoken to Jesus' mother, how he had left the Essenes and gone in search of his teacher and friend. And Jesus said hardly a word about where he had been. The wilderness, he said; that was all.

Nor did Jesus reveal any more to John. When the baptist joined them, Judas marveled at how similar the two men were, and how different. John's fist was always in the air, his voice was a battle cry; Jesus spoke softly. The one was fire; the other, water. They are riot and the River Jordan, Judas thought; yet he knew, without ever having seen it, that there was also a burning in Jesus, a flame to consume him.

"Will you now go with us?" John said to Jesus.

"I cannot."

Judas had a dread. "Where will you go?"

The man did not answer, but made a vague gesture: distance.

Later, alone with Jesus again, Judas asked the question once more.

"The wilderness," Jesus answered.

Judas could not stand the thought of losing him again. Wherever you go, I will go with you, he said. But Jesus slowly shook his head. Forty days, he promised; I will return in forty days.

Judas felt rebuffed, for it was a formulary answer. When Jews wanted to describe an indeterminate length of time, they said forty days. In tradition, forty was a mystical number; after the Exodus, Moses fasted forty days. The Israelites lived in the desert for forty years before the Lord allowed them to enter the promised land. The number had come to be a figure of speech meaning tomorrow or next year, or never.

But as Judas revealed his dread of loss, Jesus touched him. "I will never abandon you again," he said. "I will return. You must say it a thousand times to yourself, that I will return."

"Return where? And when?"

"Go to Capernaum from time to time. I will send a message to the inn."

Judas was still apprehensive. "But why do you have to go away again?"

"Today I have been given a great gift—and a burden. I do not know if I can bear it."

⁂

"I told you it would be forty days," Jesus said on his return.

"Where have you been?"

"I told you that as well. The wilderness."

The wilderness, Judas now realized, could be anywhere. The man looked ill. He was frighteningly thin, and his face looked haggard, all eyes. The wilderness could be starvation, it could be sickness, it could be an ordeal of hell. It could be in the desert or the hills of Peraea, or in Jesus' soul.

"Please—where have you been?"

There was an odd humor in his yes. "With Satan."

The man was telling him everything, and nothing. Judas tried to imitate his humor. "Did you conquer him?"

"This time, yes. I will have to conquer him many times again."

"How did he contend?"

"With temptation."

Jesus told of charms and challenges—were they real or images of a man who had been feverish?—of being defied to turn stone to bread, of being beguiled to cast himself from the pinnacle of the Temple, of being bribed with all the kingdoms of the world.

"And how did you conquer him?"

"With Scripture."

Judas knew he was being given short answers. The symbols Jesus cited were, he was quite sure, only the schemata of the trials the man had endured. And was still enduring. There had always been a gleam in him, the glow of wisdom in a mature man, but now he was strangely ageless—a being of an intense light. The flame, really, in which his new spirit was being forged and tempered, and in which his soul was being burnt clean of doubt.

And the burning was still going on. What it must have cost him, Judas thought, what pain he has gone through, and what he still suffers. You are dear to me, he wanted to remind the man, and I would comfort you if you would only allow it. Let me help you. But he could not, because Jesus could not. How selflessly the teacher endured whatever his tribulation might be; selfishly, in fact, as though he cherished it. Oh, poor Jesus . . .

"Did the devil depart from you?" he asked.

Jesus smiled. Yes, he replied, the devil departed—and behold, angels came and ministered to him.

As Jesus now must minister to others.

"We will go and find the baptist," the Nazarene said. "And I will be his disciple."

Judas felt himself going pale. "Have you not heard? John has been arrested."

"Arrested?"

"Yes."

"Where is he?"

"In prison at Machaerus."

The teacher was cast down. He murmured a despairing thought about going to see the imprisoned man. But he was too sadly sensible to pursue the impulse. He knew it would only suit Herod's purpose to ferret out the baptist's friends. Surprisingly, he made no further comment on the misfortune. It was as though he had expected it would occur, and had inured himself to the inevitable.

"Let us continue in the work he has begun."

They went down to the Jordan, and Judas was baptized by Jesus. It had a kindliness about it, and a perfection. The scrivener wondered how he could ever have considered being baptized by John or anyone other than the teacher. It seemed ordained that the Nazarene should be his preceptor always, at his baptism as he had been at his first reading of the Torah. But this last ritual was the more sacred in his heart, like a plight of troth, total and without proviso.

They would go to Galilee, Jesus said, and he would teach along the way.

At first there were few who gathered about him, but then, as they continued along the valley of the river, the crowds increased. People were confused, in the beginning, thinking him to be the baptist, John, whose name they had heard. And in fact, in those early days, he sounded like John. "Repent, for the day of heaven is at hand!" And he used many of the same warnings about death and the terrible day of reckoning. But soon he began to leaven the wrath of the baptist, for he did not preach the ministry of fury and doom, but of love and life everlasting. And he healed. When they were deep in Galilee, in the days when he was teaching in the towns and villages, in the streets and in the synagogues, he started to tend to the ailing. He mended many, a multitude, the sick and the sad and the tormented, the bereft ones who were possessed by demons. Although he bore the burdens of others and endured their travails as if they were his own, he was happy.

In those days, Judas had never seen such a deeply happy man. And his delight spread among his followers as if the Creator were newly created. He taught them to see God as the Torah said He was to be seen, not only as the Almighty of justice, but as the Father of mercy. If one side of the Lord's face had hitherto been hidden, now he turned it to them. And lo, it was the countenance of love. There was a joy in thus finding Him, as if they themselves had been lost, and now were found. We are here, they sang, we are here in the sight of the Lord! Hosanna!

However, one of the things that made Jesus sad, in fact angered him, was when people said his cures were miracles. Countless times he denied the miraculous, as though there were a terrible blasphemy in the word, and countless times Judas heard him beg his benefactors not only to refrain from using the term but even to desist from spreading it abroad that he had healed them. "See that you tell no one," he kept saying. "See that no one knows."

Judas, perceiving the teacher's distress in the matter, obeyed him faithfully, and never alluded to the supernatural powers of anyone but God. And he, too, began to wince at the word "miracle." Once, particularly . . .

Jesus had gone to a wedding where he would meet his mother, whom he had not seen in many months. He was looking forward to it with pleasure, but also with the dread of a young man who has brought worry to his family. Judas had hung behind in a small village to take care of an elderly woman ill with a fever. When the sick one was convalescing and Judas was about to leave, an itinerant tinker came to him with an inexplicable story.

In the middle of the wedding feast that the teacher had attended in Cana, Jesus' mother had come to him and reported there was no more wine. The Nazarene had thereupon told the master of the feast to fill up the six stone waterpots with water. And when the guests drew from the waterpots, the water had turned to wine.

There was more to the tinker's tale, but as the man prated about a miracle, Judas angrily cut him short. "That is not a miracle, it's a trick! And I don't believe the master performed it! What do you think he is—a street magician? Do you think he stoops to dumb show for the clapping of hands and a shekel?"

"But everybody tells it!"

"Out of my sight, you sheephead! Don't soil his name by speaking it!"

On the other hand, on the same subject of magic, there was the gratifying response of Simon Bar Jonah, the fisherman.

When they had first arrived at Capernaum, the fishing city on the banks of the Sea of Galilee was in a state of dejection. The men had been fishing the whole night and had returned with empty boats. In the daylight they had nothing to do but listen to the teacher who gathered crowds on the seashore and in a number of other places in the town. Some of the fishermen thought to follow him.

To Simon and his brother Andrew, Jesus said, "Follow me and you will be fishers of men."

He said much the same to the sons of Zebedee, James and John, whose boat had also returned without cargo.

In the afternoon, Simon Bar Jonah sailed out once more upon the sea, and returned with his boat deep in the water, and an astonishment of fish.

It was bustled about, of course, that Jesus had caused this to occur. Judas listened to the chatter, and was particularly interested in the responses of the new disciples. John, the youngest, uncertain about all aspects of his life, was troubled over the incident of the fishes, and unable to interpret it except as a miracle. But, knowing that Jesus forbade claims of the miraculous, the boy murmured indistinctly about a strange occurrence. James and Andrew concurred with this equivocation. But Simon refused to commit himself to any explanation at all. He was the oldest, the tallest, the strongest, with a massive, muscular body that seemed too enormous for his boat. Judas liked all of them, and liked Simon the best.

One evening Judas asked him, "Why do you follow Jesus?"

Simon Bar Jonah did not answer. He seemed to be watching the cranes as they flapped their broad wings, and the kingfishers hovering over the still water.

"Why, Simon?" Judas persisted. "Why do you follow him?"

"Why do you think?"

"Haven't you heard the rumor about the fish?"

"Yes, many versions," Simon said warily. "But how do *you* hear it?"

"That when Jesus arrived, he turned your luckless boat into a lucky one. He told you where to find a great shoal, and you found it. This gave you faith—and so you follow him. What do you say to that?"

"Bilge water. I do not need Jesus to point out the shoals of fish. I need lightning and thunder. I saw there was going to be a wild storm that afternoon and the fish would be in deeper water, farther from the land. So I sailed out and found them. I know more than he does about fish. . . . But I know nothing about God. And he knows everything. *Selah.* I follow him."

The Nazarene's followers became a multitude. They came from everywhere—from all over Galilee, from Peraea, from Decapolis, from many cities in Judea, even from Jerusalem.

Sometimes he spoke loudly, sometimes so softly that they had to strain for every word. One day he sat and simply taught them:

"Blessed are the poor in spirit, for theirs is the kingdom of heaven.

"Blessed are they who mourn, for they shall be comforted.

"Blessed are the meek, for they shall inherit the earth.

"Blessed are those who hunger and thirst for righteousness, for they . . ."

As Judas listened, he saw a familiar-looking man approaching. He did not actually enter the group but stood a little to one side. He was in his middle years and had a slightly grizzled beard, and for the moment Judas could not identify him. The afternoon was hot, and as the man raised his hand to wipe his moist brow, Judas saw the *P.* A chill ran through him.

When the teaching was over, the man with the marked hand remained. In measured steps, he approached Jesus. There were, at that time, only five disciples, including Judas, who were the special companions of Jesus.

"I would like to be the sixth," the man said.

"What is your name?"

"Simon. They call me Zelotes."

"We have heard of you," Jesus said. "Why do you wish to join us?"

"Because you teach the word of God with great clarity . . . and beauty."

Jesus nodded in silent gratitude, but Judas would not be silent. "Is that the only reason?"

Surprised, the man turned. "Is it not enough?"

"For others, yes. But you are a Zealot."

"That is true."

"Then, you must have another reason."

A moment. The Zealot seemed to weigh the truth against a falsehood. "Yes, I do."

"Should you not tell it?"

Simon Zelotes turned away from Judas and looked at Jesus again. "The Romans have fouled our lives, and we must cleanse ourselves. Some of us are doing it with knives and fire. But we are few, and you gather multitudes; we are soldiers, and what we need is a soul."

Jesus studied him. Zelotes was a strong man, but the teacher's gaze unsteadied him.

"I thought, at first, that we would ask you to join us," the Zealot said. "But you are greater than we are—and I ask to join you."

"We welcome you," Jesus said.

"No!"

Jesus turned to Judas with a questioning look. "No!" Judas cried again. "He is a man of violence—and you are all gentleness and peace. There will be knives and bloodshed! Please—I beg you—no!"

"I cannot turn him away," Jesus said.

"But he's against everything you teach! He doesn't want a kingdom of heaven, but of earth. Tell him no—please tell him no."

"We must say no to no one, Judas."

Jesus arose then and embraced Simon Zelotes. As if gathering him into the fold, he placed his arm around the Zealot's shoulder and drew him away. When the Nazarene and his new disciple walked down the incline, Judas turned desperately to the others.

"Why didn't you help me? Why did no one speak?"

They remained silent.

Judas turned to the oldest of them.

"Simon—you!—he would have listened to you! Why didn't you speak to him?"

"Why should *I* speak to him? God has done so."

That night, Judas could not sleep. He was more deeply troubled by what Simon the fisherman had said than by the welcoming of the Zealot. Simon's acceptance of the teacher's decision as being heaven-sent made Judas ashamed that he had questioned Jesus' decision. That he had doubted.

Am I a man of too little faith? So little that I was unable to take my vow as an Essene? Or does my belief come tardily, as I was late to my Bar Mitzvah? Will I come unpunctually to the Day of Revelation? Late and little, will I miss the secret of the vast mystery of God?

Does Jesus know the secret? Will he impart it to me?

Faith; I must have faith. It may be the key to the mystery. *Faith.*

There was rarely enough of the pomegranate nectar. She had never known anything so delicious. Nor any food or drink that had ever made her feel so buoyant. She floated. Her body lay peacefully on the surface of her visions, as on a calm and perfect water, the Lake of Gennesaret when she was a child. Sometimes, drifting, she was there with Elias; and once, in a stillness, she saw the man with the kindly face—Jesus or Judas, whatever he called himself—and he asked her again whom she wished to slay, and she could not remember, and drifted off to sleep.

Sleep was delicious these nights and days, and she was extraordinarily contented. Except on that one evening when Entemia would not give her more *elixirion.* No, my sweetling, the woman had said, you have had enough tonight, and you will get ill again.

Ill? She was not ill; why did Entemia say that? What did it mean to be ill? Did it accurately describe that she was always pleasurably dizzy, and that all times of the day seemed to be twilight? Or did it say: lonely?

She was, in all her waking states, so lonely. I am not ill, she told Entemia, I am lonely.

That evening, the two women who bathed her took her nightclothes away. Will I not be cold? she asked. No, it was a warmish spring, they answered. She had not noticed, but it was indeed quite warm.

When she was deep asleep, she vaguely thought she heard the faintest stirring in the dimness. Then someone came and lay in bed beside her. But even if he was a man, she was not frightened; when the juice of the pomegranate was in her, she was afraid of nothing. Besides, he did not disturb her; he simply went to sleep. Once, however, in the night, he touched her lightly, so lightly that she scarcely knew where he touched her. There was no alarm in it. Anyway, she sensed that it was an accident; it had happened in his sleep. Or in hers. Then, a few moments later, she felt him quivering, but she was not awake enough to know what he was doing.

In the morning he was gone. On the table beside the bed was a beautiful Roman coin. She did not recognize the object, because it was made of silver and not of brass.

"This is an old one," Entemia said, "and very valuable."

Mary handed it to her.

"No." The Egyptian smile. "He has already given me one. He left this as a present for you."

The coin was pretty, and she was glad to have it. Like the pomegranate, it made her float a little.

What seemed a long while later, although Entemia said less than a week—time was no longer measurable—he came again. Also in the middle of the night. And again he scarcely touched her, and left another coin.

She began to look forward to his coming. And she enjoyed looking at her little collection of sesterces.

One night, after he had touched her and the bed had shaken, she heard an unaccustomed murmuring. The man was crying. She was, in those times, still getting considerable drafts of the elixir, and wasn't quite sure what was expected of her, whether she should be sorry for a man who was crying in bed, or feel contempt for him. She wanted to feel sorry.

In the morning, another coin.

The man never visited her again. She missed him, and told Entemia so, and the woman said, Do not fret.

There were others. Entemia carefully selected them. They had to be men who would be satisfied merely to touch Mary, and caress her a little, and no more. One of them, in distress, begged Mary to lay her hand upon him; except for the reason of his asking, she did not know why she did it. But this was the only time it occurred, and was the most that had been demanded of her.

In fact, Entemia made hardly any demand upon her. Not that her demands upon the other women were so stringent. They led an easy, agreeable life. Besides Mary, there were eight of them, assembled with the most critical particularity. All were beautiful, and each, it seemed, was the paragon of the land she had come from—Cyrenaica, Magna Graecia, Illyricum . . . Most of the courtesans were good-hearted, two were talented with the cithara and one with the lyre, nearly all of them could sing or dance a little, one was a hoyden, one was lovably lamebrained, and only two were spiteful. Mary liked them all, even the spiteful ones. But she felt that they were all somewhat hostile to her.

Maybe it had to do with clothes. And it might have started when Carolla, the Roman seamstress, arrived to do their summer dresses. Although the women could choose the design of their own costumes—with Entemia's advice and approval, of course—a certain amount of exposure was required. From season to season their choices varied slightly, but for the most part they remained the same: what they were proud to expose did not alter materially from spring to autumn. One of them selected a bareness of bosom, to be sure; another wanted to expose an aspect of a single thigh just as another chose a single buttock. Victoria decided to show her belly, because the navel was so perfect; Ridas wanted to denude the smallest circle of herself, but when told she would have to shave, demurred and chose the exposure of both nipples. With this or that one, what feature she laid bare was a mark of her vanity, Mary thought, but with most it was a mark of their wit and their ability to laugh at themselves, and at what men prized in them. As to Mary, because she was Entemia's favorite, she was required to wear as much or as little as she liked, and she chose to be fully clothed. She was certain it did not sit well with the others.

Even though relatively few demands were made of her, she felt, at times, as if she were living among the deranged. Often she heard wild noises in the night, as though someone were being slaughtered. But apparently no real harm was done. Except that there was, occasionally, a tussle and an accident of blood.

The loudest noises occurred when Naguib arrived. He was a hulking Egyptian who looked like a farmer, one of the impoverished fellahin, but he was apparently affluent. He habitually chose the same woman, Darella. She was the smallest one in the house, and the least popular. But the instant Naguib entered, he always made a beeline for her, paid Entemia in advance, and presented his tiny courtesan with a jeweled ring or a lovely brooch; sometimes, Roman gold.

When he disappeared with Darella, demoniacal sounds would issue from her room, shouts and screams and curses so violent that the palace would tremble. He would emerge sometime later with bleeding arms and great welts on his legs, and he would wear his mantle loosely over the bruises on his back; oftentimes he limped and whimpered as he slunk away. But little Darella always emerged from the room unblemished, as cheerful and chirping as a bird.

It was not permitted for any of the men to beat the women. Never. Beating the *koykla,* however, was allowed. As much as they liked, the visitors could whip the leather dummy with the ropes and thongs that were provided, or they could bring their own canes and cudgels, so long as they paid for any damages done to the sawdust woman. They were even permitted to have a naked witness to the beating, someone they could fondle from time to time, or even lie with, so long as the courtesan was unharmed.

There were other predilections. One customer wanted to be tickled into sexual hysteria, another was gratified by burning himself with lighted candles or oil lamps, another asked for a special cincture to be tied around his private part. A man from Thessalonica always bought two women, the first to berate and belittle him, the second to flatter and aggrandize him into a braggart satisfaction.

Two customers spent their times in the palace, pretending to be ill —a slight chill, a light fever. What they wanted was an interval of nursing; and Entemia herself ministered to them. She brought them soothing gruels, laid poultices on their imaginary aches, and sometimes read them to sleep. Nursing, she said, was a motherly act, and motherhood was a role she enjoyed playing. The notion that a whoremonger could be maternal was a new one in Alexandria, Entemia claimed, although she had encountered it in Rome. Here in the city there were four other mongers. Three were men of assorted meanness, and one was a snaggle-toothed witch; none was maternal. Entemia's monopoly.

Much as she loved her "daughters," Entemia was not always kind to them. Sometimes she was crabbed and petty—because she was past forty now, and jealous. Mary thought she had no need to be. She was younger in spirit than any of them, she was the most beautiful, and she was certainly the best-educated and most widely traveled. If she had a swift temper, she also had a touching talent for remorse. Her tears of contrition after she had slapped someone or had caused a humiliation, were like a warm bath for everyone. And Mary felt that Lydia, the senseless one, was not so senseless: she knew precisely how to incur Entemia's wrath so that she could collect the woman's tears, like pearls warmed by the flesh.

If the women all adored Entemia, it seemed that they liked Mary less and less. This bothered her. She had related it to clothes, and one day asked Entemia if she should think of exposing her body a little more.

"It is not only a question of what you wear."

"What, then?"

"They do not like it that you are so special."

"I do not like it either, but what am I to do?"

"Whatever you wish."

"Why does it matter to them?"

"They think that because you withhold your body from the men, you consider yourself better than they are. They say you condescend—"

"I do not!"

"—and that you are dishonest."

"Dishonest?" She was appalled. "How?"

Entemia did not respond immediately. She gazed at Mary as if weighing whether to proceed. Her decisions came through complexity: she believed nothing, she wanted to believe everything; she was calculating, she was impulsive; she was cynical and sentimental.

"Tell me . . . before the Romans brutalized you . . . were you a virgin?"

". . . No."

"Then, why is your flesh so sacred to you?"

"It is not sacred! I despise it!"

Mary was more shocked by what she had said than Entemia was. And shaken by a truth she had not confronted. She hated her body. Irrationally, this instant, she blamed her flesh as she had blamed the Romans. It had welcomed spoliation and had been spoiled. It had demanded a vengeance she had been unable to execute, and had exposed her as a failure. It had, however indirectly, caused the death of a shining young man. She wondered why she had not tried to violate it.

"I will do what the others do," she said.

And she determined she would be the best of all of them. At first it was excruciatingly difficult. Difficult for the most rudimentary and humiliating reason: having no desire for the first men who lay with her, she was dry, and it was painful. You dunce, Entemia said, do you want to tear yourself to shreds? Why do you not use the oils? Why indeed? A matter of perverse pride, or self-punishment? She used the oils.

Then there were skills to be learned. Entemia encouraged her. "You have an advantage over the others—you can read. Read about the great courtesans, the wonderful hetaeras of the past. Read about Phryne."

She did. She learned about the hetaera Mnesarete, who was called Phryne, "the toad," because her facial skin was scaly and hideous. And how the woman had learned to distract men's eyes from looking at her face to studying her beautiful body and the sensual stirrings of it; how she had become the model for the Aphrodites of the painter Apelles and the sculptor Praxiteles; and how, when she was accused of profaning the Eleusinian mysteries, she was defended by the orator Hypereides, who ripped her robe away and displayed her bosom, which so aroused the judges that they acquitted her. Mary studied every description of the woman, every poem and painting, every Venus and Aphrodite, how the fully clothed woman used her hands as if they were hiding a naked body, and how her tongue was always slightly in evidence when she talked, and how she pretended she could not keep her eyes off the hemline of a man's tunic.

But Mary's best teacher was Entemia. "You must stay away from Egyptian customers," she said, "for they do not want a woman like you. Your eyes are too quick—you speak too well—and you are too alive.

Egyptians believe they are in love with death, but I think they are afraid of it—which may be the same thing—so they embalm themselves and build pyramids to eternity. And when they choose a woman in my house, they hope she will be a mummy. That's why Lavinia is the perfect woman for them. She was dead before she was ever born. When she lies under her Egyptian, I would wager she does not breathe and that her skin is ice. Her Egyptian fellow fornicates his death away. But you twitch with life—you would not serve his purpose."

She paused as if she had a need to be more careful.

"Now . . . you must avoid the Jewish customers as well. They will not appreciate you. A Jew wants to feel guilty. His God has told him that fornication is a sin—so his guilt is part of his custom, he is at home with it, it even gives him pleasure. But you are now so skilled in the uses of your body that a Jew will perhaps forget that he is in the midst of a transgression. So he will have a single delight instead of a double one—to pleasure his penis and beat his breast at the same time."

The Egyptian smiled. "As you know, in lovemaking it is always best to have two things going on at once."

Entemia had taught, and continued to teach, all her women. She protected them from every harm. One day, however, there was a crisis with a particularly graceful and busy one named Daphne. She had been a dancer, and it was said that she did wonderful, enveloping things with her limbs, and tantalizing movements with other parts of herself, and the men came out of her chamber as if they had been wrestling with tigers. She had a regular customer named Nikolatos who was strong and had vast endurance. He took to coming more and more often, clearly trying to take exclusive possession of Daphne's time and body. He was in love with her. On days when the dancer was indisposed, he refused to look at another woman, and it was said he relieved himself in a wadi somewhere.

At last, in a transport of love, he asked her to marry him. How can I, she replied, how can I? She started to weep heartbrokenly. "I am a slave!"

It was true. Except for Mary, all the women in the palace were slaves.

That night, when the house was asleep, Nikolatos crept back to speak with Entemia in private. He could no longer stand it, he said, seeing his beloved in bondage. It was unbearable to him to think of her having to sell her body to other men, having to torture and degrade herself. He wanted to liberate her—and he offered an enormous sum to buy the freedom of his future wife. I will have to think about it, the Egyptian woman said; she is one of my best, and my youngest, and there is much profit left in the girl.

When the man departed, Daphne was hysterical. "Please don't sell me!" she cried piteously. "Please don't sell me!"

"He says that if I don't sell you, he'll go away—and you'll never see him again."

"Good—oh, good! I can't stand him anymore. He is consuming me —all of me—and I have nothing left for other men."

Entemia winked to Mary, who was listening to the tumult. "But you're a poor, oppressed little slave, Daphne. You're tortured and degraded—and he will make a respectable woman out of you."

"I don't want to be respectable! I want to stay here!"

"Here—in this pit of evil? You'll die in the pleasures of damnation."

"I pray I will—I pray for it!"

"Good—go and pray. That's a good and pious girl."

Later, Mary asked: "Did he really offer a great deal of money?"

"Oh, yes. More than she was worth."

"Why didn't you take it?"

"I can't sell them from one slavery to another. Look at Rebecca, there. She was married to a man in Antioch—a rich merchant. She ran away and sold herself to me—for a few sesterces—just so I can say she is mine—my slave—in case her husband comes to claim her."

"Will you remain loyal to them?"

"It is not merely loyalty, it's good business. If I betray them, I won't be able to attract the choicest women."

"Does that mean you can buy whomever you want?"

"I have a secret to tell you. I never buy anybody if I can avoid it. Except for Rebecca, they are all free women pretending to be slaves."

"I don't believe it."

"It's true—ask them."

"Why do they come here?"

"For a license to disport themselves with men."

"All harlots do not love their work."

"You're right. As in any profession, many hate what they're doing. But not my women. I choose only those who love to fornicate, who want to be furrowed like the earth."

"I can hardly believe that all of them—"

"Yes, all of them. The women who are here want to be here!"

"I think you delude yourself. They're here because they don't want to be out there."

"Well, that's another way of saying it. But there's hardly a woman in this house—"

"—who is happy about what she is doing!" She saw Entemia flinch, and she relented. "It's no reflection on you, Entemia—this is perhaps the best brothel in the world. But most of us here are pleasureless in our work, and some are repelled by it."

"Then, why are you all here?"

"Because the world has treated us worse than you do! Or because we are stupid or lazy or sick or afraid!"

"Which are you?"

". . . I don't know."

The flare of vexation had passed. She thought about Entemia's question. It worried her.

"I wish I knew why I am here," she said.

"Why bother to know? Knowing is not the better part of wisdom."

"How did I get here, Entemia?" The Egyptian started away, to put an end to the conversation. But Mary insisted. "How?"

"I *wished* you here."

"Nonsense. How did I get here?"

"I had a strong need to have you in this companionship. And I knew you would be well composed here. . . . I still think you will be."

Entemia's evasions were telling Mary something she dreaded to discover. "You sent the men, didn't you?"

"I didn't mean for them to hurt you—only to rob you of your money, so you would come to me. And they would have done it skillfully, without causing you a pinch of harm. But who was to know you would fight like a *sicarius?*"

How uncanny, Mary thought, that I am not so horrified by this violence anymore. It is, I see, another way that wishes get fulfilled, another form of negotiation.

"Was Caleb part of it?"

"No, he wasn't. I swear to you, he wasn't. For weeks he didn't even know you were here."

"But he knows now?"

"Yes."

"Has he been here since I came?"

"Yes. We kept you out of sight. He played a short game with Victoria, and had scarcely laced his sandals before he was out of the house."

She believed what Entemia had told her, everything. She wondered if she could always believe the woman. She wanted to.

As the seasons changed, she got better and better at her trade. She felt in many ways like an artist, a musician playing on a complex instrument. Except that she had never met a lyrist who hated the lyre as she continued to loathe her own body. *There* was the enslavement, *there.* Her body was her slave and she was beating it as if it were a *koykla,* beating it to make it perform her self-degradations in a skillful, sensual, artistic way.

Sometimes, watching the other women and seeing how cheery and satisfied they were, how they got gratification in their work, she envied them. If at least I could have their sexual pleasures, she told Entemia.

"But they are special women," the Egyptian answered. "Do you think your ordinary woman gets any pleasure out of sex?"

"I can't believe that only the men . . ."

"But it's the fact. It's *phallari* and *alvari.*"

"I've never heard those words."

"I composed them myself," she said with mock pride. "Our trade is too limited in its vocabulary. Besides, our argot is much too vulgar. So I've created two discriminating words."

"What do they mean?"

"Have you noticed that the word for the sexual act is the same for the man as for the woman? In every language that I know—Egyptian, Greek, Latin, Aramaic, Persian—always the same tired obscene term for both sexes. Different in every tongue, of course, but why should it be the same word for both men and women? From what I've seen of the enterprise, this is an egregious inadequacy in expression. We need two terms, not one. Why not? The act is quite different for a man than for a woman. It's done differently and experienced differently. There are differences in the will and the wanting, in the aggressor versus the defender, in the sounds and the smells and the touchings, in the pleasure and the pain. Even in the length of time it takes to come to some sort of conclusion. And the conclusions themselves have about as much in common as an oyster and a unicorn. Now, understand, I'm not a linguist, but a human need is a human need, and we urgently require two separate terms for the act. So I call it *alvari* for the woman, and *phallari* for the man."

"In any language?"

"Fornication is universal. But a woman must not expect the same kind of pleasure as a man derives from it."

The only pleasure Mary derived from it came, paradoxically, from the Romans. Because she learned to work a thousand spites upon them. She asked sly little questions that unsettled their virility. Sometimes, on the contrary, she praised them in anticipation of a prowess they knew they would not have, and so they had none. Occasionally, in the midst of the act, she would make some offhand remark—about bad breath, perhaps, or a scaliness of scalp—and the Roman customer went soft. All done with the utmost charm and a loving manner, so that the men never ascribed the failure of their potency to her but to themselves, and they came back again and again to prove they were lusty soldiers in naked uniform.

She had her greatest pleasure with an illustrious Roman customer: Sejanus came.

He had not been in Alexandria for many months, and now he returned on agitating business. There was an imperial shortage of wheat. Egypt was the granary of the Roman Empire. Meetings would be held with the Delta grain merchants, who had become intractable of late. From a dozen colonies, delegates would be arriving, haggling in concert and in private. Sejanus was, of course, representing Tiberius himself.

He arrived on an especially festive evening. The main hall of Entemia's palace had been newly decorated by a Corinthian master; there were twin magicians from Byzantium; the string instruments were augmented by the loveliest voices from Thrace, and the *elixirion* had been made from the first pomegranates of the year.

Sejanus stood on the threshold, being greeted by Entemia, and Mary recalled how, on sight, she had loathed him. She thought of the story he had told and had a clear vision of him eating a living human brain. Yearning to do him some harm, some humiliating damage, she warned herself: you must stop being revolted by him; you must be like the physician who overcomes his disgust with a tumor in order to destroy it.

She hoped, she longed for him to choose her among the women. That it might be left to chance was galling.

However, it wasn't left to chance, but to Entemia. She was leading him directly toward her.

"Ah, the renegade," he said. "I promise—this time—not to tell you stories that offend."

"You must remember," Entemia said, "that Mary did not yet live with us."

"Remember? How can I forget my frustration?"

They all pretended to smile. His eyes did not undress her—she was inured to that humiliation—they did the opposite. They added a covering—a caul—she felt as if he were encasing her in a slimy membrane. I won't be able to manage it, she thought, I won't be able to go through it with this revolting . . .

But she did go through with it. For three nights in a row. And each night she damaged him a little. The first time, when his clothing was off, she looked at the size of him—neither small nor large—and pretended to hide her disappointment. Then, while fondling him, she called it dear little thing, dear little thing. At last she pretended such passion that he ejaculated prematurely. It happened twice again, almost exactly the same way, and he did not get inside her.

When he did, the following night, she made a frantic movement, accidentally, it seemed, as if he had done something hurtful to her, and he slipped away, and lost his firmness. It occurred once more and then once more, on the oddest mishaps, and each time she was so patently insincere in saying the fault was her own, that he had to blame himself.

The third night she felt free to suggest that he was something less than a Hercules, that he lacked a certain puissance, that his power was not in the bed and not his own, but borrowed from an old and ailing emperor.

Her abuse of him had a perverse effect, not at all what she intended. He thrived on it, and so did his member. He pitched battle against her, and she had memories of Roman ravage, dreading that she might lose this combat with the monster. But suddenly she realized what it was that he was trying to do: excite her to her own ecstasy. Not out of generosity—certainly not because of affection—but as a token of dominance: he could make the Jewess do exactly as it pleased him.

So she committed the most heinous offense against a risen man: she laughed at him.

He struck her once. Then, when she did not cry out, he struck her twice again.

She did not bathe him that evening; he bathed himself. And preferred it. As he was doing so, she thought: I have lost. The last action was a violence—not mine against him, but his against me. I didn't even humiliate him. I am only a whore, and who will know that he had a few minor embarrassments with me? He will not even remember them himself.

She watched him. He tossed one linen away and took another one to dry his private parts. As he did, he looked down and held himself to the light, the limp object, examining its skin. She suspected it was blotched, from rough use. Or perhaps he thinks . . . that ugly animal, he wonders if I have infected him.

She screamed, "Diseased!"

Startled, he looked at her.

She ran naked out into the corridor. "Diseased!" she shrieked. "Beware of him! Sejanus is infected, he is diseased!"

He rushed after her, into the corridor. So did others. Some were clothed, some naked.

"Diseased!"

"You lie, you harlot!"

Entemia came rushing up the stairs. A chamberwoman, bearing soiled bedclothes, scurried past them.

Mary pretended a frenzy. "Beware of him—he has the illness—beware!"

Sejanus, suddenly conscious of his nakedness, hurried back into the bedchamber. The din in the hallway did not lessen. The more frightened ones ran away as if being in the same corridor might contaminate them; others tried to calm the panic-stricken woman. Entemia shouted for the corridor to clear. Go back to your rooms, she yelled, back to your rooms!

Sejanus, a mantle over his nakedness, appeared again. He was apoplectic.

"I will send soldiers for her," he said.

Entemia stepped forward. "You would not be such a fool. Do you want all of Alexandria to know of your misfortune?"

"I am not diseased!"

"If people say you are, will you walk naked to prove otherwise?"

He turned violently on Mary, slapped her once again, and departed.

One day Caleb arrived. He did not so much as glance at any of the other women; he came only to visit her, he said. Hardly a year had gone by, and he looked wasted. His eyes were sunken and his skin was gray. She thought he might be ill, and asked him. No, he said with an untrustworthy vagueness—ill?—no, not at all.

He spoke no words of apology, made no mealy excuses about having been drunk on that ill-fated evening, but his manner spoke his sorrow—not for the act, but for loving her too much, in that one extra way that tainted all the others. He did not look at her at all. He seemed to want to touch her with gentleness, and she thought how sad it was that he probably never again would be able to do so.

He had just come back from Jerusalem. "How's father?" she asked.

"Not actually ailing, but not really well."

She smiled. "Like all of us."

He seemed grateful for being included.

"Does he speak of me?"

She could see he wanted to say yes. "No." Then, bethinking himself. "There was an incident a few months back—and then he spoke about you."

"What incident?"

"The *quaestor* arrived again. An informant had told him that you were seen in Rome."

"What did he answer?"

"That he had heard a variety of stories about you, even that you were . . ."

"Dead."

"Yes. How did you know he would say that?"

"It's a line in one of the Greek dramas. 'The fury that dreams the children dead.' . . . Not you, of course."

"I think me, too."

"There is so much rage . . ."

"Yours can be quieted a little, I think. I have some good news for you."

"What?"

"Two of the four of them are dead."

"Tullius?"

"No. Tullius is still alive, and his adjutant, Quintus Sallus."

"How did the others die?"

"There was a fire in a wing of the Antonia. They suffocated."

She smiled wryly. "Why was I not allowed to suffocate them?"

He smiled too. "There are still two left." Then, quickly, "But you must not come home to do it—the Antonia is still looking for you."

"Some way . . . Tullius . . ."

"No need. You have apparently put a witch's curse on them. You don't have to get a drop of blood on your hands."

"I want his blood on my hands!"

"Peace, Mary." He seemed as sad as if he had abandoned all hope of fulfillment in his life. "We must be at peace with ourselves."

"I don't want to be at peace. I am at war with the world, and I will stay at war."

He departed as if he were a little afraid of her; certainly *for* her.

When he was gone, she recalled how she had humiliated Sejanus, and she thought grimly: what a petty victory. She had, for a moment, pacified her appetite by nibbling at a crumb of spite, but she still had a famine for vengeance.

And here she was, doing nothing about it, paying for her livelihood with the disgusting availability of her body; here, like an invalid, she malingered in a foreign land, four days journey from Palestine, locked away from home, unable to pursue the only passion she had left.

She wished she could believe in witchcraft, believe she had actually *caused* those deaths. But she believed in nothing, least of all the miracles of sorcery. She believed in nothing and had caused nothing. Never in her life.

She was walking up the stairs, going from the main hall toward her bedchamber. Two more, dead without me—how useless I am! Halfway up the staircase, she began to tremble. I must not faint, she told herself, I must never be weakened again, I must not. With her right hand she held tightly to the railing. With her left she scratched her nails down the length of her cheek. Again, she said, you are not feeling anything, use your nails again. The pain at last. Pain, more pain, rage, blood. She did not faint. Rage and pain are fortifiers, she said; they are my only allies.

That evening she heard that Pontius Pilate was going to be a visitor.

All she could see was the face of Elias, all she could hear was his voice, telling a dream, vowing to kill the Roman procurator. I have your dream now, she murmured; sleep, Elias, sleep.

She wished for the balm of the evening breeze. At the close of day, the dusk still held the remembrance of the afternoon sun, and she was much too warm. The shawl, besides, gave her a feeling of airlessness, but she could not remove it. It hid half her face, the cheek that was healing, and, although it was draped ingeniously around her head so that it seemed another weaving of her hair, it was a stifling nuisance.

The procurator, with whom she was having wine and currant cakes, told her he approved of the exotic ways that women nowadays were concealing half their charms—half their identities, in fact. The shawl makes you part familiar, he said, and part strange.

"Which do you like better—familiar or strange?"

"The fact that you seem familiar is quite strange."

"Why so?"

"Because we have never met."

She wondered if he really thought they had never met, or was setting a small entrapment. She talked about yesterday's unexpected rain and the rainbow, and he talked about the awkward grace of the large birds, the ibises, wading in the pond.

He said that it was all very beautiful here, did she not think so? Especially the propylaeum, she replied; it was her favorite place at Entemia's, but then, porches were all rather pleasing to her, being neither outdoors nor in, and the ibises were indeed beautiful, yes, very, how tall they were, and could it not be possible that the people of the Nile were right in saying the birds were sacred?

"Do you believe in sacred birds?"

"Oh yes—don't you?"

"Do you believe in God?"

She was not going to be trapped *that* easily. "I believe in many gods—in all of them."

"That's odd, isn't it, for a Jewess?"

"You would not take me for Egyptian? Or Greek? Or Persian?"

"Any of those . . . and Jewish." He took a sip of wine and picked a currant off a cake. "We met, I think, at a feast that Herod gave for me. You ate too much."

She smiled as though they were playing a game. "Ah, that's the familiar part of me—now tell me the strange."

"Strange that you are here, yet not so strange that you're not in Jerusalem, where people pry."

Her wine might spill, she thought, and carefully set down the cup.

He saw the tremble. "No need to disconcert yourself, however. I'm not a *quaestor* and Egypt is not my jurisdiction. Besides, I have hands that cannot hold two swords at once. I'm here to fight for wheat."

"Will you win?"

"In one of your Jewish books it says that Joseph sent his sons to Egypt to barter for grain, and somehow—here—one of them was imprisoned. I think—I'm not sure of this—it is how you became enslaved." He smiled. "The Jews have learned their lesson. They don't send their sons for grain, they send a Roman."

"The Jews have not sent you."

"No, that's true. But I do this for the Jews I govern."

"You are magnanimous."

Her irony pleased him. In the gentlest way, he reached across the table and ever so slightly lifted the shawl from her cheek.

"Who did that to you?"

"A fiend."

"Yourself?"

She was surprised at his perspicacity. "How did you know?"

"There is a fiend . . ."

"In all of us."

"Oh no, not in me. I'm what we call *venerandus,* which doesn't mean I am only to be venerated, but adored. Ask Procula—adored! Even by my wife—ask Procula. Know me well, and you will love me."

"I will kill you."

He had just started to take a sip of his wine. Hearing her, he laughed into it and spluttered, splashing the ruby liquid all over his spotless, white toga.

Still laughing, he said, "That's an engaging game—let's play it."

"Play what?"

"Play how you will kill me."

"I don't know yet."

"Play why, then."

"Why? . . . Because you are a cruelty."

"Me—Pontius Pilate—a cruelty? Ask Sejanus if this is true. He says I'm too soft and sweet—he calls me the ripe fig. Ask the emperor. Ask Procula if I am cruel."

"I have asked the Jews."

"Ah yes, the Jews. They call every little blunder a cruelty. Does a cruel man bring water to a city that hates him and is dying of thirst? I built an aqueduct for Jerusalem—two hundred furlongs of expense—"

"For which the Jews paid. You pillaged the Temple."

"Not pillaged—taxed. As all of us are taxed."

"And then, when we rebelled, you sent soldiers—disguised as Pharisees and Sadducees—with daggers hidden—and they slew—how many of us?—hundreds?"

"Fewer than you mourned. You Jews—a traitor dies and you mourn a hero, a beggar dies and you mourn a priest."

"We mourn the Galileans. Remember the Galileans? The ones who were sacrificing the lamb on the altar, and your soldiers arrived and slew them—right there on the sacred altar—so that their blood was mingled with their sacrifices? Do you recall them?"

"No, I don't—because it never happened," he said blandly. "And if it did, it was a blunder. Not a cruelty—a blunder." He was taunting her.

"Tell it to Procula," she said.

"But it's true."

"All your barbarities were simply errors, is that it?"

"You don't believe me?"

"No."

"But I assure you—the mistakes of an ill-advised man."

"Misguided by his counselors."

"Yes—exactly! A bungler always at the mercy of bunglers!"

Perhaps he was serious.

He leaned forward. "You must believe me—it's true!" he said. "That's what I am—a bungler! Even in bed! Ask Procula!"

He was a puzzle to her. She had never met a man who confessed to being incompetent in bed. Ask Procula. Ask Procula, indeed. Would the wife of Pilate dare to say, even in the intimacy of women's talk, that her husband was incompetent? Yet he himself had apparently no shame in saying so. Why?

He was watching her. He smiled with studiedly clumsy charm. "Would you take a bungler into your bed?"

"I have no choice. I am a slave here."

He spoke with bitter sweetness. "I wish I were better at everything I do. Especially now . . . as I see you . . . I wish I were better."

Something wrong. "I'm sure you're better than you think."

"Thank you. You give me courage." He was wry. "I will return when I have the courage to bungle with you."

He departed, and Entemia said he left some money, as if he had been gratified. Perhaps he had.

He would return; she wondered when. And she speculated: How would he behave in an upstairs room? Would he have to prove to her that he was a bungler? Or to himself, that he was a deft and potent man?

And how would she do Elias's work—and her own? How would she kill him?

How? It could not be something overt, for daggers were telltale, and blood left ineradicable trails. A seeming accident, perhaps, to a chariot wheel or the girth of a saddle. But such would likely cause only a bruise or two, and who would perpetrate it? Who could set fire to the house of the proconsul where he was staying? She must have no accomplices. Doing it alone would give her singular pleasure, but add to the difficulty.

Poison. A woman's expedient. A dagger on an impulse, but poison in deliberation. And she would do it with utmost deliberateness. A little at a time, so that his death would be gradual and unexceptionable, a vague discomfort at first—a slight nausea, perhaps; a soreness of head or muscle; then sharp twinges, spasms in the night, blood on the tongue or in the feces, pain, violent pain, outcries and vomitings and pain, pain, pain! She longed to watch the progress of it.

But what poison, and how would she get it? And how could she administer it? Over what period? How long would he remain in Alexandria? The so-called spices added to the pomegranate—she wondered why they made one's head spin, and whether in more concentrated doses they might be noxious. She inquired of the steward of Entemia's wines: aconite, he told her, the most trifling amount of aconite, not to be dawdled with. Baneful, yes, in fact they called it wolfsbane. She studied it. How innocent its origin was, a flower, in the family of buttercups, blue, yellow, purple, and given in the East for better breathing, better slumbering, and sometimes—in excess—exhilaration, then . . . mortality. But hard to get. Even more difficult to disguise, except in the tiniest droplets, which, regrettably, would do no harm. There had to be some other bane.

She went to the library.

Meanwhile, Pilate visited. Each time he came he wore a fresh white toga, differently embroidered from the last. One day, the braid was broad and purple, studded with small golden medallions. If the coins had not been incised with the likeness of the emperor, she would have preferred that toga to all the others. It enhanced his attractiveness; he was the tallest, slimmest Roman she had ever seen.

He never asked to take her to the bedchamber. Never even hinted, by glance or innuendo, that he wanted to lie with her. He seemed altogether content to sit with her outdoors on the propylaeum, sipping wine and nibbling at currant cakes, never any other refreshment, playing verbal games about Roman rules and ruthlessness, and whether the Greeks deserved their Sophocles and statuary, and whether the Jews were disciplined by God or disciplining Him. And how the Romans understood power and would not let the enemy unify; how they divided even their god into ineffectual godlets; which was why the single almighty Jewish God could be a menace to Rome. . . . As she had suspected, he was not stupid, and not a bungler.

Finally, annoyed. "That's unbecoming—how you call yourself a bungler!"

"But that's what I am," he said. "Ask Sejanus."

"And that's even worse. 'Ask Procula, ask the emperor, ask Sejanus!' " She was in a temper. "I ask you. Why should I ask Sejanus?"

"Because he knows all about me. He is my mentor. He watches over me, he intercedes for me with the emperor. I would not be the procurator of Palestine if not for him. Sejanus understands me and he loves me. And people who love me know me for what I am. A bungler!"

He smiled in an impish way, and she realized he was taking her into his confidence. Bungling was his mitigation, his alibi, his life's excuse for everything. Ask Procula, ask Sejanus . . . how shrewd the man was. What a wonderful cloak he had found to hide his inhumanity, his cruelty to the Jews. What a costume for the actor: the mantle of a fumbler, to hide the heart of rock, a garment without sleeves, because he had no arms or hands, only four left feet. And an incompetent phallus? No, he was probably expert in everything. Even in bed.

Then, why did he not wish to take her to the bedroom? Was he really a bungler in that single chamber of his life? Wine and currant cakes and courtly disputation—was this all the erotic consummation he could manage? Or was he teasing? By titillating her curiosity, did he think he was already titillating her body? Or was he engaged in some sort of perversion with, say, the display of his white-and-purple gowns of office, or his image of the ibises? Or—this, in a brothel, the most shocking perversion of all—was he faithful to his wife? Ask Procula.

She was getting nervous. He would be leaving—she did not know when—and she had found no reasonably safe way to murder him.

Rolling a currant in her fingers, "Will you stay in Alexandria much longer?"

"Would you like to get rid of me?"

"Oh, yes!" she laughed.

He laughed also. "That's right—you said that you would kill me."

"How long do I have?"

"Unfortunately—or fortunately, if you look forward to my company—I will have to stay perhaps a fortnight. Maybe more."

"I'm glad."

She was. It gave her a bit of breathing time. But not too much, she told herself. If desperation came to desperation, would she think of a paid assassin? Might there be a Zealot taking refuge in the city, or even a *sicarius* . . . ?

The blemish on the inside of her thigh was smaller than one of the medallions on Pilate's braid. No larger than a fingernail. It was not very red, it did not itch or ooze or bleed. It came, she surmised, from a new perfume she was using, and would disappear after a bath or two.

It did not.

Another one appeared a few inches to the left of her navel. That also did not go away.

There was no need to concern herself, she decided; it could have come from eating too many of the new plums, especially the underripe ones. But, that same day, another one appeared, and overnight, a rash of them. Luckily, they were covered by her clothing and did not show. Even more luckily, none of them disfigured her mouth or any of her private parts, so they could not be true chancres. She started to ask Entemia, but an instinct told her not to.

That evening, Mary felt feverish and became dizzy. She thought it was the onset of a flux of some sort, but it wasn't. A quite different sickliness, as if she would vomit if she could. She wished that this could be something other than she dreaded.

The next day, in secret, she went to a doctor in the Brucheum.

"Fever—dizziness," he said. "They are not the symptoms. Calm yourself. No need to be frightened. You have macules, yes—but they are merely blemishes, and all in innocent places. You haven't a single token of the thing."

The thing. He would not accord the dread ailment the dignity of a name. But it needed no Latin nomenclature. It had the same designation in Entemia's house. The Thing. It was the single matter, the single circumstance, the single terror, the single vile deed and its punishment.

And she could have wept for relief that the doctor had said she did not have it. But he had told her to come back in case the macules spread.

They did.

He examined her again, and said he had been wrong. It was the sickness. There would be other symptoms after a while. There was no cure for it.

As she was leaving, the eccentric physician, a finical man, was washing more thoroughly than she thought was necessary, even parts of himself that had not touched her, his arms, for example. He refused to take her money in his hand, but asked her to deposit the piece of silver into a ceramic cup that had a green tincture in it. With a flutter of hope, she asked what the liquid was, and he replied that it would cleanse a coin but not purge the blood.

Walking through the Brucheum . . . turmoil . . . what to do, where to go? Her father? Her brother? . . . Better to die in an alleyway.

Approaching Entemia's vast house, she quailed at the sight of it, and entered not by the great door but by one of the rear ones, small and hidden. You must resist your impulse to tell Entemia too quickly, she warned herself; give yourself a day or so to know what you are thinking; no matter how fond of you she is, the instant she hears The Thing, you will be out on the street. Meanwhile, an indisposition; call it that.

The sickness was still invisible to others. Not a sign on her face or hands. But: no cure for it, he had said; and there would be other symptoms. No need to be told about them; she had seen the diseased ones in the streets. Some people could not distinguish them from lepers. Yet there were differences that even the untrained eye could see. The one kind had running sores; the other, rot. Her sores would run. She had noticed the distinction when it was morbidly fascinating to her, in Jerusalem, and had read about it. Once, she had heard a sick Egyptian shout that he was not a leper who had to cry, "Unclean," but a man who would die with all his limbs, however venereally diseased. He was partially right about the limbs, but totally wrong about "Unclean." The law said the leprous *and* the chancred . . .

"Unclean!"

There was one other difference. There were old lepers.

She wanted to weep, and couldn't. She wanted to weep so badly that she almost wept for wanting to. O God, she cried, let me weep, *make* me weep, punish me with weeping, bless me with it, let the tears roll down my face, let me be wet with crying. But she could not weep about dying, she could not care.

A brief life, then. Good. Thank the monster God for miserly mercies. A long and fortunate life—wasn't that the general prayer? A short and fortunate life—a compromise. A short one, at the least. She would find a way to shorten it.

Braggart. Find a way to do what, exactly? Kill yourself? Why, God's testicles, you couldn't even find a way to kill a pig, a Roman, a Pontius Pilate.

The next morning, she discovered a tiny chancre on her most private part.

And at last she had found a way to kill a pig.

"Why do you not wish to see me in the late afternoons anymore?"

"Twilight—I have come to like the twilight," she responded.

"I arrive at twilight and even then you don't appear. It's already dark."

"I like the darkness better."

"You didn't when we first met."

"We are not the same as when we first met."

Pilate did not respond at once. Every response would be critical now, she knew. He would be leaving in three days. One intimacy might be enough, two would be better, and three . . . But so far, not even one. Was there any romantic promise in this converse about darkness?

"You're a woman who loves concealment."

She laughed in a false little melody. "Me? Really?"

"Yes. Even in daylight—when we first met—you hid half your face behind a scarf. Now I can barely see any of it."

Let us give praise for that, she thought, for there was the tiniest blemish—scarcely noticeable—at the corner of her mouth.

"Is it important that we see one another?" she asked.

"That has a troubling ambiguity . . ."

"We prize our eyes too highly."

"What do you prize more?"

"In the darkness . . . my mouth . . . my fingertips."

She knew she had come to the right place; she had come through a silence of a perfect length. This moment, if she reached her hand across the table and laid it gently on his, he would slowly reach his other hand to cover. Then he might do a number of other things. He might raise the hand to his mouth, he might simply hold it there, not kissing it, or—kissing—his tongue might single out a finger. That would be conclusive.

Slowly, as if afraid to make the faintest zephyr, she reached across the emptiness. Slowly, slowly she lowered her hand upon his own. Stillness then, not the flicker of a muscle. His hand was warm. With her fingertips she caressed his smooth skin, counted all the knuckles, then the valleys between them, and how they got lost in the light forest of his hairy wrist. Then she softly slid two fingers underneath, so that they might nestle in his palm if he should close his fingers.

But he didn't. He removed his hand. And he performed none of the rituals she had invited.

This silence, too, was long enough.

"I think you had better go."

"I do not wish to go," he said. "I wish to carry you upstairs."

She had better not sound eager. Chill the air a bit. "I am perfectly capable of walking."

"Yes, you are capable, that's clear."

A touch of acid, she thought. And envy. Was that—after all—truly what bothered him?

"You are not as incompetent as you claim—and I am not as capable."

"At best, I am a professional procurator—that is all. You are a professional . . ."

Suddenly she knew how to catch him. The oldest harlot stratagem that ever was.

"I am a professional with others! But I want to be a novice with you. I want to begin at the beginning. I want—oh, Lord, I want—! Oh, God, what a monster you are!"

And she began to cry. The tears were so well managed that she almost believed them herself.

"I'm sorry," he said. "Believe me, I am sorry."

But she knew he was not yet convinced.

"Go away," she said. "Please leave."

"I've said that I regret—"

"Did you think that I would take your money?" She arose from her chair. "You Roman toad, did you think I would take a single sesterce—?"

"I have paid Entemia and I—"

"Entemia is Entemia!" she shouted as he got up and started to approach her. "I always get extra money from my customers—have I ever taken a shekel from you?"

"It never occurred to me that you—from what I could see—"

"You saw nothing!" she cried. "You didn't see that I hung on every word you said, that I watched your every movement, that I could feel your body through every fold of your toga! You didn't see that I would go anywhere with you! Dear God, I would go back to Jerusalem with you—at the risk of being caught—for, God knows, I am caught already."

Her weeping was in wails.

He tried to comfort her. "Mary," he said pleading, "Mary."

"Don't touch me!"

He was indeed touching her, and her efforts to break away from him seemed so real that he had to pinion her against his body with all his strength. At last, her head lay against his breast and she sobbed heartachingly, while he spoke comforts to her, and endearments.

And it seemed so natural, like lovers who had never loved before, that they held fast to one another, clutched in the tenderest of embraces, and did not separate until they were in her bedchamber.

As they were undressing, "Do you really love me?" he asked.

"I love you to death."

And for an instant it was a comedy to her, a farce at which she wanted to scream with peals of laughter—it was the jest of Elias, and he, too, was laughing. And all at once, when she and the Roman were disrobed, it was as though the three of them were nude together, and she thought: There is nothing more terrible and more disgusting than human flesh. And look at the monster in the moonlight, tall and slim and as clean as all those Roman baths could ever make him, and Elias is corrupting in the grave and—on my way to it—so am I.

Now he stood there, a silhouette against the window, with his body straight and his penis erect—the blunderer who was not going to blunder, not tonight—and slowly moved toward her.

She thought as he started to touch her: Shall I, before he enters my body, humiliate him a little, as I humiliated Sejanus and those other Romans? Shall I diminish his strength and size? Shall I speak about a scaly scalp or a bad breath? As indeed his breath was bad.

Suddenly she realized it was not his exhalations she was smelling, but her own. There was rot in her and she was breathing it, and all at once she could not endure the fleshiness of being human, the ugly degrading pus and putridity of it, and all its lymphs and bloods and semens, and the act, the terrible, ugly act of procreation which created nothing, and as he reached and touched her breast, she screamed.

"Don't touch me! I am chancred!"

And she fled.

❖

When Mary confessed her illness, Entemia was not shocked. She had noted the young woman's listlessness the last few days, and this morning was on the verge of asking about the blemish at the corner of her mouth. The older woman wept a little, offered Mary extra money, which was refused, inquired what the sick one would do with herself, only half listened to the vague answer, and reminded her to leave her bedroom key.

She would leave Entemia's tomorrow morning, and go elsewhere. If she found a small room in the Egyptian quarter, and lived modestly, the money she had saved would last, she imagined, until she no longer needed it. Living frugally, she could take a longer time dying.

There would be a saving grace in her own death, she thought: she would not be left to mourn. Grief was always a belittlement, and she felt small enough. Insignificant.

Even what she was packing—a minimum of clothes—was insignificant. The sickness, however, would have some significance: something she would have to deal with and watch develop, as she might watch the spreading of a mildew or a mold, or a fester growing on meat, which of course it was.

She wondered when the real pains would begin. Some had already started—an aching in the joints, and last night, vomiting, she was reminded that bile is green.

As she opened and closed closets, she thought how odd it was: how difficult it used to be to choose between a purple mantle and a blue one, and now how easy it was to discard nearly everything. She kept only the simplest things, the lightest weight, the ones she could wear in the Rhacotis.

The women in the house accepted her dresses with arms outstretched, not sure they wanted to wear the clothing she had worn. But she assured them that those she offered had been untouched by any tainted part of herself. Besides, they were so beautiful: mantles of silk from Persepolis and from lands more oriental, damasks from Syria, intricate weavings of lace and velvet, scarves and ribbons like gossamer, and a tunic embroidered with spun gold overlaid with scarabs of amethyst. There were gloves and gloves, one pair made of leather so thin and soft that she had always worn them as a second skin.

She returned the gems that Entemia had loaned her—rings and necklaces, bands of brilliants to be worn upon the forehead, five sets of earrings, one of jade.

"Keep the jade," Entemia said.

"Thank you, but I will never wear them."

"Keep them—I beg you—please."

She would not. Truth to tell, she wanted no memory of herself in jade, no memory of how she had dressed up to be another woman, however beautiful. She could not wear mummery to her grave; there was little time left for pretense. This is what I am, she told herself, a Jewess with an ailment; it is, likely, what I have always been.

In the afternoon she went to the Rhacotis and found a room. She left a little money and said she would return tomorrow.

That night, her last one at Entemia's, she could not sleep. She ached a little and cried a little; not much. She tried to bring back only the loveliest memories. The hills of Magdala, of course. A belt of primroses her mother had made for her to wear around her waist. Your mother makes such fragile things, her father had said. Caleb's Bar Mitzvah; how beautiful he looked dressed in his grown-up tunic and his silken prayer shawl and his shining innocence. And the first time she had been able to read a Greek poem . . . and that boy Judas, could he write a poem? And the soft ferny light in the tabernacle Jesus had built for her outside the walls of the Essenes, and the paleness of his face. And Elias. If only she could believe in eternity or afterlife or heavenly encounters . . . with Elias waiting for her. She wondered if heaven was childhood and death, a divine contrariety. She thought of how, one day, her mother plaited Mary's hair in exactly the way that her own was done, and how alike they looked, and how happy they were. You make such fragile things.

Her weeping, however quiet, was soon past control. I want to be in Magdala, she said, with my mother and my sweet hills and my crocuses. I don't want to spend my last days in the Rhacotis, crying my life away in Egypt, I want to cry at home, I want to cry at home. . . .

She returned to Palestine. Entemia had begged her not to do so: You will get caught, she kept saying tearfully, don't do it, you'll get caught. But Mary wondered wryly what difference that would make, and said goodbye—no, don't embrace me. But Entemia took her into her arms and held her close and even kissed her forehead and murmured gentle things through tears and caresses and regrets. Don't go to Magdala, she said.

. . . Mary did not actually go to Magdala, nor even to her onetime home in Jerusalem. Not because she had a fear of being apprehended, but because she did not want to be seen by her father or even by the old servants. She felt there was something inexplicable about wanting so desperately to be back in the land of her birth when, in fact, she would deliberately be avoiding all the places in her birthright's memory. Why did she want so achingly to be here, and to be buried in this earth of Israel?

Was she, after all, a Jew? When did she cease being one, when did she start to eat on fast days? When did she stop admitting to herself that the sweetmeats nibbled on Yom Kippur always had a taint of bitterness? How could she be a Jew in so many ways and a heretic in so many others? There was hardly a line of the Torah, except for the Psalms, perhaps, that she would not gladly erase from her memory; the Ten Commandments seemed a crass morality for wanton children; and now that she was dying, there was no solace to be drawn from any of the Jewish lore or ritual she had ever learned. Then, what was she coming home to?

Not to her father, certainly. She would only bring him disgrace and pain; and pain for herself as well. He could only view her as an apostate and a sinner—and how could she let him see the lesions of her punishment?

How could she let anyone see them? The progress of the sickness, the physician had said, is various; with some, slow; with others, swift. Her "progress," it would appear, might be mercifully swift. For the first two days of the voyage, nobody had seemed to notice that she was in any way different from anyone else; one of her fellow voyagers had, in fact, preened a few feathers. But, in the last two days, she had been shunned. It was from them, rather than from her polished silver disk, that she knew that the skin of her face had altered. For the rest of the voyage she wore a heavy veil.

Where could she go, and disappear? Where would she not be looked upon with disgust? Where would she not be looked upon at all?

Where there were others like her. Where the cripples lived, and the sick and the leprous. Where she would be undistinguishable from the maimed and the poor and the mad and the dying.

She went to the Valley of Hinnom.

She lived on a hidden street in a hidden house in a hidden room. Hiding was her name.

But achieving the state of invisibility was not as easy as she had hoped, even in Gehenna. The poor still saw her, they knew her presence. Not that they openly stared; they hadn't the courage for that. They simply blinked and squinted with distrust; suspicion gave them cats' eyes. She thought, at first, that they hated her, but hatred required a vigor they did not possess; resentment was the most they could manage; it was natural for them; resentment was their customary condition.

At first, she tried to believe she was different from them: She washed her crusted sores; they didn't. They lived in a truce with the rats and roaches; she warred. They ate the refuse from the taverns, some even scrabbled in the middens; she could afford a loaf of bread and a bowl of gruel and even, if she did not squander otherwise, a speckled fruit. Most important, she did not cringe. They cringed in doorways, they cringed as they walked, they cringed in everything they did; but her demeanor was always straight. She drew back from nothing, not the ignominy of her sickness, not its pain, which was getting worse each day, certainly not the imminence of death. She would not cringe.

One night, however, she realized that her *mind* was cringing. She cowered from thought. Whenever a question started with why or wherefore, her brain recoiled from it. It was as if she was afraid to know what had caused her torments, why her joys had been so short-lived and mostly in her childhood, why she had not had a lasting love, why she had not been chosen to bear a child, why she had been so beautiful and was now so ugly, why she was dying at such a young age. And on that particular night, all those questions came rioting in upon her, making a chaos in her mind, and a pain in her body so unbearable that she wailed.

When it was over: I must not be afraid to think, she said. I must remember that thinking used to be my joy, and knowing was my quest.

I must go in search of *knowing.* I must discover why and wherefore. I must seek out all the great *becauses,* or even a single one. I must find God, if only to spit at Him.

Then she did a wonderful and unexpected thing. She bought a book. It took more than she could afford—half of her money, half. As if she were gambling half her remaining sustenance upon the felicity of a single thought. It was an odd papyrus, a single roll, not a double, exquisitely lettered all in Greek, poems from a score of sources, a few proverbs, a single psalm for the Sabbath, and a vivid design of wild poppies done in brilliant inks. The miscellany made her feel as though all her pockets were full of surprises, and it was worth every coin she had paid for it. Let me live only half my allotted days, she said, but let me read a little and ask a final question. Let me hope for a single answer. Let me have another flash of knowing before I die!

On a day when the sky was sodden, she wandered eastward in Gehinnom and came upon the lepers. This was where they had to remain, crowded together and forbidden to stray, by the muck-infected waters of the Kidron. There was a multitude of men and women, and many children, too, afflicted with the sickness. The stench of their disease was suffocating. Insects hovered by the millions, making black clouds and a buzz in the atmosphere. They clung in swarms to the rotted skin; the leprous had to keep their tired bodies in constant motion or the flies would blacken and torture them.

As they saw her approaching, they spoke their warning to her. "Unclean!" they whimpered. "*Tameh!* Unclean!"

Then they asked for bread, for clean water, for anything at all that they might eat or drink. Some of them approached, but not too closely; the law was strict. A legless woman came nearer than the others. Her reek was almost intolerable and it seemed that one of her beseeching hands was no longer attached by anything but a tendon, the bones were eaten away. Bread, she said, bread.

Mary went away and returned with five loaves. She broke them into tiny morsels and tossed them out as if to birds. The lepers scrambled and made terrible little noises, liquid, mucal sounds, and suddenly there was a quarreling and a fighting over crumbs.

"No!" she cried. "No—I will go for more! Do not quarrel—do not fight!"

Abruptly—with no previous sign of them—a *quadrum* of soldiers arrived. They carried long wooden poles which they used to prod the lepers apart from one another, and back from the margins of their permitted space. Shouts and screams and proddings. Suddenly—she could not stand seeing it—a pole poking at a man's dangling arm—and as it prodded, the limb wobbled lifelessly and fell to the ground. Animal noises then, and throttled shriekings.

One of the soldiers, approaching, started to drive her off. But as he came closer, he saw her disfigurations.

"Say, 'Unclean'!" he shouted.

She was confused and afraid, and not swift enough.

"Say unclean as I approach you!"

"I am not a leper."

"Harlot! Say, '*Tameh*'; say, 'Unclean'!"

"Unclean," she murmured.

"Louder, so we are warned."

"Unclean! Unclean!"

She had not spoken it aloud until that day. And thenceforward she uttered it always, whenever she was out of doors. At first it was an announcement that someone else was arriving, not any person she had ever been. Then, at last, she knew that she, Mary of Magdala, was unclean, and she stopped bathing. She became loathsome to herself.

All that she had left was the book. But soon she was unable to read. A few minutes perhaps, all being fine and clear and delicate; then the letters would merge. She took to looking only at the pictures, the poppies, but one day the individual flowers flowed together and became a single blob of redness. They were blood and she was bleeding. It was only a nosebleed; after a while, she halted the flow.

Three days later, at dusk, she stood in an alleyway and heard a running through the streets. It is a woman, she said; a crowd is pursuing her. She shouts for them to let her alone, that poor fugitive. Someone rips the creature's mantle, her bodice, someone tears her hair. She falls. Oh, let me be, she cries, but they beat her. Her face is full of terror, her mouth wails piteously, her eyes are dying. Why don't they let her be? Or—why is she so desperately clinging to her life? Let go, she advises the woman, why don't you let go?

The pains got worse and worse. She could not read the book at all, she could not see the flowers. Then, one day, when she simply wanted to hold it in her hands, to touch it, she could not find the book anywhere. Perhaps it was here in the room, in an unaccustomed place, hiding. But, nothing. Or perhaps she had dropped it on the street. Nearly blind, she went outdoors, trudged for hours, and still found nothing. Lost, the beautiful book, lost even to the touching.

Then there was a falling in her mind, a dropping out of her brain's grasp, and she thought: part of me will drift below being, and will be lost as the book is lost, and I will never discover it again.

I wish I were dead, she said, I wish it were tomorrow. But I won't know when death has come, will I? Death is the tomorrow that never comes.

Still, longing to die, she clung to things. A learned phrase, a memory of the way she had played with numbers, a fugitive melody, the meter of a poem. And Magdala.

She yearned for Magdala. Clearer than any image in her mind was the soft sweep of a meadow of home. The hills of Galilee, I want to die in the hills, somewhere.

So she started to walk northward to her dying.

She walked and walked.

"Unclean," she said as she trudged onward.

But she would not be unclean in Magdala.

Judas was fond of all the disciples except Simon Zelotes. There were twelve of them now, including himself. Simon the fisherman had said Jesus had chosen twelve as a symbol of the twelve tribes of Israel; but Judas believed he had chosen that number in commemoration of the Twelve Elders of the Essenes, and he often wondered but never asked whether Jesus regretted leaving them.

Judas did not. His life with Jesus was nearly an all-pervading peace. He had never known a time so free of turmoil. He lived in the freedom of knowing that what he did, how he tended the sick and ministered to the poor, how he learned and taught, how he prayed, all had one quality in common: goodness. Even how he sang. It used to be that he never sang aloud. I have a camel's voice, he once said, all croak, no resonance. Bit by bit, however, as Jesus and the disciples would sing the lovely psalms, he started to sing with them, and hark, there was melody in his voice.

There was much singing among the disciples; they were a cheery, warmhearted lot who needed only a snatch of melody to conjoin them in a chorus of loud, uplifted voices. Everyone sang—save Zelotes. Silent and detached, he would take close heed of the music as if spying for a hidden half note of treachery. He trusted nothing, Judas decided, because he himself was not to be trusted. In his presence, Judas was always tense. With the others, however, he was at ease; they were his friends. He had little chance to speak intimately with the four fishermen, Simon, Andrew, James and John, for they scarcely ever left Jesus' side; but he had something in common with Matthew, who, like himself, had been a publican, a collector of customs taxes in Galilee. Philip and Thaddeus, and James the son of Alphaeus had all done a number of things, and even had had a number of names, so there was talk about their questionable pasts. Still, Judas believed them to be honest men—honest sinners, he called them—if not as bright as he would have wanted them to be. None of us is bright enough, he told himself, to understand the deepest meanings of the man who teaches us. Possibly the slowest-minded disciple was Thomas. Frequently he would ask the same question again and again, in various versions, because he did not comprehend the answer. This uncertainty made him seem skeptical to the others, but Judas was convinced he was not a doubter, but a muddlehead. Bartholomew, whom Judas still called Bartholomew of the Bread, was his favorite. The boy had been a follower of John the Baptist, and when the preacher had been arrested by Herod and thrown into the prison at Machaerus, the lad had been saddened into misery. He spoke rarely, and when he did it was a forlorn question, always about the baptist: Are they torturing him, do you suppose? Dungeons are damp and cold and he is so thin; do you think it will sicken him?

Judas and the Zealot, discordant from the beginning, came no closer to being friends. They had different views on nearly everything. For example, what to do with the collections? They all subsisted on what people gave them—food, a place to sleep, a cast-off cloak, occasionally a shekel or two. Sometimes the disciples were able to get a few days' employment, but being on the move made it difficult to find work, especially for the fishermen. But there was no privation. Now and then, when Jesus spoke to a particularly large throng, there was a sizable quantity of coins. Judas had been put in charge of the money, and he knew exactly what to do with it: what they did not need to survive on, he gave to the poor. Even if he were not certain, without asking, that Jesus would have done the same, he still would have made the donations; it was how they lived. When Jesus sent them forth to heal the sick and spread word of the Kingdom of Heaven, he bade them provide neither a bag for their journey nor extra tunics nor sandals nor staffs. Money was not needed. Simon Zelotes, however, disagreed. He said that action would be costly, and when the time came . . .

The Zealot always sounded as though he was making threats and issuing warnings, and his subversion of the Nazarene's teachings offended Judas.

But he had to admit that the man was an effective rabble-rouser. Sometimes he would disappear for a few days, and for at least a week after his return the crowds who came to listen to Jesus would multiply. Of course he did not spread the word entirely on his own; he had his helpers, and it was tacitly understood he was still one of the Zealot leaders. That was another thing Judas disliked about the man, his divided allegiance.

"You ride two horses," he said.

"You walk."

"Where do you gallop, in such a hurry?"

"To Jerusalem."

"Why Jerusalem? Is there no God in Galilee?"

"God is everywhere, but the Roman fortress is in Jerusalem."

"Jesus does not believe that the Kingdom of Heaven is in a Roman fortress."

"Judas, you're the dupe of heaven. You don't see the ground at all. You look up there, and you get an azure notion of what Jesus believes. You hear him talk only about lilies of the field and how blessed are the meek. But you suddenly go deaf when he tells you to clench your fist."

"I've never heard him say that."

"You don't listen. On the day that he said he did not bring peace but a sword, what did you do? You turned away. I saw you leave the crowd. You turned your back on him."

It was true. He heard what he needed to hear—all of them did. Jesus had words of comfort and instruction that would apply—in distinct and seemingly discrepant ways—to nearly everybody. Not that the teacher himself was inconsistent, but his image of salvation was illuminated by a thousand lights, all of different colors and intensities. The image that Simon Zelotes saw was lighted only by an incendiary fire, which, Judas had to admit, had in recent weeks burned hotly in Jesus.

What worried him most about the Zealot was the kind of crowds he assembled. It rankled that many of the spectators had little religious purpose, and that some of them were probably criminals, even armed. Why were they so indiscriminately mustered; hadn't Jesus' popularity been blooming like a sudden summer, even without Zelotes' help? Something frightening was happening. Sometimes there was a feeling of riot in the air. Why did people of that sort come to the teachings of a quiet, peaceable man, as if he were a gladiator in a Roman circus? What did they see in him? One day, Judas realized what it was they were coming to watch:

Miracles. That's what Simon Zelotes had promised them. Judas was incensed. "You are bribing them with miracles!"

"Nonsense! I'm not bribing them at all." The Zealot was affronted, but did not lose his temper. "When they come and ask me about the miraculous, what am I to tell them—it's a trick of the eye?"

"It's not a miracle. He hates that word. And he has never—not once —called them miracles!"

"What does he call it? And what are *we* to call it? What is it when he heals a leper? What is it when the blind can see and the mute can speak? What is it when he raises a young girl from the dead?"

"She was not dead!"

"Her father said she was—and she was cold as stone."

"She was sleeping. Those were Jesus' words. 'The girl is not dead, but sleeping.' "

"Because death is not death to him," Simon said quietly. "He believes in life everlasting."

That Simon Zelotes should believe this—Simon, the worldly fighter, the iron-brained man of arms—that *he* should believe this—! And that I, Judas Iscariot, a man of the spirit, should not—?

If I do not believe Jesus makes miracles, it is because he has forbidden me to do so, Judas said, and whatever he tells me to do, I will obey—I have given my whole mind over to him. More, I have given him my essence, I have put my life into his safekeeping. I have told him everything about myself, I have opened my heart and soul so that my whole being is known to him; there is no dream nor any hope of heaven, no sin I have committed or even contemplated that is unfamiliar to him. I have given him all that I am, down to my smallest secret.

Then, why does he keep his secret from *me?* Why is he so unknown to me? He is a Nazarene, a *nozri,* and the Hebrew root *nzr* signifies something kept or guarded. A keeper of a mystery, a guardian of an enigma. What mystery, what enigma? What secret of the Essenes did he learn, in those days, without ever having taken his vows?

One evening he and Jesus argued. Why do you conceal what you mean and what you are? To which the teacher answered that he concealed nothing. Yes, you hide, Judas said, you hide even from the multitudes. You do not speak openly to them, but in parables. Why?

This time Jesus' reply was not so ready. It was given to the disciples to know the mysteries of the Kingdom of Heaven, he said, but not to the throng. "Seeing, they do not see; and hearing, they do not hear; nor do they understand."

Therefore the parables? To Judas it was even less clear after he had explained it. He was reminded of the secret within a box, within a box, within a box. What would be in the innermost box?

The Kingdom of Heaven, of course. But what *is* the Kingdom of Heaven?

Again the master answered in parables. The Kingdom of Heaven is like a man who sowed a mustard seed, it is like leaven, like treasure hidden in a field, like a merchant seeking pearls, like a dragnet cast into the sea that gathers some of every kind.

Box within a box, within . . . But what if the final, infinitesimal box held nothing?

Or everything. The secret of the Messiah.

Whatever ark of the covenant was closed to Judas, this was the one he prayed that Jesus would unlock. When will the Messiah come, and how will we know him? Month by month, the scrivener grew more certain that the teacher knew the answer to this. And if he refused to reveal it, there must be danger in the question—and in the revelation. But what could the danger be?

On a stormy afternoon, by the sea near Gergesa, a Pharisee shouted to Jesus in a hectoring voice: "Do you say you are the Messiah?"

A trap, of course. The fates of false Messiahs were various—exile, execration, hanging, stones.

There was a silence.

Then Judas saw Zelotes, followed by two of his men, slipping through the crowd, and as the Pharisee made a frightened noise, he was whisked away. Later, it was said that the questioner had been beaten, but the Zealot denied it.

Judas worried. It might be the start of a plot against Jesus. A case against him. But it would be built on falsity and illogic. The man was innocent. He had never claimed to be the Messiah. And he would not. He satisfied none of the criteria for a Christ:

First, he was not of the house of David. It had been prophesied that the Messiah must be a direct descendant of David, and Jesus made no claim to such a heritage. On the contrary, when someone asked him the direct question, he had answered with one of his typically cryptic replies, to the effect that everyone was the descendant of the Lord.

Second, he did not conform with an alternate prophesy that the Messiah would be a Levite; Jesus did not come from the priestly class.

Third, the Nazarene could never satisfy the criterion that the Messiah would be Moses reincarnated, who would open up the earth, disinter the true Temple of the Jews, and rededicate the sacred vessels to the Holy Name—for Jesus put no store in ornate temples and holy vessels made of gold.

No matter how the Pharisees or the Sadducees—or even the Romans—might plot against him, they would not find him culpable in any way. Jesus did not even pretend to satisfy any of the Messianic criteria. He would never be so false or so foolhardy. Thank God.

Not always could Jesus mend the ailing and make the cripples walk. There were times when the blind remained blind and the deaf could not hear thunder. On such occasions, Judas could hardly bear how stricken Jesus was. Unable to diminish the distresses of the sick, he took all their pains upon himself. How terrible it was for him to be such a gatherer of agonies.

When he had first become a disciple, Judas had thought that Jesus was like the Stoics, indifferent to pleasure and pain. Later, in a changing view, he saw him as a man who did not know the difference, because he was *made* of pain; it was his essence. Then he saw the underground spring of love that flowed within the man.

It occurred on a day when Jesus was ministering to a leper so diseased that the man could not hold himself erect, he was corrupting away. One side of his body was open flesh, and he stank. As the teacher ministered to the disintegrating creature, Judas shuddered and could scarcely remain present. Jesus knelt beside the sick one, raised a suppurating hand and held it to his own breast, stroked it, kissed it, then took the leper in his arms and ever so gently rocked, murmuring, murmuring, while the helpless one gazed at him. For a long time, it seemed, he rocked and murmured. Moment by moment the man's trembling ceased. At last, through the features that were almost unrecognizable as a countenance, a smile began to spread. And the sick one slept.

The man was still a leper. His flesh did not mend. His limbs did not strengthen. His sores did not heal. But something had healed in him. Some other sickness in him was comforted, if not cured.

Later, Judas asked if Jesus' love had been the remedy.

The Master smiled sadly. "If that were only enough," he said. "I tried to take his sins upon myself . . . as if *that* were enough."

"What *is* enough?"

He contemplated the question, but did not answer. Judas wondered if he might say that nothing was enough, that only in heaven was there a sufficiency.

There was a little girl who went along as one of Jesus' followers. She did not know how old she was; sometimes she said ten, sometimes eleven. Alone in the world, she scarcely remembered her parents; they had been taken by the plague. She was not a sad child; she rejoiced in everything, mostly the small things she could manage. She nursed a fallen bird, she tended an ailing lamb; she believed it a pity that beautiful, tiny minnows could grow into terrible crocodiles; she thought a crocodile was a carp that had been cursed.

The child fell ill of an unrecognizable ailment. Whatever doctors were summoned, whatever supplications Jesus made to save her life, did not serve to improve her health. One morning she was dead.

As Judas and Bartholomew were digging the child's grave, Jesus sat on the grass with the deceased child in his lap. All the sunlight of Galilee had left his face. He was dust. In the past few days, his little more than thirty years had doubled; he had become old, too feeble for his task. And stricken with penalty. It was as if he had gathered up all the sins that his hand and mind had committed, and they did not add up to one fault so great as his failure to save this single child.

Whatever else he was—teacher, prophet, priest—he was first a healer. Judas suspected that this was what he loved most about himself. Yet—also—what he most distrusted. So that he could see Jesus, day by day, moving further and further away from the pride of healing the body to the aspiration of healing the spirit. The soul was becoming everything. He could see—almost palpably—the falling away of substantive things. He was purifying. Words, deeds, the daily phenomena were becoming incongruous to him; neither food nor raiment nor sleep was within his soul's reckoning. Only to be one with God.

⁂

There were rumors that John the Baptist had been spirited out of the dungeon in Machaerus and that he was now free in Ephesus. There were rumors that he had died in prison. There were rumors that the Romans had starved him to death, that he had starved himself, that he had escaped and shaved his beard and become an itinerant singer or leech or ironmonger, that Zealots had stormed the fort of Machaerus, had killed a score of Romans, and that John was now the leader of a Zealot band. Ridiculous rumors with the leer of mockery, sober rumors with wisps of hope.

One day, two followers of John appeared before Jesus and his disciples, and brought the truth. The baptist was still alive in Herod's prison and had sent them as messengers to the Nazarene. He had heard about the good works of the one he had baptized, and his emissaries had been instructed to ask a single question. The eldest of them stepped forward:

"Are you the Coming One, or do we look for another?"

A silence fell on Jesus' disciples. It was as if, through all the recent seasons, there had been no other question on their lips, and they had never dared to ask it. Judas, trembling, wished the question had never been uttered.

Jesus was answering it:

Go and tell John whatever you hear and see, he said; that the blind receive their sight and the lame walk; the lepers are cleansed and the deaf hear; the dead are raised up and the poor have the gospel preached to them.

Judas's heart leapt with pleasure. It was the perfect answer. *Whatever you hear and see.* Jesus did not ask for praise for what he had not accomplished, he did not lay claim to being the Messiah, or to being the Coming One.

If the spirit of Judas was lightened, the spirit of Jesus was on wings, but for another reason. John, whom he loved, was still alive. And he called the baptist a prophet, and more than a prophet: John was God's messenger who would prepare the way.

"Prepare the way for what?" Simon Zelotes asked after the emissaries had gone.

Jesus did not answer. Judas did. "For the Kingdom of Heaven."

"Or for the Messiah," Zelotes said.

"Jesus did not say that."

The Zealot ignored Judas. His attention was solely on the master. "Did they not ask you if you were the Messiah?"

Still the master did not speak, and Judas spoke for him. "They did not ask the question, and Jesus did not answer it."

"Did he not imply that he was the Messiah?"

"No!"

"Did he not say he was the Coming One?"

"No, he did not even say that." Judas could feel the roiling of his blood. "And it's wrong to suggest that he did."

"Why wrong?"

"It's reckless—and you know it!"

"If courage is wanted—"

"Damn you, Zelotes!"

Suddenly Zelotes had him by the throat. "Don't you damn me, Judas—don't you dare to damn me!"

"Halt!"

It was Jesus' voice. The two men separated. Judas's tumult would not easily be quieted; he moved a few paces from the others. Zelotes, however, was more skilled at mastering himself. He took a moment or two, then spoke evenly.

"I did not mean to sound reckless. I was puzzled by what message the master was sending to the baptist. Did he not imply that he was the Coming One? Am I asking such an evil question?"

"No, it is a good question," Simon Bar Jonah said. His voice was quiet, judicious. The fisherman from Capernaum spoke rarely, but when he did, the disciples listened.

Judas, too, was inclined to pay heed to the man. He returned to the center of the group. Relenting, he turned to the Zealot. "I'm sorry I cursed you, Zelotes."

The Zealot also tried to be conciliatory. "We will all end by cursing one another unless we know what message Jesus sent to John."

He turned squarely to Jesus, who responded quietly. "Did you not hear what I said?"

Exasperated: "I did not *understand* it!"

"To some it is given to understand; to others it is not."

Judas's tension broke away like an eggshell. He laughed heartily. Simple as the master's mind sometimes appeared to be, how complex it was! The most clarifying teacher, he was also the most mystifying. He could send a ray of light through a black tempest, but he could also wrap a raindrop in a cloud. And how stubbornly, how steadily he hewed to his own untold design while the others shifted and wavered and floundered among their ifs and maybes and supposes! The scrivener did not even try to contain his pleasure, his merriment. And a number of the apostles laughed with him. But the two Simons did not laugh.

One summer afternoon, many people fainted. The crowd was so huge and densely packed, and the sun so blistering hot, that Jesus, fearful of calamity, had called out that he would speak at another time. But they shouted back to him that they must hear him teach—now, this minute; they had come from far places, and they were in need of him.

As always, Judas marveled at how intently they listened. This day, they lifted their heads to his lesson as if it were a zephyr refreshing them against the hellish heat. They were enrapt, making not a murmur or a movement, thousands of human beings turned to statuary. No matter how loudly he had to speak in order to be heard by the multitude, his listeners felt that his words were intimate, one teacher to one student. As Bartholomew said, He speaks only to me.

There were times when he roared to the firmament, when he bellowed about the impenitence of cities or those who vilified the spirit of God, or despoiled the innocence of children. Then his voice was a brass trumpet. However he spoke—sweetly or in wrath—it was exactly how they yearned for him to speak. He dazzled them, he irradiated them with his light. They gave him all their heedfulness—their eyes, their ears, their hearts. When they listened, they scarcely breathed. When he asked them to respond, they shouted, they cried out, they wept.

He was their savior. They had been nothing before he came; even those who had had a sustenance: nothing. It was as if they had all been waiting on a threshold somewhere—exiles, banished forever from their homes—not knowing where the next step would take them, except that it would be another place of anguish. And he had come along and given them a refuge, he had invited them into the kingdom of glory, the country of God. Jesus was their beloved, and they were his.

On that day of dreadful heat, Judas and his disciples carried jars of water among the people, bringing succor to the old, the feeble, the sick, the women who nursed children. Go home, Judas would murmur to the saddest of them, he will not heal you today, there are too many, there are too many. Always too many, and, even among the believers, too little faith.

Then, at the edge of the crowd, there was a terrible outcry. Judas thought at first that someone else had fallen unconscious. But the shouts continued, and a sound of raging, fighting. He hurried.

"Stone her!"

The phrase was always hateful to him. Stones were the weapons of cowards; they lent anonymity to the murderer.

He pushed his way through the crowd.

"Stone her!"

No need to stone her, Judas thought. She was dead. Twenty paces away, separate from the others, she lay on the ground, motionless, not a breath stirring, a clump of soiled rags.

One of the men had a stone in his hand but waited for others to join him. Some were already stooping for their missiles.

Judas reached for the man's stone.

"Let be," he said.

"She's a harlot." The man meant for everyone to hear him. "She tried to join us—without saying, 'Unclean.' "

"Unclean!" a woman shouted. "She did not say, 'Unclean.' "

"She's a whore—she tried to sicken us!"

"Leave off," Judas said. "Can you not see that she is dead?"

As he turned from the crowd to look at the woman once more, she stirred. Moaning, she moved a little. Seeing her in new pain, gasping, he hurried to her side. Her breath had begun to return, and she opened her eyes. But the sun was too much and she closed them again. Now she tried to struggle to her feet, but she had no strength for it. When Judas knelt to help her, she made a gesture to put him off. Again she opened her eyes and attempted to squint against the sun. She was filthy in every way, clothes, skin, hair. Her face was a mass of sores. She seemed bereft of her senses. There was no sign of knowing in her eyes.

Once more she made an effort to rise, and did better this time, except that she stumbled over her ragged mantle. At last, struggling, panting, she allowed him to help her to her feet. Stumbling again, apparently almost blind, she made a movement toward what she must vaguely be seeing as humanity. As she took a step toward the throng, and another step, the people backed away and flinched from her. Others, those who held their ground, raised stones.

The same man took up the shout again: "Stone her!"

Suddenly another voice. Jesus.

Over the noise of the crowd, he spoke softly but firmly. What words he spoke were unclear to Judas. Something about sin and the casting of stones. The waves of people parted, as if for Moses, and Jesus advanced toward the woman.

As he moved, so did she. But she fell again. And nobody helped her to arise, not even Judas. He was looking at the master.

Jesus walked, and continued walking. Then he was beside her. He glanced up into the blazing sun, as if to say that she needed shelter from it. Then, stooping, he lifted her into his arms, and carried her to where the tents were pitched on the hillside.

There was no sleep for Judas that night. While Bartholomew slumbered silently, Philip frequently had bad dreams and shouted in them. Earlier, he had snored and quarreled. Besides, the tent was too small for the three of them. Judas wondered how the four fishermen, one of whom was the huge Simon Bar Jonah, could manage in a tent of similar size.

Jesus had the tiniest of the five tents, but he was alone in it. Except tonight, watching over the harlot. Judas hoped that in ministering to her, the master would not be infected by her disease. What a strange notion it is, Judas mused, that I have never worried about lepers infecting him, and yet, this woman . . . Perhaps the infection I am thinking of is not disease, but sin.

As if the night were not warm enough, just thinking of the chancres made him hot with nerves. He needed more air. Softly, so as not to disturb the others, he slid along the ground and went outdoors.

The moon had been too young to last, and the stars seemed not as luminous as usual. The hillside was quite dark except for a slit of gold, a taper probably, through a chink of Jesus' tent. Was he going to endure a whole night of hopeless vigil over the dying woman? If so, it would be Jesus who would need the comforting, not the irrecoverable one.

With a shudder of loathing, Judas started toward the tent. He did not want to get there. In a moment, close enough that the slit of light felt like a knife blade on his cheek, he whispered Jesus' name. There was a murmur for him to enter.

Jesus did not turn his head. His gaze was on the sleeping, dying woman. He watched her as closely as if he were reading words in the lineaments of her face.

The tent was oppressive, stifling. The taper had burned down to a puddle of paraffin in the dish, and had consumed all the breathable air. What was left was the rank smell of the woman's sickness.

Jesus looked weary to exhaustion. There was no illumination in his eyes, and he stared so fixedly that Judas wondered if there was sight in them. He seemed like a man slowly disappearing into his own stupor; any moment, he would vanish.

"Go to our tent," Judas said softly. "It is cooler there."

Jesus scarcely stirred: no.

"Go—please. You must sleep."

"She is going to die."

The fact was so foregone that it needed no utterance. "Please go," Judas said. "I will watch over her."

It was empty. No need for anyone to watch over her; no use. But apparently Judas's offer gave Jesus leave to suspend momentarily his custody of the sick one. He arose unevenly, as if his bones and sinews had been gnarled, and left the tent.

For a while, Judas resented that his own impulse had committed him to an unavailing ministry. It was not the loss of sleep he minded, nor even the futility, but the stench. He opened the flap to get more air. It was a night of such doldrum that the candle flame did not even flicker.

He sat in Jesus' place upon the ground and did not look at her. Strange, he thought after an interval, the stench seemed to have lessened. The reason was, clearly, quite simple: he was getting used to it. Or was it stupefying him, as it seemed to have done to Jesus?

He stole a glance at the woman's face. It was too horrible. He must not look at it again or it would make him ill.

But you must gaze on suffering, a voice said to him. It could have been the voice of the Teacher of Righteousness, stern with piety, or the voice of Jesus, aching with compassion.

He forced himself—with main effort of mind and will—to turn his attention upon the face. Breathe, he told himself, but not in the slow rhythm of the dying woman, breathe deeply, quickly, to your own measure, *breathe.* And look at her—do not turn away.

It helped if he thought her face was not real. It certainly did not look real, and again he had the sense that he was staring at a mask. What lay behind it, what true countenance was hidden behind this hideously false one?

He made himself imagine real features and a real visage. He created in his mind an unblemished forehead and cheeks that were clean and flawless, and a nose as fine as if it had been carved out of glowing pearwood. And the mouth—see how the sores vanished!—and how beautifully curved the lips were, and how they puckered as if they had a taste of citron on them. And—best of all—behind those closed lids, he envisioned eyes so shining, so deep yet so radiant, so glittering with a defiance of life—!

The lids opened. They flickered as if the first breeze of the evening had fluttered the candle flame; then they closed again.

Had he imagined that?

Had he imagined as well that he *knew* those eyes as—for an instant —he had imagined that he knew the face his fantasy had created? Fantasy, yes, he told himself, not real. The scars and the sores were real; the face was a vagary his mind had made.

The eyelids flickered again, and opened. The eyes were quite still; they gazed at him.

He felt ill. It is the heat and this torpid air, he said; it is a fever. I am seeing an apparition that I myself have devised. I do not know this face

. . . and yet I do know it. I have seen it and I cannot remember where, it is real, it is false, it is my own imagining.

Then her eyes closed again.

Hours later, it seemed, although not yet dawn, Jesus returned.

"I think I know this woman," Judas said.

Jesus did not answer.

Judas shook. "I do not know who she is, but I know her!"

"I, too," he said. "She came to us once."

"Came . . . to . . . us?"

"The Poor."

"Who is she?"

"Mary of Magdala."

"Oh, dear God!"

Suddenly none of it was imaginable to Judas. He could no longer see an exquisite woman behind the hideous mask, he could not identify that radiant creature in a black and golden chariot, that flame of living beauty with this ugly, ashen, dying thing.

"I don't believe it."

Jesus nodded as if to say it was better not to believe it; and randomly, given permission to doubt that it was she, Judas no longer doubted it. Oh, dear Heaven, he said, oh, dear God.

Jesus grieved. "She is dying."

They had said before that she was dying. But this was Mary of Magdala, a different person, and now it needed saying differently.

"Can you help her?"

"I have prayed for her all night."

He said it with the desolation that he had done all he could, and that it might not even be enough to cleanse her spirit or help her to die in peace.

"Can you make her live?"

Gently, Jesus touched him. "Give her over, Judas."

"Can you make her live?"

"Judas . . . she can scarcely breathe. There is not the faintest sign of . . ."

"She opened her eyes!"

"There is no hope in her."

"And no prayer."

Neither of them had said it. It was the voice of the sick woman. "No prayer." . . . Scarcely a whisper . . . difficult to hear the words, clear enough to hear the despair.

Judas turned to her, as Jesus did.

Not despair, but cold bitterness. As he took a step toward her, her voice seemed to surface through a phlegm of hatred.

"Do not pray over me."

Judas knelt beside her body, and as Jesus, too, approached her—

"Get away from me," she said. "You stink of sanctity!"

"Mary—"

"You both stink worse than I do!"

Weakly, her arms fumbling at the air, she tried to strike Judas's hands away.

"Let me die!" she cried. "Why don't you let me die—without pissing your prayers all over me—!"

"No, don't—!"

Gasping, choking for air, she cursed them. Her words were as foul as her breath and body. She was profane, hurling one obscenity after another, shrieking at them and at their God.

Then sudden silence.

So, Judas thought, she is dead.

A flickering of eyelids . . .

"Help her," Judas whispered.

Jesus started to depart.

"No—I beg you—help her!"

"There is nothing more I can do."

"Yes—help her—save her!"

Jesus closed his eyes. "I cannot."

"Yes you can! You've saved lepers and cripples! You've taken criminals into your bosom—and publicans like Matthew and myself—and strangers who have reviled you! This is someone we both saw when she was healthy and young and lovely to behold! If you can help the ugly and the sick and the malformed—can't you help one of God's most beautiful?"

"I have tried, Judas, and now—"

"Now you turn her away?"

"I do not turn her away!" He was wounded. "But you ask for another miracle!"

"Another! You used the word—another! Then, you *have* made miracles! Yes—I ask for a miracle!"

"But she blasphemes—she reviles God! She has no faith."

"I have faith! I—Judas—I have faith! Do it for me!"

Jesus was still. Until, with a look of pleading, he gazed upward and began, almost inaudibly, to beg for release, for mercy, comprehension. "Dear Father . . ."

The following morning one of the ulcerations on the sick woman's face began to close.

Would it be another miracle? Judas, his mind fixed upon Jesus, asked the question of which he was most afraid: Could he be the Messiah?

11

Only part of it was screaming. The pain in her bosom was screaming. The bleeding animals, screaming. Then there were the eyes blazing down at her out of blackness, burning her, and the question from the faceless questioner:

"Why are you in such a haste to die?"

The tightening of her skin as if her body were being confined into a smaller and smaller container, crushing all her tissues together, bones, blood, organs, brain, compressing them into a single substance of flesh, letting the blood run out like the squeezing of wet curds in a sack of muslin. The feeling faint, her heart beating too loud, an echo in a chasm. The needing of air, of some word or other that was constantly missing, of more fingernails to scrabble with, the need to sleep forever, to cough something up, to see a new spring lamb getting to its feet.

Someone always seemed to be pleading, beseeching her to do something or reach for someone; it disgusted her. She choked, she retched, but vomited nothing. One day they took leathers to her; she thought she would be beaten, but they tied her to some object and she could not stir. That time she wanted desperately to speak, but her tongue had swollen and was so engorged in her mouth that there was not the slightest space for a word to breathe in, and her screaming was silent, an aching, stifled shrieking in her throat, her breast, her belly.

But not all of it was screaming. Sometimes she heard a little girl laughing, a delicious sound, and the more her attendants worried and comforted her—as if she needed comfort on such exhilarating occasions —the more she laughed. Sometimes, wanting a child, she felt a rising in her womb like the rising of bread that her mother would be baking, such a lovely aroma and warmth of home, and she was back in Magdala with Caleb and her parents, and Mary was the mother and Mary was the child, and the hills were all surprises, and her joy was a boundless meadow.

Sometimes the teacher came and she hated him. He was too white and pure, and she felt that he did not sorrow for her half so deeply as he pretended, that he battened on her misery like a maggot feeding on her rotting flesh. He spoke of angels and devils as though they were his intimates, and she needed to drive him off, so she often cursed him. But after a while, when he seemed willing to suffer the punishment of all her maledictions, she surrendered them as redress for his patience. Less and less she screamed when he was near.

Then there was the time when the dead came to life again. Judas and Elias—they were quick once more, they ran, they reached for boughs, they ate apples, one of them spoke to her:

"Why are you in such a haste . . . ?"

"Are you Judas?"

There was a glow through the shadows: the beaming of his smile. "Yes, I am Judas."

"You are the . . . ?" She could not find the word. "The one who writes."

"The scrivener, yes."

"And you have come back from . . . there?"

He looked puzzled. "Yes."

"Where is Elias?"

"Who?"

"The other one . . . Elias."

He paused and she wondered if he was going to be sly and pretend he had never known Elias. "You mean the one from Kerioth?" he asked.

"Yes, that one," she said. "Which of you died first?"

He looked troubled, but she was not going to let him avoid the question.

"Which?" she insisted. "You or the one I killed?"

"You didn't kill anyone."

"He did not come back with you?"

His trouble deepened. Instead of replying, he reached toward her and put something on her forehead, something warm and cool at the same time, deeply comforting.

"What is it?" she asked. Before he could reply, she knew: a compress. There had been many such, now that she recalled them. And every time she had been aware of the pleasantness, he had been nearby.

After a while, he removed the damp cloth, which he set down in the stone basin. He dried her forehead with a softened linen. Then he placed his hand on her brow to see how warm it was.

"You had better not touch me," she said softly.

"I have been touching you for months," he answered.

She could not believe it. But she had no way of knowing; she could not recognize anything, not the place, not the bed she lay in, not the clothes she wore.

She looked at her hands. They were clean; even her nails were clean. There were a number of scabs, but no running sores. Slowly, with a tremor, she raised her fingers to her cheek. There was a tiny damp spot on her cheekbone, but the few incrustations that remained were dry. Her other cheek was somewhat the same, and her forehead felt free of any blemish.

"I . . . am I getting better?"

"Yes," he said. She had never known a smile could come out of so many hiding places.

"Are you sure?"

"Yes, I am sure."

"My body . . . ?"

He flushed. "Your body is like your face."

"You are sure of that as well?"

He was befuddled with embarrassment. "Yes. You have a few unhealed spots on your back." He could hardly continue. "And a few . . . others." Then, recovering. "But they are healing—everything is healing."

Her head began to swim again. Nothing he had told her was true, she was sure of that. It was all apiece with her dreams of having a child and having been one, of the carefree little girl who laughed; part of the tender touchings of the past, when one had a cold and was wrapped warm, when a knee was skinned and bandaged, when parents made a miraculous ministry to ailing children.

She wept that it was another of her dreams, and wished she were not awake at all, and tried to go to sleep again. She wondered if she would open her eyes upon some other region.

They were always moving her. When she first became aware of the transfers, she did not like them. No place is better than any other place, she would have said if she could talk; you busy people, don't you know that? Then, when she was able to speak a few words, they were always the same: Go without me.

But they never failed to take her with them. There were so many tents in so many pastures, there were walls of baked clay and walls of stone with mortar crumbling, and walls of wood. One day there were old cedar planks between her and some animals, and she wondered what kind of living things they were. Then, through the sleepy buzz of afternoon flies, she recognized the snorts and snufflings, and a cow made a mooing sound. Not far away, she thought, just beyond the wall, a close and friendly neighbor. She listened and she smiled. It was the first time she had smiled in—how long?

In the later weeks, when she was out of bed and walking, she was not certain what occurred around her. She took no part in anything. Some days she simply sat and watched the dragonflies. She tried to predict where they would land and how long they would remain. She counted them. Distinguishing one from another was extremely difficult, but she did her best. That might be all she would do in one day. And it would tire her.

Some days she made lists of things. An accounting, for example, of how many ways, in how many languages, she could say "however." Judas said it was a good sign. "However" signified the other side of things.

"Why should I see the other side when I don't see this one?"

Jesus had been listening to them, and he grinned. Smiling was easy for him, but grinning was almost impossible. His eyes and facial muscles were not built for it, but sometimes—rarely—he seemed to trick them into doing things they were not meant to do. When it happened, his eyes capered.

She wished she could like him. She remembered that she had liked him years before, when they had first met. But he was different now. He lived with destiny; this made him pompous.

But there was not a single puff of pomposity in Judas, and she was deeply fond of him. He was the most woundable man she had ever met; he walked through life in his naked skin. Even if she wanted to, she could never be unkind to him—it would be like torturing a deer. And so selfless he was, so full of devotion! He was ready to die for anyone he loved—for Jesus, surely—and, she thought, for her.

One day, when all her scars were mended, they walked together along the shore of Gennesaret. In the whispering winds from the sea she could feel the shrouds of her illness slip shiveringly away. She wondered aloud why the breeze from the water tangled her hair but did not in the least bit ruffle his beard. He raised both hands to his face as if the reference to whiskers could not apply to him, and seemed absurdly surprised that he had hair on his face.

They laughed, and she thought: he has forgotten what he looks like; he has no vanity. He bathes as often as the Essenes told him he must, he cleans his teeth, he runs his fingers through his hair, but he never studies a silver image of himself, never gazes in a pond. No vainglory, none at all.

Nor would he even take the credit that life owed him. That day, in particular, he rejected a gratitude that was due him. A dozen times she had started to thank him, and on each occasion he had found a way to skirt the subject.

"Why will you never let me thank you?"

"You have thanked me enough."

"Enough? For saving my life?"

"Not I. It was Jesus."

"It was the doctor who came—how many times? And you."

"No. . . . Believe me."

"I do not believe you," she said quietly. "It was you—all the time—nighttimes, daytimes—you—washing my sores—bathing me—you."

"As your sores were healing, mine were too."

Did he know how touched she was? "You healed me."

"No. He did more than I," Judas said. "He prayed for you."

"Didn't you pray?"

"Yes. But it was his prayers that were answered."

"His—oh, murder!—will you stop kneeling before him? If you both prayed, why couldn't it have been your prayers that were answered?"

"Mary—please—"

"Please what? If your prayers are useless, why don't you stop praying? What good are they? Let him say them for you!"

"That is unkind."

"What sort of partisan God do you pray to? How dare you say you both prayed and He listened only to him!"

"Because you had an incurable disease and Jesus cried to God."

"You—*you* cried!"

". . . I do not make miracles."

"Nor does Jesus!"

"He does," he said softly. "He did."

"You're a fool!"

For all her musings, for all her fervid resolutions that she would never hurt him, it was as though she had struck the man.

And he had no guile to cover up the smart. He simply looked at her, and away, and back at her again.

"Oh, Judas—forgive me!"

She lifted his hand and kissed it a dozen times, forgive me, she kept saying, forgive me. And then, because she saw the ache unmended, she embraced and held him. His arms were tight and close and she felt that his hurt was far too great for the provocation, and it could only mean that his love was too much, that his love—not her affront—was the torment he was suffering. And she wanted to beg him, to warn him: Don't love me too much, for I have too little to return.

⁂

Now that she was well again, why did she not continue onward to Magdala? Had Magdala, when she was a child, truly been a paradise? Or had she, in the delusion of her illness, made her childhood home a fantasy of Eden which now—in her more logical mind—she was afraid to see in its reality? Was Magdala only a place to dream of? And now that she was awake . . .

She wanted to be dreaming . . . and awake. Not that she was enamored of consciousness. But life among the followers of Jesus was satisfactory to her, even if she was an unbeliever. For the first time, she was one of the simple working women. Among the hundreds of steady followers, many of them were females. Some were there with their husbands, some with their parents; but a few were unattached. They cooked when there was food to cook, they tended the sick, they cleansed whatever they could lay their hands on. Many of the women, like many of the men, did not work at all; they begged. This was a more formidable labor than Mary could ever think of doing, so she did manual things. She washed. She could not count the streams she beat the clothes in, the well-copings; she could not count the soiled mantles she made clean, the tunics, the bodices, or the number of heads she scoured of vermin. Among the other women who were laboring, she discovered that the hardest-working were the ones who had left their husbands; and the two who had left their children as well—they, especially, labored ceaselessly, in a frenzy. At a stream one day, she saw one of them beating a wet tunic against a rock as if she meant not to cleanse the garment but to cleave the rock. She worked like a slave. It occurred to Mary: She certainly was not fleeing the slavery of housework; then, what slavery . . . ? Mary wondered why the woman—Zilpah, her name was—why she was here. She suspected, without knowing any reason, that it had nothing to do with God, and that there were many followers—women especially—who were unbelievers like Mary herself.

One day, when Zilpah was frantic with more work than she could finish, Mary took some of the woman's soiled clothes and put them on her own pile.

Zilpah tried to get them back, but Mary said, "If you're going to work so hard, you may as well go home."

Sober as the statement was, it was spoken lightly, so that the woman could dismiss it. But she did not.

"They don't need me at home," Zilpah said.

"Are you sure?"

"Yes. I have no daughters."

The response was oblique. Mary turned quickly.

"My husband is comfortable in every way," Zilpah continued. "My children are boys—both past their Bar Mitzvah. They own everything."

With only half a smile: "Even God."

The woman grinned. "Oh, yes, He is theirs."

"And this one?"

"Which one?" Zilpah clearly knew that Mary had meant Jesus, of course, but the woman was distressed. "I don't know."

"Then, why are you here?"

"I don't know that, either." Her discomfort was becoming more acute. "Except—Jesus—he speaks to us. Sometimes he even speaks to me. One day, he asked me if I knew who God was. He asked *me.*"

"What did you answer?"

She turned crimson. "I didn't know any answer. I couldn't even speak—I was embarrassed."

"Was it so important to you that he asked you?"

"In all my married life, my husband never wanted to know if I ever asked who God was. It never occurred to him that I *could* ask such a question."

"Did it occur to you?"

"Oh, no!"

"And now you can ask."

"But now . . . I am afraid to."

As I may be, Mary thought. Better not to ask the question at all, but simply to assume there is no God, no deity she had to deal with, pray to, blame, bargain with, curse at. Love.

"Will Jesus help you to find God, do you suppose?"

Zilpah's brow knit. "I don't know. I think yes. Whenever I know the right question to ask, he always answers."

"Satisfactorily?"

She smiled self-deprecatingly. "Well . . . I am so grateful for *any* answer." Her face clouded. "Except once . . ."

"What was the question?"

"I said to him, 'You always talk to us—and you listen. You treat us not like sisters, but like brothers. We are not only important—we are important to *you.* Even, perhaps, to God. Then . . . why is none of your twelve apostles a woman?' "

"What did he answer?"

"He did not answer."

"Nothing at all?"

"He looked troubled, and went away."

Mary wondered if Jesus used this as a conscious stratagem: look troubled and walk away. She had seen him do it often. Well, far better than answering a question with a lie. But he was scrupulously faithful to the truth. She wondered whether he was honest on principle or on pride. His rejection of sham might be part of his pact with God, or he might be brain-arrogant, so swift and direct of mind that he never had to move circuitously by way of falsehood. Lies took too much time, and he was in a hurry. She wondered where he was hurrying.

There was another stratagem he used, which was like a lie, yet wasn't. He gave obscure answers to simple questions. Mary thought it was elusive and somewhat slippery. But Judas believed he was always giving a direct answer to another, unasked question, one that Jesus himself was hearing in his mind, and that he was always trying to quell some tempest that was storming there. For example:

One day, Bartholomew and a few others who had been disciples of John the Baptist asked why the Pharisees fasted—and the baptist's people as well—yet many of Jesus' followers did not fast. And why did he not upbraid them for this? To which Jesus suggested that the friends of the bridegroom need not mourn as long as he was with them; time enough when he was taken away.

It irritated Mary. Fasting was fasting, as she recalled the Law, and jabber about bridegrooms seemed to her a bit of Sophism. But not to Judas. To Judas, the teacher was not answering an inappreciable question about fasting, but a vital one that doomed about in Jesus' head: How long will I live?

It was true, she realized, that while the man was offering everlasting life to everyone, he spoke often of his own death. She wondered if he did it to gain sympathy, or if he was struggling, somehow, with an obsession.

She wished that Judas did not love him so much. How odd, she thought: I don't want Judas to love me—or to love Jesus. Not so much, not with such a wrench of heart and soul. Whom can Judas love, then? God? First, he would have to create Him. Perhaps that was what Judas and Jesus and all the other poor hopeful fools were trying to do.

Simon Zelotes hardly ever spoke to her. When she had been ill, he had rarely come to see her—inquiring about her health, but maintaining a detachment. He had never revealed that, in another place and in another connection, they had been accomplices.

His aloofness wounded her. She construed it as contempt for a woman who had failed him and his cause.

But perhaps he merely did not want to betray that he knew her as a Zealot who had been involved in murders. If that was the reason, she was grateful to him. During the days when she was getting well, finding herself in the first self-respecting time of her life, she dreaded that her new existence would be ruined: someone would recognize her and name her a criminal. But she had nothing to fear from Simon Zelotes. He told her so one day.

"I no longer know you as a Zealot," he said, "only as a harlot regenerated."

She stiffened, and he was quick to give a reassurance. "Don't think I say this with the same feelings as the other disciples have. Yesterday, they threw stones at you; today, lilies of the valley. They sentimentalize everything, have you noticed?—even whoredom."

"I have not noticed." Her manner was wooden.

"Then, notice. Look how they treat you—with much more regard than they give to Zilpah, for example. They think because the sin of the flesh is one of the more interesting ones, that the sinner is also interesting. She must be more than she appears—a more golden heart, a victim of misfortune, a sufferer of wrongs—and be capable of great pity and understanding and devotion."

"I don't believe they feel that way."

"Yes, they do. When you were sick, they considered you filthier than dung; when you became well, you were cleaner than their mothers."

"And to you?"

"You are not my mother, and you were never dung. I know what you are because I know what you were. That you went through a time of harlotry does not make you a different woman. You were bright and brave—and I still know you that way." Then he smiled grimly. "But I dare not know you too well—or some will think you are a Zealot. Which you are not."

Mary's gratitude—and admiration—increased. She regretted that she and Simon could not be closer friends. But she agreed that the better part of wisdom would be to keep her distance. And she did.

One twilight, however, in the shadows, like a thief, he beckoned her to come away from the others. She was helping in the preparation of an outdoor meal for some two hundred people, and it was difficult. But when night came, with embers glowing in the fires and stomachs full, she drifted away toward the tiny grove of locust trees, and met with the Zealot.

He had a present for her. He groped for her hand in the dimness, and placed the object in it. The thing was hard, metallic, and felt like a buckle.

"Yes, a buckle," he said. "A *fibula.*"

She had forgotten the meaning of the word; then its companion came to mind: a *cingulum.* The buckle off a Roman soldier's belt.

She shrank from asking whose it was. "Tullius?"

"No," he answered. "The other one—Quintus Sallus."

"How was he killed?"

"I will not tell you that."

"Did you do it?"

"That, either."

"Whoever did it—I am not grateful."

She handed the buckle back to him, and he hefted it in his hand.

Surprised, he did not speak for a moment. "Have you decided to forgive the Romans? Are you turning your cheek?"

She was insulted by the irony in his voice. She knew that Zelotes was not a cheek-turner, but he *was* a disciple, and mockery did not suit the role.

"No," she said. "I'll never forgive them. And I want no one to kill them—except myself."

He looked momentarily confused, and she wondered why. She knew the source of her own confusion: ineffectuality—and rancor at those who had been slain without herself as executioner.

"Tullius is still alive?" she asked.

"Yes."

"Where is he?"

"What difference? You don't mean to kill him, do you?"

"Yes, I do."

"It will be done for you."

"No! Myself!"

"Mary, please—"

"Why do you doubt me? Because I failed before, does that mean I will fail again? Why do you doubt me?"

"Because you have changed—the teacher has cured you. He has cast out your demons."

"That's not true! I still have them! All seven demons—as if they were alive!"

He was silent, and she yearned to tell him how she ached to believe in a man who could cast out demons, or in a God who cared enough to do so. If the Nazarene was able to heal the lesions on her skin, why had he not healed the lesions on her soul?

As he looked at her, Simon's confusion seemed to have cleared. In its place, pity. "Give over, Mary," he said quietly. "Let us do this for you. Take the buckle, and have done."

"I will not have done." She tried to sound calm. "I say that I will kill him—and I will."

"When the time comes . . ."

"I will do it."

"Very well." She was not altogether sure he was accepting her promise. "Meanwhile—here—take the buckle—only a token—take it."

She took the thing and he started away from her. "Wait."

He turned.

"You said that Jesus has changed me. Has he changed you?"

"He changes all of us."

Only a half answer. "Why are you here?"

He made an ambiguous gesture.

"Why do you claim to be one of his disciples?"

"Because I am one of his disciples."

"I think you lie, Simon."

"Oh, no. I believe in him."

"I don't think you even believe in God."

"No, not in God—but in Jesus."

"And when he says, Turn the other cheek, you go and kill a Roman."

"No. When he says, Not peace but a sword."

"I think that's a way of hiding that you don't believe in him at all."

He retraced his steps and came so close that she could see his breath in the chill night air. "You've been listening to Judas," he said. "He's a troubled soul who lives either in heaven or hell, but never both at the same time. Which means he doesn't live on earth. He thinks a man should be either a soldier or a priest. He's wrong: a Jew must be both. He thinks the devil can be prayed out of existence; I think he must be stabbed. He says, Let the Romans rob us and kill us and shame us on earth; and we will have our heaven. I think the Romans will also rob us of heaven." He was silent an instant. Then: "But Jesus—! The Nazarene is not a babe in arms. He knows that there are those to whom we turn the cheek, and others in whom we turn the blade. He says we're a scattered multitude, like sheep without a shepherd. He's right. And when Jesus sings the psalm about the Lord being *his* shepherd—Jesus is *ours*. He will lead us and he will take care of us. Where there are wolves, there will be staves—and where there are Romans, there will be swords!"

There was a jarring dissonance between the Zealot's martial music and the peaceable harmonies of the teacher from Nazareth. For days, she could not get Simon's portents of bloodshed out of her mind. When Pharisees came to mock Jesus, she wondered when their taunts would turn into brickbats. And a more frightening phenomenon was happening: more and more Romans were appearing among the multitude of listeners; soldiers, for the most part, and their insolences.

She wished that Judas, whose mind was always at war with the Zealot's might, would not be satisfied with the naïve comfort that the energy of Jesus' love was stronger than Simon's sword. The fact was, the swords were *there.* The Romans carried them, the *sicarii* in the crowds were armed with daggers, and every hillside had its slide of stones.

But Judas pointed out a progression she had not noticed. Often now, after a particularly inspiring session and after the crowds had departed, a single Pharisee might remain. He would talk quietly with Jesus, and they might walk apart somewhere; and next week, perhaps, he would appear again. No mockery anymore. But he might be a single Pharisee in a month, and the Pharisees that hated Jesus were many, and always there, buzzing about like hornets.

"What about the Romans?" Judas asked.

She had been unable to believe it, the first time she saw Romans joining as followers. There had been a centurion. Catching sight of the uniform, she had felt a clutch at her throat, but it was another Roman of the same rank, not Tullius. Since that time, there had been a few more Roman soldiers, with shifty eyes, trying not to be seen or recognized. One day, watching two of them at prayer, Mary wondered what language they prayed in.

The simplest, if they prayed according to the model the Nazarene had set. It was another source of her irritation with the teacher. That particular prayer, for example, in its utter artlessless, its naïve innocence—how did he expect mature people—? How had he had the effrontery to distill out of all the ancient, scholarly, closely reasoned, time-honored formularies of Hebrew ritual a concourse with God that was so childlike? Childish, in fact. Did he think that Jews were such simple people, and that God, if He existed, was simpleminded? Did he think that neither the Lord nor the people would understand a mode of address more manifold than he had given the worshipers to speak? It piqued her to watch them praying—many of them kneeling to do so—with words so simplistic.

"Our Father who art in heaven, hallowed be Thy name. Thy kingdom come, Thy will be done on earth as it is in heaven. Give us this day . . ."

Naïve, ingenuous. Yet . . . she had to admit . . . the prayer had beauty. Heard as verse, it was filled with grace. She said it often—as a poem—not to God, of course—but to herself.

She had noticed, toward the end of her stay at Entemia's—how long ago it seemed—that her breasts were becoming heavy and slightly pendulous. But now, even though she was older, there was no longer any slackness in them; hard work had made her leaner and her bosom firm again.

Her skin was clear. One day, alone, bathing in a brook that leveled into a pond and became a brook again, she leaned over the calm water and gazed at herself for a long time. All she saw reflected was her face, her arms, her torso to her waist. She was entirely well at last, she told herself, and something of her youth had returned to her. Her neck and shoulders, like her bosom, had been restored to a slimness that was pleasing, as succinct as a well-turned sentence. She was once more beautiful.

But she was no longer young. Her skin, unblemished as it was, had aged. Not that her face had wrinkled, nor that there were any of the tiny discolorations on the backs of her hands which might hint at the passing years; merely that her skin had lost—what was it?—the signs of a caress. Or even the need for it. Gone. Gone the hunger to be touched, to be stroked, gone even from her mind the fantasy that the love in a man's fingers was magical with . . . what magic had she dreamed?

Yet . . . sadly . . . she knew that Judas longed to touch her. If only she had the yearning to be caressed that she had had when there were tutors teaching geography and the enigma of zero and the difference between Cynics and Stoics— how gladly she would satisfy it with Judas.

Beware, she thought. You said the same about Elias once, and regretted not having satisfied anything. Beware of what, then? Beware of yes or no? Beware of loving and not wanting?

"I want to go to Magdala," she said.

Judas was surprised.

"Are you sure?"

"Yes. I'm ready now. I want to know if it was as beautiful as I remember it."

"It won't be."

"I'm prepared for it not to be."

"Yes . . . go."

If he had tried to convince her not to make the trip to her childhood home, her disagreement would have fortified her. But now that he was, in a sense, giving her permission to be brave, she suddenly felt cowardly.

"Will you come with me?"

She had not expected him to look so pleased; had, in fact, imagined that he would view the chore much as if she had asked him to accompany her back home for a funeral. But even that, she suspected, would be a felicity for him: whatever she felt deeply, he wanted to be close to.

When she was afraid to approach the place, Mary had pushed Magdala a world away. But now that she was going, it was only across a shallow valley, a few miles distant, a few hours' walk. The time was spring at its earliest, but spring in a rush. Green raced with green to get there first. Buds burst and flowers jostled for attention. There was such a precipitance in everything, that Mary and Judas approached Magdala before she wanted to be there. Wait, she said, I don't want to see it too suddenly; could we just sit awhile?

They lay down in a shaded glen, beside a busy stream. He's pretending to be asleep, she thought, so that I will pretend as well, and unbind my muscles, and breathe deeply, and relieve my heart. He is smiling. A dapple of treetops obscures the sun and his smile is gone. He is so available, so tender that a misplaced leaf can take the sunlight out of his life. And yet, he is so capable of happiness. This morning, as we started down the hill, he danced. He somersaulted in the cedar needles, and came up stung and laughing and embracing me and somersaulting once again. What a child he is, how inexpert in the world; he has lived too long in the shelter of a commune and a cause, too much with God and too little with man. I want to touch his face, but I am afraid he may actually be asleep and I will awaken him. I want to smooth his hair and beard, I want to soothe him, strengthen him. Be strong, Judas, be strong on your own, without . . . him. Without God, too. I beg you, because I love you and tremble for you, be strong.

Not yet noon, as they turned the shoulder of the ridge, she beheld her childhood home. Half a hill away, and halfway down, it was exactly as she remembered it.

In the old days, until early afternoon, there was always a mist in the sheep meadow, so that from the western windows of the house one could never be certain that the flock was there. Only the tinkle of the bellwether was the assurance. Now the meadow wore its mist and, so faintly that she felt she might only be remembering, she heard the gentle clinking sound.

She must beware, she told herself, of the serene sense that nothing here had changed, everything had remained friendly and familiar. She had had the same sentiment about Jerusalem once, and had discovered that it was alien. But this . . .

It was exactly as she remembered. The house itself was bathed in the same forenoon light as in the olden time, the shutters were still open as they would be this hour of the day, even the poplar trees did not seem to have grown. The same, the same, everything the same.

She would go closer, then, indoors perhaps. Her heart pounding at her ribs, she started down the hill, Judas following.

Abruptly—! Stop, she said. What an idiot you are! Nothing can be the same. What a simpleton to imagine otherwise. Your mother is dead, so are the two bondspeople. Your father is more absent than he ever was. Your brother is lost . . . and so, perhaps, are you.

She closed her eyes to the house, and opened them upon the hillside—her mother's hillside. It was as though the woman was an arm's length away. With a wild distraction, Mary's glance darted across the ground, the grasses, the weeds, whatever verdure lay upon the springtime, searching, seeking for only a single flower. But—again—too late in the season. There were no crocuses.

What? Did you come for crocuses? To see things as they once were? No, you came to see things die—as you yourself will. You came to be punished with the knowledge that you are mortal!

Uncontrollably, she began to weep.

Judas hurried close to her. "Don't. Oh—beloved—don't!"

"Hold me," she said. "Hold me."

He took her in his arms and held her against her quaking.

"Hold me."

As his hands moved over her, she thought: Nothing that my body is, is worth what it means to him.

"Touch me—touch me."

As they lay together—she in her silence, and he in his outcries—she tried to hear what he was saying. Oh, God, was all she could descry, oh, God.

She wished that she, too, could call on Him, but there was no prayer in her. Then, because she wanted it to be more beautiful than it was, she told herself:

"Our Father who art in heaven . . ."

But it was only a poem.

12

Judas felt blessed. He was in love in all the ways he wanted to be in love. With a woman, with a friend who was the Son of Man, and with God. And *they* all loved *him.* He flourished, to his felicity, in a world of benediction where he could sing gratitude to the Lord, and praise to His creation, which had turned pure and kind and bountiful.

True, he had a shadow on his life, a sin—he was committing fornication. But it was only a temporary impiety, and the tarnish on the bright coin of his life would be rubbed away as soon as he and Mary married. Which could not happen soon enough for him. But for Mary . . . he must not broach the subject with an insensitive and reckless haste. Let well enough alone for a while, until she had completely committed her mind to the fact that she was no longer ill. Odd, he thought, that a state of health should demand as much dedication as a state of illness. No matter how totally her body had been restored, her soul was still ailing in some distant and inaccessible place. Except for Judas, who did not use his masculinity as a coercion, she had not as yet made peace with men or God. Sometimes, seeing her alienation from the Lord, he wished that the Almighty were a woman. For Mary's sake.

For Mary's bright, loving, hard-working, charitable sake, he wished all men were humane, all hands gentle, and that all hearts beat with the same throb of compassion. That all men were Jesus.

Not that Mary wanted a world of Jesuses; she would deride such a thought. But then, he and Mary did not agree on everything. In fact, their appraisals of people were nearly always discrepant.

For example, she thought Thomas was one of the most interesting of the disciples. He had been so teased and put to ridicule for his incessant questioning, that he had shrunken into a sulk. Mary felt sorry for him, she liked him; he was a doubter, she said, a young man of unsounded depths. Judas said he was a dunce.

Another difference: Judas recalled with awe how quickly the four fishermen had become adherents of Jesus. It had all been done in a single day—scarcely a glance from the Nazarene, and they had tossed away their nets and followed him. What a wonderment! Nonsense, Mary said. All four had sprung from the same steamy soil—Galilee—a hotbed of insurrection. They had probably been rebels for years, maybe even secret Zealots, waiting for a safe and subtle leader, someone who did not rashly brandish daggers the way Barabbas did. And when Jesus came . . .

They particularly disagreed about Simon Bar Jonah, the fisherman. She disliked him because she thought Jesus overvalued the man. He gives sententious advice, she said, and he intones. But Judas was fond of the disciple and, in a way, even revered him. Simon is a tall man, he said, who does not know his own height, bumps his head on lintels, and when he is uncertain what is expected of him, falls short of his stature. But when he knows precisely what the master wants, the fisherman is a giant. A giant minnow, she said.

They almost concurred in their feeling about Bartholomew. Didn't she find him the most considerate of all the disciples, Judas asked, the most generous, the most delicate? Yes, she answered, because he is girlish. Judas was shocked and annoyed. He lost his temper.

"Don't bring Alexandria to Galilee!"

The outburst was so beyond provocation, and he was so ashamed of having abused her confidences about her past, that he spluttered with apology. But Mary was oddly unperturbed. "Why were you so angry?" she said mildly. "If I say he's girlish, do you think I like him the less? Or are you afraid that if you thought it true, *you* might like him less?"

She had the mind of a rhetorician. This ruffled him, and he told her so. They had been walking by the Dead Sea, on a desolate, salty shore where nothing grew, no weeds, no water plants, for the sea was sterile. They walked away from the beach, where only tamarisks could struggle for their lives, and in the suffocating heat they lay under the shade of a spindly tree.

Frequently, he said, she made distinctions that did not exist.

"Or that have not occurred to you."

"Take the distinction between Matthew and me," he continued as if he had not heard her. "You see a vast difference, but I see very little. Both tax collectors, both scriveners, both with styli in our heads."

The similarities were superficial, Mary said; in their vitals, they were totally different. Matthew lived in his mind, he was an intellectual; Judas lived in his heart and in his visions, a mystic.

He had never thought of himself as a mystic. Hadn't he been the last of the disciples to use the word "miracle"?

"But now you're the one who most fervently believes they are miracles."

"They are."

"And the one who believes most devoutly that he is the Messiah."

"I have never said that."

"But you believe it."

"I will not believe it until he tells me to believe it."

"Oh, Judas . . ."

He heard the pity in her voice, and was hurt. "This is a bad subject for us. You can't talk about the Messiah without scorn, and I can't talk about him without heartache."

"Heartache—?"

"Sometimes I dream of the Messiah with such hope and such joy that it's torment."

"But why, Judas? Why do you need a Messiah? As a messenger? If you believe in God, do you need a messenger to tell you He exists?"

He was confused, he was hot; his head swam. She laid her hand on his forehead to smooth away the anxiousness. With her fingertips she closed his eyelids as if to shut out whatever might be irksome to his sight. He wished she were in love with him.

"You are very dear to me," she said quietly.

He tried to smile. "Like a pet lamb?"

She was distressed. "I've never lain with a man who truly loved me. Do you think that touches me so little?"

"I want to touch you more deeply than I do."

"Why do you try to measure the depth of my love? Can you measure your own?"

Again, wanting not to sound too grave: "Fathomless."

"I think you think so. . . . Sometimes I see that you're in love with me, and sometimes with Jesus." Her face shadowed. "But you are really in love with the Messiah."

"I love all of you."

"But the Messiah is your passion."

The matter so disturbed both of them that they agreed not to discuss it anymore, although Judas knew it was a pact they could not keep.

Only a week later, walking through woods at the foot of Mount Tabor, they had another, more turbulent disagreement. He had pointed out that, considering her disdain for the teacher, she worried unnecessarily about his fate.

Darkly, she turned to him. "His enemies will do him in."

Judas hated her to say such things. Convinced that her alarm was unjustified, he pointed out that the Nazarene's quarrel with the Pharisees and Sadducees was already being pacified. There were clear signs. While the poor, as Jesus had said in other contexts, had always been with them, now even the middle class and the rich were joining the master. Only last month, a Sadducee named Joseph of Arimathea had become a follower, and he was a member of the Sanhedrin!

"Does one Sadducee mean the whole Sanhedrin?"

"I loathe it when there's acid on your tongue—I loathe it!"

"They'll do him in, Judas."

"No! They will all be reconciled!"

"Reconciled? Jesus and the hypocrites? Don't you hear what they say about him? 'He heals on the Sabbath! He takes up with publicans and whores. He doesn't fast when he's supposed to. He says he can forgive sins and cast out demons.' "

"He says no such thing!"

"That's what they *say* he says!"

Judas did not dispute the importance of the charges, but they were all merely differences in the interpretation of the Law, and Jews had squabbled over them since time beyond memory. The Greeks had their contests at the Olympic games, the Romans at chariot races, the Jews at the scrolls.

"Scrolls! What idiot talks about scrolls? He talks about life and death —about who should make sacrifices and who should be sacrificed. He talks about who should eat and who should starve—"

"No!"

"—who should survive and who should perish. He talks revolution."

He was incensed. "Don't you dare to say that! It's not true!"

"Ask Simon Zelotes."

"I don't have to ask that fanatic! I listen to Jesus himself. I hear only about kindness and love and the Kingdom of Heaven!"

"Not anymore, Judas. He talks about hell and damnation these days. The wages of evil."

"And the triumph of good—the prize of heaven!"

"The prize of heaven will be exile and persecution—God's wrath and God's judgment."

"That's not what I hear him say."

"Then, you don't listen."

"Yes I do. I hear a man who is so full of love—"

"And anger! He has become full of rage. And if you don't hear that in his voice, you're deaf. I think you *want* to be deaf to him—and blind —and stupid!"

All at once, she started to quake. She made a sound as if she were wracked with pain. Afraid she was becoming ill, Judas hurried to steady her. But when his hand touched her arm, she violently struck it away.

"Don't touch me!" she shouted. "I can't stand you when you shut your mind to the truth! I can't stand you!"

She ran through the woods, away from him.

Perhaps Mary was right, he thought: deaf, blind, stupid. Yet, if Jesus was preaching such unpopular homilies as damnation and unpardonable sin, why was he so popular, why did the crowds multiply? Could they all be deaf, blind and stupid? Why do they—why do we all—follow him? One day he asked the master himself.

Jesus was disaffected by the question. Popularity was a philistine measure of achievement; he did not see its value, nor did he care to interpret it. But when Judas pressed him, reminding him that worldly attainments had to be weighed on worldly scales, Jesus retorted curtly:

"Then, go and ask my mother."

What an oblique answer. "Why your mother?"

To which Jesus replied with a wry smile that if the worth of his ministry were measured by his family in Nazareth, he would be judged a total failure. His brothers and sisters would call him a disgrace, deny that he was one of them, and say that his memory would be better forgotten. And his father, if he were alive, might pause at his work, lay down his hammer, take the tacks out of his mouth and say that his son was a disappointment, to have brought such heartache to his mother. As to his mother herself . . .

Sadness enveloped Jesus. It was the first time he had talked openly about his family. There had been a time, early in his ministry, when he had perpetrated an act that was so unkind, so unlike the master that, for many days, Judas was troubled. It had happened at a synagogue where Jesus had been called upon to speak. As the master entered the building, someone brought word that his mother and brothers had arrived and were waiting for him outdoors. Jesus was on the way to the bema and—unnerved—he halted. He had not seen his family for a long time. Taken unawares, off balance, he seemed torn between going out to them and starting the lesson. Then Judas saw the master's jaw tighten as his eyes went deathly still. Tell them to go back to Nazareth, he said, for he had no mother and brothers, except for these, his disciples. He was cold as ice.

That night, long ago, when he had asked Jesus how he could so chillingly reject his family, the master had replied that they were not his family. While his mother was indeed his mother, he had long ago ceased to think of himself as being related to his sisters and brothers, for blood was not all of life. Suddenly, in mid-sentence, he had stopped talking, as though he was having difficulty in reconciling thought, feeling, aura.

But now, today, as he and Judas were walking along the sea, he appeared willing, almost desperate to speak substantively of his relatives. He told how he had left Nazareth in something less than a nimbus of glory. His brother James, who was two years younger than Jesus, but starting to act like the head of the family, had practically driven him away. Jesus had shamed them in the synagogue, so James had said, with his interruptions of the service and his slanders about hypocrisy. Their neighbors did not approve such disturbances; Nazareth was a peaceful, orthodox place, not rife with radicals and Zealots like other Galilean towns. Jesus was as much a troublemaker, disturbing people at their prayer, as if he had gone bareheaded onto the bema, or ripped the tassels off his *tallith.* His two younger brothers, Simon and Judas, had agreed with James, but Joses had offered an extenuation for the blasphemer, saying that perhaps this was only a phase Jesus was going through; he might be unhappy about being a carpenter. Or about a secret love that had gone badly, one of his sisters said, and the other sister thought this might be so.

Mary, his mother, had wept. On his last day at home, as she had made him food for his journey and sewed a rip in his mantle, she tried to console herself and him, and to make peace in the family.

There was, however, no chance of peace. And even later, on that day when Jesus rejected them at the synagogue, he knew that they did not come as a peaceful, loving family, but to force their will upon him, to make him desist from what they considered his shameful teachings.

But perhaps—and Jesus spoke with deep yearning—perhaps if they were to hear him preach today, they would not think his teachings were so shameful. There might be something impressive to James in the fact that the crowds were now large, and it was no longer considered so disgraceful for Jews—even Pharisees—to listen to him. If only his *family* would listen . . . they might even be a little proud of him. He knew that pride was vanity and a sin of sorts, but forlornly he indulged himself for an instant, and nursed a dreamer's thought that one day they would take pleasure in him, they would ask him to come home, they would welcome him not for what they wanted him to be but for what he was.

This gave Judas pause. He had never seen any sentimentality in Jesus. Warmth, tenderness, yes, and deep compassion; but never reality so idealized, so sweetened by a yearning. Uncharacteristic as it was of the man, Judas suddenly understood:

Jesus was homesick. He longed for Nazareth, and to be with his family once more. He needed to forgive them and needed their forgiveness. He wanted them to know that he had long memories of their growing up together, of happy holidays when there were children in the house . . . and that he loved them.

Toward the end of summer, a neighbor came from Nazareth. He brought tidings of Jesus' mother. It would be Succoth soon, the Feast of Booths, she had said, and two of his brothers had been building little pavilions all over Nazareth, arbors and tiny bowers in hidden places, and there would be a lovely celebration of the gathering of summer fruits, and the gathering of families. Would Jesus come?

Judas watched as a doubt crossed the Nazarene's face. Then it was suffused with pleasure. He had hardly had a chance to accept when the neighbor added:

"And you have been requested to read the portion on the Sabbath."

Jesus could not believe they wanted him to do so. Who has requested? he asked; and when he was told that the elders of the synagogue had sent to Mary, he repeated the words of honor to Judas as if his friend had not heard them. They sent to my mother, he said with a glow in his eyes, they *sent.*

The next two days were a time of flurry and exhilaration. All through his travels, Jesus had had only two cloaks, one of natural homespun which had, with age, faded into a dunnish brown, and a second one of sackcloth, the color of tree bark. They were more than he wanted, and more than he advised his disciples to carry with them. But now he asked Mary Magdalene if she could make him a mantle of white muslin—white for a special occasion, white so that his family would know he respected them and that he himself was respectable, not a vagrant out of the wilderness.

The day came to go to Nazareth. Mary, with the aid of Zilpah, put the finishing touches on the new white robe; then, with Jesus trying it on, took up the hem so it would not drag. The teacher stood in his new garment, and beamed. How beautiful he looked, Zilpah said, and Mary smiled to see him blush.

There was a loose thread of white muslin on his beard. She reached for it and stopped herself.

"A thread," she said.

He lifted the wisp of cotton and playfully handed it to her as a gift. She smiled a little, and rolled it into a tiny ball.

"The mantle fits him well," Judas said. "Doesn't it fit him well?"

Zilpah, beside herself with pleasure, giggled and agreed, and Mary mumbled yes.

They were ready to depart now, all the disciples, and a few others, men and women. It would be nearly a full day's walk, and as Jesus led the way, there was a babble of talk and merriment, as if all of them were being tickled.

Looking to the right and left, Judas did not see Mary. Puzzled, he turned around.

She was perhaps fifty paces behind them, standing very still, watching them depart.

"Mary—hurry!"

She did not move, she did not answer.

"Mary."

Still no answer, only a slow movement of her head to signify she wasn't going. Something is wrong, he thought with a catch of nerves; she's ill again.

Hurrying back to her, he looked closely at her face. There was no sickness, only grayness.

"Is something wrong?"

"Nothing wrong, Judas. Go with the others."

"But you—? Why?"

"I don't care to go."

"But why—why?"

"Please . . . it's not important . . . I simply want to stay."

"Here? For what? What will you do?"

She smiled unevenly. "There's always something," she said. "There are sick people in the village. I'll go there." Then quickly, as if she wanted to have done with leave-taking. "Jesus said Naim—after Nazareth—I'll meet you there."

She must have seen his worry, and laid her hand on his cheek. "Don't fret," she murmured.

She kissed him gently on the other cheek, took him by the shoulders, and affectionately, as if he were a small boy, turned him around. Go, she said.

Rejoining the others, he was hurt that she was not coming with them. And a little provoked. Most of all, bewildered. Why would she not go? All through the long day of walking, bothered and fretful, he could not join the pleasures of the journey. At times, he thought, the followers sang too loudly.

But, late in the afternoon, when they arrived in Nazareth, his spirit lifted. What a festivity it was! Embraces, cries of pleasure and surprise, a child born to a sister Jesus had not known was married, and two more children to another one, and Joses' new wife, and the improvements to the workshop that had been their father's. And Simon, the youngest brother, saying this is a new clinching tool that I made from a worn-out hammer; giggling, he showed how it turned down soft nails. And Jesus smiling at his mother, who was kissing and weeping and laughing, and trying not to do everything at once. And how pathetically grateful she was to Judas for having heeded her plea and taken care of her son, as if Jesus' health and well-being were totally Judas's accomplishment.

Then, showing Judas—and Jesus, too—the youth of her famous son. Look, Judas, she said, this is the room he used to sleep in. There, see that window?—when he was a tiny boy—how old would you say, Jesus, three or four?—he used to climb through and shoo the geese. What a gabble! Jesus, let them be, Jesus come back, come back! . . . It seems I've always been calling him back.

Then James. In a variety of ways, he had taken their father's place. Younger than Jesus, he already looked older; his face and carriage had settled into middle age. He was the sternest in the family, and the most creed-bound. More than all the others, he disapproved of the renegade —and it was James's welcome that was the most conditional, and most judgingly withheld.

"You're taller," he said to Jesus. "Can you still be growing?"

Jesus smiled. "I am perhaps a little thinner."

"You don't eat good things."

"Less."

They both tried to smile. Unless they spoke of faults and differences, they had little they dared say to one another. Yet, it was a homecoming, and they yearned to make exchanges of some sort. Friendly, if possible; neutral, at least.

"Come," James said. "I will show you something." He made the invitation general, but the other disciples were taking water from the well, and some were drinking wine. James inclined his head to Judas. "Bring your friend."

As he led them past the carpentry shop, James pointed out a mattock he had fashioned out of ash; also a plow and coulter made of oak and iron. However simple and beautiful these tools were, what the man was most deeply proud of was the *succah* he had built.

Unlike other booths, which were tiny shacks randomly improvised of rough boughs and tree branches to commemorate the temporary shelter of the Jews in the wilderness, James's little edifice was elegant. Standing a dozen feet from the shop, it was meticulously fabricated of polished cedarwood, with carved knobs on the pegs that held the joints together, and with a door of incised panels and mitered moldings. And inside, hanging from the rafters, were a number of carved amulets of wood: a Decalogue of elm, an Aaron's rod engraved with leaves and serpents, a *mezuzah* made of birch. There were other wooden decorations, many of them.

Judas looked at Jesus, who was trying not to comment on the overelaborated *succah*. My brother, Jesus said, is as good a carpenter as my father was, and all I know of tools I learned from him. But Judas could see that his friend could not find any other compliment to pay. How sad, Judas thought, that the mattock and plow had been created with such purity, each object hewn to its use, no ornaments; yet the *succah* . . .

so gaudily garnished. He sensed that Jesus was poignantly troubled over this. Why did James have to hang so many trinkets on his religion?

What a master craftsman you are, Jesus said. And James thanked him, not in the fancy mode of the *succah,* but with the simplicity of the plow and mattock.

Until this moment, the two brothers had conversed without looking at one another, not so much as a glance, as though a meeting of the eyes was a confrontation they were at pains to avoid. But suddenly, for the fleetest instant, they frankly gazed at one another, and seemed to share a yearning; a kindness passed between them.

James said softly, so that Judas scarcely heard: "It is not true that you don't keep the Sabbath, is it?"

"No," Jesus said. "Not true."

"The Commandments?"

"All of them."

"I knew they lied about you," James said. "I knew."

"Yes, some lies have been told."

James seemed to be shedding a heavy burden. "They say you have many followers."

"There are . . . yes . . . many."

"That must be a satisfaction to you." Then, as if to show he was not insensitive. "But this can also be a worry, yes?"

"Yes."

"We hear about you a great deal these days. Sometimes I am . . . confused." He was on the edge of a confession, difficult for him. "It is not—you understand?—that I do not like people to speak your name. I do—I often get a pleasure when they mention you. But only if they bring tales of honor . . . not . . . shame."

"People will say what they will say."

"But you must not give them cause to . . ."

"I will try not to, James."

Suddenly, desperately, a small muffled sound. "We want to be proud of you!"

". . . Yes."

"Tomorrow—I will be so pleased." Normally a slow-speaking man, he was now talking rapidly, his words tumbling as he tried to keep ahead of his emotion. "You will be on the bema—you, Jesus—my own brother—you will read the portion—! So pleased—I will be so pleased."

Jesus was silent; he was touched by him.

They stopped talking, uncertain how to continue. James fingered the new robe. "It is good, this weaving—is it not?—and of an unusual whiteness."

"Yes, it has hung in the sun."

Tentatively, James touched his brother's cheek. "Too thin. I can see what you do—you eat badly!"

In a rough, bearish motion, James took his brother in his arms, held him in a suffocating embrace, swayed for an instant, broke away, muttered a few more words, then left them in the *succah.*

The afternoon waned. Neighbors arrived, not many, to greet the visitors, and a number of small boys walked past the house to gawk. Toward sundown came the time for the Sabbath candles. As Mary of Nazareth covered her eyes with her palms, Jesus moved close to her and laid his hand on her shoulder. It was so full of love and intimacy and longing that Judas could not bear to look, and for a moment turned away.

"I had hoped we could eat in the *succah,"* Mary said. "But there are so many of us, God be praised . . ."

"It will be good to eat outdoors," Jesus said.

"Once, I heard you bless a meal outdoors," she said.

He looked at her quickly. "When?"

"That last time . . . when you said no mother . . ."

She did not refer with any ill feeling to the time when he had sent his family away—as if she had not taken his words as a rejection.

"The others went home," she said. "But I stayed a while—to have a look at you. You came out of the synagogue and shielded your eyes from the sun. The shoulder of your mantle had a rent that wanted mending. There was quite a crowd at the midday meal—outdoors. I lost myself among the people, so you would not see me. It was a lovely prayer. Such a hopeful one." Her eyes gleamed; then they shadowed. "But afterward—I don't know how you lost your cheerfulness—you talked of hypocrites. . . . How do you see so many in your mind?"

"There are so many."

"Do you really think so?"

He nodded.

"I don't know." She smiled wanly. "People are of two minds, so they have two faces. Sometimes I am of so many minds that I forget what I look like."

"When I say 'hypocrite' I mean someone who does not tell the truth."

"Ah, the truth . . . It is so difficult. Why do you need to make your life so difficult?"

Jesus did not answer, and she turned to Judas. "Why does he?"

When Judas also was silent, she went on. "He has always been too curious, always turning the stone. There is no beauty under the stone, only . . . hypocrites."

Jesus smoothed her hair. He took a ewer down from a shelf that was too high for her to reach. As she accepted the pitcher, she held the hand that had extended it to her. She looked closely at her son.

"Are you well, Jesus?"

"Yes."

"James noticed that you are thin. Joses says you are pale. I do not see those things, but I do believe you are afflicted."

"I am not."

"You're not really a heretic, are you?"

"Heaven forbid."

"Your brother Simon thinks . . ."

She was having a deep difficulty. Her eyes misted over, and she let his hand go. When she turned away from him, Jesus said softly:

"What does Simon think?"

"That you are . . . possessed."

"Do you also think so?"

Trembling, she avoided his glance. "I don't know. . . . Are you?"

"The mad are not good judges of their madness." He was trying to treat it lightly. "Ask Judas."

"Is he, Judas?"

"No."

"Then, why is he afflicted?" She turned with a helpless, unhappy sound to her son. "Why are you afflicted?"

"Please . . . do not cry."

"Why are you afflicted?"

He took her in his arms, and she wept. "I am not," he tried to reassure her. "I am not—you must believe me—I am not afflicted. Perhaps—more than many others—I am blessed. Please—you must believe me."

Her weeping subsided a little, and he continued. "And you will see —tomorrow—you will hear me reading, and you will know that I am indeed blessed. And you will be glad."

She patted him a few times—his hand, his cheek, his shoulder. Blessed, she kept murmuring, as if to cling to his assurance, blessed, my son is blessed.

The following morning, when Jesus rose to the bema, his family had cause for pride. In his white robe, and with the sunlight pouring down upon him, he seemed translucent. How clear he looked, and what a wonderful day it was. Hear, O Israel, all the voices were chanting, and his among them; all Jews, all addressing the same and single Father in heaven. Hear, O Israel.

And the tones of Jesus the Nazarene were single and pure, like a shepherd's flute, as he chanted the words of the Torah. When he finished the portion he was supposed to read, there was some confusion about how he continued. Was he reading from Isaiah; and if he was, why was he doing so?

"The Spirit of the Lord is upon me, because he hath anointed me to preach the gospel to the poor; he hath sent me to heal the brokenhearted, to preach deliverance to the captives, and recovering of sight to the blind, to set at liberty them that are abused, to preach the acceptable year of the Lord."

Something was wrong.

There was a whispering. Who had asked him to read such an untimely text? Now, as he closed the book, he did not descend from the bema, but gazed steadily at the congregation. Someone, whispering, asked if he was going to preach. Who had invited him to do so?

"Today this scripture is fulfilled in your hearing," he said.

A man was moved to ask in a muted voice: Was he boasting that he was the healer mentioned in Isaiah? Someone said aloud that this was not fitting, it was blasphemy. Another yelled his shock that Jesus would vaunt himself in this way—Jesus, the nobody, the son of a poor carpenter whom they knew as they knew him, as they knew his mother, Mary, and his brothers and sisters—who was he to lord himself over them?

Someone shouted for James, and when the carpenter arose, he was pale and shaking, and could not answer when they asked him why his brother had departed from decorum. He started to speak, but no words came. The same loud complainer turned back to Jesus, demanding to know what rights he had, what special gift had been bestowed upon him, what healing he had done in Capernaum. When Jesus suggested it was the same as he would do in Nazareth, someone laughed and another shouted, "Heathen." Then other taunts: gentile, heretic, pagan. Jesus, too, was shouting—a prophet was not without honor except in his own country—and for their disbelief in him his own people would fare worse than the gentiles—the widow of Sidon and the lepers of Syria would do better than Nazarenes.

Suddenly, hearing this, the townspeople thought he was cursing them, and they surged around him—shouts and fists—profanities—violence in the synagogue—and he had to be carried away by his disciples. On the street, the crowd pursued them, threatening to seize the blasphemer, kill him, drag his body to the cliffs above Nazareth, cast it down. Some started to stone him—but there was an outcry, "Sabbath, Sabbath!"

Hurrying away, they could still hear the voices, the taunts, the mockery, the threats. And one voice, more terrible than the others, was Mary's outcry to her son, "Come back, come back!"

She is bereft of reason, Judas thought, to call him back. Back to what? To stones and curses? And as he heard her voice, still calling when all the others had gone—*come back, oh please come back*—Judas knew that all she wanted was to touch her son once more, to hold him, to say farewell.

"Turn to her, Jesus," he said.

But the master trudged downward from the hill of Nazareth.

"Turn—wave to her."

The tears rolled down Jesus' face, but he did not turn.

As the Sabbath was ending, the teacher and his followers plodded southward to Naim. Nobody seemed to understand how the terrible thing had come to pass, or why. Where had everything gone wrong between the white-mantled intention and the dirty, dusty fact?

When they approached the wider road that entered into the town of Naim, they saw Mary Magdalene and a few others at the northern gate. How odd that she fell in step beside Judas without asking a single question, as if she knew exactly what had occurred. But how could she? Had she really learned the tenet, ahead of all the others, that a prophet is without honor in his own country? It was a tenet an unbeliever could easily believe.

Trouble followed trouble these days, Judas thought; these were days of unforgiveness.

One afternoon, messengers came.

John the Baptist was dead. For the first time, there was no veil of hearsay, the image was bare. Herod had sent men to John in prison. They had beheaded him. A lovely young girl had asked for his head upon a platter, and Herod always paid homage to beauty. No, no rumor; the messengers had buried only the limbs and the corpus.

Jesus' face was still. He murmured questions softly to himself, asking whether this was true, and could it be true? Then he turned from the others and went away from them.

He trudged along a narrow pathway, upward on a hill, and, at a far distance, Judas followed him. When Jesus got to a wood of hemlocks, he disappeared among the heavy growth of dark greenery. The hemlocks were in bloom with small white flowers.

Judas came to the edge of the wood and did not follow him farther. Then, at a distance, he heard the terrible sounds. It was so heartrending that Judas, too, cried out. He ran to him. Oh, Jesus, he said, I know what he means to you, I know he was your rabbi and your baptizer, I saw how he opened the heavens for you on that day, but oh—beloved friend—do not break your heart for him!

The weeping did not cease, and Judas felt as though the whole wood were weeping, and that the white flowers and the tiny leaves of the hemlock were falling from the trees, and that this woodland would ever afterward be barren.

After the death of John, the Nazarene underwent a grievous alteration. Thitherto, he had always spoken with a firm authority, as if he had been born with intimations of how the world had begun and how it would end—whence and whither, as one of the followers had said. But now, when he addressed a throng, he occasionally paused and hesitated, as though he had lost his place, or was listening for a voice to prompt him.

One day, a group of scribes and Pharisees presented themselves to him when he was in the midst of a lesson, and they heckled and badgered him, asking for a sign, a sign.

Judas wanted to shout at them—as he expected Jesus to shout—a sign of what, you fools, that he is speaking what all our priests should be speaking, the word of God? But it seemed to Judas that the master's reply was oblique: The only sign that would be given to an evil and adulterous generation would be the sign of Jonah, three days in the belly of the great fish, as the Son of Man would be three days in the heart of the earth.

They had asked for a sign and he had given them a foreboding. It was as if they had struck upon the identical, agonizing question Jesus had been asking himself—and the Lord. A sign, dear Father, give me a sign.

As though unable to deal with the matter alone, the teacher turned the selfsame question upon his followers. They were in the region of Caesarea Philippi, north of Galilee, toward Mount Hermon. The mountain loomed. Clouds lowered. In the distant sky, beyond the hills, fine golden hairs of lightning twisted and vanished.

The disciples were peevish and out of temper. Something was wrong with them, or with their leader. They talked about omens and portents. They muttered about vague forewarnings they could not understand, and how there were more gentiles in the crowds these days, more strangers who might not be as friendly as they pretended, how there were fewer emanations of the Kingdom of Heaven and more of a vale of bitterness. And there was a feeling among the multitude—so Bartholomew and Matthew reported—that the teacher was withholding something from them . . . the acknowledgement of who he was.

Jesus had been silent. Now he asked the question: who did men say he was?

There were furtive glances among them. Nobody wanted to answer him. When they did reply, they were evasive:

"Some say John the Baptist," Andrew said.

Another one: "Some say Elijah."

"Jeremiah."

"One of the prophets."

Judas, who had not answered, was nettled by them. How could they lie to him about what the crowd—like all the rest of them—wanted to hear? He could see that Simon the fisherman was also annoyed by the shifts and shuffles of the disciples, and had turned his back on all of them.

But Jesus would not accept their subterfuges. He confronted all of them. "But who do *you* say that I am?"

No one answered. Judas had a need to let the word vent itself from his throat, but something choked him. And in the silence he could not fill, he heard the fisherman's voice:

"You are the Messiah, the Son of the Living God."

Yes! Judas wanted to yell his agreement at the top of his voice. And now that Jesus had heard it spoken, *he* would give forth in full voice. Yes!

But the Nazarene didn't. Not in any clear and single word. Simon Bar Jonah was blessed, he said, for flesh and blood had not revealed this to him, but Jesus' Father in heaven had done so. And he called Simon by the name of Peter, and said that on this rock he would build his church, and the gates of hell would not prevail against it.

The sky over Mount Hermon went to darkness. Black horses of the storm stampeded toward them. Lightning inflamed the sky, thunder pursued it. The disciples scurried away for shelter. But Jesus remained as if to commune with din and fire. The rain poured down on him.

Judas could not take his eyes off the man. The Nazarene did not seem to know that his disciple was there. I must charge him, Judas decided, with having given Simon an acceptable evasion or an evasive acceptance, a hundred descriptions of the word *yes,* but not yes itself. I must demand a direct answer. I must make him speak out, I must make him acclaim himself! *Now.*

Now the event would happen as it happened in the Torah. Now, as in the lore of the prophets—with lightning and thunder and the heavens on fire, there would be a blaze of revelation. He would hear the one word out of the mouth of Jesus: Messiah!

So he shouted over the tempest:

"Jesus! Who are you?"

Jesus did not look at him, only at the lightning. It was as if he had not heard his disciple's question, only the thunder.

Judas could scarcely catch his breath. His heart was near bursting.

"Who are you?"

The storm passed over. And Jesus did not answer.

Jesus' favoritism was a vexation to Judas. It was not the particularizing favoritism that he minded, when the teacher singled Peter out for special affection because the fisherman was the worthiest, or John because he was the youngest, or Matthew the most repentant. Those individualized gifts of his love Judas understood, and he marveled at how discriminatingly the Nazarene knew when to lay a benevolent hand upon the worthy or the needy.

Another favoritism worried him. There had been a time when little distinction had been made between Jesus' twelve closest disciples and the rest of his followers. They were all taking instruction from the master, all students. But then, when the master sent his twelve selected ones forth as messengers to preach his gospel, he bestowed a partiality upon them and they became his most intimate witnesses. His council meetings with his disciples, which had been easy and casual, open to anyone who cared to sit at the perimeter and listen, now turned into closed sessions. Judas disapproved of this. It offended him that the thirteen would steal away somewhere—"steal" was Mary's word—and have their meetings apart from the others, a locked room in an inn, behind a thicket in the wood, a boat on the Lake of Gennesaret.

He especially disliked the furtive secrecy, which suggested that a danger hung over them, some indeterminate menace that had not as yet taken shape. That the Pharisees and Sadducees hated Jesus and his friends, and that the legalistic scribes were constantly scheming cases against them, was by now taken for granted. But their quarrel did not go to the heart of heresy, no matter how serious Mary thought it might be. Mary was wrong—Judas was convinced she was wrong—for Jesus had repeatedly affirmed his loyalty to "every jot and tittle" of the Law, and there could be no real peril from their fellow Jews.

Nor even from the Romans. Why should there be? What civil crime had Jesus and his followers committed? There had not been a single breach of the Roman law, no counterfeiting of Roman coins, no destruction of property, no insolence to the soldiery, no disorder in the city streets. As to streets, ever since the rise of his ministry, Jesus had not even set foot in Jerusalem. Nothing. Certainly—and here again Judas knew Mary was wrong—no threat of insurrection. Jesus was a man of God, not politics. He was not a leader of a revolt, not a general of armies, not a secular sovereign of the Jews. He was not concerned with a kingdom on earth, but of heaven. The Romans, whatever they might be, were not stupid; they knew he was no threat to them. So why would they be a threat to him?

Then, why the clandestine meetings and the queasiness? Sometimes he believed that the mere feeling of guilt engendered guilt. The fear of a danger became one.

Besides, such fears and guilts caused dissension. Which he was witnessing this very moment in a shadowy glade among alders and locust trees. The question now was whether to spread the word among the gentiles. Already, there were many foreigners in their midst, pilgrims from Idumaea and Tyre and Sidon. Romans, Syrians. Peter was of the opinion that unbelievers should be encouraged to believe, wherever they came from. His brother Andrew agreed with him; so did the sons of Zebedee, James and John; but Thomas and Philip were opposed to such a proliferating growth, and lamented the days when they were a small Galilean band of worshipers who knew all their fellow faithful by name. Those days are over, Peter said, albeit sadly, and the Kingdom of Heaven is vaster than Galilee. Saying this, Peter looked at Jesus, who returned the fisherman's glance with a silent regretfulness.

Which carried the notion onward to the necessity for more disciples to spread the gospel. And when it was suggested that there be as many as seventy more—

Judas gasped. "Seventy?"

Simon the Zealot had been silent through all this. Now he said quietly, "I think before we consider spreading ourselves abroad, we should think of what we must do here at home."

"Such as?" Peter asked.

"Jerusalem."

Silence. No one dared to speak. It was as if they were afraid that whatever they said would damn them—as cowards or revolutionaries.

Judas was the first to respond. "We will not be welcome in Jerusalem."

Zelotes, generally under easy control of himself, was having a difficulty today. He was tense, his smile was forced. "On the contrary," he said. "The people have been waiting for us."

"The Pharisees and Sadducees? The Romans? I'm afraid you're right."

"Don't be afraid, Judas. I said the *people.* You know who they are. You've collected taxes from them. You've been one of them—with your parchments torn and your ink spilled and your head bloodied. You've seen them begging in the streets, you've seen them in Hinnom, you've seen them under the hoofs of Roman horses."

Affronted by the rabble-rousing speechment, Judas retorted, "Don't tell me about the poor, Simon. I'm still one of them."

More placatingly, Peter said, "The poor are many, Zelotes, but they are not strong."

"They will be strong. All they lack is a leader. And they know about Jesus. There isn't a beggar in Jerusalem who hasn't heard the name of Jesus. There isn't a blind man or a cripple or—!"

"Would you have an army of cripples?" Matthew asked.

"They won't be cripples. The minute Jesus appears in Jerusalem, they'll throw away their cups and their crutches. They'll stop whimpering and start shouting. And they won't be alone. The Zealots will appear from everywhere—and the *sicarii*—and suddenly, out of nowhere, there will be men with swords and men on horses. And the many will become the mighty!"

"And what do we do?" John's voice was frightened. "Take up swords?"

"Whatever we take up, we march with the others. We'll march behind *him.*" The Zealot pointed to Jesus. "We'll make him our commander—our liberator—another Maccabee. We'll make him King of the Jews."

"No!"

An outburst like a curse. It was not one of the disciples who had uttered the word.

It was Mary.

She and Hannah and Zilpah had brought the apostles their midday meal. They carried trays of steaming barley and marrow soup, and loaves of hot bread.

At her protest, there was a murmur of displeasure among the disciples. It was unheard of for anyone outside the circle to interrupt their meetings, especially a woman. Matthew muttered, not unkindly, that she should leave the food and go.

But she did not. The tray in her hands was shaking. She set it down. Still she did not depart. She looked at Jesus.

He nodded.

She took a breath, and spoke. Not to him, but to the others. "If you call him King of the Jews—you make war on Rome. Only the Emperor makes kings, only Tiberius. Not Pilate, not Herod—and not you, Zelotes. Only the Emperor of Rome. Judas thinks you do no harm, you do nothing dangerous, and therefore the Romans won't hurt you. He is naïve. You *are* doing something dangerous—and Zelotes knows you are. So does Pilate. He's sitting in the Antonia waiting for you to do something wrong—a terrible crime—anything—something grossly illegal. Calling Jesus the King of the Jews will suit him perfectly. You may as well throw the teacher into chains, and deliver him to the Romans. And yourselves as well. You will all be annihilated."

Not a word. Hardly a rustle of clothing. After a moment, a clatter of earthenware as Zilpah and Hannah served the bread and soup. Then, not looking at the faces of the men, Mary helped them. When the food had been given to each of the disciples, none of them took so much as a mouthful.

A strange thing: Jesus was the first to start eating. He did not look at the men or at the women. He did not seem at all agitated by what had been said. Not disconcerted in the least; as if none of them had spoken even vaguely to the point, and nothing that had been uttered could make any difference.

At last someone offered the tentative opinion that Zelotes had perhaps gone too far; Jesus was not King of the Jews and did not want to be. Someone else suggested that any thoughts about Jerusalem were premature.

Judas said hotly that they were not only premature, they were out of the question. It was foolish talk, wanton and reckless.

Most of the others agreed. But Zelotes argued to the end.

Jesus and Peter said nothing.

They all ate in silence.

In a little while, Mary helped in the gathering of dishes.

She had not meant to meddle in their meeting. But once the words were said, there was no calling them back, she had to chase after them, the fugitives, and suddenly the pursuers were also in a rout, and the chase was chaos.

She knew she didn't sound like chaos; that was a blessing. Every word she uttered had made sense, not only to herself, but to all of them —even to Zelotes. He realized—she could see the exact moment when the man realized—that he had overshot himself and lost the argument:

King of the Jews. If he had not used the expression, if the demagogue had not been seduced by a slogan, he would have won, and they would already be on their way into the snare of Jerusalem.

But she mustn't crow too soon. It was uncharacteristic of the Zealot to fall from his horse. And sooner or later, collecting himself, he would mount another charger toward Jerusalem. Next time, however, he would not be subject to his passions; the others would be. She could imagine, too clearly, how Zelotes would wield his emotions like tempered blades, shredding every argument, every plea for caution, for wisdom . . . and the life of Jesus.

The life of Jesus—he would value it at a shekel; sacrifice the man as relentlessly as he had sacrificed other Jews to the cause of freedom, as he had had to sacrifice Zealots, his own companions, his friends. Elias. The man had trained himself not to care.

As Jesus himself did not seem to care. She was infuriated by the Nazarene, how he simply played spectator while his disciples were ordaining his destiny. Hardly a word from the man. When he was more perceptive and wiser than all the others—yes, and even shrewder—not a single expletive to show them what foolish, reckless creatures they were; when he was always so full of profound advice—not a solitary counsel to save his own life. He was their leader, and they would follow him anywhere, into anything; then, why did he not lead them to a haven of self-survival? Not a syllable of caution, not a raised finger. Only that simpering smile, that superior way he knit his brow in sorrow, as if to say: How sad—all my children are idiots. She hated him for not telling them precisely what they might do with his life, and what they dare not. She hated him for not fighting more bloodily to live. As if his life was worthless to him, as if he would just as soon shuck the whole integument of living like a husk of corn— Well, if that's all his existence meant to him, let the heaven-hoping dreamer go to hell, for all she cared!

For all she cared was all she could care for anyone, she realized. Or for life itself. She was in love with him.

How grim not to know until her anger at him had become unbearable. Until she was desperate at the thought that the man might do deadly harm to himself, or let himself be harmed. How perverse that her love should be expressed in all the negatives she felt about him. Not only did she hate his indifference to his own mortality, but hated how he prattled about God and kingdoms of heaven, and how he did not deny half the miracles that had never taken place, and allowed the myths to gather about his head, and permitted them to make a godhead of him.

She shrank when people used terms like king or savior or Messiah. They frightened her. Besides, how could she be in love with a sovereign or a god or an idol? Or even with an idea? For it was not hard to see how an idea—even a noble, sublime one—could rob a man of his humanity.

His humanity. That he was a human being, that's what she loved about him; that he had weaknesses and a vanity or two, that in the midst of his wine he might have a sudden thought and there would be a wine stain on his beard, that he clung to his favorite tunic too long and would not let her wash the thing until it stank a little, that he could make a majestic ascent to a mountaintop and stumble over a pebble, that his kindness, his sweetness, were so illimitable that he often seemed a fool. That's why she loved him. Not for the miracles. He could have performed a million of them or none at all, it was the man himself who was miraculous: the old sage who was still a child, the tender lover in a time of wrath, the messenger not of God but of goodness. That, that was what she loved in him.

Before she knew it herself, Judas knew. It seemed to her he took her love of Jesus for granted. Everybody loved the Nazarene; the wonder was not in loving him, but in taking so long to realize. She was quite sure that Judas considered her feeling for the master to be as spiritual as anybody else's, not at all sensual. Not desire but devotion. Instead of separating them, her love of the teacher brought her and Judas closer together; they now had a commonality of feeling for the same symbol . . . even if Mary was a doubter.

Yet, as they grew closer in their love of him, inexplicably she and Judas drew apart in a physical way. She could understand her own need to abstain from lovemaking with Judas, but why—if he did not suspect her womanly feelings for the man Jesus—did he stop touching her? Could he have gone so far in his holiness as to feel that someone who had sewn the hem of the master's white mantle must be sacrosanct in bed?

It never occurred to her that before either of them knew she was in love, Jesus might know. She did not believe in his omniscience. In fact, she often felt that she knew more about his feelings than he knew about hers.

He can know everything about me, she thought, all about my time of harlotry, my hideous sickness, even my devils—without knowing the single most important thing: that I adore him. And she must keep this from the man. For reasons she could not resolve—her ineradicable taint and his purity, her indeterminate relationship with Judas, her demons —Jesus must not be told.

Her demons especially. No matter how Judas believed that Jesus had conquered her sickness by casting out her devils, she knew they were still with her. Even the dead ones. Nighttimes, they often came alive again, and she knew the raping would never cease. Nor her rage against the rapists. Seven demons of rage are still within me, she thought, and now another one, a rage of love.

A rage and a tenderness. Sometimes all she wanted to do was touch him, comb his hair, wash his face and hands and feet, give him cool water to drink after he had spoken for long hours, put oil on his parched, cracked lips, whisper peace, Jesus, peace.

Hold him, hold him.

Sometimes she had fantasies. I have a vision, she might say to him. I am a young girl, a child, and I am riding on your shoulders. We pass under a tree. Halt a moment, I shout, so that I may catch a leaf. You halt and I hold heaven in my hand.

I have another vision. I am old, and you are not.

Another. You take me in your arms, you kiss me, I start to laugh and cry because I am having and wanting and having.

The terrible thing about his not knowing was that he had no need to respond to her. He could ignore her very existence. There were the times when he would not even know she was in the meadow where he spoke, or on the seashore or even in the room. Days would go by, long days, when he did not seem to know that she was alive. Not a word, not a sign. And in those times, she wondered why—if he was so sentient about everything that happened in the world—he could not hear the thumping of her heart, hear her outcries as loudly as she heard his silences.

She thought: He noticed me when I was sick. He was near me always. If I were sick again, he would come back to me. He is in love with the sad and the lame and the ailing. Oh, I am all of those, she wanted to cry, and if you love me I will never allow myself to get well again!

One day, wanting him to talk to her and to her alone, she did a terrible thing. She said she needed to discuss something with him. God. Would he help her to understand Him?

They went walking along the shore of Galilee, and the sea was in a turmoil, so that he had to speak loudly over the noisiness of wind and waves. She couldn't stand how thrilled she was to hear him outshouting nature, laying down the law that God exists, *exists*.

But as he yelled above the imminence of storm, she was ashamed of having tricked him. For suddenly she saw why he so often spoke in parables—they were his clothes. Which he was not wearing this day. As he uncovered himself, she saw that he could not reckon the world without reckoning with God. Nothing could be sensible to him. Good and evil would not be distinct, and would have no meaning. Love would be a well run dry, without a source, and his soul would perish of drought.

As he spoke of a nightmare life without the Lord, his pain was there, like an emptiness that had become a substance. It was as if his agony had made him say farewell to his senses, farewell to everything. Believing in God, death was not finite to him, but a continuance of life; disbelieving, death would be a separation from himself, and unendurable. She ached for the man, for the *man,* as if he were already gone, realizing that he was an exile on earth, that heaven was his true home. God was his whole existence.

And now, because she had asked him about his God, he had exposed himself to her. She hated seeing him so agonizedly vulnerable, and hated herself for having stripped him naked. And began to cry.

He turned quickly, and in a flash of insight saw that she had duped him. But he also saw her shame and her remorse, and she knew that he forgave her.

She wanted to view him differently after that. It hurt her to watch him counting the days until apocalypse, studying the signs of heaven, hearing trumpets, carrying on secret discourses with the Lord. She began to distrust his daily conversation; how could he speak to mortals in the same language as he used with the Almighty? As if he were addressing his followers—and her—in a tongue that was foreign to him.

Sometimes it sounded like babble, which no longer had any meaning for him . . . or was it meaningless only to her?

She could not stand the separations any longer, so she took to staying close to him. Wherever he was, she was always nearby. She brought the world of objects to his hands, so that he never had to reach for anything, a dish, a crust of bread, a cloth to dry his face when he perspired. But still she felt too far away from him, too distant to feel the warmth of his body, to trace the veining of his hands.

"When did you start to love me?" he asked one day.

"When I was born."

She had not meant to sound so girlish. She did not upbraid herself for having said something inanely romantic, but for having missed the opportunity to say something real. He had given her a chance to describe the actual and ordinary ways in which she loved him, and she had lost the moment. She could have conveyed to him so clearly, how palpably she worshiped him, that it was a tangible thing of fingertips and skin and mouth and organs, that she wanted him to hold her and kiss her and lie with her, so that he would know her body in all its healthiness as she would know his.

But she avoided talking of physical things, for this would drive him away. He would stop beckoning her when there was a special wonder to behold, a newness in the sky, a distant music in a brook; he would stop calling her to come and see the woodland. Once, when his neck was wry, she had rubbed it without his asking her to do so, and in the midst, he had taken her hand and kissed it; once, at a peal of thunder, he had embraced her and held her close, against the fury; once, he had kissed her hair. But as though a spirit had blessed her, there was no body there. How could he be such an immanent presence in her life and be so physically nonexistent?

Sometimes he seemed totally unaware of the substantive. As if flesh were not a part of being. One afternoon, he watched a child killing a mouse, and she thought that Jesus would scold the youngster, but he didn't. The little boy had become a body to him, that was all, and so was the rodent; neither concerned him overmuch. Another time, when a young mother died before his eyes and he could do nothing to bring her back again, she saw a terrible look in his face. He had come to hate corporeality. His own and others'. And she had a dread that if—even once—she could not restrain herself, and were to touch him too intimately or kiss him too sensually, he would hate hers as well, that her body would disgust him.

But how could she keep from wanting him? What could she do about her ravening need to love him and be loved? She tried to confine her desire to a small part of herself, as if a disease had to be sequestered or it would infect all of her. But it had already done so. She had thought:

the heart desires; the head perhaps. But this was everywhere and in everything, coursing through her blood, ringing in her ears, her mouth was wet and dry with it, it invaded her womb, her belly, deep, deep inside her, such a wanting! Touch me, love me, come into my heart, my body, come inside!

One morning, before preaching to a large crowd, he talked longingly about promenading in a nearby woodland. She took for granted that, when his lesson to the multitude was over, they would go walking together among the trees. But in the late afternoon he was gone; he had left without her.

Hurt, nettled, she followed him. She suspected where he might be —there was a little clearing by a stream. As she approached, she walked quietly, in a circuitous way, like a creeping thing.

He was lying in the mosses on the open space. His head rested on his folded arms and he was gazing skyward. Nearby, there was the purling stream. It made the only sound; the trees were still. No birdsong, nor the flutter of a wing. How silent he was.

She knew how sorely he needed to be alone at times. She could remember when she had been the same. But no longer; now she never wanted to be away from him, never, not for an instant. She despised herself for being so dependent upon him, and for the moment she resented his need, his *ability* to be alone.

So she had her revenge. Step by silent step, she walked a little bit away from him, through the woodland. Then she threaded a path toward the flowing water, somewhat upstream from where he lay. She took her clothes off and went naked into the stream. Pretending not to know that she was within view of him, she bathed herself. And lest he not notice she was there, she sang a little, with seeming heedlessness.

For what was an endless time to her, he did not stir. Then, at last, he slowly rose to his feet, and just as slowly walked down to the water's edge. He paused to gaze not at her but at her body, as if he knew that was what she wanted him to do. There was no haste, no furtiveness in either of them now. They met each other's glance. Then quietly he turned and went away.

She wanted to drown herself.

He asked her once if she foresaw the time when she might love God.

"Not until I know Him."

Not a thought-out answer, it had simply come to her, the truest thing she could have said about herself: knowing was everything. Mystery was a violence to her; knowing was love.

He said she was too troubled by the unknown, and the unknown would one day be knowable . . . and something about our Father's promises.

"I don't believe your Father's promises," she said. "I don't believe He means for us to know. I have greater faith in the serpent—he offered the apple of knowledge. The Almighty exiled us for eating it. We're still in exile."

"Our Father—"

"Please don't use that expression. It doesn't endear him to me. I'm not a great lover of fathers."

"If I call him by another name—"

"Call him Jesus."

A quip, no more. But it bothered him so deeply that he went silent.

Afterward, she realized that the jest was serious. It was another way she loved him—as a father. Which left behind such a wake of turbulence that she rocked. Her father, yes, the only one she had ever unreservedly loved and who unreservedly loved her, and— The father of her child!

She wanted a child by him so desperately that if she could pray— Pray, beg, go down on her knees in supplication to gods or mysteries or the unknowns of anything—a child, I want a child by Jesus. One day she tried to strike a bargain—with what?—with destiny. Not a perfect child, she said, or even a beautiful one; I will gratefully accept an infant marred or slightly misbegotten—and you will see what a wonder I will make. I will caress and rock such love into it, I will sing such a melody into its heart—

One day—midafternoon—her bodice was damp. The milk was flowing at her breast. I am with child, she cried to herself, I am with child! My Jesus has loved me only with his soul—and yet I am with child! A miracle!

But, the same day, the blood flowed, and she loathed herself for being a woman, and not being one.

Barabbas came in the night. Nobody saw him come, no one had asked him to come. When he appeared in the early dawn, nobody seemed to notice him. Perhaps he was not recognized, except by Mary. And by Simon Zelotes.

There was something dreadfully friendly and wrong. It seemed so out of joint that the two men should walk toward the sea together, as though they were old companions, as though one had not prosecuted the other at the trial of Zealots, as if the black-bearded man had not been banished by the very design of the man with whom he strolled so amiably.

Then, when the crowd was gathering for the morning lesson, she saw them trudging up the incline from the shore, and heard them laughing—old friends who shared their memories of pleasure and foolishness. How could this be, she worried, and what could it mean?

As Jesus appeared and stood a little higher, on a mound of rocks, the multitude was starting to shush itself. And a few instants before he began, another man came hastening toward Barabbas and Simon, and the black-bearded one introduced him. As the third man turned a little and made a gesture, she saw that his cheek was badly scarred as if by knives or scourges, and that from time to time, pretending contemplation, he raised his hand to cover his disfigurement. She had the errant thought: his beard has grown everywhere but where he needed it the most.

Then she heard Jesus' opening remarks and his invitation to the prayer. Some people knelt, some did not. Of the three men, the scarred one remained upright, but Zelotes and Barabbas knelt and prayed together, like brothers.

When the lesson was over and the crowd had dispersed, Barabbas had disappeared. So had his scarred friend.

All afternoon, she was uneasy. She brooded over the visit, as though some offense had already been perpetrated. At last she went to Zelotes.

"Why was he here?"

"He is a follower," the disciple replied.

"He is not a follower."

"Why do you say that? Because he has never appeared among the crowd? Jesus has many followers who have never even seen him."

"Zealots?"

"Yes. And others."

"Sicarii?"

"Even *sicarii.* And still others. You underestimate our teacher."

"So do you. You're going to use him as a tool for your riffraff and your cutthroats. You don't think him worthier than that."

"You're wrong," he said. "I think him worthier than you do. When he says, 'Let us pray,' I kneel. I kneel and I pray as I have never prayed since I was a child. Can you say the same?"

"No, but I would not hurt him—and you would."

"I wouldn't hurt myself if I could help it. But if I have to die for being a Jew, I will do so. I ask no more from him. If I love myself no better than I love him, isn't that enough?"

He had spoken in the rhetoric of a leader, but she believed him. His coolheadedness had misled her about the man; she had not taken him at his definition: he was a Zealot full of zeal. There was not a nerve of hypocrisy in him. He could not believe halfheartedly; his faith had to be fervent, or not at all. Faith in Jewry, faith in Jesus.

"If you're honest, what are you doing with that thief?"

"Using him." He smiled grimly. "Jesus is not a tool, but Barabbas is. He says it's time for a revolution—with which I agree. He says in time of revolution, his followers must join ours—with which I do not agree."

"But obviously he thinks you do."

He shrugged in a self-deprecatory way. "He serves us."

"How?"

He said evasively, "He has a score of Nahums."

"What is a nahum?"

"The man with the scarred face—his name is Nahum. He's a vandal, a pickpocket. But—most of all—a spy."

"For Barabbas."

"It doesn't matter, does it?—as long as he spies against the Romans. And tells us when they spy against us."

She had known, of course, that there were always informers among the crowd. And even when there was nothing to inform—at least nothing that the Romans had cared to prosecute—there was always a sense that every stone and blade of grass was treacherous. But that was a generality of existence in an occupied land, taken for granted. Now there was a particularity.

"Is there a special Roman . . . ?"

"Yes."

"Who?"

She knew the answer even before he said the name:

"Tullius."

The centurion had been to two meetings, Nahum had told them, and he would certainly appear again. He would not be wearing his uniform, of course, but would be dressed plainly, in a sackcloth way, like one of the followers. Whatever criminal he was looking for, he had not found. Certainly not a young woman who had been involved in a murderous raid against Romans, or he could have uncovered and recognized her. He would come, she dreaded, for the greatest catch of all: Jesus, in some terrible culpability against Rome. Or in some culpability Tullius would devise.

She couldn't bear the thought. Now there was more reason to hate the Roman, and fear him. The terror that the centurion might do harm to Jesus quickened all her old rages into havoc. It was as if she felt Tullius at her body once again. She wanted to kill him now, this minute, she wanted to make amulets of his bones.

"I need to do it without any help from you or anyone," she said. "I need to kill him by myself."

Zelotes nodded as if to make a special note, told her to wait patiently, and went away.

On a morning when there was a hoarfrost on the ground, she

awakened and could not stand the waiting any longer. If it is not today or tomorrow or the next day, my frenzy will send me raving to the mountains.

But, that afternoon, Zelotes came and said the time had come.

A lesson was just beginning, and the Zealot reported that Tullius had arrived. If she truly meant to do the deed alone, he would tell her where the Roman could be found. It would be singularly easy today, because of the place where the centurion had stationed himself; nobody would even notice he was dead. She would have to come up from behind. Embrace him, as she had once been trained to do, tighten her left arm around his throat, choking back any possible outcry. Then, her right arm around him and to the front, and the knife below the breast bone.

Zelotes handed her the dagger.

The multitude was dense on this occasion, too dense. She could not believe it would be as easy as Zelotes had described. The Roman would be wearing a brownish gray cloak indistinguishable from hundreds of similar ones in the crowd, but his tunic would be a grayed-down orange color. It need not be bright, she thought, for her to single out the man. His face would flare at her like a lamp in darkness, even if there were millions in the throng.

She threaded her way through the thickest part of the multitude, just as she had been instructed. In all this human gathering, there were no faces; she had only one countenance in her mind.

Moment to moment, she heard Jesus' voice, but only in disconnected phrases. Wheat and tares, he said . . . sowers of seed . . . birds devouring . . . She had heard those parables before; she wondered if he was repeating himself, which he sometimes did, or if she was remembering wrong.

The knife, under her mantle, was cold in her hand. She thought: by now it should be warm.

The mustard seed . . . the pearl of great price . . . she had heard those parables as well. How beautiful his voice was.

The centurion—where was he? Not where he was supposed to be. There was no orange tunic, nor was there anyone who looked like Tullius.

Now . . . here . . . on the perimeter of the crowd . . . pausing among the shrubs where the hill rose toward the woodland . . . standing exactly on the place where the monster should have been. No sign of him.

Distantly, the echo of Jesus: Let us pray.

She saw the blur of orange as the man knelt.

He was far away, scarcely within earshot of the teacher's voice. On the edge of the greenwood, just within the grove, as if seeking the shelter of the trees, asking them to hide him.

But why? If he was here to spy on them, of what good was his detachment from the crowd, how would he be able to define the faces if he ever had to identify them? How could he be certain of the words the teacher was saying?

She sidled along the edge of the woodline, at an angle where he could not see her. Getting closer, she slipped in among the trees. It was winter and she wished there were more foliage to hide her and that the dead greenery on the ground were not so noisy.

Closer, closer.

Why was he kneeling?

Closer, and she could not descry what he was murmuring.

His body trembled a little.

Now she could hear him.

He was praying to the Jewish God in his native tongue. *Mea culpa,* he was saying, *culpa, culpa.* And he was sobbing, grieving as if over the dead.

She turned away and ran deeper into the woods.

As the crowd was dispersing in the late afternoon, there was a scream from one of the women and the slain man was discovered. His tunic was more red than orange.

The dagger under Mary's mantle was as cold as before; no blood had warmed it.

Toward sunset, in a widow's garden, east of Bethsaida, Jesus said: "Who has done this?"

Only the twelve disciples had been summoned. And Mary. It did not bode well that she had been invited to attend.

"Who has done this?"

His voice sounded like Sinai. And no one answered him.

He spoke quietly then, but with a tone of execration. A person was slain in the midst of prayer, he said, and if one of their number did not ask for whatever absolution God and man could give, then the blood of the dead would be upon all of them, like a sacrifice to evil.

Why should he suppose that one of them was guilty? someone asked.

His voice thundered at the sophistry. "Is it not one of us?"

Matthew said quietly that if he said "us" this could mean all of mankind, and which of them could deny it?

While Jesus scarcely looked at her, Mary felt that she was foremost in his mind. She trembled. No choice but to answer him.

"I'm never asked to be among you," she said. "Today I was asked. It can only mean I'm the one you suspect. But I swear to you—"

"Who has done this?"

The third time he asked the question, he looked at Simon Zelotes, only at Simon. The Zealot went white. With a gasp, he fell to his knees before Jesus.

"I swear to you, Master—I swear I did not!"

"Are you lying, Simon?"

"No!" he cried. "No! I could not lie to you, Master! And do you think I could kill a man in prayer—do you think I could?"

"Then, you know who has done it."

"I . . . think I know. But he's not among us."

"If you know, then he is among us!"

Suddenly—unbearably—Jesus let out a cry, clutched at himself, clutched his mantle at the throat and rent it. And rushed away.

She ran after him, toward the same woodland where Tullius had been killed, and she called, "Jesus—wait—please wait!"

As she realized that nothing could make him wait for anyone this moment, he disappeared among the trees. But some dread kept her in pursuit of him. Jesus, she called, where are you? Wait, wait.

For hours, it seemed to Mary, she looked for him. But he was lost to her, and as the sun was setting, she turned about to leave the woodland. She had gone perhaps half the distance when, in the gloom of nightfall, she heard a muffled sound. It was a strange noise, like the thrashing of a beast, but a human voice as well, as though in a struggle.

She turned toward the disturbance—in a barren place, behind a huge boulder as tall as a man. She could not see the living thing that made the noise, but here the sound was louder and more terrible. Approaching the great rock, she slowly went around it, frightened of what she might behold.

Jesus knelt upon the ground with his arms upheld against the boulder, as if with his own will, with his own might he must keep the great rock from rolling over him. And he wept. And cursed himself. Give me their sins, he cried, give me their sins. Have mercy upon them, and give me their sins. She could not endure—he beat his head against the rock. Oh no, she said, oh no! Blood flowed from his forehead, down his cheeks, upon his mantle. Their sins, he cried, torturing himself, inflicting penalty upon his body so that his blood blinded him; give me their sins.

"Oh, beloved!" she cried. "Oh, my beloved!"

She tried to lift him to his feet, to draw him away from his torment. But he did not know her, and with the strength of a wild thing he struck at her and drove her away. She tried again, and again he drove her off.

His blood was on her clothes and upon her hands. I'll go for someone, she thought in her frenzy, someone will help me, someone will help him, help him!

However, when she returned with Judas and Simon, the rock was still wet with his blood, but Jesus was not there.

He vanished.

For days they searched for him in all the well-known places, the towns, the tiny villages where he had touched upon people's lives. But he was not to be found.

She knew that his disciples were as harried by his disappearance as she was, but she became rabid one evening and accused them of hiding things from her. She said to Judas: "You know where he is, don't you?"

"No, I do not."

"Yes, you do." She felt feverish. "Where? Tell me where."

"He has . . . gone there again."

To that special loneliness again, that desolation. To the desert, to the wilderness. Gone to spill his blood on the mountain. Mount Hermon, someone said, where last spring a wild boar had eaten the insides of a mind-wandering shepherd. Mind-wandering shepherd indeed. Gone to collect the sins of all mankind, the poor crazed guardian of the unworthy sheep. Her beloved, out of his wits, and lost.

Gone to seek what? The curse of heaven? Solace, more likely, not allowing her to offer it. Needing someone to behold his heartbreak, and hiding it from her; needing someone's love, disdaining hers. How could he—even if he loved her so much less than she needed him—allow her to love him so little?

I cannot stand my love of him, she thought; I'm as brainsick as he is. She screamed at him: I hope you never find what you look for, I hope you're destroyed without me, I hope you ache so much—!

As I do.

No. I hope someone comforts you, and puts cool compresses on your brow, and cradles you, as I would. Oh, poor, loving man, who cannot be loved nearly so much as you have love to give. And pity. Oh, dear God, pity!

Just as she had not known when he went, or where, so she did not know when he returned. Suddenly, one day, there was a shouting, then a running, and she saw Simon Zelotes race across a meadow, toward a road that led to Capernaum.

Then more shouts and more running, and people chattering and yelling to one another.

"What has happened?" she cried. "What—what?"

"He has come back," Judas said.

His eyes danced.

"Peter and James and John say he was transfigured."

She hated words like that. "You mean his wounds—"

"No, no! They are healed. The man himself—transfigured!"

"What does that mean?"

"They say he saw God—and that he heard His voice."

"Whose?"

"God's—the Lord's."

"How does he look?"

"The Lord?"

"Jesus."

"As he did . . . except . . ."

"Except?"

"We are going to Jerusalem."

She thought: I must not fall.

"Are you ill?"

"No. The sun's too bright," she said. Then, as if all the decisions in the world had to be made in the next few minutes. "We must talk him out of this."

"I tried—but his mind is made up." Then, quickly: "And perhaps just as well. When he knows something is right, it *is* right—and we must follow him."

"Judas, Judas!"

While they were all prating about rightness, calamity would strike, one kind or another, and what could she do?

Judas saw her suffering and put his hands on her arms. "Mary—dear love—try not to be too anxious. I felt as you do, but it's different now. He has had a message—he has talked with God. He must do as he is told. And the Lord will look after him."

She went numb. She said the words without giving them any thought. "The Lord will not care."

She went to find Jesus. There were scabs on his forehead, but his skin was otherwise clear, and his eyes were luminous.

"I am going to Jerusalem," he said.

He spoke detachedly, as though he had not recorded that she had tried to keep him from smashing his brains on God's boulder. Seeing how estranged he was, she could not speak.

"Have you heard that I am going to Jerusalem?"

"Yes, I've heard."

"It is time."

"It is a bad time. It will be Passover," she said, as if that were the whole point. "Don't you know what happens in Jerusalem at Passover?"

"Yes. All Israel will be there."

A million people, she said hotly, will swarm into the city, to cram themselves into the Temple or to smell the incense on the terraces. Pilate will call soldiers from barracks all over the country. The streets will bristle with swords. There will be dagger men in every crowd. The Roman horses will trample a trail of blood. If you cause a disturbance—the slightest little racket in a thoroughfare—they'll throw you into the Antonia and beat you with chains.

He was scarcely listening; he knew everything she told him.

All of them did. They all knew, yet they didn't know. They were people whirled into an ecstasy, a lunacy, by their damnable Almighty. They were going to carry the word of God to the sacred city, they were going to bring the Kingdom of Heaven to the Holy of Holies.

Jerusalem, Jerusalem, we are going to Jerusalem!

Then, on the evening before they were to leave for the capital, when she was altogether convinced that Jesus had only a demented notion of the risk he was taking, he gathered his disciples together. He asked for Mary to be present, and she felt that, while he spoke directly to them, his words were meant for her alone.

I must go to Jerusalem, he said, and suffer many things, and be killed, and arise again on the third day.

That night she awoke with blood in her throat. She spat and rinsed her mouth, and tried to be very still, but an animal within her howled. She thought she might be having a seizure, and welcomed it. Let it come, she said, let me madden. But it went away.

On their way to Jerusalem, on the outskirts, near the town of Bethphage, she could not believe what she beheld, how preposterous. He was dressed in the white mantle she had made for him. It was spotless and gleaming, and so was he—aglow with cleanliness and his dream of the glory of God. And he was riding on an ass.

On an ass, in the name of everything ridiculous, he was going to make his triumphal entry into Jerusalem—on an ass!

Judas was shocked at her laughter. It is written, he kept saying, it is written. It is predicted by the prophet Zechariah. And he quoted:

"Rejoice greatly, O daughter of Zion. Shout, O daughter of Jerusalem: behold, the King cometh unto thee: he is just, and having salvation; lowly, and riding upon an ass."

But this daughter of Jerusalem did not rejoice.

However, she had the amazement of her life. Nobody, on any pathway to Jerusalem, ridiculed the man on the jackass. On the contrary, they spread clothing on the ground to soften his way, they strewed the trails with flowers, they sang from the Psalms and gave him wine to drink. And when he passed through the gateway into the holy city, the other daughters of Jerusalem did rejoice. Indeed, it seemed to Mary that the whole city rejoiced that Jesus had at last arrived.

14

Not that I've become a partisan of Simon Zelotes, Judas thought, but right is right. And it was right for Jesus to go to Jerusalem. His reception proved it.

Moreover, with Passover only five days away, this was the perfect time to come, the perfect festival. It marked every kind of release: spring's release from the bondage of a cold winter, the release of the children of Israel from slavery in Egypt, the release of the Jewish spirit from a frightened idolatry.

One day, in the lower city, as he and Zelotes were watching Jesus pass through a cheering crowd, the Canaanite asked: "What do you think they see in him?"

"Deliverance."

"Yes. I agree."

Judas realized they were agreeing on a word, not on its meaning. To the scrivener, deliverance meant redemption from sin, from sorrow, affliction; to Simon, it meant only liberation from the Romans. He felt affronted by the Zealot's narrow construction of the term. Not only was his meaning a diminution of all that Jesus signified, but Zelotes used it belligerently, even in public places. He waved a flaming torch at a haystack. Jerusalem was crowded and dry and hot—combustible; one of the Zealot's sparks, thrown into this Passover tinder, could set the Temple afire.

"You're asleep, Judas," the Canaanite said. "If you dream that these people have come to pray with Jesus, you'd better wake up. Look at them. Most of them don't know the meaning of prayer. They were born hating God and they'll die that way."

"Their souls will be redeemed."

"They don't care a damn about their souls. They're hungry, they're filthy, they're sick."

"They will be fed and cleansed and healed. That's what they came for."

"They came to kill."

"I don't believe it," Judas said. "But even if it's true, their malice will cease when they hear him speak."

"It's one thing to speak softly to a peaceable crowd on a green hillside in Galilee, and quite another to satisfy a smoldering mob in Jerusalem."

"He will satisfy them."

"With what?"

"With what he tells them."

"What can he tell them that he has not already told the others?"

Judas knew what he would tell them: one word. The scrivener could barely say it anymore, for the Nazarene had not as yet spoken it. There was a rumor that Jesus had actually called himself by the sacred title—in secret. But Judas knew it could not be true. The master would never have uttered it in a guilty whisper. When he announced himself, he would speak aloud, on a hilltop, or from the highest bema: *I am the Messiah!*

Judas's vision—Mary was right—he was in love with it. Right, too, in calling him a mystic. It had come as a consternation to him that he was not the reasoning man he had once thought himself to be. Hard to believe that his brain had misled him all these years, that it had almost reasoned away his soul. Indeed, the excellence of his mind had been its most terrible defect; it had deluded him. Even by the rational law of opposites and balances, a world of hatred argued a heaven of love. But don't look for "arguments," he admonished himself; stay with the vision. Which now he did. Thank heaven he had caught himself in time. If his brain had once made him doubt that a Savior would ever appear and there would be a Kingdom of Heaven, made him doubt that there would be a forgiveness of sins, an end of contention among the Jews and even with the Romans, and that there would be a glorious vision of God the Father—his soul now told him all these benisons would come. And soon.

Soon, this very Passover. That, Judas was convinced, was the reason the Nazarene had decided to come to Jerusalem. For this was the home of the Jewish heart, the sanctuary where God would show Himself.

Once Judas had forsworn what he saw to be the trickeries of his mind and committed his whole being to the dream of the Messiah, how wonderfully the muck of earth fell away from him. He felt he no longer had to comfort himself with corporeal things. He need no longer be enslaved to food or bodily comforts or sleep. Even his love for Mary lost its physicality and became a spiritual thing. For a brief time, when he had first realized that she was in love with Jesus and might have lain with him, the thought was a wretchedness. But then, even if he had not discarded the notion as being unlikely, it no longer related to his deeper existence. Anyway, he meditated, with a wry smile at the balances, whatever flesh-bound gratifications Jesus might have deprived him of, he had recompensed with exaltations of the spirit. Earthly love was not the meaning of Judas's life; his love was Jesus, the Son of God. And his promise of heaven. Which would be fulfilled.

It should have made him blissful. But he was in a torture of waiting. When would it happen, when? He was constantly tense, every nerve drawn tight as a trap string. At first, back in Galilee, he had believed this nervousness was part of his new life force, his new aliveness to a vital spark within himself. But he began to get jumpy and too easily startled. Sometimes, trivialities—an unexpected noise or a dog darting out of an alleyway—would make him shake. On a number of occasions, he felt that a rein was about to snap. Having prided himself on needing little sleep, he was now worried through long nights of wakefulness. He took to drinking wine at bedtime.

On their second day in Jerusalem, he and Jesus were praying in the Temple. They sat beside one another, so close that the tassels of their *tallithim* had become entangled with each other. When they noticed it —in the midst of prayer—they started to disentangle their silken cords and, because they were making it worse, began to smile to one another. At last they disentwined themselves and went on with their prayers. It was a loveliness they had had between them, and the smiles continued, when suddenly—such a small thing. A young boy, toying with the ram's horn, blew a raucous note. Judas arose and shouted, "No—no!" And there was such a loss of temper, such a loss of himself, that for an instant he did not know where he was. Jesus' voice—whispering, comforting—brought him back again. It's nothing, he said to Jesus, and to himself as well, nothing.

But a similar outbreak occurred again, yesterday. You've been overburdening yourself, Mary said, carrying every beggar on your back, not eating, drinking too much wine, and why do you awaken before sunrise?

This morning he had awakened early because of the soldiers. Cavalry, clattering through the street in the middle of the night. They had no right to be there. Jesus and the disciples were staying in the house of the Bethany Simon, the one who had been a leper. Some slept in the cottage, some in the small lean-to that had once been a calf cote. It was a tranquil place, the nearer side of Bethany, a few miles walk from Jerusalem, and hardly a place to cause suspicion. Close as they were to the

Antonia, there were people in that little town outside the city who had not seen a Roman soldier in many years. Then, why were the horsemen there?

They were passing on their way to somewhere else, Thomas had said. From where to where by way of Bethany?—it wasn't logical. Then Judas had the sense that, wherever they went, there were Roman soldiers following them.

"Not following," Bartholomew assured him. "They are simply there. They are everywhere."

"No. Following."

Though the men all disagreed, Mary was silent. But she had always been afraid of coming to the capital, so her apprehensions must be disallowed. Yet, his own . . .

His worst disturbance, however, was the change he saw in Jesus. Three times now, he had prophesied his own death. And with the predictions had come a kind of acrimony which did not seem consistent with his nature or with the glorious resurrection he said would follow his decease. If resurrection meant the realization of his paradise . . . ?

Sometimes Jesus was hotheaded in a way that was inexplicable. There was the incident of the fig tree, which Judas had not witnessed. The tale was told that Jesus was hungry and, noticing a fig tree from afar, went to see if he could find some fruit to eat. But the branches were fruitless; he saw nothing but leaves. So he cursed the tree, and it withered.

The story upset Judas, and he would not believe it. There was no such violence in the man. When he asked Jesus if the account was true, the teacher repeated what he had said to Peter: Whatever things you pray for, believe that you will receive them, and you will. It was one of his evasions. Why does he equivocate with me, Judas complained to Mary, why doesn't he *tell* me?

Each day, Jesus went among the poor in Jerusalem, and the misbegotten. He gave, as always, all the riches he possessed of prayer and comfort. On the day of the fig tree, the Nazarene did not rest, he did not eat, he did not pause for breath. He is getting too thin, Judas thought, even thinner than I am. There were ridges of white on his cheekbones; his bones might burst the skin. His eyes looked feverish, as though they would burn to ash. He went like a man demented by grief and heartache, he healed and failed and prayed angrily and wept and healed again.

One day, when they were walking in the heat and Jesus was a step ahead of him, the master halted. His whole body seemed to fold in upon itself, and he started to sink to the ground.

Judas, rushing forward, caught him.

"Don't let me fall," Jesus murmured.

"Lie down—Master—lie here."

"No . . . no . . ."

Judas held him, not knowing what to do. With one arm in a close embrace, he raised the other to comfort him. He wiped the perspiration off his face, kissed his brow, murmured something about water . . . and the moment passed. Jesus smiled his recovery, and they continued onward.

The next day, havoc.

He and Jesus had passed through the colonnade of the Temple on a number of occasions, and it seemed incredible to Judas that the master had not commented, indeed had not seemed to notice, how execrable the place was. The beautiful galleries—tiled pavements, walls of the most exquisite mosaics, columns of the whitest marble veined in azure—were like the filthy pens of a slaughterhouse. There were beasts for sale—first quality for sacrifice, the hawkers shouted—calves and sheep, pigeons and turtledoves. The vendors prodded their sheep with pointed sticks; with whips of leather they herded the calves into frightened huddles; the crates of doves and pigeons were thrown like bales of hay. The animals bawled, bleated, shrilled in terror; the tiles were slimy with their dung and urine; the air reeked with ordure and fear. A bird seller held a pair of doves aloft; their feet were tied together; male and female, he cried, man and wife, more lovable to the Lord. A calf seller cut a slit in a heifer's ear; so young that the blood is still crimson, see how crimson, he shouted, for favor with the Almighty.

The moneychangers were close by, under the portico, and even inside the vestibule of the Temple itself. Temple money, they yelled, sacred money for sale—we trade anything, anything—shekels, drachmas, denarii—good money, bad money—if it clinks, we trade it. Pilgrims from everywhere bartered their secular coins for the so-called holy money with which they paid their Temple tithes. Sometimes the moneychangers dealt fairly with them; more often, when the pilgrims were from distant places and did not speak the local Aramaic or understand the currency, the dealers gave them short change or light weight or coins that were wrongly alloyed or counterfeited. Since the moneychangers' booths were adjacent to the Court of the Gentiles, where non-Jews were permitted, the dividing line was not always recognized, and many of the traders were Egyptians, Syrians, Phoenicians.

On this particular day, as Jesus and Judas were passing through, a young heifer balked at being stabbed for the sample of testing blood, and attempted to break loose. The tradesman lifted his whip and started to strike her across the eyes.

Suddenly the whip was in Jesus' hand, and he flailed. At everyone in sight—calf dealers, bird sellers, customers, worshipers, Levites passing through, Jews and foreigners, anyone, everyone—lashing, slashing with the leather thong.

There were shouts—outcries—a scurrying for animals—bleats and screams—mayhem.

And still he didn't stop. The moneychangers now. Lifting tables and dashing them against the pillars of the Temple. Money—everywhere—gold and silver—lead, brass, iron—flung against the tiles and out upon the stones of the Court of the Gentiles.

House of prayer, he shouted, not a den of thieves, house of prayer!

The crates of the doves were broken, and the finches. The birds went free, the calves and sheep ran loose along the colonnade and into the courtyard, and through the portals of the Temple.

The beasts are in the Temple, someone shouted, and Judas yelled no, they are being driven from it!

A crowd gathered. A few laughed and screamed in a delirium of pleasure. But most of the people were silent and frightened, holding their hands over their mouths, pulling their children close.

When the wildness was over, and Judas was no longer exhilarated, he, too, was alarmed. Not so much by what Jesus had done, but by the fact that there were no consequences.

There had been outcries for order, but no summoning of soldiers. Priests had appeared on the fringes of the crowd, but they had not lifted a finger. The melee had spilled over into the Court of the Gentiles. Many gentiles were, in fact, involved, and a number of them had suffered losses. Toward the end of the commotion, two members of the Sanhedrin had appeared, on the perimeter of the crowd. And half a dozen Roman legionaries.

But not a single hand of authority had been raised. Not by the priests, by the Sanhedrin or by the Roman constabulary. Jesus had not been arrested. He had not even been rebuked. Silence.

The silence was more worrisome to Judas than if the perpetrator of the disorder and damage had been apprehended. It signified to Judas that the punishment would not be waived, but delayed. A writ would be served, or a warrant; more official and more terrible.

Yet the day passed without anything.

Then ensued a buffeting by the winds—questions from all directions—sharp, gusty onslaughts from Sadducees and Pharisees, from priests and elders, interrogators sent by the court of the Sanhedrin or by Caiaphas, the High Priest.

"By what authority," they asked, "are you doing these things?"

"I will answer you if you will answer me," Jesus replied. "The baptism of John, where was it from? From heaven or from men?"

If they said John's authority had come from heaven, then why had they not believed in the baptist? If from men, let them answer to the multitude who now accounted John a prophet. He had trapped them and they went away.

"What about mammon?" the Pharisees demanded. "You teach the way of God, but what about mammon? Is it lawful to pay taxes to Caesar?"

He knew them and their mealy mouths. "Show me the tax money."

Someone handed him a denarius. He pointed to it. "Whose image is this?"

"Caesar's."

"Render therefore to Caesar the things that are Caesar's, and to God the things that are God's."

This was the question that troubled Judas the most. Taxes. No matter how the interrogators had tried to ensnare him with questions about resurrection and the Torah and the priority of the Commandments, those were always legitimate religious matters. But taxes were political. Roman. Why had the Pharisees examined the master on such a totally civil issue? Had they been prompted by the *quaestores?*

It made Judas more anxious than ever. He started to behave in discrepant ways. When Jesus fomented too violently in the Temple and Judas was reluctant to criticize the master's courage, he criticized the disciples instead: Why do you indulge yourselves with luxurious unctions and oils, why do you waste money that can be used on the poor? One day, he quarreled with Peter because the fisherman would not beg Jesus to mitigate his anger against the Pharisees, who were becoming more powerful in the Sanhedrin. To which Peter answered, Why do *you* not beg him?

Judas tried. It was no use. Jesus merely listened to his friend as if in disbelief, and went forth that day to call the scribes and Pharisees a brood of vipers. Serpents, he shouted, murderers, scourgers, crucifiers. On their hands was the blood of prophets, whom they slew in the Temple and on the altar.

"O Jerusalem, Jerusalem," he lamented, bewailing the murderers' city, "You shall see no more of me till you say, 'Blessed is he who comes in the name of the Lord!' "

Then came the auguries of doom:

He warned that not one stone of the Temple would be left upon another, that all would be thrown down—

He warned of wars, of nation rising against nation, and kingdom against kingdom—

He warned of famine, pestilence and earthquake—

And all would be merely the beginning of sorrow.

Then, when his warnings hung like a dust storm in the air, the inevitable happened: His prophecies were viewed as maledictions. He was laying a curse on creation, and it would wither. As he had cursed the fig tree and made it wither.

The priests and the Levites saw him as a danger; the Pharisees and Sadducees also saw him as a danger. And what terrified Judas: So might the Romans. In fact, it was rumored that warnings about him were being bruited about the Roman offices and garrisons.

Mary—in a wildness—came and reported:

"Do you hear what the soldiers are calling him? King of the Jews!"

A *quadrum* leader had spread the word. Any day now, he said, Jesus was going to be anointed. By whom, the military men were asking, by whom? It was said that the Emperor Tiberius was asking the same question, and Pilate was going to arrest someone, to root out the answer.

It was clear to most of the disciples—not to Zelotes, of course—that if Jesus was arrested, his answer would be what it had always been: he had no interest in an earthly kingdom, only in the Kingdom of Heaven.

But Judas knew that saying it again and again would be of no avail and that the time was becoming more and more perilous. Twilight, toward darkness, as he and Jesus were walking in the lower garden, at the foot of the Temple, he said to the teacher:

"If Pilate is distrustful, do you think it puts his mind to rest when you speak so vaguely about a 'kingdom of heaven'?"

"I do not speak vaguely."

"Forgive me. I simply mean that it's not enough to tell Pilate you are not the King of the Jews. You must tell him who you *are.*"

"Who do you say I am?"

It was what he had asked Peter. Suddenly—uncontrollably—Judas lost his temper.

"Don't ask me that!"

"But I do ask you."

"No! I'm sick of your evasions—sick of them! You ask us to believe in you—and to follow you—and to love you—"

"No!"

"—to love you! But whom are we to love? Who are you?"

"Who do you say I am?"

Frenzied, distraught, Judas snatched at a branch of a blackthorn bush. He tore it from the ground and slashed at the wall against which it grew, whipped the wall, whacked again and again, as if to make the mortar bleed. He himself bled, however, his hand torn by the spines of the blackthorn.

Quietly Jesus took the branch from Judas's hand. With his cloak he wiped away the blood and the bits of leaf and white sloe flower from his friend's palm.

Judas quivered and did not know how to make himself be still. But Jesus gave him no quarter.

"Who do you say I am?"

How can I answer him? Judas thought; I must answer him or run away. But where will I go to without him?

"I think you may be the Messiah." His voice was unsteady; he was quaking. "But if you do not tell me that you are, then I know nothing about you. And I think that it is now time."

It was as if a cloud crossed the man; his eyes were veiled with distress.

"No," Jesus said. "I am waiting for . . ."

The pain was too much; he could not finish the sentence.

All night, in Bethany, and into the next morning, Judas could not get Jesus' uncompleted sentence out of his mind.

Toward noon, he separated himself from the others and walked the hills alone, toward Jerusalem. As he was entering the city, a *quadrum* of soldiers approached him. They asked him if he was Judas Iscariot. He nodded. And he was arrested.

15

She didn't know what was happening. Things seemed to be falling apart. The disciples were behaving in ominous and unpredictable ways —vainglorious about their popularity with the crowds, yet fearful about being too conspicuously exposed to the public view. It was a perplexity of pride and terror, as if they did not know whether to strut in the sunlit courtyards or scurry back into the dark alleyways.

People were getting separated in the city, lost, gone for hours. Judas, for example; not lost, for he knew Jerusalem, but gone a whole afternoon. He had told nobody his destination, and nobody had seen him depart. Not at all characteristic of the man, especially not in a city full of soldiers, where it had been deemed wise for people not to straggle off into unknown byways.

And Jesus, too. Not physically disappearing; he was present in body, well enough, but these days he had been lost to view in a more chilling way, seeming to have evanesced out of her life. Out of everyone's life, she told herself, as if that were any comfort. What an emptiness he had left. Formerly, his attendance in a room had filled all the available space. Now, even when he was there, he was elsewhere; as if some essence of him, some vast hope, had shriveled into nothingness and had left a void of despair.

She wanted to help him if she could; she would do anything to bring him solace. If he were an ordinary man, she would have arms to hold him with, she would have a mouth to kiss him, but it was as though she were unendowed with such things, born armless, crippled, mouthless, totally unfit to offer love. Sometimes she touched him just to let him know that she was there; sometimes he even touched her in return, to let her know he knew. But his eyes were caves.

She could barely stand to hear him preach anymore. While she was always in the crowd, she would have to close her ears. When, occasionally, she heard a phrase or two, it was all wrath and desolation. She mourned the passing of the sweet singer of psalms, the man who loved his enemies, the gentle soul who suffered the little children to come unto him. How could he have altered so unrecognizably? Or was Zelotes right, that there had always been a fury in the man? We take what we need from him, he said.

Take everything, in fact. She felt as though they had all eaten away at the beloved teacher, had gnawed at his goodness and love and kindness, every sustenance of his heart, and left him nothing but his wasteland.

Everyone had done it, in every town and village. And now in Jerusalem. They gorged upon him. The people in the city, natives and pilgrims, were ravenous for everything he brought them, greedy for his words of wisdom, for his easily remembered prayers, for his censures of sinners who were other than themselves, for his promise of salvation, even for his revilements. They were especially greedy for the new Jerusalem he seemed to be offering them. They wanted it, they wanted to possess and consume it, to steal its holiness, to spirit it away in their bloodstreams and brain pockets.

She hated being among them. She resented them almost as much as she resented the Roman soldiers, many of whom were strangers to the city, wearing the insignia of Tiberias and Caesarea and Joppa. Often she understood the Latin of the soldiers better than the alien-accented Aramaic of the foreign Jews. But, no matter how unintelligible they were to her and to one another, they all understood the language of calumny. Hearsay, tattle, slander—their universal language. They gossiped about one another and about the obscenities of the Romans and about the corruption of the priests and about how the taxes would be raised or lowered. They believed some of the rumors; some they doubted. God was a rumor they believed.

But they were not sure about His prophets. Especially the new one from Nazareth. Savior? King of the Jews?

When, once again, last night, she had heard the rumor of his being King of the Jews, she had wanted to go off with Jesus and speak to him alone, but Judas had gotten to him first, and they had slipped away together. She was left with a few of the others, with Simon-named-Peter, as usual, intoning. In his opinion, Jesus had always been the King, had always been the Messiah, Peter had never had a doubt of anything. Oddly, Zelotes had agreed.

"If he has not *become* our leader by now—after all the uproar he has caused—then, this is the end of him."

"And of us, perhaps," the oldest disciple had said.

John had concurred. "He has to be our Moses now."

"What if he is not?" she had asked.

"Then, this is not our Passover," Peter replied. "And we are still in Egypt."

The fisherman had spoken with an unaccustomed note of criticism, and they all made sounds and signs of qualified agreement. She wondered how Jesus would have answered them if he had been present.

In discussing his plans for the *seder* tonight, he had talked with a sense of occasion, giving Peter and John instructions more ceremoniously than usual. They were to go to the city, find a certain man and tell him that Jesus' time was at hand, and that he and his disciples would keep the Passover at the man's house.

She wished he would not use such forbidding expressions as "my time is at hand," and she wished she had been invited to the Passover supper. She thought how sad that she would not be present at such a great festivity, but she was not at all self-pitying. In fact, it had nothing to do with her self; another person had been slighted, someone to whom it had at one time seemed important to be included in social gatherings. Once, there was a Jewish girl who had slit the bodice of her dress and gone as a seminaked Roman woman—uninvited—to an obscene revelry. And later, in Alexandria, to bacchanalia of one sort or another . . . thinking she was naked in those days, when what she was was hidden, smothered in disguises.

How wonderfully unadorned she felt. Without mask or mummery, she was at last what she was.

Older, however. Youth gone and vanity discarded. The crow's-feet, no matter how Judas called them laughter lines, were the wrinkles of suffering, not only for herself but for others, and she knew they would grow deeper. She wondered, with the first strands of gray in her hair, and in the simple clothes she wore, how she could be so truly convinced that this was Mary of Magdala . . . and yet not quite recognize her. And if, by chance, her father and brother were to see her in a street of the city, would they know who she was?

Once, on the day following the arrival in Jerusalem, she thought she saw her father; that same day, Caleb. But they were other men. Daytimes, nighttimes, they clung to her mind. How could she be so close to her father in Jerusalem, and not go and see him? She had an urgent impulse . . .

But she resisted. He would not recognize her; she was another person. The Mary who had lived in the splendor of the great house on the hill no longer existed. Nor the Mary who had lived in the filth and disease of Hinnom. In both places, she felt, she had been a stranger to herself, unhealthy and unclean. And now . . .

Oh, beloved, she said, I thank you and I thank Judas—for I no longer hate myself. I am a long way from liking who I am. But not to hate myself—!

A woman shrieks, then a shrill whistle. There is a swirl of motion in the crowd, a maelstrom. Everybody violent and whirling toward the center, where the body lies. Shouts and screams, make room, give him air, no, he's dead, he's dead, call officers, make way, please make way.

More whistles, men's voices shouting, a legionary beats his sword against his shield to sound a warning noise, make way, make way. From both sides they come, mostly on foot, a few on horses. The beasts rear, shy, whinny. One of them refuses to go forward into the crowd, into the blood.

He's dead—the Roman merchant is dead.

Suddenly another shout—quite different—someone sees the murderer:

"There he is!"

The woman points to the low roof of the ironmongery. The killer is running. Crouched, head low. Jumping roof to roof.

"There! He did it! That's the one!"

The shouts are louder now. They are no longer interested in the dead Roman, but the murderer. Their voices—horror gone to hunt.

"Get him! Get him!"

It looks as though they won't. The soldiers are in the crowded thoroughfare, almost immobile, while the murderer is running free.

One of the horsemen starts to wave his sword into the crowd, threatening with it, shouting make way, make way.

A clatter of steel. Something stops the fugitive. There are soldiers on the other side, perhaps. He turns back toward the swarm.

Mary recognizes him. So do others. Someone shouts:

"Barabbas!"

All at once, everything is reversed. Nobody shouts against him, nobody yells get him. A woman screams, "This way, Barabbas—this way!"

They are his allies now. They pinion the soldiers by their very presence. Even the horses cannot move.

"This way!"

He falls.

Someone tries to help him up, but he resists. A path is made for him, but he does not run. His leg has crumpled. They raise him to his feet, and he can stand, but barely that.

"Make way! Make way!"

Now that the fugitive cannot move, there is nothing else to do: they make way.

One of the soldiers grabs him. As he starts to maul the prisoner, the crowd growls, and a mounted legionary curses the stupid one, while the other soldiers surround Barabbas. For an instant, apparently, he can no longer stand. But as he starts to fold, someone from the crowd shouts an encouragement, and he limps among the soldiers as they lead him away.

All at once, the shouts again, from where the dead Roman merchant lies. The dogs are at him. Mongrels, alley hounds, are licking at the blood, and two are chewing at the stab wounds in his belly. One of them is eating at his cheek.

Shrieks now, rampant. There is a horror and need for horror. With no warning, as if the Roman soldiers are the carrion-eating dogs, the crowd starts at them. Stones, fists, feet—and swords. Blood mingles with blood, then more soldiers from all directions, horsemen and terror, and, of a sudden, the street is empty, except for the cadaver and the dogs.

"I can't stand the city anymore," she said. "How long do we have to stay?"

He said that they could leave after the *seder* tonight if it weren't for the Sabbath. She replied, without consideration, that the Sabbath had not been known to deter him overmuch. When Jesus did not dignify the remark with any comment, she was chagrined.

"Who was the man?" he said.

That also irritated her. With all the things that should be worrying him right now, all he could think of was an unknown Roman merchant who had been dead for hours. At first she had thought the horror of the dogs had usurped his mind, but she realized it was the sadness of death in anonymity, a corpse unclaimed and unwept, and she saw that the abandonment spoke to him in a way she could only surmise.

She felt a heaviness of pity for him and wondered how she could soothe him a little, what lightness she could bring, however she might have to twist it.

"Don't worry," she said. "When you die, you will not be abandoned. You will be claimed and wept for, and you will not be lonely."

The sadness stayed. "I will never die," he said.

She smiled at his inconsistency; sometimes he spoke of his death as if it would come tomorrow, or an hour hence; sometimes he would live forever. Sooner or later, she realized, she herself would have to state the undeviating fact. State it now. His death was imminent. Soon. Somehow, somewhere, soon.

No. Smoke in a room where the fire does not draw. Dispel it. Open the lattices.

"I will be so happy," she said, "to be back home in Galilee. . . ."

"It is spring."

"Yes—only in Galilee. Jerusalem has no seasons."

"What if we never get there?"

"Where?"

"Galilee."

Smoke again. It was choking her.

"Why would we not?" she said.

"Jerusalem . . . and the thing to finish. . . ."

"Finish what, for God's sake?"

He smiled at the inapt expletive. "Yes."

"What? Finish what?"

When he did not answer, and she could barely stand not knowing, she asked another question:

"Do you love me?"

"I have never not loved you."

"I wasn't asking God, I was asking you."

He winced. "Yes, I love you."

"Then, tell me. Finish what? What did you come here to do?"

"It doesn't matter," he said. "I think I may have failed."

"Failed to do what?"

She was lightning-struck. She knew the answer. Knew it, and refused to believe it.

He had come here to make the apocalypse. Not to see it, not to watch it come about, but to *make* it. To ask for and be shown God's revelation, to be given the key with which he would open the gates of heaven. And despite how abjectly he had begged, how devoutly he had prayed—despite all his adjurations to others that if they sought they would find, if they knocked it would be opened unto them—he had not found what he sought, and the gates were locked.

"You will find the way," she said.

"To where?"

"The Kingdom of Heaven."

"You think the path is through a vale of madness, don't you?" he said.

"I do not think that you are mad."

"Are you sure?"

". . . No."

"Do you think that *you* are?"

"No," she replied. "I have been ill, but I am the sanest person I have ever known. I see what is. Sometimes, when things become too terrifying, I try to call them something else—but then they become more terrible."

She touched his cheek. How warm he was.

I have to see what is, she said to herself.

He is going to die.

There was no denying it. Nor denying when the event would happen, saying it would be ten years from now or in his dotage. It would happen soon—days, hours—right here in Jerusalem.

She could not stand it. What he had said to her—I have never not loved you—was what she should have said. For it seemed to her that through all her life she had loved some undiscovered teacher as unlike her as the dream is to the stone. And now that he was found—no, she couldn't stand it.

They had been speaking rationally, as if he were telling a parable and she was trying to parse it like a complicated sentence. Then, suddenly, she saw the stark thing: no parable—this was his dead body they were trying to make a grammar of, his cold flesh, his rigid limbs, his staring eyes like pebbles, his death, his death.

"Jesus—please—I beg you—let us leave Jerusalem."

He seemed stunned. "Leave—and go where?"

"Where? There is all the everywhere—!" All at once—wild—her words were wild. "Please—they'll kill you—come away—!"

"I cannot."

"Please—oh, please—!"

"I have my Father's work."

"I hate your Father!" She was all scream. "I hate Him! Your Father who art in heaven is in hell! If He is God, I hate your God! I hate Him—and I hate you for loving Him!"

She started to beat her fists upon him as though he were the Almighty she must destroy. He made no movement to stop her. The longer he did not try to restrain her, the more violently she beat at him. Until she had only strength enough to weep. She wept and sobbed and cried out how she hated God and hated Jesus. And at last she turned away from him.

Later, she had no mind for regret. She saw, in fact, the defensibility of lunacy. It filled an urgent need. She envied all those others who could take insanity in small measures, all those lucky ones, the slightly demented, who could believe in God and witches and resurrections and divine revelations. How smug of mind she had been to try to make a world of order and reality out of chaos, when it was only intelligible as a madhouse. All those arguments she had marshaled for reason and fact and substantiality, so that she could see existence for what it was, without hypocrisy or superstition. Well, now she needed both. She needed illusions, she needed a faith of any kind, she needed lies, so that her life could be sufferably human; she needed gods and angels so that anything could be possible, so that she could have one intimation of eternity, not for herself, but for the man she so deeply loved. Let him, O God, let him live forever, she said. Let me be mad.

16

The *quadrum* of soldiers would not tell Judas on what charge he was being arrested. They led him in the most circuitous way—to avoid the crowds, they said—to a northeastern gate of the city. He knew this section well. He had collected taxes near the Sheep Gate on a number of occasions, but he did not know the Antonia fortress, except from the outside.

Nor would he get to know it on the inside. As they came in sight of the vast Roman edifice, the *quadrum* turned southward toward the Sheep Gate and entered the Court of the Gentiles.

The Temple, Judas asked, why were they taking him to the Temple? The one who carried the tablet on which Judas's name was inscribed replied that they would not be permitted inside the Temple, but others would.

The others were already waiting for them. Two men, Ahira and Helon, they said they were, the one a Levite, the other a scribe. You will come with us, they whispered. Walking ahead of Judas, leaving the soldiers to depart, they did not even look back to see if the arrested man was following. Abruptly, in the swift transition from the Roman soldiers to the Jewish clerics, he had ceased being a prisoner.

They led him through a part of the Temple he had never seen. The passageway was long and narrow, without illumination except for a lighted taper at the farthest end, where there was a single door. As they were approaching, the door opened and an old man stood on the threshold, waiting for them. He wore the robe of the High Priest, except that there was gold embroidery on white silk instead of white on gold, which signified he no longer held the office. The metal threads glistened as though the tiny candle were a blazing torch.

"I am Annas."

That was all he said. Then, as he made a peremptory gesture of dismissal to the guides, he cleared the doorway. Since he was a former High Priest and venerably old, Judas could not precede him. But the elder waved at him, the same peremptory gesture as before, and the younger man took precedence.

The chamber was huge, yet all its light and space seemed to converge upon a single table and its single oil lamp. There were no windows; midday was a dark night. And it was only later that Judas realized this was a library of sorts—shelves laden with scrolls and papyri and ancient dust.

The middle-aged man who sat at the table wore white on gold, and a golden coronet. He did not rise, he scarcely moved, as though he were studying his own rigidity.

"This is my son Caiaphas," Annas said.

He was not his son, as Judas knew, but his son-in-law, and he thought it was an affectation of modesty to introduce him as a younger relative instead of as High Priest.

He felt a reeling puzzlement. Arrest by soldiers, and then—in the presence of the two most sanctified mantles of the Temple.

"You are welcome here," Caiaphas said.

"Under arrest, they told me."

"Not so," Annas said.

"Yes, arrested," his son-in-law corrected.

Judas looked from one to the other, not knowing which to believe. The old man smiled, but apparently he had caught the knack only recently, and his features were still uncomfortable in amusement. The younger priest had not learned how. But he did things to compensate. He nodded on a few selected occasions, sometimes yes when he meant no. Infrequently he made small, friendly gestures of accessibility, as if to open a portal to himself, but it was unclear whether any door existed.

"The Roman keepers of the peace have been reporting some . . . disturbances," he said. "Normally nothing would come of such complaints. A few arrests by the local legionaries, and that would be the end of it. But this being Passover—and Pilate in the city—and Herod . . . the streets are in a frenzy. Some special tact is required—or anything can occur. In fact, the occurrences have begun. Two robberies—yesterday a man was beaten—a Roman storehouse raided. Less than an hour ago, there was a murder. And one of your master's followers was arrested."

"Who?"

"His name is Barabbas."

"He is not one of Jesus' followers."

"It is said that he is."

"It's not true. He is a *sicarius.*"

"Ergo?"

"Ergo, a murderer—therefore, not one of us."

"I am glad to hear it," Annas said. "We are both glad to hear it, are we not?"

He turned for concurrence from his son-in-law, but the man withheld it. "How about Simon the Zealot? Is he not one of you?"

"Yes."

"And is he not a murderer?"

"If you have questions for Barabbas and Simon the Zealot, why don't you ask them instead of me?"

"Because we do not want Pilate to ask the questions."

There was something so askew about everything that Judas was lost. The old man came to guide him.

"Pilate gets alarmed, you know," he said. "Every little disturbance is a riot to him—every riot is an insurrection. He was on the verge of arresting the whole lot of you—"

He stopped. For all his pretense of calm, the old man was shaken.

"Why didn't he arrest us?" Judas asked.

"Because we begged him not to," Caiaphas said quietly. "Until we could be sure of . . ." He hesitated, reconsidering.

"Be sure of what?"

The older priest seemed to burst. "Who is this man Jesus?"

He had thought, at first, that they were both angry at Jesus, but now perceived something worse. They were frightened. And confused by something they had not, as yet, fully measured. There was anxiety in the room, like an illness that could be communicated. Judas tried not to become infected.

"Why don't you ask Jesus who he is?" he said. "Why have you brought me here to bear witness upon the others?"

"Because we told Pilate that you were the one."

"The one for what?" They did not answer, and he became unnerved. "In the name of heaven—what?"

"We need you to tell us about your teacher," the old man said.

"Let him tell you. Go and hear him preach. Listen to what he says about the Torah. Or talk to the others. There are eleven other apostles and countless followers—"

"We do not care about the followers," Caiaphas said quietly. "They are only sometime people—they are yours, they are ours, they are anyone's. And the apostles—forgive me, Judas—there is an insufficiency of brain among them. John, perhaps, but he is young—not one to influence his master. Matthew is still a collector at heart—taxes, wise sayings, other men's opinions. Not likely to be influential. As to the fisherman, the one that you call Peter, the rock—well, a rock is good for sitting on and building upon, but not the best for moving. You, we think, are the brightest of the lot, and the most movable."

"Where do you want me to move?"

"Not you. Jesus."

"In what direction?"

"That depends on where he wants to go," Caiaphas said.

The older man leaned forward. "And who he is."

"He is a simple man—a carpenter, a builder—he comes from Nazareth."

"Is he a blasphemer?" the old man asked.

"No."

"He sins against the Torah." Caiaphas consulted a papyrus. "Breaks the Sabbath. Consorts with sinners. Claims the power of forgiveness."

"And that terrible disorder on the very threshold of the Temple!" Annas spluttered. "Money and animals violated—that's vandalism!"

Caiaphas shrugged. "I must confess—and I ask your discretion, Judas—that I was pleased about the animal sellers and the moneychangers. While I know we must have them—and the Temple profits from their presence—I've been troubled by how they abuse their privileges. All of the merchants do. The pens of the animals are slovenly—the Temple tiles are filthy—they are not gentle with the birds. But the moneychangers are the worst. How many times have we told them not to bring their tables past the portals—how many times?"

The question was rhetorical, but the old man answered. "Countless," he said.

"So—if they were chastened—splendid. The disorder was a civil matter—let the Romans deal with it. As the Romans will deal with whether he is the King of the Jews."

"He never claimed to be."

"Come, Judas."

"Never—never."

"Zelotes—Peter—hundreds of your followers—"

"Not Jesus—never!"

Caiaphas puckered his lips; it was as close as he came to a smile. "Well, a Roman matter. But . . ."

He paused to look pleasant. Then he said, with disarming easiness:

"Why does he diminish the majesty of the Almighty?"

"I do not believe he does," Judas said carefully. "Unless you mean he magnifies the stature of man."

"It's occasionally the same." His smile was unsuccessful. "If the glory of the world was created out of the might and omniscience of God, does Jesus believe he can create a glory out of man's frailty and ignorance?"

I must be careful, Judas thought; this is the palaver of priestly politics, and I must not get caught in it. "I don't know what you mean."

"Doesn't he take advantage of the unenlightened?"

"I don't think so. In what way?"

"He tells them he performs miracles."

"He tells them no such thing."

The old man said, "But *does* he perform them?"

For a moment, fearful of a trap, Judas was silent.

"Miracles—miracles!" Annas's head moved with birdlike twitches. Alert, excited, he looked at Judas, then at his son-in-law, and back to Judas. "Does he perform them?"

"Patience, Father."

"But I have to know." The old man was aquiver. "Does he make miracles? Does he, Judas?"

". . . Yes."

"You've seen them?"

"Yes."

"Lepers healing—cripples walking—?" Annas trembled. "You have really seen them?"

"Yes."

"If he says he makes miracles—and doesn't make them—you know that is a sin?"

It was the first sign of the old man's senility. Judas smiled gently. "What is it if he makes them and says he doesn't?"

Annas bridled. "You are laughing at me."

"No—please—forgive me."

Caiaphas conciliated. "Never mind," he said. "We're inclined to weigh the so-called miracles too heavily. We're a nervous people these days. It used to be that we would listen to the counsels of the Law, but now—only to the counsels of superstition. If superstition says we're blind, the world grows dim; if it says leprous, we start to rot. And if superstition says we're healed, we are miraculously restored to health."

The old man leaned forward. "What if it's not superstition?"

"I beg you, Father—"

"What if he is really the Messiah?"

Caiaphas, seeing the old man's agitation, tactfully withdrew a little. In a politic manner, he turned to Judas. "My father-in-law, like all of us, is not untouched by the prevalent lunacy. The Messiah has always been the Jewish madness."

"That's a profanity, Caiaphas!"

"I'm not profane, Father. I admit that if we are insane, we've been demented by God. But I don't foresee a Messiah in our time."

"What if he does come in our time? What if this man *is* the Messiah?"

"Is he, Judas?"

". . . I do not know."

"Then, why does he say so?"

Judas flared. "He has neither said that he is King of the Jews nor that he is the Messiah."

Caiaphas spoke evenly. "King of the Jews—let the Romans worry about that. But the Messiah—that is *our* concern. And there are rumors that he has claimed—"

"The rumors are untrue!"

"How do you know? Have you heard every word he has ever spoken?"

"Because if he had ever said such a thing, he would have done so to me."

"Why, necessarily?"

Concerned that they might see his nervousness, he tightened every muscle. "Because he knows how I want him to be."

"And I, too—I, too!" The old man shook.

"Father, if you cannot contain yourself—"

"I will not! What if he is the Messiah—and we refuse to recognize him—and we miss our single chance for salvation?"

"And what if he is a false prophet?"

"Because we've had false prophets, does that mean we'll never have a true one? Have we not had true prophets? Why can we not have a true Messiah? If God has promised us a Savior, isn't it sinful for us to say that none will ever come?"

"I did not say never, I said not now."

" 'Not now' can be 'never' in the lifetime of one man." As he lowered his voice, he became more intense. "And my lifetime is short, Caiaphas. You will live five hundred years—or so you think. I'm past seventy, and as good as dead. I've lived a long life, and I'm still in love with it. And if someone comes to me and says, 'Old Annas, live!'—if someone says life is eternal—heaven is now, heaven is always—and such a man has made some miracles—shall I be deaf to him?"

"Not deaf, Father—no. But not witless."

The old priest was wounded, and drew upon what dignity his feebleness would allow. "I think I'm prudent, not witless," he said. "If a man were to come to you and say, 'I am the Messiah—recognize me or perish'—wouldn't you be foolish to use your last breath to shout the man away?"

"He has not said, 'I am the Messiah.' "

"Because he is afraid!"

"How do you know that, Father?"

"Because I know! And Judas knows. Do you not, Judas, do you not?"

"Perhaps—I cannot tell."

Annas's voice turned pleading. "Tell him not to be afraid, Judas. If you think he is the Messiah, encourage him to say so. Tell him he is safe —we do not slay Messiahs."

Caiaphas said grimly, "There have been none to slay."

"Tell him we've prayed for him and prayed. He knows that, but remind him, remind him. Prevail upon him, Judas—beg him to tell us!"

"If he does, will you believe him?" Judas asked.

"I will—oh, dear God, a man of miracles—I will!"

Judas turned to Caiaphas. "And will you?"

"Let us say this." The High Priest spoke measuredly. "If he is the Messiah, he has committed no sins, he has not infracted the Law. Breaking the Sabbath, consorting with sinners, disputing the Scriptures—who says the Messiah may not do these things? Who knows what our Lord sends his Messenger to do? A Messiah's law is the Messiah's."

"What if I ask him—and he says no?"

"Then, he is a sinner. He has blasphemed, he has broken the Law, he is a heretic."

"What if he does not answer?"

"He will answer," the old man said. "Sooner or later, he will have to answer—if only in extremis."

"Extremis—no!" Judas shuddered. "I could not bear it if he were hurt."

"We are talking about a Messiah, Judas." The old man's voice had become gentle, fatherly. "A Messiah cannot be hurt."

Annas moved closer to him. There was an intimacy about him, as if he felt he could make a warmer attachment to Judas than he could to his own son-in-law. Judas felt sorry for the old priest, he liked him, he understood him. Most important, he believed him.

The elderly voice, soft and quavery, had gathered strength. "Don't worry over your friend, my son. Let God do it. No harm can come to him. The man has made miracles and he will make more. If he is the Messiah, nobody will be able to hurt him. They can lock him in chains, and he will burst them; they can put him to the sword and he will not bleed. If they try to kill him, his words will save him. 'I am the Son of God,' he will say. And as he is saved, so shall we be."

"What am I to do?"

"Where is he now?" Annas asked.

"He will be here in the city tonight. We will sit at *seder* together."

"Good. Go to him—do not wait. Tell him you have been with us. Beg him to speak. And promise him—if he is the Messiah—our God will protect him."

"And then?"

"After the supper is over—return and tell us."

There was a man named Joachim who owned a well not far from the marketplace of the lower city. The water was clear and cool and, until recently, it had been for sale; Joachim did a good business. When he became a follower of Jesus, however, he began to give the water freely to anyone who had no money, and his well became a meeting place for the poor. On the last two afternoons, toward twilight, Jesus had gone there.

But when Judas went to seek him at the well, the master was not present, and, of his followers, only Mary was there, ladling water and washing children.

"Where is he?" Judas asked.

"I haven't seen him for hours," she replied. "They said he was with you."

"With me? Not since the morning."

Once more, she looked oddly at him, he thought, as if at a puzzle. Shaking her hands of the wetness, she dried them on her apron.

"You're tired," she said.

"No—no."

"And dusty. Would you like some water?"

"No. Some wine. Can you change it?"

"Bad jest." But she smiled. "I was certain he was with you."

"No—I've been looking for him. The Temple. Bethany. Did he say he would be with me?"

"I thought he did. . . . Where have you been?"

"With Caiaphas."

"You are full of jests today."

"Bad ones."

"You mean it? Caiaphas?"

"Oh, God."

Marginally he saw her handing him a ladle of water, and he did not know why she was doing so. He ignored the offering, and she set the ladle on the coping of the well. Why did she do that? His mind was—where?

"When Jesus and I were among the Essenes," he said, "they used to talk of a mystery. We would know the secret if we took our vows. But neither of us did. Still . . . I believe he knows the secret. Has he told it to you?"

Once more, she looked oddly at him. "No, Judas."

He wondered if she was lying. "Please—Mary—it is of the heart . . . Please—did he tell you the secret?"

"No."

"I think it had to do with the Messiah—when he would come—who he would be. Did he tell you?"

"I swear to you, no."

"I know you're lying—I know it!"

"Judas—?"

He began to cry.

"Judas—Judas."

She took him in her arms. "What is it—are you ill, dear friend?" she asked. "Are you ill?"

"No," he said. "How warm you are. Is my skin cold?"

"It's burning. Here—come here."

She led him closer to the well. There was nobody there. It was already sunset, toward the eve of Passover. Again she went to the well and brought him water, this time in an earthenware dipper; she wet her hands and cooled his face. Burning, she kept saying, burning. He wondered if her hands had caught the gift of healing.

He was feeling better now, more calm. Night would be coming soon, the shadows were lengthening, there was a farewell descent on everything. Goodbye, he wanted to say to Mary, as though they were parting forever. Except that the departure had already occurred between them, without his knowing exactly when. He wondered if she had noticed the precise time. He had thought, at first, when she said she loved Jesus, it was as all of them loved him. Now, this moment, he felt such a pity for her, wanting the man as she must, the corporeal man, and having to make do with a fleeting emanation. One day, he saw her looking at Jesus with a glance that told him all her wanting and her emptiness, and he felt an ache for her which had never gone away.

"I must go and find him," he said.

"Shall I go with you?"

"No—I have to speak to him—I think not."

She looked downcast and excluded, and he wished there were a way to make them all one, the three of them, as parents make a family. There had been a time when it did not seem such an unwonted image; where Jesus was, there was a promised hearth. But now . . .

He was already quite a distance away when she called something after him. He turned.

"Levi's." She raised her voice. "If you don't find him, you're to meet for the *seder*—Levi's!"

He called back that he already knew, and hurried onward. He didn't know where onward should be, for he had looked for Jesus in a dozen places. So he turned toward Bethany. And just as he started upward on the Bethany road, he saw the master coming down. How odd that he was alone; he hardly ever was allowed any solitude these days. No retreats, except his wildernesses.

"I have been searching for you," Jesus said.

"And I for you."

"Since early morning."

"Yes."

"Where have you been?"

"With Annas and Caiaphas."

The teacher was silent. Unlike Mary, he did not consider this a jest of any kind, bad or good. And Judas thought: nothing surprises him. Could he really have foreseen it, could the notion even have crossed his mind? And would he continue to hold his muteness on the subject without asking a single question?

"You don't care to know what they wanted?"

"Yes, I do."

"They want to know if you are the Messiah."

"And what did you tell them?"

Do not shout, Judas told himself. And do not go blind, get water for your eyes, they burn like coals. And do not, do not run—or fall—or shriek.

"I told them I did not know."

"And do you not?"

The shriek: "Don't speak without speaking!"

"I do not want this cup."

"You are the cup—you!"

"Judas—I beg you—"

"You are the torture—you!"

"Be patient, if you can."

"No! No patience! No time left, no time! Don't wait for the apocalypse, Jesus—it has come! You are the death and the life everlasting! You are the apocalypse—you!"

"Did you tell them that?"

"No! You have to tell them! You have to say your name! Messiah! Say it! Oh, please—I beg you—say it! Messiah! Messiah!"

There was anguish in the master's face. He seized his disciple by the shoulders. "Judas—dear Judas—do you think I do not know your pain? But I cannot answer to your pain—or to my own! But the time will come." Abruptly he lifted his head and looked upward. Then a cry of torment: "Oh, Father in heaven—tell him that the time will come!"

When Jesus released Judas, the disciple fell on his knees, his body twisting this way and that, as if to find some posture in which he might not be in agony. With his face in his hands, he wept; he wept and he rocked.

Jesus was still. At last, he knelt to the distraught man. In a little while, Judas had regained himself, and together they continued toward the place of Levi.

When Jesus and Judas arrived at Levi's, the other eleven were already there. The night had become a little damp, and there was a small fire on the hearth. Some of the disciples were drinking wine, the new wine of Passover.

Levi's place had once been a hostelry of sorts, a small one, but now that the owner was old and his wife dead, he had given up letting out the rooms except for special occasions or to favored people. Sometimes it might be a friend whose granddaughter was being married and there were visitors from a distant city; sometimes for a feast after the Bar Mitzvah of a grandson. For such festivities, Levi, with the help of someone or other in the family, would cook and serve, and remember bygone times when his inn was always full and his wife was bustling.

This was such an occasion, with the Nazarene and his friends. The old man had aired out the largest upstairs room, and had set two tables together to make a long one, as there would be thirteen people at the *seder.*

He had even cleaned the stable and brought in fresh hay. Not that there would be cattle or horses, he said; there had been none quartered for many years, but in case other followers might appear and want to spend the night. He marveled at how many people he had seen at the Nazarene's last lesson on the porch of the Temple, and might even consider going along with them when they left Jerusalem after the Sabbath, if his legs were not too stiff and the wandering was not too far. Yes, he might decide to go; a few aches and stitches in the legs were a small price to pay for what the teacher offered. He giggled that eternity to an old man was offered at a bargain.

He made a great fuss about clearing away the *chametz.* Judas, touched, remembered the old ceremony on the eve of Passover, how his father and mother had gone about ridding the house of its leavened bread, saying the prayer aloud, making a clean place for the unleavened *matzoth.* Every room of the house, as if he and his brother had lumps of risen bread squirreled away in their winter shoes. And he thought what lovely games they used to play with their Lord.

Passover was always his favorite holiday. He loved everything about it. How the table was set with ritual plates: One with *matzoth,* of course, three of them, to commemorate the bread of the wilderness, yeastless and tasteless, the bread of affliction. Another with a shankbone and an egg, either cooked or roasted, and some horseradish and celery or parsley; a little to one side, a rosy little hill of chopped nuts, fruit and wine. That was the best plate of all, he always thought, and he stole from it. The third dish was either vinegar or salt water, and symbolized the years of bitterness. He hated it.

But there was nothing else he hated about the ceremony; it was as nearly perfect as anything could be. He loved the way they were all dressed up in their first spring clothes, with new leather belts that Tubal had made in the saddlery, and even new sandals, more open to the air than the winter ones had been. These are the best sandals you ever made me, he would say to his father; he would say this every year. And he loved, too, the way his father sat higher than usual on a bed pillow, and was nestled in among two more pillows so that at the *seder* he might imagine he always dined in the comfort and luxury of a king.

Best of all, he loved the story. And how it never varied. It would be told in answer to the questions of the youngest child. Judas, being the youngest, would ask them. Four questions, all having to do with why this night was different from all other nights: Why the unleavened bread, why the bitter herbs, why do we dip into them, and why do we, on this night only, dine only in a leaning position?

Then his father answered his questions with the story of the slavery in Egypt, and the Exodus; of the bitterness under the yoke and in the desert; of the sweetness in freedom; of the glory in deliverance. No matter how often Judas heard the tale, there was always the suspense of whether Pharaoh would keep his promise to Moses and let the Jews depart. Always the hot blood and frustration and heartache when the Egyptian monarch broke his pledge and added heavier chains. Plague after plague, blood and frogs and lice and beasts, and did the King of the Egyptians want still another devastation, did he not know that there would be more disasters and more, since the Jews were God's chosen people? The death of the cattle and boils and hail and locusts and darkness—the Jews still enslaved, the Pharaoh's vows unconsummated, and the Almighty's vows as well. At this point in the story—knowing every turn and nuance the tale would make—Judas always felt a trembling. What if, this year, his father would tell him that it was only a tale for children, and that it had never ended in the way it had been told at *sedarim?* Pharaoh had not finally relented, the Jews had not been freed, and there had never been a Moses. Witness, his father might say, that we are not free; the new Pharaoh's name is Tiberius, and the Egyptians are now called Romans. What if his father should say: Judas, you are old enough to know the truth: The Exodus never happened, we are still slaves. The boy could barely endure that moment of suspense, that moment of terror.

Then came the final plague, the most terrifying, the most cruel. The slaying of the firstborn. Early, he did not know its meaning. Then, when he understood, he tried to close his ears, tried to misunderstand, to say it was part of a fable that had only been imagined. But no: real, his father said, all the plagues were real, or the Jews never could have turned their backs on Egypt. Plagues, he said, were the price of freedom. And Judas had at last believed him.

But after the whole story had been told, then came the best part of the ritual—the most exciting, the most unnerving, and it promised the greatest marvel.

This part of the story—this was the only part—was truly unpredictable. Admittedly, in the past, it had always ended in the same way. But there *could* be a different ending, couldn't there? Every year, Judas asked his father the same question: it *can* end differently, yes? His father always reassured him that it could.

What was done was in the hope that the wonder would indeed occur. At the conclusion of the meal, when wine had been drunk by everyone, even by the children, and every sipping had been blessed, one special cup was poured. It was the only tall goblet in the house—made of silver—the only beautiful cup his family had ever owned. Nobody in the household had ever used it; untouched by anyone's lips.

The cup of the prophet Elijah. Every year, at the end of the *seder,* wine was poured for him. Then the front door of the house was opened, so that the prophet could enter, drink the wine and say that the time had come: Israel was redeemed.

Each year, the same. The pouring of the wine, the blessing, the opening of the door, the wind of early spring gusting in the night, the waiting for the footstep, the waiting for the figure at the door. Each year, the aching hope for deliverance, for the living sign of God, for Elijah, for the Messiah. . . . And each year, no one.

But it *could* end differently. On some beautiful Passover evening, on some lovely equinoctial night, Elijah might—he might appear!

Abruptly, this year in Jerusalem—as they all sat down to the festive table—Judas shivered as though a gust of the prophet had chilled him. Light burst his brain.

He knew when it would occur! He knew when Jesus would declare himself!

It would be tonight. Tonight, at the *seder,* when the wine was poured and the door opened, the Messiah would appear! Not Elijah, but someone greater, the vastest hope of Israel, God's son and Messenger—the Messiah! And he could see exactly how it would happen. Jesus would walk to the door and stand in the doorway, and tell them: I have come. The Messiah has come, and I am with you!

How beautiful the *seder* was. And all as he remembered. The three dishes on the table, the shankbone, egg, herbs, nuts and fruits and wine, and the salt water of bitterness.

When the time came for the four questions, he wished that he could ask them, but John was the youngest, and his voice the lightest, so that the questions seemed never to have been asked before. Or answered, as Jesus answered them.

He read nothing from the Haggadah; he told everything. As if it had happened yesterday and were still happening, and tomorrow would be the time of Moses once more. He told a tale for children, until he came to the plagues, and then it became a fact of age, and terrible.

When it was over, his eyes were old, the eyes of Exodus, and Judas thought: I was right, this is his time, for he has found his timelessness. Then everything Jesus said made Judas feel more certain that it would occur tonight, for all his words were prophetic. He prophesied betrayal; whoever dipped with him into the dish of bitterness would betray him. They all dipped.

When he broke the unleavened bread and shared the dry crusts he said: Take, eat; this is my body. Then, when he had sipped at his wine, he passed his cup to the others and bade them drink, for this was the blood of his new covenant, shed for the many, for the remission of sins.

He predicted that they would stumble because of him, that the sheep of his flock would be scattered, and that Peter—tonight—before the rooster crowed three times—would deny him.

For all his auguries of doom—the betraying, stumbling, scattering, denying—there would be the last, sweet, saving grace: the pouring of the wine, the opening of the door, and—the Messiah.

Jesus poured the wine himself. He did it slowly, as if measuring each drop. When it was done, he set the goblet upon a cleared place on the table.

Then he nodded to John and the young man went to the door. He opened it.

Jesus lowered his head and spoke a prayer so soft that the words could not be heard.

Judas tried not to breathe, not to blink his eyes.

Then Jesus raised his head.

The doorway was empty.

There was not a sound in the corridor, nor, it seemed to Judas, in any of the corridors of the night.

Jesus did not speak. He did not stir from his seat at the table. He nodded once more to John, and the young man closed the door.

And once more Judas wept.

17

This is a day, Mary thought, when everyone is searching for someone. Now Jesus' mother, down from Nazareth, searching for her son.

Mary Magdalene saw her first on the steps of Solomon's Portico. People told the woman that Jesus had been there but had departed; there were differences as to when and where he had gone. Toward dusk, she appeared again at Joachim's well; once more she had missed him. His mother might be fifty, Mary thought, but she looked older. Not because her hair was gray, but because she was so worn. She had had a ride on a carter's wagon from Naim to Jericho, but had walked the rest of the distance, a good ten miles. The walking would turn out to be worth it, she said in a disconnected way, if she could find her son and convince him to come home. Her smile, however, said she knew it was a futile errand. She had simply come to see him, that was all.

Since night was fast approaching, Mary took the woman under wing and they plodded upward, toward Levi's. A *seder,* indeed, the Nazareth lady said, impressed that her son would be preparing one without a woman's help. She herself had just finished making the preparations back home in Galilee. And you not there? Mary asked. My sons have wives, the other answered.

They slowed down a little; the woman's feet hurt and the hill was steep. She hummed softly in a childish voice, and scolded a bird that she thought was mimicking her; Mary wondered if she might not be a little giddy-headed.

"Do you like Passover?" the woman asked.

"I used to like it very much. As a child, I was never sure whether it was a story or a prayer."

"It's neither—not for women," she said matter-of-factly. "It's only something we do at springtime. Different dishes, different pots to cook in. Passover's a form of housecleaning, that's the most of it." She laughed. "Don't say I said it."

Having been sensible, she turned a little witless again. "If my name is Mary and yours is the same—how shall we tell each other apart?"

Mary decided to treat the question soberly. "We will simply talk to one another."

"How will I know I'm not talking to myself?"

"I'll call you Mary Mother."

"That is very nice," she said.

By the time they got to Levi's it was early evening. There was a dim light at the entrance and a bright light in the upstairs room. Now and then, the men's figures passed in front of the window, shadowy forms not identifiable.

"They have not sat down as yet," Mary said. "Shall I go and tell Jesus you are here?"

"No."

"Will you go up, then?"

". . . No."

Mary thought it was the evening chill that made her shiver. But she saw that the poor old woman, having traveled and trudged, had suddenly lost courage.

"The last time I came uninvited . . ."

"He won't send you away this time," Mary said, trying to comfort her. "Anyway, it wasn't you—it was his brothers."

"I know, I know."

The awareness had clearly never set her mind at rest, nor did it now. She seemed not to know what to do about anything.

"Come," Mary said. "I'll go in with you."

"No. They've already started. I don't want to interrupt him."

"We won't, then. We'll wait downstairs. Come along."

"No."

She was quaking, cold, tired, in an alien place, feeling as simple-minded as she might actually be, perhaps, and on the verge of tears. Mary was at a loss: what to do with her?

"Wait," she said.

As the younger woman started for the other building, the older one called, "Don't tell him I'm here!" There was a note of panic.

"I won't."

Indoors, she spoke to Levi, engaged his help and his promise of secrecy—and the use of one of the bedding places in the stable. Also, she arranged for him to bring some food.

The stable was clean and cozy and not the least bit chilly. If hay has a little life left in it, Mary Mother said, it offers up a bit of warmth.

In a short while Levi came shuffling in, laden with a tray on which there were a lighted candle, food and wine. He had a cloth on his shoulder which he spread over a bale of hay. He cautioned them about straw and the open flame, and when he left, they drank a little wine and a little more, and it suddenly struck Mary Mother funny that he had had to warn two grown-up women about something so obvious as hay and a bale of fire. She stopped to confide that she had mixed up the words, and they both giggled.

Starting to eat, Mary Mother suggested that they might pretend to be having their own *seder*, just the two of them. They were pleased with the idea, except that Levi had not provided them with all the Passover accessories—in fact, necessities. There were *matzoth*, but no *haroseth*, the mixture of chopped nuts, apples, raisins, cinnamon and wine; and no water of bitterness. Mary regretted the absence of the *haroseth*—she always ate what was left over; but thought they could do without the water of bitterness. If she went to ask Levi for them, she might consider asking for the first and not the second. But Mary Mother said if you get one, you have to get the other, and they both decided they didn't need either, they could imagine whatever they wanted, since they weren't altogether certain how the story of Passover should actually be told.

Together they told it to one another, like an old tale they had heard at the well or in the marketplace and had each heard somewhat differently. They didn't tell the occurrences in an unbroken sequence, as the men upstairs were surely telling it, but in bits and pieces, the way people gossip, sometimes getting the order of things mixed up. Occasionally they stopped to speak of other things, the food, the wine, the lovely spring night, and Jesus. Once in a while they disagreed about motivations and morality—whether it was wrong or senseless for Moses to smite the rock in violation of the Lord's specific instructions, and whether it was justifiable for his punishment to be that he never got to see the promised land. Mary of Nazareth said it was wrong of Moses, and the other one said senseless, but they both agreed that they didn't care about "justifiable"; the punishment was terrible, and very sad. After Moses had given his whole life, his heart and soul—and then, never to see the promised land—! Mother Mary said she did not see how the Lord had the heart to go back on such a promise. But He occasionally did things like that. Then they were silent.

The woman kept puzzling Mary. Sometimes she was wise and sometimes silly. Mary wanted to attribute the silliness to the wine, but she remembered a certain disconnection even before a drop had been tasted. Whenever she was on the point of deciding conclusively that the poor lady had drifted from reason, Mary Mother would say something so well observed or so sensitively understood that Mary had to revise everything. I could really find out about her, Mary thought, if I broached that ridiculous tale about her virginity at the birth of her firstborn. . . .

"Oh, dear heaven," Mary Mother said. "We forgot the four questions."

"If you had to make up your own questions, what would you ask?"

"I would probably start with something doltish, like 'Are two pillows enough, or do you want three?' "

Mary smiled. "Maybe asking about pillows is as good as asking about plagues."

"What would you ask?"

"I don't know. We keep saying that Passover has to do with deliverance and resurrection. Yet, whenever we talk about someone resurrected, it's always a man. Do women get resurrected?"

"Is that your question?" Mary Mother asked.

"Well, no. . . . What I'd really like to know . . ."

She halted.

"Go on."

Somehow, Mary felt sure she would not shock the woman. "I'd ask my father, 'If you were born a woman, which would you rather be, a virgin or a harlot?' "

"Do you think that's such a useful question? Generally, a woman neither stays a virgin nor becomes a harlot."

"Generally, she disappears on her wedding day."

"I never disappeared."

It suddenly occurred to Mary what an extraordinary thing had happened. Until this time, in discussing a man's forebears, all the talk had to do with who his father was, his grandfather, his male antecedents. Never, who was his mother? Now, for the first time in Mary Magdalene's experience, she heard people talking about the mother. However they spoke of Mary of Nazareth, as blessed or cursed, the woman was the one for special designation.

Seeming to be within range of Mary's thought, the older one asked, "Does my son ever speak of me?"

". . . Not often."

"I didn't think so," she said. "Does he talk to you from time to time?"

"Yes. Frequently."

"I mean really talk."

"He doesn't speak a great deal, except to multitudes. But when he listens, it is a kind of speech."

"Yes. . . . Does he do so with other women?"

"With everyone. He makes no distinction among us, men or women."

"I think there's a special goodness in that. And yet . . . here we are, and there they are—upstairs—all men."

"Yes."

"We can never be certain about anything, can we?"

" 'Goodness,' you said. That's certain enough for me."

"But why doesn't everyone see him as we do? It's plain enough." Mary Mother was distressed. "But they don't, do they? They carry so many tales about him."

"Don't listen."

"But how can I not—my own son? They say devils and damnation—they say that's all he talks about. Now, that's not true! And that he likes sinners better than righteous people."

"I think that may be true."

"I don't believe it."

"You think sinners should be shunned?"

"I'm afraid I do, yes."

"I don't think he does. I think he tries to have an equal affection for everyone."

"Except the Lord, I hope. The Lord's a different matter."

". . . Yes."

Something seemed to bother her. *"Does* he like sinners as much as other people?"

"Sometimes I think he likes them more." Mary smiled to herself. "I think he likes me more."

Silence. The woman's mind was hard at work. "Are you . . . that Mary?"

"Yes."

The Nazarene woman nodded. There wasn't the slightest hint of disapproval. For all her small-town righteousness, the precept that sinners must be shunned was something written in the Law, not in her heart.

She leaned across the dishes and touched Mary. "I think you have it wrong. Having been a sinner, you imagine he loves you better for that very reason. But I'm quite sure it's another thing: he loves you not for your sins, but because you are naturally lovable."

Mary felt herself flushing. As a child she had sensed that her worthiness to be loved was something she had come by naturally; as an adult she always had to work for it. Could it be she need not have to work so hard?

She went back to the Jews in the desert. "And then there was Joshua and the walls of Jericho."

"I never believed about the trumpets, did you?"

"Not really," the younger woman said.

"How these tales ever get started . . . like the one about me."

Mary laid down the morsel of *matzah*. She did not want to make a crunching sound, or any at all.

"Have you heard them . . . about me? . . . The tales?"

"Yes."

Mary Mother leaned forward a little. "What do you think?"

". . . I do not know."

"Could you ever believe that a virgin could give birth?"

I must be very kind, yet very accurate, Mary thought. "Once, when I thought I was pregnant—without having lain with a man—there was milk at my breast. Was that a miracle?"

"You know it was not. It's a thing that happens."

"Were you miraculous?"

"I don't know. . . . Sometimes I try to recall how I was in those days, and I can't remember. . . . I hear the talk, and I don't know how to answer. Some say I was a virgin; some say I was a sinful woman who fornicated before marriage. Whether I was a virgin or a harlot may make a difference how you think about me. But it shouldn't make a difference how you think about him. He is pure. He has always been pure. Whoever I lay down with, his Father was God."

"Then, you don't say it was not a miracle?"

Suddenly the woman was in a storm. *"I don't want to talk about miracles! So much evil in the name of miracles—!"* She started to come apart. "I don't want him to die! If God had miracles to make, why did he have to make one about being or not being a virgin? There are better ones to make! If I give the world a child—and nobody wants him—why can't I have him back?"

She was gone now, shaking, weeping, and Mary gathered her to herself and held her close. For a long time, the woman sobbed and shook convulsively, and Mary made no effort to restrain her. At last the sounds had stilled, and the troubled one nestled in Mary's arms. Then Mary Mother removed herself, and did not know what to do with her body, where to lodge it, where to go. So, at length, she lay down on the straw and folded herself together like a child. She was as still as slumber, but Mary knew she was not asleep.

There was a wind rising and it rattled the stable door. Mary lifted the wooden latch, took a step out into the darkness, and closed the door behind her.

The sky was sharp and bright. Each star was a command.

She had asked the woman if she had been a virgin at the birth, and had been given . . . an evasion. Like her son, who often replied to a question that had not been asked, bypassing the real one, she had added an elusion to an enigma. No wonder Jesus was so good at it; he had learned at his mother's knee.

But what if it wasn't subterfuge? What if the woman had told what she honestly believed and understood; what if she had related the mystery according to her total comprehension? And what if the lack of a reply was Mary's inability to hear, to grasp the woman's meaning with her mind? Or grasp it with a part of her spirit she had not learned to use . . . or lacked?

Suddenly it occurred to her: None of it was evasion. Never, when Jesus spoke, did he shuffle and equivocate. He was telling what he comprehended, which was a world beyond worlds. He was a mystic in touch with intimations there were no words for—with the language of firmaments, with beginnings beyond history and endings beyond time, with the language of God. And if none of them understood . . . how alone he must be.

She looked across the distance to the lighted window on the second floor. It became dimmer. One of the lamps had been extinguished, perhaps, and the *seder* was over. Another lamp, and now there was only the faintest glow.

The downstairs entrance door opened and closed with a clatter.

Judas, with ungirted mantle, hurried out and rushed across the roadway. As he ran, his long hair blew in the night wind of Nisan, and he looked bereft. She wondered where he was running in such reckless haste.

18

Locusts—darkness—lice—the dying of cattle—

He had his plagues mixed up. And some were missing. He had known them perfectly in childhood, each one in proper chronological order, and the list complete. But now—

Hail—beasts—

The wind was too biting for the time of year. Though the *seder* wine had made his head hot, his body was cold. He wished he had not thrown away his worn-out winter tunic; there was still some warmth left in it. His hands, oddly, were the coldest parts. If he reached inside his mantle, he might warm one of them in the pocket, but it was awkward, and what to do with the other one? He had not remembered that the Temple was so far away.

Frogs—locusts— No, he had counted locusts. Boils—blood— None in their proper order, and not enough. Only nine. An insufficiency of plagues. What was the tenth?

The slaying of the firstborn. Had he counted it? Had he taken that one into consideration—considering that Jesus was a firstborn?

There would be no slaying. And no betraying, either.

Count it as a plague, and you've got ten of them, the list complete, but don't count it as something that will be done tonight. Certainly not by me.

"One of you who eats with me will betray me."

That was a dread of Jesus, and would not be realized. No reason it should. All Jews want the same thing, Judas said, all want the Messiah. No matter what their differences, no matter how good or evil they are, no matter how they keep the Law or break it, they all concur in the single hope. And in this yearning, he was not in discord with Annas. The old man had trembled when he talked of everlasting life, as Judas trembled.

So he must trust him. Regardless what tales of corruption he had heard about the high priests—and most of them true, he was sure—the revered one had to be virtuous in this singular respect: true to the one vast dream. The old man might betray everything, but not his final, most desperate vision.

What was more: Irrespective of what Jesus' charges were against the Sadducees and Pharisees, the teacher was still a Jew, and a high priest was still a high priest. The Temple was still a holy place to the master; he preached in it, he had tried to cleanse it, he loved it. And there, perhaps, would be unfolded that most sanctified secret they had spoken about when they were Essenes together. Not to an ordinary man like Judas would the Son of God entrust the hallowed intimacy that he was the Messiah, but only to those who were entrusted with the most precious mysteries of the Lord, the highest of high priests. Only in the Temple could he really make the pronouncement—there, in the most consecrated place, the Holy of Holies. Hear, O Israel—the Messiah has come—and I am the one!

And Judas, his cherished friend, would be there, a favored witness, one of the blessed.

Blood, frogs, lice, beasts, dying cattle, boils, hail, locusts, darkness, the slaying of the firstborn. All of them, and all in order! A good sign!

It was warmer here, in the denser part of the city. And there was not far to go. He saw the flaring lamps of the Temple on the mount. What an enlightenment in the darkness. And the lamps would burn even brighter when the word was spoken. The world would be even more gloriously ablaze than on that day, at the Jordan, when Jesus had been baptized and had become the beloved of God. Beloved of God, beloved of all of us, beloved of me, of *me!*

The guard stopped him, another one brought a lantern and held it to his face, asking if he was Judas, and they let him through.

Fumes from the nearly spent candles and from the burning oil of two braziers were thick in the old man's private chamber. His wasted body needed the extra warmth. But to Judas it was stifling in there; he had had too much wine. His head went round; the air was suffocating.

He looked about him. There were no others in the room, only he and the dotard priest, Annas, sitting deep in cushions, huddled and cold.

Silence. Judas delayed answering the question he had been asked this afternoon; Annas delayed repeating it. As though the elder was afraid of what he might hear. But at last he could not endure the waiting:

"Is he the one?"

"He did not tell me so."

The priest leaned forward and cupped an ear with a hand. "Do not mumble," he said.

Judas felt sure that the old man had heard him. The younger one had difficulty speaking more loudly; his throat was dry. But he repeated the words more deliberately.

The priest got smaller. "Did he say that he was not?"

"No."

"Ah!" He snatched at the wisp of hope. "If he has not told you, do you think he will tell us?"

"He must."

"Yes, exactly—he must, he must! Even if we have to take him to the Sanhedrin."

"Please . . . no."

"Only the inner Sanhedrin, of course. Not make this a court matter, understand, or cause him any harm. Discretion."

The door opened and Caiaphas entered. He barely nodded, then turned his unspoken question not to Judas, but to his father-in-law.

Annas said heavily, "He did not speak."

"Of course not," Caiaphas said with impatience. "It was foolish to expect he would."

He turned with precipitance to Judas. He reached into his mantle and came out with a little leather pouch.

"Here."

"What is it?"

"The prescribed amount. Thirty pieces of silver."

"For what?"

"For knowledge you have brought us."

Judas wished the candles would not flicker so unsteadily; the quavering light made Caiaphas appear to be swaying. "I do not want it."

The old man's voice was conciliating. "Take it, Judas. This means nothing. It is written that we must give it to you."

"For what, for what?"

Caiaphas said, "It is betrayer's money."

"No! I do not betray him!"

Again the assuaging voice of the old man. "It's only a term, Judas, a compliance with formality—don't let such a thing disturb you. The law is crassly written. It says that an informer must be paid or he will allow himself the comfort of a noble intention."

"I do not have a base intention!"

"Of course not. What is more important, you have a noble cause. Please—I beg you—take the money."

"No."

The old man's voice sounded desperate. "Please. We cannot proceed unless you take it. And all that you've done—all that *he* has done—will go for nothing. Please, Judas!"

He still did not reach for the money.

The venerable man changed his tactic. He reasoned as if with an old friend. "We want to know if he is the Messiah. Do you not want this as well?"

". . . Yes."

"And if he tells us what he has not told you—is that not better than no word at all?"

"Yes."

When the syllable was spoken, Judas was not sure what answer he had given. The fumes from the braziers seemed to be thicker than before, there was a smoke in the air—an illogic he could not comprehend—things left out—the objects in the room not holding their definition. Nor, for a moment, could he speak. When he found his voice:

"No harm?" If only he could understand. "No harm will come to him?"

"Why should he be harmed? If he is not the Messiah, it is not a sin . . ." Then, heavily, ". . . only a heartache."

Heartache he understood. Judas took the money.

In the corridor, Caiaphas turned him over to Ahira the Levite and Helon the scribe, and they led him outdoors to the Court of the Gentiles.

Not a sin . . . only a heartache.

Outdoors, his head cleared a little. Four legionaries were waiting. You will go with them, Helon said, and show them where he is. Before they went, one of the legionaries, the leader, went apart with Ahira and they whispered.

When they returned, "These men are not from the Antonia, they come from Tiberias," Ahira said. "They have never seen him."

Judas smiled wanly. Of course not; of course they would not send local legionaries to apprehend the master, for next week they might have to deal with an unruly crowd who would know them as the men who had apprehended a beloved leader. These soldiers from Tiberias, however, would be gone by then. . . . But how about himself?

No harm . . .

The *quadrum* leader peered at Judas and, in halting Aramaic, said that when they approached the man, they would stand at a distance, and Judas was to go ahead and identify him. How would he do it?

"The one that I kiss," he said.

Helon and Ahira turned back toward the Temple, and Judas went forward with the soldiers.

Marching with the legionaries, he thought, It is all going to be done quickly and silently. Not a word spoken among them, not a sound except their footsteps, and the clink. The money pouch was in his mantle pocket. As he walked, it kept striking against his thigh, and each time . . . the faintest tinkle of metal.

Yes, it was going to be done softly and secretly. Before the crowds knew anything, Jesus would be plucked out of their midst, and tomorrow . . . For all Judas knew, for all anyone knew, tomorrow might be . . . revelation.

Clink.

It was a small enough sound to deal with, and luckily the rest was quiet.

But not for long. The city hummed with the Passover. Some *sedarim* were still in progress—lamps in windows that would usually be lightless now—families in reunion, noisier than usual; only on Passover would there be such a babble in the night. The older children were allowed to stay awake, even to have a little wine. Judas could hear their voices; many were singing; they did not all sing the same song; better, he thought, if they sang the same song. Some of the feasts were just terminating, visitors were calling their farewells, carrying tapers to light them home. Nearing midnight now, yet there were people on the streets.

"Where are you taking him?" someone called to the legionaries.

"Is he arrested?"

"What has he done?"

A few boys followed them, then others, adults as well. The stalkers who were farthest away threw taunts at the legionaries; one boy picked up a stone, but his older companion made him get rid of it. The mockery, however, did not cease; it was part of the festivity, to bedevil the soldiery, and hail them as fools. *Ave, fatuus,* they jeered. *Ave, fatuus.*

As they approached the Jerusalem gate, some of the younger boys dropped back and disappeared, but many of the newly bearded ones continued in the *quadrum*'s footsteps. They were silent now, however, simply dogging the soldiery, keeping the rhythm of the march. The loudest sound was the soldiers' feet as their nail-studded sandals stirred the gravel in the dirt.

Judas led them away from the city to where it had been planned they all would be. It was upward, not far from Kidron toward Olivet, where there was a walled garden. Called Gethsemane because there had once been an oil press there, it was partly an orchard for figs and olives and partly a walking place, with hidden bowers and havens of quiet. The man who owned it had recently become a follower of Jesus, and allowed him access to its serenity.

As they got close to Gethsemane there was a smell of sap from other orchards, and Judas felt that the trees, the buds, the very earth itself were bursting into spring.

At the turn of the road, Judas told the *quadrum* leader how close they were and where he would be, and asked them to hang back, for he did not want Jesus or the disciples to know that he had come with soldiers. The leader looked doubtful and said something about having control of the legionaries, but not of this little rabble that was following them. But he waved the Jew onward.

Judas went ahead, alone.

Clink.

Be still, he said.

One wall of the garden was a high hedge. As he came alongside, he heard a muted sound, the sighing of a gentle wind, as soft as a Sabbath.

No, not a wind, but a voice whispering on the other side of the tall shrubbery. It was Jesus. Halting to listen, he heard, yet scarcely heard: ". . . Father . . . all things possible . . . Take this cup away from me . . . not what I will, but what You will."

His voice was somewhat strange, not as the disciple remembered it; softer than usual, as if he were not speaking to God, but to himself, or the God within himself. He might be crying.

Judas also prayed: "Dear Father, be kind to him."

Suddenly he heard the crowd behind him. And the soldiers' voices. They were surging toward him. Hold them, he started to shout, hold them back.

He must hurry. He ran.

There was a frenzy then, and he did not know what happened.

The soldiers, running, the disciples, the crowd. Jesus seeing them—and him.

The kiss. The master calling him his friend. Then swords, and Peter wielding one, and blood, and Jesus crying for them to put up their weapons or all perish by the sword, and some of the crowd shouting in defense of Jesus, and some against him, hating him, calling him blasphemer, and an outcry about legions of angels.

Then, all at once, they were gone, everyone. And he did not know where to go or what to do with himself, so he remained there, in Gethsemane. He wondered if one of the disciples might be left behind, someone awake or sleeping, anyone. He did not want to be alone. But there was no one there.

19

It was still darkness when the disciple Thomas came running and weeping, to find Mary and tell her that Jesus had been taken. Mary Mother cringed in a corner of the stall, as if to get as far from the news as possible. And Mary Magdalene tried to make reason out of what Thomas was saying.

There was no sense in the man. He pulled witlessly at his beard and wailed that he had never understood the master, yet had offered to give his life for him, but when the moment had come, he had run—as all of them had run.

"Run from what?" she said.

"From them, from *them!*"

"Where is he?" For the third time, she asked. "Arrested, you said—by the Romans?"

"No—yes—some say the Romans—there were legionaries—but Caiaphas—I don't know!"

She left him quaking, and rushed away. As she was some distance from Levi's place, she heard the old woman:

"Wait! Wait!"

"Go back!"

"No—please—wait!"

"I must be quick—you'll hobble me!"

She heard the woman crying, asking what she should do, go back or follow, and did not stay to see what choice was made.

Arrested on what charges and by whom?

She would go to the Temple first, she decided, not because it was more logical to go there than to the Antonia, but because it would be more accessible to a Jew.

In the narrow streets, the morning crowds were stubborn and spiteful; they slowed her and would not let her through, the damnable holiday celebrants. And all their garbled information. He was arrested, they said, he was dead, he had been caught with the *sicarius* Barabbas, he and his followers had started to tear down the Temple, he had been stoned in the marketplace. Or: he was the Savior, he was the King of the Jews, he was last in the line of the Maccabees, he was their long-awaited deliverer, and gone, arrested, killed by the sword of a legionary from Tiberias, from Ascalon, from somewhere.

She had her own rumors. The ones she told herself in black revery, and a particular one that kept recurring: The soldiers come and ask for him; she lies and tells them he is dead. When they have gone, she finds him, and it is true, he is dead, and her falsehood has betrayed him. She cries, "The truth, the truth," and it does not reawaken him. So much for lies and resurrection.

At the Temple, they gave her contradictory information or evaded or simply did not know. She asked one Levite and another, she asked an old scribe who had a circumstantial look, she asked congregants; some knew and some did not, that an arrest had taken place, but that was all of it. Everybody, it seemed, was cautiously holding back, hiding words like stolen coins.

"Someone!" she cried in desperation. "Someone knows!"

The animals were at the altar. It was the time of the morning sacrifice, and her voice was like a dying bleat. Any moment, her blood would pour upon her mantle.

"Someone knows!"

Two men came, took her by the arms, and put her outdoors.

In the crowds again, she let them move her anywhere, it did not matter. Then she saw the tall one—the tallest in the crowd—and she shouted:

"Peter!"

He turned as if he had been caught by soldiers. A voice was calling him, he did not know whose, but everyone was his enemy. When he saw her, he hesitated, then propelled himself—away from her.

"Peter—wait!"

Only once he looked back, and in his face there was the panic of a fugitive.

"Peter!"

She pushed, she tore her way through the crowd, in pursuit of the man. He disappeared and appeared and disappeared again, like a boat that was sinking, bobbing, sinking. Now, certain that she saw him, she raced and called, but he was gone. Out of the crowd and onto a deserted street where there was nothing and nobody, she heard—from somewhere—a murmur, a weeping.

The sound was clear, but she could not find him. Then there he was, the mammoth man in a tight alleyway, crouched like a scared and ailing dog in a cellar, whimpering in misery.

"Peter!" She ran to him. "Where is he?"

"I don't know."

"Where—what—tell me!"

"He said that all of us would stumble, but I vowed to him I wouldn't. And he said I would deny him before the cock crew—and I did."

"Peter—where—what?"

He moaned and wrung his hands. "Three times! They asked me in the courtyard if I knew Jesus of Nazareth—and I said I did not know him. Three times they asked me and three times I denied him. I denied him!"

He was senseless in his anguish. She would have ached for him if he were not thinking only of his own misery. Tears, she thought, everyone rent with tears; what good were they doing Jesus? And she vowed she would not let her fear and her sorrow prevent her helping him, and she would not shed a tear, *no tears.*

She saw the blood on Peter's mantle.

"Whose is that?"

"I don't know—they came to seize him—and I struck at someone."

"Where is he—try to tell me—where?"

"He was with Caiaphas—then they said Sanhedrin—but it was after midnight—and someone told me Pilate—"

She left him there, and ran.

The lictor did not believe a word she said. He would not let her through.

"If you have evidence against the Jew, then speak."

"Only to Pilate."

They had been around the matter twice, and now the magistrate looked out the window as if hoping that, when he looked back, she would be gone. But she refused to depart, and begged to be allowed inside the praetorium—while the crowd outside was increasing. She could hear them shouting for the Jew and against him, and this was upsetting the administrator; he did not want to deal with them or with her, or with anybody. He was youngish, he spoke Aramaic with a cultivated Greek accent, and he was trying to be courteous. He hid his nervousness with a show of affability.

"I like Jerusalem, but I hate this time of year."

"Yes," she said. "Please let me in."

She could see he was unsure of his position, not certain how to handle her; there might be some truth in what she was saying.

"We could compromise," he said. "I might have you talk to the chief magistrate."

"Only Pilate."

"What if I arrest you—or simply have the guard remove you?"

"I'll inscribe a tablet to Rome and see that the Emperor knows that a lictor named Erminius prevented me from—"

"Can you write?"

"Yes."

"Latin?"

"Yes."

"Where did you say you met the procurator?"

"I did not say."

She was reluctant, but now she knew she would have to use part of what little influence she had. "Tell him that I have evidence against the Jew—and that I am a friend of Entemia."

"Entemia?"

"Yes."

He sent a soldier off with the message, and talked with a surprising lack of discretion about how he hated it when Pilate came to live here for the holidays. Somehow, there were always more disturbances then, more troublemakers.

In less than an hour, she was in the presence of Pilate.

The wall hangings in the enormous room—carpets with the likenesses of Tiberius on every one of them—were so thick and heavy that they ate the voices. Besides, the crowds on the terraces below the balcony were noisy, sometimes muttering, sometimes shouting in unison, whatever the momentary sentiment might be, for or against the prisoners. Two of them. Jesus and Barabbas.

It was a high-ceilinged room, the proper scale for the tall procurator, although he seemed smaller than she remembered him. He had made higher gestures then, in Alexandria, broad and flowing movements above his shoulders, his hands were not as wearily floor-bound as they now appeared to be.

He had recognized her instantly, despite all the changes in her appearance, and had said openly that he had felt tricked when she said she had no evidence against the Jew but for him.

"Why should I believe you, since you say you lied to the lictor?" he asked.

"Because it will be to your advantage to believe me."

"You mean yours."

"You owe me an advantage."

"Do I indeed? Why?"

"I served you once."

"As I recall it," he said with a wryness, "you did not serve me."

"That's how I served you," she said. "I was diseased."

"Ah yes," he said blandly. "I heard all that. And how that country wizard miraculously cured you—and others—and how he feeds a multitude with a herring or two—and makes good wine from water or urine or something—and heals the leprous. Excellent, all quite excellent. Even admirable from a Roman point of view—he improves the body politic. Those are not our charges."

"What charges, then?"

"Only one. Treason."

"He is not treasonous."

"He calls himself King of the Jews."

"He does not. I will bring a thousand witnesses—"

"If that's your evidence, go home."

"—who will say they never heard him utter such a claim! Never!"

"I will not listen to them."

"Then, Rome will listen. They will shout so loud that Tiberius will hear them."

It worried him. Things had gone badly for him of late. Some said he would be called back to Rome.

"Go away! What do you want?"

"Let him out of prison."

"It's not in my hands—I can't."

"Please. I'll see that he goes home. Back to Galilee. Next year, he'll be forgotten in Jerusalem. Let him go."

"I tell you I can't. It's too late for him—for me—for all of us. If I let a dangerous man go free—"

"He's not dangerous!"

"—what will I tell Tiberius?"

"Tell him—" She paused. Sobriety was not succeeding with the worried man; perhaps if she lightened things for him . . . "Tell him that you . . . bungled."

But, for Pilate, there was no longer any sport in that fiction. It got him angry. "Don't make a joke of that."

"I don't," she said quickly. "It was an excellent mitigation."

"It's no good anymore."

"Why not?"

"Because I've lost my mitigator. Sejanus is out of favor." His fright was worse than she thought; his voice shook. "My mentor—any day now he will be fed to the jackals."

"Don't worry. You will eat the jackals."

"No. Many times he saved me from Tiberius. He was my protector—he loved me, he owned me. And if I am forced to own myself—!"

It was a prospect too terrible to contemplate. "Perhaps Sejanus will get back in favor," she said.

"Not this time." He started to laugh in a manic way. "Do you know what they say about him in Rome? That he eats living brains—and soon he will have to eat his own!"

"Don't let anyone eat yours, Pilate." She was exploiting his terror. "The most hazardous thing you've done was to allow them to arrest the Nazarene. The safest would be to let him go. If you don't—you see that mob outside the praetorium—?"

"I'm not afraid of the mob, I'm afraid of the priesthood." Suddenly he lashed at her. "I hate this thing! I don't want this matter—I don't want it! I'd like to toss it out the window into the faces of that mob down there. I take it in bad part that your miserable Sanhedrin has shunted that little Jew upon me. He's their concern more than mine. It's their damn Law he broke, it was their priests he insulted, it was their God he blasphemed, it was their Temple he threatened to destroy!"

"He did not. He predicted it would be destroyed, but he never threatened to destroy it."

"To a Jew a prophecy has the terror of a threat. And if the Messiah prophesies—"

"He never said he was the Messiah!"

"Talk to your people—not to me. You all disagree on that point. The members of your Sanhedrin hear the evidence they want to hear. Some hear him say yes to the question, some hear no. Some want a Savior and some want a more favorable rate of exchange. In any event, I don't care what he calls himself—as long as the word 'king' is not in the title. For that belongs exclusively to the emperor."

"Then, let the emperor keep it. Jesus wants none of it."

"What stupidity! You think it matters what he wants? Or what he is or what he says he is? It's how the people perceive him. And too many have begun to call him 'king.' "

"That is not his fault."

"Fault? Who cares about fault? Who cares if he breaches the peace a little, and sets a few beasts free and flutters the feathers of a turtledove or two, and upsets the tables of the moneychangers? I don't need a cohort to quiet a riot like that—a *quadrum* will do. If only that were the end of it. But quietly—overnight—people attach great words to these little things—freedom—deliverance. And suddenly—everywhere—all over the province—pillage and murder. It's an earsplitting noise—they hear it in Rome."

"He speaks quietly."

"They take him for a prophet—and prophets don't speak quietly.

There's a saying among the Greeks, that a whisper in Delphi can cause an earthquake in Africa. I don't believe that to be true, but *they* do—that is the danger."

"I wish you could think of yourself as a courageous man."

"I don't because I'm not."

"Lenient, then."

"Ah, there you've caught me. My leniency. I could have ruled this province better if I had lived here in Jerusalem and kept a chain around every throat. But I said: let them breathe a little. Once, when I was new here, I set up the Roman standards in this holy city, and the graven images of the emperor offended your Jewish elders. So those old Jews came up to Caesarea—thousands of them—and they stormed my palace. A dozen soldiers could have done away with them, but when my legionaries drew their swords, the Jews knelt and presented their necks to the drawn blades. I should have given the order to slay a few score of them. But I was moved, I was *lenient.* Everybody—Jews and Romans—took it for weakness, and I've never convinced them otherwise. I won't be lenient again."

"What will you do with him?"

"It is being done."

"What?"

"They are scourging him."

"Oh, no!"

"Don't shake. A few lashes might save the man's life."

"Let him go—let him go!"

"If he denies he is King of the Jews, he is a free man."

"No—he will not—no—"

"His task is easier than mine. All he has to do is deny—"

"No—I beg you—no—"

Abruptly, a terrible noise. Drums, rattleboxes.

Pilate rushed to the open window and out upon the balcony. She hurried after him.

Below, on the topmost terrace, many feet above the crowd, a detachment of soldiers appeared. Two of them carried scourges.

Pilate shouted. "How many have you given him?"

"All thirty-nine."

"And?"

"Nothing, Pilate. Neither yes nor no."

"Bring him here."

In a few moments, they brought Jesus. He could barely move; his walk was a shuffle, like the stirring of an object. Finally he came to rest on the terrace below the balcony. His back was bleeding, and his legs. As he seemed about to collapse, a soldier offered to hold him, but he gestured the man away. He stood alone. His white mantle, which he carried in his hand, trailed on the ground; the blood upon it was encrusted with dirt. They had lashed his face as well; there was a wet redness on his forehead; his hair was matted with it. There was nothing in his eyes, nothing. It would not have seemed so terrible to her if, through the drying blood, she had seen pain in his eyes, or rage, or tragedy. But there was nothing.

At the place where they had brought him to a halt, under the window, he glanced about him, now one direction, now another. He did not know where he was, or where he was meant to look. Then Pilate called to him:

"Nazarene! Up here—look up here! Have you heard what they asked you?"

Jesus did not look upward.

"Have you heard the question?"

No sign from the man below.

"How do you call yourself? King of the Jews? Or not?"

And still the man did not glance upward. She could not stand how beaten he looked, how emptied.

"Jesus!" she cried. "Jesus—oh, my beloved—tell them no! Tell them no!"

He did not raise his eyes.

All at once he began to tremble. Only a little, scarcely a tremor, and it made him appear small and shattered, and too mutilated to be taken for someone human.

"Behold the man," Pilate said.

Oh, God, she kept saying.

"Take him away now," Pilate said.

She did not know what the order meant, but the legionaries were turning him, pushing him downward, down the steps. She screamed and turned upon Pilate. Before she could reach him, hands were upon her, soldiers' hands.

Then confusion, and motion of a kind she could not understand, and she was outdoors, in the middle of the crowd.

Some had recognized her as the one who had been on the balcony with Pilate; some tried to hurt her, some to help her; she could not tell which was which.

Then she heard noises about saving one of the prisoners. Shouts and rattleboxes again, and voices raised. There was a legal forgiveness—someone was yelling the Greek word *amnestia, amnestia*—it was a pardon that the Romans granted once a year, on Passover. One condemned criminal could be freed, as a symbol of the deliverance of the Hebrews from Egypt, and as a sign that Rome could dignify the Jewish servitude. Forgiveness, the crowd shouted, Passover pardon, *amnestia,* pardon for a Jew, pardon, pardon.

Salvation. Jesus might still be saved.

Then she heard a loud voice shout:

"Barabbas! Save Barabbas!"

The man who yelled was hoisted so he could be seen. She knew him. Nahum, the scarred one, the friend of the *sicarius.*

"Barabbas!"

Here—there—spotted through the crowd—*sicarii,* like a hundred Nahums, shouting:

"Barabbas!"

She started to shriek Jesus' name, save Jesus, save the Nazarene, and some shouted with her. But then:

"Barabbas, Barabbas!"

Her voice was small; it seemed that all those who shouted with her had small voices.

From other directions, she heard other sounds and other outcries and did not know what they were saying. Then, like a thunderclap, it was too close and too clear.

"Crucify him!"

As long as I keep my reason, Judas said, heaven will not be lost. There may be havoc on earth, and in me, but there is no havoc in my master's heaven. And I can save him still. As long as I remember cause and root, and keep in mind the thing that must be said and done—

—they will not scourge him. And if they do—as it is said they have already done—it will cause him no pain. They will not dress him in a robe of scarlet, and put a crown of thorns upon his head, and a reed for a scepter in his hand, and call him King of the Jews, and mock him and spit on him and revile him. As it is said they have done. And they will not—as long as I keep my reason—they will not crucify him. As it is said—

As it has been done.

I have seen it. I have seen it with my mind or with my eyes. Seen him carry the cross and fall with it, and the young man taking it up for him, and the crowds reading the sign and mocking him:

"King of the Jews!"

I have seen them spit upon him and revile him, and the thorns, and the blood on his forehead and in his eyes, and the stripes on his back.

Seen all of it, and now I must see more, must go up there, on the hill, on Golgotha, and must talk to him. Tell him—reason with him—make him know that he can save himself. Remind him how many times he has prophesied that the Son of Man would come in the glory of his Father with his angels. And this is the time of his coming! I have not betrayed him; only marked the appointed moment for him to speak. Sooner or later, the High Priest said, he will have to answer, if only in extremis. This is the sooner and the later, Jesus—I will tell him—reason,

reason—this is the extremis. And when he hears me, he will say the word—Messiah.

He will say, "I knew it, Judas, when we were Essenes together—*this was the secret!* I have known it all along—and now you, too, can know: I am the Messiah!"

And he will step down from the cross and his wounds will be as memories, and there will be a shining.

Clink.

The clinking sound was only an impertinence, Judas told himself, and nothing more. It reminded him that he was still of the earth, and had not yet escaped from the evil of his flesh, nor had he any right to do so until the word was spoken.

The hill, then, upward. It was fitting that the way went upward, toward the highest firmament, closest to our Father; every sign must count for something. Golgotha, the place of the skull: that, too, a sign—of death vanquished. The midday darkness: a sign that there would be an eclipse of the sun and a quaking of the earth, and at last . . . apocalypse.

At a distance . . . three crosses, not one as he had expected. Ah yes, he remembered now, the thieves. It was not fitting, not *reasonable* for them to crucify him in the company of thieves. Abruptly he changed his mind: most reasonable; when had Jesus ever turned away from sinners? Come unto me, children, sinners, misbegotten, thieves—publicans. He was always calling them, so he could give them his love, his sweetness. Did they know his sweetness?

Closer now.

Thunder. Everything suitable to the occasion, everything sensible, answering every test of fitness.

Oh, dear God, he bleeds!

He is on high, but his voice does not ring; he mumbles. The soldiers imitate his gibberish, they jeer at him. They are kneeling on the ground, playing a game with dice, gambling for the purple gown that has replaced his white mantle, the gown of mockery. It does not matter. He will not need his clothes; he will be arrayed in sunlight. Sunlight, you brutish ones, you heedless of the earth!

He bleeds.

But blood is his lesser agony; the rest is so terrible that the sky shrieks and the hilltop shudders with pain; the rest is loneliness and betrayal—someone has betrayed him.

Who? What monster has done this?

Clink.

The master speaks. He asks God to forgive them, they know not what they do.

But the master is wrong, Judas calls to him. You are wrong, Jesus, we know what we do—and we do not betray you, we bring you your salvation so that you may bring ours!

Forgive them, the master says.

No! Oh no, beloved teacher—speak—say it—save yourself—save all of us—save me!

Forgive them.

"Tell me who you are! Say, 'Messiah'!"

The master does not speak, but makes a moaning sound.

"Save yourself! Come down from the cross! Come down into my arms that I may hold you, love you. Save yourself—save *me!*"

Judas reaches his arms up as if to take him down. You are my beloved, Judas says, and I will release you from your pain. I will save you! I will save you, save myself!

He is at the cross. He reaches up and grapples with a nail. There is blood on Judas's robe and on his hands. The soldiers shout at him, someone drags him away, he falls. Save him, he cries, save me!

The master speaks, but not to him. "My God, my God, why have You forsaken me?"

The man whispers something then about thirst, and they give him sour wine. And he yields up the spirit.

In Judas, a temple is torn, the earth quakes, the rocks split . . . but there is no apocalypse.

⁂

The soldiers drove the bereft man from the hill.

He thereupon went in search of Jesus—in a more reasonable way, he said—to find him where there would be no blood, and his own mantle would be stainless.

He saw the master teaching on a hillside, and he walked with him by the Sea of Galilee—he and Jesus and Mary, the three of them—and he heard the start of the beatitude: *Blessed are the poor in spirit, for theirs . . .*

Clink.

Then he saw himself in the synagogue of the Essenes. I am standing on the bema, he said, and Jesus is beside me. I am having my Bar Mitzvah, I am reading my portion as Jesus has taught me, and I can feel his pride in me like the warmth of wine. I cannot stand how happy I am that I am a Jew and Jesus is my friend. And now I have reached my manhood, and my teacher kisses me, and I am so joyous that I ache. And then—as if my cup has not already flooded over, he leans toward me and whispers in my ear, and starts to tell me—joy of joys!—the Secret!

But he speaks too softly and I cannot hear him. Louder, I beg him, louder—!

Clink.

He reached inside his pocket, snatched at the purse, held it by its leather laces, and struck himself with it. He beat himself, he beat and beat his mouth that had spoken against his teacher, he beat his brow where the evil had been, his eyes that had looked upon the tortured body of his beloved friend.

Bleeding from the mouth and eyes, and bleeding in all his body—if only blood could cleanse him—he walked he did not know where.

He was throwing the money at a door, a great wide golden door, silver pieces against the gold, until all that was left to him was the empty pouch. He let the thing slip away, to the ground.

He couldn't stand how people talked to him, so he went to Levi's, in search of Jesus once more, and tried to find out whether the *seder* had happened, or was yet to be, and wondered who would ask the four questions and who would answer them.

He went into the stable then. He did not know what the leather object was that he held in his hand. It might be a belt, or part of a harness of some sort, or a collar. There were brass objects he did not comprehend, but it was of careful workmanship, something his father could have made. If he were to ask his father what this thing was in his hands, his father would know, and surely tell him.

He wondered if the leather would cause him pain, and smiled wanly at how long his pain had been, and how brief it now would be. As if speaking to a small boy in Kerioth, he said gently, "Don't be afraid."

The thing fit tightly around his neck.

21

The soldiers allowed the men to approach as closely to the crosses as they liked, but not the women. Women were prone to cause disturbances, it was said, so they were kept at a prudent distance, more than a stone's throw away.

The two Marys did not cause a disturbance. The younger one did not even weep. Not only because she needed to console Mary Mother, whose weeping was like the scream of gulls, but because the man suspended was too distant—long paces from where she stood and miles beyond her mind's imagining. She could barely see the blood, she could not believe the pain. And when she tried to feel his agony, when she tried to take it from him and engulf it within herself, there was a barrier through which it would not pass. So it was a dry and distant horror, without tears.

Once, without knowing her own voice, she shrieked, "Let him down, let him down!"

Nobody paid attention, except that Mary Mother raised her head and lowered it again.

Another time, Mary threw a stone. It fell short of anything, and again nobody noticed. Too far for a stone, she thought without being sensible, too far for a stone.

Once or twice, when she heard Jesus' voice, this was the closest she came to being intimate with his pain, but she could never clearly make out the words; she did not even know whether they were cries of wrath or torment or benediction.

There were not many visitors; she would have expected more. A few women came and went. Old. She was surprised at how few young ones were even curious. The men, nearly all of them, were people of function, scribes and Pharisees, to see whether the commission had been discharged, and satisfactorily. Midmorning, two Sadducees and a Roman centurion. Quick glances, slow and studied noddings, then departure.

Of the disciples—nobody. They were afraid of capture, of course, afraid of the fate of Jesus. Not a soul all morning, until later, when Judas arrived. She heard him screaming at the dying man, and again the words were unintelligible. They sounded, first, like curses, and she thought what waste, to be cursing at the crucified. But then she knew them for what they were, pleadings, supplications. He was out of his wits, raving, tearing at his clothes, running to the cross, trying to pluck out one of the nails. With that, she knew him as the betrayer. She wanted to rush at him with her claws, except that she was torn between rage and pity, and was not sure whether she would excoriate him, or—worse—forgive him. Fury, she said, do not lose your fury. But so much of it was gone that she felt cold and naked, and her compassion was only a shred to keep her warm. Of what use is pity, she thought, except in the heart of Jesus, and look at him now. She wanted to ask him the question—what use pity?—but his murmurings were incomprehensible, mocked at by the soldiers, and his voice would not carry this lengthy distance.

Then, because the wind shifted or because he shouted to be heard, his words made an aura upon the hilltop, and she heard them: My God, my God, why have You forsaken me? She gazed at the perishing man across the empty wasteland, and wondered who had forsaken whom?

Then he was dead.

There were no visitors anymore. Even the soldiers deserted, all but one.

She and Mary Mother waited because his body was there. The void was a hole where her heart had been, and at times she felt that she, too, had perished. Only the wind had a feeling, a rage to be elsewhere, and the earth seemed to be dying of despair.

Later, when she could not tell whether the dark was tempest or night, Joseph of Arimathea arrived with two men. He brought news that Judas had hanged himself, and she could not comprehend the words—an alien language—the death of her two most beloved ones within scarcely more than a heartbeat of time—her brain refused the tidings. And she could not make an outcry that would respond in any measure to her agony and desolation.

Joseph carried a lamp in one hand and, in the other, a bit of papyrus which said he was permitted to remove the body of Jesus. But the soldier could not read, and the Arimathean was at pains to persuade him. At last the sentinel nodded wearily, and Joseph and his men took up the shovels that were on the ground and dug around the base of Jesus' cross. Then they slowly let it down. She could not see all that they were doing. When they lifted him from the ground, his hands and feet were wrapped in linen, and his body was enshrouded in white. Now he was borne in the arms of two of them, and they were carrying him down the hill.

The two women stirred and followed.

It seemed far, and it must have been truly night by then, when they arrived at a sheltered garden embanked against a gentle hillside. Where the rising ground met the flatland, there was a tomb—Joseph of Arimathea's, perhaps—hewn out of rock, and a great stone had been rolled away from the opening.

Inside this cave, Jesus was laid. Then the three men heaved at the stone and rolled it against the opening, and that way the tomb was closed.

Sometime during the night she imagined she saw him in the white shroud, and it became the cloak she had once sewn for him, the resplendent whiteness of her mantle and the man. Then she wept. Oh, my love, she said, I will cry forever, I will use up all the tears in the world, and leave none for children.

What use, your death, what use? Behold the man, indeed; if only you had been content to be a man. And why did you die alone, why could I not have been closer, to draw away some of your suffering? Always alone, forsaken. Behold, not one of us close enough to touch your hand, except your betrayer. See how you were deserted—oh, behold.

Deserted by your disciples, all of whom had implied, one way or another, that they would die for you. But only one has done so: Judas. Do not tell me, beloved, that they have done exactly what you would have wanted them to do: save themselves, the better to spread your ministry. You were your ministry. And now that you have gone, your heaven will be only a parable, one of your grand evasions, misremembered. And no one will mourn for you, all the weeping will go quiet. Except mine.

How will I live without you? I could not feel your pain before, but now your scourges are on my back and they have driven nails through the palms of my hands. Your outcries are in my throat, your blood is on my breast. Come, let me hold you, let me give you breath, let me bind your wounds, let me kiss your eyes, your mouth, let me love you unto my death. See, I have you in my arms, where no one will hurt you. I promise, no hand will touch you, and I will shut out every angry sound. Oh, let me love you!

Gone, forever gone. . . .

The next day was the Sabbath. On the following morning, she and Mary Mother gathered some spices together to anoint his body. They walked down the hillside to the garden of the Arimathean. How will we move the stone? Mary Mother asked. Someone will help us, Mary answered.

It had been night when they had seen the place, the gardens were vast, and they did not know their way. There would be a gardener somewhere, she imagined, and she would look for him. Then, before they realized, they were there—all as they remembered, the sheltered garden against the gentle hillside, everything the same.

Except that the great stone had been moved.

Not totally moved, as it had been when they had first seen it, but far enough from the opening that they could go in.

They entered. There was scarcely light enough to see. But his shroud was white and lying on the ground. It glistened in the single ray of sun.

He was not there. The tomb was empty. All that filled it was the shroud and stillness.

Mary Mother trembled.

Mary comforted. "Don't worry. They have taken him away."

"Where?"

"I don't know."

"Who?"

"Joseph, it is likely."

They came out of the tomb. The old woman was shaking. She had her hands clasped tightly over her heart as if to contain it within her breast. Her face was ashen.

"Don't be afraid," Mary said. She led her to a bench under a tree and begged her to sit down. "I'll go and find the gardener. He will tell us where they have taken him. I won't be long. Catch your breath, now. There, that's good. Rest."

She went one way and another and did not find the gardener. Perhaps there was no gardener to find. She came upon a footpath that led into a little wood. It was green and shadowy in here. It was cool. There was a promising goodness of early spring. It should have been a comfort, but the spring was gray without him. It made her weep again.

As the path turned, she heard a rustle of leaves and saw the gardener in the shadow.

"Woman, why do you weep?" he asked.

"If you have taken him elsewhere, tell me where he is, and we will carry him away."

"Mary."

She knew the voice and could not endure it. She cried his name, she cried, "Teacher, Teacher!"

And she rushed to him and threw her arms about him.

"Do not cling to me," he said gently, "for I have not yet ascended to my Father."

"My beloved—my beloved!"

He stroked her hair, he told her to be comforted. What more he said she was not sure of, except that she was to go and tell the others, his mother, everyone.

Then he was one of the shadows, and he was gone.

Oh, dear heaven, she said, oh, my dear discovered heaven!

It had happened as he had foreseen, as he had foretold. Exactly as he had said it would.

No matter whether he had made a miracle, no matter whether this was resurrection or apocalypse, no matter what it was named, she had seen him, she had touched him, and it was Jesus—no one else—it was her love.

She had asked for an illusion, a madness, and had been given an even greater gift; she had received what she had always yearned for:

A knowing. It was Jesus.

If this was madness in disguise, she did not care. There were too many names for too few things, and her love was singular and had been too ambiguously labeled. I love him and he is there! He was reborn, the birth out of the blood, the life out of the tomb.

He is in me and he surrounds me; his spirit dwells in me, and he is my shelter. It is as if he needed no resurrection, he has never died.

She remembered her fantasy, that she had grown old and he had not. Now it would be revised. Now I can love you forever, she said, and you will not grow old—nor will I. I will be a hundred, and you will still see me as the woman you made clean again, and young. And oh, how I will love you—as though we have just been wedded—I am your bride! And each moment that I live will be filled with you, each breath I take will be a breath you have breathed in me, and I will love you, love you!

It was too much to contain within herself. I will share it with the others, she said, and tell them he is risen.